But W

by
David Kevill

ISBN: 978-0-244-60640-4

PublishNation
www.publishnation.co.uk

Chapter One

Sarah was shivering from head to toe with the cold damp atmosphere but the worst thing was not being able to see a thing. She could hear noises, like the drip, drip, drip of water but she had no idea where it was. She needed water to survive, she knew that, which only added to her anxiety.

She heard living things scurrying about but she had no idea what, occasionally something would run across her arm or leg, increasing her shivers. She panicked that she would reach the stage when she would have to catch, if she could, one of these creatures and eat it, just to survive.

Despite being of what many people call 'a mature age', Sarah was a tough character, used to surviving alone, used to walking these remote moors, but this was her biggest test yet – or so she thought.

The morning had begun as every other morning did, this much she could remember, but how many days ago she had no idea. How long had she been in a daze? Her head hurt like hell and although she couldn't see it she could feel the sticky blood.

She got up at 6:30am as she usually did at weekend. It must be weekend as she remembered that only Betty was with her. She had no dogs to pick up on Saturdays and Sundays so she could have the luxury of an extra half hour in bed. She cleaned her teeth and splashed water on her face, she would have her shower after she had walked Betty. As she always walked long and hard a welcome home shower was always something to look forward to.

She enjoyed her breakfast of muesli, the kind with lots of fruit in, toast and black coffee whilst watching the birds out of the window. The robin hopped onto her window sill to say his daily hello. At least it seemed like the persistent rain of recent days had stopped, which was very welcome. Betty enjoyed her usual breakfast of natural organic dry food; only the best for her. In no time at all she had devoured every morsel and was hopeful of at least some of Sarah's toast. She adopted the pleading look that was hard to resist, head on Sarah's knee, eyes looking up, Sarah knew she couldn't ignore that look and would give her some toast, but only when she had finished her own breakfast. She had to teach her some manners.

"It's impossible to fill you," Sarah said whilst stroking Betty's head. She knew she had to watch what she ate otherwise she would end up over weight, which wasn't good for the dog's health, but a piece of toast wouldn't hurt.

Sarah assumed that they set off on their walk over the moors at about 7:30am as they usually did, it would be the first of their two walks today. She always walked in the remoter areas of the moors as she liked the solitude there, just herself and Betty. They walked along Moorland Road, past the two cars parked at the start of the lower moors. Later in the day the number of cars here would make it resemble a small supermarket car park; many people found the climb from the village to the lower moors too much so drove to the top of Moorland Road. She remembered exchanging a 'Good Morning' with the elderly gentleman she saw regularly walking his small terrier. He always wore a woolly hat with a bobble on, and for that reason Sarah called him Bob, although she didn't know what his name really was.

Sarah and Betty walked perhaps half a mile along the gravelled path before turning right and climbing the steep narrow trail that led up to the higher moors and away from the village. It was tough climbing here therefore it was very rare for Sarah to meet anyone in this area. In addition to her two or three walks on the moors every day with the dogs she cared for during the week Sarah also loved going to her Zumba classes, as a result she was very fit and healthy therefore the climb presented no problems to her and she continued to make a fast pace.

The landscape up here was made up of short tufts of tough grass which made walking difficult if you strayed from the narrow paths trodden by the sheep. Sarah stayed on the paths but Betty coped with the rough ground well and loved nothing more than chasing her ball across it. Sarah wondered how she had so much energy.

Sarah's memory was slowly becoming clearer despite the injury on her head. She remembered picking up the tennis ball in the ball thrower, you could get much more distance with a thrower than throwing the ball with your hand, but this time unusually Betty didn't run after it. This had never happened before and it puzzled Sarah. Maybe Betty had hurt her paw but Sarah couldn't find anything when she examined them.

"Fetch Betty," Sarah said, pointing to the ball, "there it is," but Betty sat there flatly refusing to go for the ball.

They normally had at least three balls with them as lost balls were a frequent occurrence but she had forgotten to grab some extras this morning leaving them with just the one ball left from yesterday. Sarah decided that there was no option but to go and fetch the ball herself. She trod very carefully, making sure she didn't disturb any nesting birds, or worse still tread on a nest and break the eggs. She knew the meadow pipit nested in this area and their nests were very difficult to see.

She reached the ball and was bending down to pick it up when the ground gave way beneath her. Was Betty aware of the danger? Was this why she wouldn't fetch the ball? Dogs are often credited with sensing someone's illness so maybe Betty could sense that there was danger.

Before she could grab anything to stop her fall she was down in the underground space she could now see no way out of. The descent was so fast she momentarily thought of the containers her mother used to tell her about that they used to put money in in department stores when she was a child, whoosh they used to go, where to she didn't know, and whoosh they came back with your change.

She now began to wonder if this was an accurate event of what happened, could her mind be playing tricks on her. Did she fall accidentally or was she pushed? If she was pushed what had her attacker done to Betty? Her mind flittered between the two versions of the story, did she fall or was she pushed? Her surroundings weren't conducive to making rational decisions.

Now in her cold damp dark prison hope was fading fast. She wished she had a thick coat on, her mother always nagged her to wear warmer clothing, especially when she was a teenager. It was her way of rebelling against the unhappy childhood she'd had. Somehow she had never got the sense to dress for a worst case scenario.

She had no idea how far underground she was. Despite her damaged ankle she had tried in vain to climb out but the space seemed to be shaped like an overturned funnel making it impossible to get a grip to climb. She was too far down to reach the hole she had fallen through, she could judge where the hole was because of the faint very narrow shafts of light she could see high above her, light that disappeared well before it hit the floor. At least these shafts gave her an idea when day turned to night and vice versa. She decided to try and keep count by moving one of Betty's treats to her now empty pocket each time the shafts disappeared. It wasn't fool proof of course because thick cloud cover would obscure the light, and there had been plenty of that in recent days. At least she though there had. She seemed to remember frequent flicks of an imaginary switch turning the downlight through the hole above on and off but she couldn't be sure of anything. It was easy for her mind to play tricks on her in these horrific surroundings. That pocket had held her mobile phone but it had smashed when she landed, although she couldn't see it, she could feel the damage. In exasperation she threw the phone across the underground space, something she now regretted because she had no idea where it landed and it contained all her contacts' phone numbers – "Damn," she cried in frustration, "you stupid woman!" She would need those contacts if she ever got out of here alive.

There appeared to be no way out and no one would miss her until Monday evening when her clients realised, due to the puddles on their floors, that their dogs hadn't been collected for walking. She shouted "help" over and over even though she realised no one would hear. After what seemed like hours of shouting, although it was probably only minutes, she felt a tear running down her cheek, then another and another until she was sobbing at the sheer desperation of her situation.

Sarah only remembered crying once since she had moved out of her parents' home which was when her previous dog, Sam, had to be put to sleep, a victim of cancer. That was the toughest decision she had ever had to make and she cried for weeks. She sometimes wondered if it was wrong to cry for the death of a dog when she never shed a tear when her father and mother died, she felt she had shed enough tears as a child, because of them, that they didn't deserve any more.

Slowly, despite the increasing cold and damp, Sarah drifted into a shallow fitful sleep. "Where's Betty?" her subconscious asked. How is she? Has she found anyone? Has anyone found her? Had someone hurt her, or worse? Sarah had never trusted anyone enough to form a close relationship, she had her parents to thank for that, therefore Betty was her relationship, her close friend and her constant companion.

"Betty, I love you. Please get help," she cried out in her sleep, but Betty couldn't hear.

Chapter Two

John loved the early hours when the light of day was just appearing. He loved sitting outside, when the weather permitted, drinking his first cup of tea of the day, strong and very milky was the way he liked it, listening to the dawn chorus. He could make out the repetitive high pitched call of the meadow pipit, the sweet song of the skylark and the dramatic song of the rare and elusive Dunlin.

He would sit out here every dawn except when it was raining hard. He didn't mind the cold, having been born and bred in this high remote farmhouse. In any case the surrounding hills protected the farm from the worst of the bitter winds that almost daily battered this barren landscape.

The isolation served him well. Although he was friendly to the people he met on his trips to the village, he really did prefer his own company. He guessed that this came from the fact that his parents had both been happier isolated from the outside world with just their own and each other's company, only mixing with other people when it was essential. They frequently told him he was different to other children, although even to this day he had no idea why. He thought that everyone did exactly the same things he did, but he would soon find out otherwise.

This had never been a large farm, simply surviving on the income they got from selling the milk from their ten or so cows, which his dad used to take to the local dairy in the tractor and trailer John still used. It must be over thirty years old now but it managed to transport him on his infrequent trips away from the farm. The trips were never more than five miles each way although over very rough ground for the first mile, from the house to the gravel track that ran down to the nearest village.

After he had finished his early morning tea he went indoors to cook his breakfast, bacon, eggs and fried bread as always. To say John was set in his ways was an understatement. The bacon had to be crispy, the eggs turned over to make sure the yolk wasn't runny and the fried bread not too hard nor too soft. His mother had always made it the way he liked it and, although he had never cooked anything until his mother died ten years ago, five years after his father had passed away, he taught himself to cook it exactly the same way, although the first few months were littered with disasters.

His breakfast was washed down with another large cup of tea whilst he listened to Today on Radio 4. The radio was his only entertainment, they had never had a television and in any case it is unlikely that the reception in this valley would be sufficient to receive many programmes well. Who needed television anyway, John was more than happy with the radio and his books. As for those computer things he'd heard mentioned on the radio, well they were completely foreign to him, he had no idea what they were.

Breakfast could be a leisurely affair as John had no work schedule to cope with. The remaining cattle were sold when his mother died and he had been left sufficient money to survive without working. Working would involve mixing with other people and life was easier if he didn't have to.

On one visit to the village he got talking to old Harry, who walked with a stick, and indeed helped him home with his shopping. Although John was a loner he did like to help people when he could. Although he had seen Harry many times this was the first time that they had spoken, and certainly the first time Harry had invited him into his house. They had a cup of tea, a piece of cake and a good chat. John was surprised that he was really enjoying the company. He began to think that he might have been wrong keeping himself to himself for so long. Why had his parents told him he was different, he seemed just the same as Harry.

Harry asked John if he would like to accompany him on his walk along the canal. He tried to walk every day to help his health. He didn't go far but it tended to take a long time when you factored in his chats with everyone he met. Unlike John, Harry was very lonely living on his own and welcomed the chance to talk to anyone. John had nothing to rush back to the farm for so he agreed to walk with Harry. They both stood up from the old but comfortable easy chairs and put their coats on, it was sunny but chilly, and that is when John's panic set in.

He was horrified that Harry didn't check that the gas cooker and fires were switched off at the wall as well as on the appliance itself. Also he only did one cursory check to see that his back door was locked. John wasn't sure that he had checked properly, not like he would have done. All through the walk John worried in case someone broke into Harry's house, how could he be sure the back door was locked by just checking it once? He was terrified that the gas cooker or one of the gas fires might not be switched off properly and might explode. How could Harry be so careless? John was so glad that he had only electricity at the farm, and even that was a worry since the council had run the cable to the farm about twelve years ago.

The walk was very difficult for John. Every time Harry stopped to talk to someone he really wanted to hurry him up but he couldn't be that rude. If something bad happened to Harry or his house it would be John's fault. Why hadn't he made him check things properly? Was he so careless every day? Should John tell him to warn him for the future?

John accepted the offer of another cup of tea when they returned from the walk but only so that he could check that everything was alright. He so wanted to say something to Harry but he didn't know him well enough. John quickly drank his tea and made an excuse to return to the farm. He worried about Harry for weeks, in fact he still worried about him. If anything happened, it would be his fault because he didn't tell Harry the foolishness of his ways. Harry's welfare, and the welfare of anyone who visited his house, and the welfare of the firemen, paramedics and policemen who would visit Harry's house when something bad happened was now John's responsibility. If anything went wrong he would have to confess that he could have stopped the bad things happening but stood by and did nothing.

Most days John didn't eat lunch so spent the time between breakfast and tea wandering round the valley near the farm. He loved to check how the tadpoles in the small pools dotted around were progressing, he hoped not many had been eaten by the birds, foxes and the other creatures that inhabited this part of the moors that were always on the look-out for an easy meal. He also kept a look out for any abandoned young birds. He had hand reared young birds many times although he failed on more occasions than he succeeded, but every one reared and released was one saved from certain death. He loved spring, especially after experiencing several periods during winter when snow had trapped him in the farm, there was no possibility of going anywhere then, and this could last for weeks in a severe winter.

He also used the afternoon to undertake jobs that needed doing around the farm. The farm was weathered but generally in a good structural condition. John didn't worry about flaking paint or a few planks missing from the gates, no one came here anyway. Even serious ramblers didn't come near the farm, they preferred to walk up on the tops to get a better view.

Following his evening meal, he would settle down to listen to the news and then the Archers, again on Radio 4. After that another cup of tea and a read of his current book, usually something either historical or nature related, would lead nicely to his 9pm bed time. "Early to bed, early to rise makes a man healthy, wealthy and wise," his mother always said.

Just as he was scraping the remnants of his meal into the dustbin he thought he heard a bark, it was faint but it certainly sounded like a dog barking. No it couldn't be he reassured himself. It was so dark at this time of day that no one could be walking up here now, he must be mistaken. After a short silence he heard it again. Still he could see nothing. He went back into the house and sat to have his bedtime cup of tea.

No matter how he tried he couldn't get the barking out of his mind. He thought it was probably the wind playing tricks on his ears but it did sound like a dog. He didn't like uncertainty, John liked 100% guarantees. He wanted to know that it definitely was the wind. He couldn't settle, he had to go outside again to check. He stood outside in the dark listening to the silence. There was no wind he noticed, it couldn't have been the wind. The silence continued which unnerved him. He turned to walk back into the house but then he heard it again, fainter than before but he had heard a bark, he had definitely heard a bark. He scanned the surrounding land but it was difficult to see far in the dark. This was one of those rare places where light pollution didn't penetrate the jet black of night. He wished that he had opened the curtains. That would have cast a little light, but only on the yard and there was no dog in the yard. He looked into the distance for some time, hoping that his eyes would adjust to the dark and be able to see clearer. Then he saw it in the corner of his eye. There was movement, only slight, but there was movement. He stared towards the movement and then very slowly a shape began to form. There was a faint shape coming up the valley. As it got nearer he saw that it was a black dog. Its colour made it really difficult to clearly see it at this distance. The dog came very slowly closer and closer; he didn't know if it was frightened or injured. He slowly walked to meet the dog, hoping it wouldn't run away. As he got nearer he could see that the dog was very weak and looked like it hadn't eaten for some time.

"Hello little one," where've you come from? The dog nestled its head into John's hand to show that it was very friendly, and to rest its head to be honest. It was very weak, very wet and very dirty. Suddenly it turned and started to walk away, looking behind at John every few seconds. It really looked like it wanted him to follow, to where he had no idea. Where did it want him to go? He couldn't go anywhere in the dark, that was madness, the rough ground meant there was a more than average chance of breaking your ankle or leg. No, whatever it was would have to wait until tomorrow.

He picked up the dog and carried it into the porch of the farm house. He had no dog food so he gave it some bread and milk; it ate this faster than he ever thought possible. The bowl of water he had also provided again quickly disappeared and had to be refilled. After the dog had eaten and drunk it's fill he had to bathe it. No way could it go into the house without a thorough bath. That would be very unhygienic.

It was now 10pm, way past John's usual bedtime but the dog wouldn't settle. It just stood at the door wanting to go out. No matter how much John talked to it and tried to calm it down it remained unsettled – John knew something was wrong, but the investigation would have to wait until tomorrow. He desperately wanted to start the search now but he knew that was complete lunacy during the hours of darkness. A sleepless night was a certainty but he couldn't go until it was light.

Chapter Three

The cold was the worst, strangely even worse than the dark. It felt like she would never be warm again, chilled to the bone. The dark in a strange way was comforting, at least Sarah couldn't see if there were any dangers in her underground prison. As long as she stayed still surely nothing could hurt her.

She was certain at first that Betty would go and find help somewhere, it was just a matter of time, but time had a limit, she drifted in and out of consciousness, every wakening accompanied by severe shivers. How long had she been here? She found three treats in her previously empty pockets, did that mean she had been here three days or had she missed some or counted some twice, she had no idea.

She was very hungry and her mouth felt like sandpaper. She suddenly realised that she could eat the dog treats, surely they wouldn't do her any harm. How on earth would she get them down her throat without some form of liquid?

Her clothes were completely soaked from the damp, only adding to her discomfort. Everything was soaked, right down to her underwear.

Drip, drip, drip was her constant accompaniment. Annoying yet comforting, hearing it meant she was still alive. Drip, drip, drip as the seconds, minutes and hours went by, drip, drip, drip as her terror intensified. She was terrified, if she had to die she didn't want it to be this way, she didn't want to die not knowing what had happened to Betty.

Suddenly she had that light bulb moment! If her clothes were damp so the ground beneath her must be damp.

Sarah felt around her to make sure that if she moved she wouldn't fall off the edge of her current 'bed' and fall further into the abyss. As she felt around something moved under her fingers which caused her heartbeat to race, something cold and hairless, what the hell was it? She'd never been in any place as dark as this, even her childhood cupboard didn't seem this dark, at least as far as her mind recalled.

She began to shake as panic set in, the shaking intensified as she tried to shout for help. Her throat was so sore that her voice was weak and croaky, there was no one to hear anyway.

Water was now a desperate need, an essential need.

After what seemed like a long time sat in frozen animation after her encounter with the creature she calmed enough to continue feeling around her. She eventually decided that she could, and should, risk turning over in order to be in a position to face the ground beneath her, to see what water it held.

Her ankle hurt like hell, it felt like the furnace she imagined the devil to be stoking in readiness for her arrival. She slowly and steadily completed the manoeuvre.

She couldn't feel any vertical around her, and there was no standing water she could try and scoop into her mouth. She had no option but to lick the ground beneath her, the ground she had been lay on for an unknown number of hellish days. The ground was damp rather than wet but she licked and licked getting a miniscule bit of gritty brackish liquid into her mouth each time.

She licked until her tongue was bleeding, she could taste the blood. She didn't care what creatures may have urinated or defecated on this patch of subterranean prison, any disease she may get would be preferable to dying in here. The thought of something eating away her flesh as soon as she took her last breath was unbearable.

If she wasn't rescued at least a disease should bring her final breath earlier, although probably more painful.

"For fuck sake what am I doing here?"

Chapter Four

When he got up the next day John found the dog still lay behind the door. He had no idea what the dog was called, it had obviously had a collar on at some time, he could tell that from the lie of the fur around its neck, but there was no collar now. It must have snagged on a bush or tree and pulled off. He hoped it didn't trap the dog too long, or hurt it too much, before it managed to get free. The dog rolled on its back to show John that it trusted him, he could see it was a bitch so decided to call it Flora, his mother's name, at least until he found out its real name.

"Come on Flora, breakfast is ready," he said. They both devoured their breakfast, one of them in double quick time, one very leisurely. He let Flora out into the farm yard to go to the toilet whilst he finished his breakfast and cup of tea. Whatever they were searching for would still be there he thought. Flora constantly whined and scratched at the door, he assumed to hurry him up.

Breakfast over he put on his coat and made sure to get his torch off the sideboard, just in case.

"Come on Flora, lead the way."

They walked for what seemed miles over the rough ground, Flora dashing left, right and round in circles trying to pick up a scent, not just any scent but the scent she wanted to pick up. The strong wind wasn't making things easy for Flora.

"Time for a rest Lass, my old bones can't keep up with you."

John sat on a rock but Flora wouldn't settle. Nose in the air, sniffing all around. Suddenly Flora froze, her nose in the air pointing towards the top of the hill forming one side of the valley. Off she ran, at a pace far faster than John could manage, even with the help of his walking poles. She never let John out of her sight though, constantly turning round to make sure that he was still there. When she sensed the distance between them was too much she waited for John to close the gap.

He sensed that Flora knew where she was going and was on the right trail. Then she stopped about 300 hundred yards in front of him and started running round in circles, barking all the time. She had found what she was looking for.

Chapter Five

Her eyes closed, weaker by the hour, only semi-conscious of what was going on around her. Could it be real, was the barking she heard real or just a figment of her imagination. She shook herself awake, there it was again. "Woof, woof."

"Betty," she whispered. She would recognise that bark anywhere. Was Betty still lay by the hole? She would be starving by now poor thing, or had she gone to get help? Either thought brought tears rolling down Sarah's cheeks. Was Betty real or just a figment of her semi-conscious imagination?

Silence. She must have been mistaken. The barking was obviously part of a hallucination. She had been having more of these as time went on, slow minute by slow minute. She wasn't even sure when she was awake or asleep any more. She wasn't sure of anything anymore except the fact that being trapped in this dark cold prison with no idea what was going on in the outside world was driving her crazy.

Where was her water bottle? Sarah always brought a water bottle when she went walking. Did she forget today, did she drop it as she fell, did it fall further into this hellish place. The only liquid her mouth had tasted since her accident was the dirty, gritty liquid she had managed to lick from the ground and the salty liquid of her tears, and surely these would dry up soon. She hoped that it had rained so at least Betty could lap water off the vegetation around her.

"Someone please help me," she whispered, to no one.

Sarah couldn't be certain of anything anymore. Had she really heard Betty bark? If not, she hoped that if she had gone looking for help she had found someone nice and caring. There were too many people these days who wanted dogs for all the wrong reasons and treated them in a way that no living creature deserved to be treated. She sobbed at the thought of Betty being cruelly treated or even worse, heaven forbid, being used as bait for dog fighting. At least she was no use to anyone running these horrible puppy farms, but they wouldn't know she had been spayed when they first took her, what

14

would they do when they found out. Betty was so trusting; she wouldn't think badly of anyone.

"Someone please care for Betty," she whimpered, to no one.

Being trapped here brought frightening flashbacks of her childhood. She thought she had managed to train her mind to push the happenings of her early years to the archives of her memory, but this brought it all back. Her childhood certainly couldn't be called happy, although at the time she had no idea it was any different to anyone else's, until she went to school. Even then, when she realised that other children were not locked in a cupboard for the slightest transgression, she daren't say anything or bad things would happen to her parents, or so they told her.

Being trapped here vividly brought back memories of being locked in the under stairs cupboard for hours or even, for really naughty things, like spilling a drink on the floor, a couple of days, without food or water. Speaking without permission, or leaving the dinner table without asking, or disturbing her father whilst he was reading the newspaper was certain to result in at least four hours in her 'den'. They said it was for her own good, to teach her how to behave for when she grew up. There was no light in the under stairs cupboard nor was there a handle on the inside, she was trapped, completely at their whim as to when they felt like letting her out.

She daren't cry, or shout for help, or bang on the door, all those would have added more hours to her torture. She simply had to accept her punishment. Just like now, there was no one to hear her crying, or hear her shouts for help, she simply had to accept her 'punishment', only this time she didn't know why she was being punished.

Although she was a very friendly person she had never formed a close relationship with anyone for fear that she would change if she got married, or even lived with someone. Was she a nice person during the chase but a horrible one once she got her man? She had also never wanted children, she loved children but feared that her parent's attitude to children may be hereditary.

At least in the cupboard she knew she would get food and water before she died, but here there were no such certainties. She knew water was more necessary than food, she had to find water before she lost the sense of being thirsty, that was a sign that the body system were starting to shut down and death may be just days, or even hours away. If rescue didn't come soon she would have to find the source of the drip but she had no idea where it was coming from or what was between her and the drip, there could be an even deeper chasm, was it even water. Certainly licking the ground wouldn't be sufficient.

Drip, drip, drip. Like a metronome, like counting sheep it sent her into a shallow sleep.

Suddenly she heard it again, the barking. She was sure it was barking and she was sure it was Betty. She shook herself awake, even though her head still hurt like hell. She thought it was probably infected by now in this far from sterile atmosphere.

She knew she was awake, no doubt now, and she heard it again. Woof, woof, woof.

Drip, drip, drip. Woof, woof, woof. Her two chances of survival.

It had taken John several minutes of prodding the ground with his walking pole around the area indicated by Betty before it went below the surface. The grass was an excellent camouflage of what lay beneath.

"Hello." She couldn't believe her ears, was it real?

"Help."

"Hello, is there anyone down there?"

She cried tears of joy this time. Through those tears she returned, as best she could, a weak 'Help'.

Could they hear her; her voice was very weak.

"I can hear you, just," John shouted.

"Oh thank God, thank God."

"You have this beautiful black Labrador to thank for me finding you. She wouldn't give me a minute's peace until I followed her."

"Thank you Betty," she sobbed. Betty had helped to save her life. She was going to get the biggest treat Sarah could find.

"Do you know how far down you are?"

"I've no idea, a long way down I think."

"OK I will go and get my rope ladder. I'll be back as soon as I can. Hang on in there."

16

Before he went to get the ladder he shouted into the sink hole, "Try and catch these. They will help you until I get back."

He reached into the hole and dropped first his water bottle, then a chocolate bar he always carried.

He couldn't see anything down the hole so had no idea where the 'captive' was.

Despite her best efforts she missed both items.

"Please, please don't go," she cried. She knew that she had to stay strong, her rescue was underway.

"No," she screamed "don't you dare go."

"Help," she cried out, to no one.

John had stuck one of his walking poles into the ground by the sink hole so that he could easily find it again.

Strangely Sarah was more scared than ever. Would he come back? Would he find her again?

"Why me," she sobbed.

Time passed so slowly; not like her normal days that flew by. She was getting more desperate minute by minute. Logic told her that he would come back but long containment can easily flick the mind's logic switch to the off position.

She thought she heard movement above.

"Hello," she heard. Was it a dream or reality?

"Now then let's get you out of there and get you to hospital. Not long now."

God had answered her prayers. Sarah thought her rescuer sounded like a really nice man. She wanted to ask him so much, particularly about Betty, but she needed to save her strength for the efforts of getting out of her 'cell'.

John lowered a rope ladder, which he kept at home in his bedroom to help him escape if fire broke out whilst he was in bed. He had always had a fear of fire.

She struggled to reach the ladder. The sink hole wasn't wide enough to let him move the ladder from its current, and only possible position. Sarah was scared of moving too far for fear of falling further down, just as she was about to be rescued.

At last she caught hold of the ladder and painfully managed to get her feet onto the bottom rung. She couldn't climb, she didn't have the strength. Even if her ankle hadn't been damaged she didn't have the strength.

John had returned in his tractor. It was the only vehicle that could navigate this terrain. Luckily he had thought to hook the end of the ladder on to the winch positioned at the front of the tractor. They used to use the winch to pull out any of their cows that became stuck in ditches.

"I'm on the ladder," she shouted as loud as her throat would allow.

"Hang on tight."

He switched on the winch, putting it on its lowest speed, and slowly Sarah inched her way to safety. John lay flat on the ground ready to grab her hand as soon as he could reach it to help steady her as she was pulled through the hole.

After a few minutes he could see the top of her head. Her blond hair, although dirty and unkempt, caught the sunlight. Once her head was half way out of the hole he stopped the winch and very gently placed his sunglasses over her eyes to shade them from the brightness.

The more that happened the more kind and caring her as yet nameless saviour appeared to be. She knew from instinct that she could trust him. In fact she was trusting him with her life at this very moment.

Once the sunglasses were securely in place he restarted the winch. He reached down to grab her hands to smooth her passage through the opening of the sink hole. By now he could see that her hands and her face were covered in cuts and bruises.

Just as he was grabbing her hand the ladder snagged his fingers. He felt blood run down them.

"This changes everything," he whispered.

Chapter Six

Steve picked Katy up at 5:30 as normal. They could only afford one car so, as Steve worked further away, and as a teacher, started later and finished earlier than Kate, he took the car. Katy always teased Steve about being a part time worker, even though she knew he did lots of lesson preparation at home, in his own time.

Steve worked at the local high school which he joined five years ago as Assistant Head of Geography, having transferred from a school in Preston. His job was quite ironic really because he couldn't find the way to anywhere without the use of a sat nav.

When they moved to enable Steve to take up his new position Katy was lucky to get a transfer with the company she already worked for, in the same department, credit control. Even though this meant a step down in status and, of course, salary and benefits she was very grateful. Steve's pay increase was such that their combined salaries were much higher than they used to be.

They had just had a very busy weekend with a visit from Katy's parents and sister from Somerset. It was always nice to see them but also very nice to have the house to the two of them again. Peace and quiet, well except for yappy little Cuddles. Steve hated the name Katy had insisted on for their west highland terrier but when they first got him Katy said all she wanted to do was cuddle him, hence the name Cuddles. Steve still couldn't bring himself to shout Cuddles when they were out with the dog, he called him Del. Mind you they only walked Cuddles at weekend, they both worked very hard so used a dog walker Monday through Friday. The dog walker had been recommended by someone Katy worked with, in fact dog walker was probably a misnomer because she looked after Cuddles all day, not just during a walk. Sarah was indeed a brilliant find, she was excellent.

They were both tired after their hard Mondays. They usually found Monday more tiring than the other days, so, as was quite common, they decided to get a take away for tea. The choice between Chinese or Indian took almost all of the forty-minute journey home but finally, by utilising a game of rock, paper, scissors whilst stopped at the traffic lights about a mile from home, Steve won, and Chinese it was.

Katy sat in the car playing games on her mobile phone while Steve went into the shop to get a set meal for two. It had been hard enough to decide the nationality of the food, it would have been impossible to decide what actual food they wanted, so a set meal for two was the easy way out. The shop was busy as usual and the aromas of all the different flavours being cooked stirred Steve's taste buds and made him feel very hungry. Not far to go home though once they had the food.

It was just before 6:30pm when they arrived at their stone built home. It was only about twenty years old but had been built of stone to fit in with the old village. They loved that home, the first they had owned rather than rented, even though it was small it was perfect for them. Tucked away down a quiet cul-de-sac yet only a short walk from the village shops, pubs and restaurants. They loved the village too and often, at weekend, walked along the canal that went right through the village centre. That's when Steve wasn't watching his beloved football team. Katy didn't understand football, nor did she, if truth be known, like football but she went along because she loved to be with Steve, no matter what he was doing.

Just time to eat the take away before settling down to watch the One Show and then flicking channels to watch Coronation Street. These were both compulsive viewing, after which Steve would do any work he had to do to prepare for tomorrow's lessons.

Katy turned the key in the lock of the back door, their preferred entrance, which led straight into the small but modern kitchen. As she stepped into the house she slipped on something wet on the floor.

"What was that?" she asked.

"It looks like dog wee," Steve said, "but Del never wees in the house, he hasn't done since a few weeks after we brought him home.

"It's Cuddles, not Del," Katy said in exasperation.

"Never mind that. Why has Del weed on the floor? "

Steve took Cuddles out into the garden and immediately the dog did another wee and a gigantic poo. Gigantic in comparison to the dog's size.

"Do you think that Sarah didn't come today? Maybe she was ill."

"Sarah is never ill," said Katy, "and in any case she would have rung us to let us know. He must just have a bit of a tummy upset. I'll contact Sarah tomorrow at lunch time to ask her if he has been like this all day. She should be back from her morning walks by then."

Cuddles sorted out they settled down to eat their take away. "Wang Foo do the best spring rolls I have ever tasted," Steve said. Katy just nodded her agreement to avoid pebble dashing Steve with chewed up sweet and sour chicken.

They were always on the last minute every morning so they always washed up after their evening meal. They couldn't bear to face a pile of congealed pots first thing in the morning. Today Katy did the washing up while Steve took Cuddles for a long walk.

Washing and walk finished Katy snuggled up on the pink leather sofa with Cuddles on her knee. Steve was upstairs doing his lesson preparation, as usual. Katy's eyes were half on the television and half watching the beautiful sunset over the village – life was as close to perfect as possible. Right at this moment they didn't have a care in the world.

Chapter Seven

Sarah felt a sudden judder and the winch stopped. Why had she stopped her upward move to freedom? She panicked, what had happened? She couldn't hold on much longer.

"Help," she cried out. There was no reply. Why had he deserted her? Fear made her shiver.

John took care to make sure his hand was bandaged well enough to avoid any more of his blood falling onto Sarah, although the damage was already done.

Just as suddenly Sarah started to move again. Inch by inch she sensed the light increasing as she slowly moved further through the sinkhole entrance. She had never sensed anything better than the smell, the taste of fresh air as she emerged above ground. It was like the best wine that she had ever tasted, it was like the best day she had ever had, it was pure luxury.

It didn't take long for the rest of her body to emerge above ground. She so wanted to see her rescuer, this unknown man she had never met and knew nothing about but she took care to keep the sun glasses on to avoid damaging her eyes as she emerged into the bright daylight. John had told her to do this and she trusted her saviour completely. How could she ever repay him for what he had done? She was sure that she would think of a way as she recovered in her hospital bed, when John got her to hospital. That surely wouldn't be long now.

She lay on the ground sipping the water from the bottle John had given her while he packed away the rope ladder and the winch. She gulped the sweet tasting fresh air and welcomed the breeze on her face. Her hands were very sore from gripping the rope ladder like her life depended on it, in fact her life had depended on her maintaining her grip. She looked at the cuts and bruises on her hands and arms and wondered just what state her face was in. She began to feel the world swirl into faded and blurred images then disappear altogether.

She regained consciousness to find John supporting her shoulders to keep her partially off the ground.

"What happened?" she said in a faint, weak voice, "Where am I?" Momentarily she had no idea what was happening but slowly as her mind came back into the real world. Memories of her horrendous ordeal came back into focus.

"I'm sorry," she whispered.

"There's nothing to be sorry about lass," he replied. "You just rest here until you feel strong enough to help me get you into the tractor. There's no hurry."

Sarah drifted in and out of reality for the next hour or so. John spent the time thinking about how the future would be with this anonymous woman, he didn't even know her name yet, he knew nothing at all about her but he knew that he, and he alone, had to care for her for the rest of her life, she was his responsibility now. John was feeling a mix of emotions, all of them negative emotions, but panic was by far the prominent feeling.

The rest, the water she drank and the chocolate bars John gave her to eat gradually helped Sarah regain some strength, both physically and mentally. "I'm sorry," she said again, this time a little stronger than before. Still very weak she managed a fading, "Thank you, thank you."

She had no idea who her rescuer was but she had no option but to trust him without question. It was highly unlikely that anyone else would pass this way, it was far too remote. She had no reason not to trust him anyway.

"What's your name?" she said very quietly.

"John." He didn't ask her name, he had more important things on his mind than to ask her name, at least for now.

After a further period of silent rest John thought she looked strong enough to manage to get to the tractor.

"I think I should try and help you to your feet now. It's better that you get somewhere warmer," he said.

Caringly he helped her up into a standing position, advising her to put her weight onto her left foot, her undamaged ankle.

"Now try and put a little weight on your other ankle please so we can judge if you can hobble over to the tractor or if I need to carry you." She tentatively put her right foot on the ground and although a pain shot up her leg it was bearable.

23

Slowly they made their way to the tractor with John supporting her and trying as best he could to avoid the clumps of moorland grass and heather. It wasn't far to the tractor but it seemed like she had walked a marathon by the time she reached it. Now there was the problem of how to get up into the cab. Being an old tractor there was no easy way of getting up there, John would have to help her again.

"Grab the door and I will try and push you up. Try and pull a little if you can." He knew she would be very weak but hoped she would be able to help a little. She did her best but the main propulsion came from John. He pushed with his shoulder as he would when he was winching a cow out of a ditch. She noticed this and also that he was very careful where he put his hands. She didn't care where he touched her as long as he got her into the cab and on her way to hospital, all modesty went out of the window at times like this as far as Sarah was concerned.

At last her bottom and the seat formed a union. She hadn't expected Rolls Royce comfort but this was ridiculous. She was sat on a seat of metal with just a thin cloth over it. There were no seat belts and nothing to hold onto. How on earth was she going to get to hospital without flying through the windscreen, a windscreen that was so splattered with mud and animal excrement that she couldn't see through her side and John's wasn't much better.

"Where's Betty, is she alright?" How could she forget Betty? She should have been the first thing she asked about and she felt guilty that she hadn't been. Her one true friend and yet she had forgotten her, how could she.

"Betty! So that's her name. As she had no tag on I christened her Flora, after my mother. Flora, sorry Betty is fine now. She was very weak when she found me but now she's recovering and I'm sure she can't wait to see you again. She's a lovely dog, a credit to you. I'm more than happy to take care of her for as long as is necessary."

"I hope I'm not in hospital too long so that I can see Betty again soon," Sarah said.

John didn't reply. The tractor started first time, which was quite a feat for something so old. Slowly, very slowly, they set off across the rough ground with John doing his best to minimise the jarring on Sarah in general and her ankle in particular. As he drove he pondered what he was going to do with her ankle, he had to do something but had no idea what yet. If only he could have taken her to the hospital they would have sorted her out in no time, but that was impossible now.

After what seemed like hours to Sarah, during which the pain in her ankle had increased to an almost unbearable level, they reached a gravel track. Sarah knew this path well, she had walked it frequently, usually with three or four dogs in tow. She knew that there would be about a mile to go along this track then they would turn right to drop down into the village before taking the main road into the next town, and the hospital.

The surface here made the journey less painful for Sarah and at last she felt she could try and strike up a conversation. John hadn't said a word since they set off. Sarah notice that he appeared to be deep in thought, but not in a nice way. She saw the tense frown that spread across his face. The last thing he had said to her was before they had set off. He told her then that he would just be a minute while he went and hammered a sign into the ground by the sink hole to warn others of its existence. 'Always thinking of others', she thought to herself. She thought he was a really nice person. Not to mention that she probably owed her life to him. John had said she owed her life to Betty, not to him. Kind and modest.

As they steadily moved along the gravel track Sarah took the opportunity to look around at the wonders of this part of the world.

She saw Skylarks hovering high up in the sky, singing continuously before plunging steeply downwards. Skylarks are often the first birds to sing at dawn, hence the expression 'up with the lark'. She even saw an adder, recently emerged from its hibernation, slivering fast across the ground no doubt in pursuit of its weekly meal. The newly hatched chicks of ground nesting birds were easy pickings. The adder is Britain's only poisonous snake but luckily it is more afraid of humans than humans are of it. It is rare to see one but small dogs who pester an adder are in danger, something she is always acutely aware of on her walks.

She felt alive for the first time since she fell into her underground prison. Alive and glad to be so. Everything was going to be fine. In a few days she would be back walking her clients' dogs, even though she had lost their phone numbers at least she knew the addresses she picked the dogs up from. She would have to visit each one to apologise and explain what had happened. She hoped her absence hadn't inconvenienced them too much, she knew they would understand.

She even managed to have a conversation of sorts with John while they were travelling along the gravel track. She put his monosyllabic answers down to shyness.

Yes, not long now until things were back to normal.

In the distance she could see the junction where the gravel track met the road into the village. It was a T junction with the right fork going into the village and the left fork meandering onto even remoter areas of the moorland, soon becoming a gravel track again.

200 yards to go, 100 yards to go, she counted down knowing each yard was nearer to the hospital and the start of her recovery. 50 yards, right turn. RIGHT turn, why had John turned left.

"John why have you turned left?" No reply.

"John why have you turned left," she ask nervously.

"For everyone's protection," he whispered. A whisper she could barely hear.

"What did you say?"

"For everyone's protection," he said a little louder this time.

"What do you mean?" she asked, a little afraid of what the answer may be.

Her question was met with silence.

"What the hell do you mean? Please tell me."

Again there was no answer. She was scared. Was the kind man turning into a weird man? What did he mean?

"For fuck sake answer me John. You're scaring me."

Her alarm seemed to make her much stronger. Adrenaline kicked in to help her fight the danger. She sensed danger but had no idea what lay ahead.

"Don't be scared, I will take good care of you."

"The hospital will take better care of me, take me there now."

"Don't worry, I will take care of you. I just thought you might like to say hello to Betty, surely a little delay won't do any harm."

26

"Oh yes, yes please." She couldn't contain her excitement. She was going to see Betty. To see those soft brown eyes, that wagging tail, that.....well everything that is Betty." She loved her and she knew Betty returned that love unconditionally. The type of love that doesn't exist between humans. She would talk to Betty and explain that although she would be going away again it wouldn't be for long. She knew she would understand. Above all she would take the chance to thank her for saving her life.

How thoughtful of John to take this detour. What a kind man. The thought of seeing Betty again pushed all concerns about what John meant by 'for everyone's protection' to the far reaches of her mind, at least temporarily.

Chapter Eight

The excitement of seeing Betty again acted as an anaesthetic against her aches and pains. Her excitement levels grew as each yard crunched under the wheels of the tractor. They had long ago left the short stretch of tarmac road and were close to the point when they would turn off the gravel onto the rough track up to the farmhouse, or so John told her. She had no reason not to believe him.

John said little else except to give her advance notice of directions, and even these were few.

"Not far now," John said, but still she could see no buildings. No animals. No trace of a farm. They took a tight left bend in the track and suddenly it came into view.

"This is remote, no one would know you were here," Sarah said.

The farm was in fact what she would describe as a small holding. Just the farmhouse, a barn and a small outbuilding. All the buildings and their surrounds seemed in good condition although a bit rough around the edges. As they turned into the cobbled yard she noticed how clean and tidy it was and yet she saw badly peeling paint on the woodwork of the farm house. She noticed that what few items of farm equipment she could see were neatly lined up side by side in one corner, almost as though they were on parade. Tidy meets run down, it was hard to explain.

There was no sight nor sound nor smell of animals nor did she see any sign of crops growing. In any case crops wouldn't grow in the harsh weather experienced so high on the moors. Maybe John was a hill farmer but she could see no signs of sheep anywhere. What kind of farm was this?

John reversed the tractor close to the other farm equipment that was lined up in the yard. He inched it forward, then he inched it backwards, then he inched it forwards, then backwards, on and on.

"What are you doing?" Sarah asked.

John was making sure that the tractor was parked exactly in line with the other equipment, the right distance away and not too far forward or too far backwards. It's positioning had to be exactly right, it just had to be. How could he tell her why? He knew he couldn't. He wasn't sure why himself, but he knew it had to be just right.

"The coal delivery may come tomorrow and I need to make sure that the wagon can get through," he told her. She knew that wasn't true as there was plenty of room to get any vehicle through, but decided not to pursue the matter. She had only known John for a very short time but already there was so much about him that she didn't understand. So much that concerned her.

With John's help she slowly and carefully stepped down from the old tractor, now neatly parked alongside the other equipment. As she made her way towards the weathered green door of the farmhouse she finally heard it. That unmistakable sound. Woof, woof. There was no mistaking that sound, it was Betty. Sarah went as fast as her ankle would allow.

John unlocked and opened the door and like a greyhound leaving the trap out shot a bundle of wriggling, wagging fur. There was no 'where the hell have you been?' as would be the case in a human relationship. Betty was just pleased to have her companion back, unconditionally. Sarah sat on the cold damp cobbles so as not to get knocked over by the canine missile. The ground momentarily brought back thoughts of the cold damp surface she lay on for days in her underground prison. How many days? She realised that she still didn't know. Those thoughts weren't allowed to surface for long before Betty jumped at Sarah in a unison of unbridled joy and excitement. Canine licks galore joined human hugs. Neither had a care in the world, they were just happy to be together. Sarah momentarily forgot that very soon she would have to leave Betty again to go to hospital but soon that thought returned and made her feel very guilty. Betty had been so excited to see her and now she was going to desert her again. Poor Betty wouldn't understand. Sarah could feel a little tear slowly flow down her cheek. She wiped the tear away, determined not to let it spoil the mutual happiness and excitement of two very close friends meeting again. Not just friends, soulmates.

At last the reunion calmed enough to allow Sarah to ease herself off the ground and make her way into the farmhouse, taking care not to be tripped by the circling twirling bundle of fun.

As soon as she was over the threshold John rushed to shut and lock the door. Sarah wondered why he felt the need to do this in such a remote setting, what was he afraid of? As he slipped the keys into his pocket she considered asking him but thought better of it. That was a question for later.

As she stepped into the room she saw a picture of time stood still. It reminded her of her grandmother's house. Her maternal grandmother was the only grandparent she had ever known. Time with her Grandma was the only happy time in her young life. There was no need to be afraid of the under stairs cupboard, there was nothing to be afraid of. Grandma was very kind and caring, she wished that she could live with grandma all the time but that wasn't possible. When she asked Grandma if she could live with her she would always ask why and say that her parents would miss her very much. If only she could have told her what life at home really was like but her parents had said that if she told Grandma she wouldn't see her again. This scared her. She didn't know if they meant that they wouldn't let her visit Grandma or was it something more sinister? She couldn't take the risk, she had to keep the secret.

Grandma died when Sarah was in her late teens but sitting here in John's living room brought all the memories flooding back. There were the stone floors covered only partially with a threadbare rug in front of the fire. There was the farmhouse range fireplace. She loved Grandma's fireplace and used to create imaginary friends who lived in the various compartments. She would also imagine pictures in the flames created by the burning logs.

There was an old sideboard which reminded her of Grandma's dog Sally. Sally was a cocker spaniel and would spend hours asleep under the sideboard. Sarah loved Sally, she was the only living thing that she could confide in. When Grandma was out of ear shot she would tell Sally all her secrets and Sally always responded with big sloppy kisses, as much as to say don't worry everything will be alright one day. Life had been alright once she left her parental home, although a fear remained that her parents would in some way damage her life until they died, close together ten years ago. Despite everything she missed them. It's strange that you can miss someone who was so unkind to you.

Sally was the catalyst for Sarah's love of dogs and Betty was her current true friend.

Here she was in a strange house with someone she knew nothing about. John seemed a really kind caring man but her knowledge of him was zero. She needed to find out more about him but that would wait until after hospital. She did however have a few questions she needed to ask now.

"Does your wife not mind you bringing me here?"

"No wife."

"Your parents then?"

"No parents."

"So you live here alone."

"Yes."

His curt monotone answers concerned her a little. It seemed to go beyond shyness somehow but perhaps she was being over sensitive.

"When are you taking me to hospital?"

"After a brew."

She was shocked that she had a damaged ankle, cuts and bruises widespread on her arms and legs and her hair matted with dried blood, indicative of a large wound on her head – and he wanted a brew!

"Can't you wait until after you have taken me to hospital before you have a brew?"

"No. You need liquid."

"I've had water, I'm fine."

"Trust me."

She had no option but to trust him. She had no reason not to trust him – yet.

As he went to the kitchen to make tea Sarah noticed that he went and checked that the door they had just come in through was locked. He had only locked it a few minutes ago. He pulled the handle down so hard and for so long that she expected it to fall off. When he was half way to the kitchen he turned back and tried the door again, several more times. Sarah thought that this was very strange behaviour especially since this farmhouse was so remote you could probably leave the doors open all day and all night and have no unwanted visitors, well at least not of the human variety.

This behaviour made Sarah more alert despite her headache and other aches and pains. She took the opportunity of his time in the kitchen to have a hobble round the living room. Could she find anything that may tell her more about John? She saw that the only form of entertainment was an old radio and books, lots and lots of books – all in alphabetical order.

As she heard the kettle whistle she made her way back to her chair. A comfortable but well-worn old beige cloth chair. A little grubby in places but this was inevitable considering its likely age. Betty curled up at Sarah's feet again having escorted her on her walk around the room. She felt Betty was guarding her somehow.

As John made his way back from the kitchen carrying an old wooden tray containing two mugs of tea and a plate of rich tea biscuits she noticed that he took a circuitous route back to their chairs and the little table that separated them. As she watched she began to realise that he was taking a route that would make sure that he didn't step on any cracks between the flagstones.

What the hell was wrong with this guy she thought? Her anxiety was increasing but she thought she needed to stay calm or at least appear to be calm.

"Thank you," she said, for the tea and biscuits. It was a good brew of tea. He certainly knew how to do that.

The tea was drunk in silence. She watched John all the time out of the corner of her eye to try and judge his emotions, she could judge nothing. He seemed void of any emotions and yet he seemed caring. This conflict concerned her a little.

After they had finished their tea and biscuits John got up, walked over to the dresser and reached down a book. She thought he was getting a book to read at hospital in case he had to wait there for some time. Why wasn't he talking?

He sat down again in his chair and opened the book. Sarah noticed it was a medical book. 'The Home Medical Encyclopaedia' she saw the title was and she also noticed the date 1920 on the spine of the book. The book was in far from pristine condition indicating that it had been well used.

As he flicked through the book he kept looking up at her. She felt he was trying to determine just what was wrong with her and how bad the damage was. Now she really began to panic. The man she thought was going to take her to hospital, the man she trusted to take her to hospital was sat reading a medical book that was almost 100 years old. What the hell was going on?

"John what are you doing?" she said as calmly as she could.

"Just a minute."

"John you are frightening me."

John sat bolt upright and looked Sarah straight in the eye. She thought she saw fear in his eyes or was it shock? Had she shocked him by telling him he was frightening her?

Her comment also shocked him into verbal overdrive. "Please don't be frightened. I won't harm you, I will take care of you and Betty."

She thought he really meant it but his words and his actions weren't in unison.

"You need to bandage your ankle tightly and bathe the wound on your head," he said. "I'm sure your ankle is only badly bruised." He had no idea if this was true or not but he had to try and persuade her that a trip to hospital wasn't necessary.

"What the bloody hell are you on about 'I need to bandage', 'I need to bathe'?"

Betty sensed the atmosphere and sat up to put her head on Sarah's knee. In her way she was trying to comfort Sarah, to tell her everything would be alright.

"John, when are you going to take me to hospital?" she asked with a hint of panic in her voice.

"I'm not, I can't. You don't understand."

Chapter Nine

Sarah's world just went into a spin. She couldn't comprehend what John had just said. Suddenly her injuries didn't feature in her mind, recovery became survival. Thoughts bombarded her like a meteor storm. Was she dreaming, was this a nightmare like the ones she had as a child in her under stairs prison. Forcing her mind back into the current situation she tried to decide her next move. 'Think you fool', she said to herself 'you can't lie back and accept this'.

"What the hell do you mean you can't take me to hospital?"

"I can't. It would be dangerous."

"Dangerous for who? It could be dangerous for me if you don't take me." John was scaring Sarah, Betty looked up at her with concern in her eyes. "Don't worry Betty, we'll get away from this madman," she whispered. She said these words more in hope than conviction.

"I'm not mad and I'll take good care of you. I won't harm you."

"Then let us go. If you won't take me to the hospital, then take me home or drop me where someone will find me."

"You don't understand. I can't let you go from here. You are a danger to everyone out there. You could make them sick."

Sarah thought back to what had happened in the last few days but couldn't think of anything that could have given her a contagious disease. She felt a whirlwind of emotions, anger, fear, revenge, sadness. Should she choose fight or flight? She quickly realised neither would work. John appeared too strong for her to try and fight without the help of a weapon and the flight option seemed equally hopeless. All the windows appeared to be screwed into a closed position meaning the only way out was through the door and the only key she knew about was in John's pocket. Right at that moment her situation seemed hopeless.

"Don't be so fucking stupid. I don't know what's going on in your head but its madness. How can I make people sick?"

"Just trust me, you could." As he said this Sarah noticed a tear slowly rolling down his cheek.

This shocked her. She was the captive but he was crying. What was going on?

Fight with a weapon seemed the only option. Why was he crying? She looked around for a suitable weapon and her eyes rested on the poker lying on the fireplace. He was crying more now. She would have to bide her time so that she could catch him off guard. Now he was sat with his head in his hands sobbing.

"You might be contaminated now. I'm sorry."

Fighting wouldn't work she realised. How could she explain walking into a kind man's house and hitting him over the head with a poker? She didn't want to spend the rest of her life behind bars. What would happen to Betty? No, there had to be another way.

"It's all my fault," he said, "It's all my fault." As he said this he began standing up then sitting down over and over. Up then down, up then down, up then down.

"Will you stop constantly standing up and sitting down. You're driving me crazy," she screamed. "I can't stand it, I can't stand you. Why of all people did you have to rescue me? I wish I was back in the sinkhole." She knew that was a stupid thing to say but fear got the better of her. She was becoming increasingly concerned that John was unstable and feared that he could snap at any time.

"I care for you," he said softly.

35

This really freaked her out. "No, no you don't. If you cared for me you would take me to hospital now. You would let us go." Was John going to stalk her when she did eventually gain her freedom? This thought terrified her.

"I do care, I need to protect you and the world."

"Who do you think you are, Superman? Saviour of the world. All I can see is a weirdo who has kidnapped me and is keeping me prisoner."

"I'm sorry Sarah. One day you will understand, one day."

The room went silent. There was nothing else either of them felt able to say.

Bringing her anger under control Sarah realised that for now being a captive was what she had to accept until she could plan and execute her release. Her first priority was the need to attend to her wounds and she needed a shower and some clean clothes. How was she going to get clean clothes?

She couldn't bring herself to look at John but she could sense he was upset by her angry outburst. The silence went on for what seemed like hours until John asked nervously what she would like for supper. Just like she was his partner and he was being the dutiful husband making supper before they went to bed.

'Oh my god no!' she thought. Was that how he thought of her?

'Play the game Sarah' she reminded herself.

"Please may I have a cup of tea and some toast?" This seemed to please him.

"Would you like jam on your toast?" he asked.

36

"Yes please John."

A scene of domestic bliss.

Conscious that she was still in the state she had been when John pulled her out of the hole she decided, after supper was finished, to remind John that her ankle needed binding and her wounds cleaning. She asked could she have a shower first to clean herself and wondered if he had any clothes she may wear. Goodness knows what clothes he would give her but she had to get out of the stinking damp clothes she was wearing.

A smile appeared on John's face. It was the first time she had seen him smile. He seemed really pleased to be able to help her.

"I don't have a shower but I will run you a nice warm bath. You just wait there while I do and then I will help you upstairs."

John's absence gave her the opportunity to look around the room to see if she could find a spare key. She had no idea how she would find her way across the moors in the dark but she sure as hell would give it a good go. She checked drawers, she checked the toby jugs that lined the old dark wood dresser, she checked under the paperwork on a small table by the door but nothing, not one thing that would help her escape. Constantly keeping her ears alert for the sound of John coming back down the stairs allowed her to be back in her chair before he reappeared.

"Come on Sarah. Your bath is waiting. I will help you upstairs and show you your bedroom on the way. Then I will put some clothes on your bed for you to wear after your bath."

John knew that he had to help Sarah but he was certainly not enjoying doing so. He was concerned about the contamination risks and worried about how he was going to accommodate Sarah into his life and his home.

Chapter Ten

Katy and Steve's day started just like any other working day. They woke up at 7am as usual but then had the usual battle as to who got up first to make the breakfast. This usually resulted in a tickling match which, as always, Steve lost.

"I don't even need to touch you to tickle you, you're a wimp," Katy goaded him in fun.

"I'll get you up," he said as he opened the curtains wide to let the bright watery early morning sun shine straight onto Katy's face.

She knew it was best not to let Steve know his little games irritated her. If she did he tended to push things a little too far. The child that still lurks in every man. She rolled onto her stomach and kept her eyes tightly closed as she ordered "Bacon on toast please."

"No way," said Steve, "It's your turn, I made breakfast yesterday."

"Bacon on toast please, pretty please?"

He wasn't going to give in. He had to walk Cuddles so he sure as hell wasn't going to make breakfast as well. If only they had a garden, then he would only have to open the door in order for Cuddles to have his morning constitutional. He wasn't going to lose this one.

"Watch out or I'll put Cuddles under the covers with you. That will get you up."

"You wouldn't dare," Katy laughed.

"Who wouldn't?"

Steve knew he would be in the dog house for the rest of the day if he did put Cuddles in bed with Katy but he was so tempted. The grief he would get would be worth it.

"What do you think Cuddles?" he said, "Does Cuddles want a cuddle."

Katy quickly turned over to put her in a better position to push the dog off the bed should Steve carry out his threat.

Mischievousness got the better of Steve and under the covers went one wriggling excited dog. Before Katy could move she felt the trickle of warm liquid on her stomach. "Shit," screamed Sarah, "He's dribbling wee in his excitement.

"Just wee?"

"Isn't that enough?"

"But you said shit."

"Stop being so stupid, I've got a naval full of wee," Katy shrieked, "Get him out of here now! You're dead Steve Mills."

Katy was wriggling out of discomfort and anger, Cuddles was wriggling out of excitement. Steve was shaking with laughter.

"Don't just stand there, do something. I'm all wet and warm between my legs."

"Nice," Steve said with a cheeky grin on his face.

Katy managed to wriggle from under Cuddles and shot up into a standing position to avoid a repeat of Cuddles' antics. She jumped up and down demanding that Steve got hold of the dog. Never being one to do what he was told immediately he stood there enjoying the sight before him. He wasn't the only one.

Steve saw the look of horror on Katy's face. She was frozen to the spot.

"What is wrong with you," he asked.

"Look – Men – Roof," she stammered, "Curtains – Shut - Now!"

Steve looked through the window to see three workmen on the roof of the industrial unit behind their house. Their eyes were popping out of their heads, never had they had such a wonderful start to the day than the sight of a naked attractive young woman jumping up and down on a bed.

Katy couldn't move from horror. Steve couldn't move for laughing. After what seemed like a lifetime but was probably only a few seconds she jumped off the bed and ran into the shower room. Steve closed the curtains, much to the dismay of the workmen. What a tale they would have to tell in the pub tonight. He had no doubt it would be embellished.

Steve took Cuddles for a short walk while Katy had her shower. It would be a longer shower than normal he was sure. He was also sure that she would spend the time plotting her revenge.

Katy loved Steve but she really wished he wouldn't be so childish at times. He thought these childish pranks were funny but she didn't. She was covered in dog wee, the bed was soaked in dog wee and dog wee had dripped all across the carpet as she made her way to the shower. It would take ages to sort it all out and that would have to wait until tonight after work by which time it would stink. She also knew she would end up cleaning it up as Steve would use his usual excuse of lesson planning to show he couldn't possibly spare the time to clean.

She met Steve on the rebound from a former boyfriend who had been kind, sensible and caring but boring. He had no fun in him, no life. Now she was married to Steve who had too much fun in him, or at least what he thought was fun. Would he ever grow up? She loved him so much though that she tolerated these occasional stupidities.

"Why are men so infantile?" she whispered to herself but she knew she couldn't stay angry with him for long. She was determined that breakfast and the journey to work would be silent affairs however. Steve hated her silences which made her love them just to annoy him.

Having had her shower and now smelling like a human rather than a wet dog she made breakfast while Steve had his shower. Bacon on toast today. She had changed her mind and offered to make breakfast for when Steve came back from his walk.

After walking the dog and having his shower Steve crept into the kitchen looking sheepish and waving his white handkerchief in surrender. "Hello love," he said with a coy grin on his face.

Silence.

He sat at the small round table to eat his breakfast but whilst he could see Katy tucking into a delicious toasted bacon sandwich he couldn't see anything on his plate except a few crumbs.

"Where's my breakfast?" he said nervously.

"On your plate."

"There's nothing on my plate."

"Well I put it on your plate, "she said with a cheeky grin.

"Stop messing around Katy, where is it? I can't go to work without breakfast."

"Cuddles was on your chair a few minutes ago. Maybe he has eaten it."

He looked down to see Cuddles licking his lips and realised immediately where his breakfast was.

"Why didn't you stop him Katy?"

"He seemed excited, just like he was in bed earlier. How could I disappoint him?"

"That's why you offered to make breakfast."

"Touché."

Despite all that had gone on this morning they were only five minutes late setting off for work.

The journey was, as expected, silent. Steve tried his best to engage Katy in conversation. He hated her being annoyed with him. He couldn't see why she didn't share his sense of humour. He was hungry and ostracised.

Katy arrived at work at 8:50, again just five minutes later than normal. Steve waited for her to wave him off to his work as she always did, but not today. Sarah walked straight through the reception doors without a backward glance.

"Good morning Katy," Julian on reception cheerfully greeted her, "how's your morning been so far?"

"Don't ask," she replied. Julian always gave a bright and cheery welcome. She wondered if he ever had problems himself, if he did he hid them well.

Her morning was largely uneventful. Her job was to chase customers for late payment. The lesser of two evils she thought. She much preferred to chase than be chased for money. She had heard every excuse under the sun from mice in the computer to the boss's dog had died. She even once had a customer tell her they couldn't pay because snow had blown into the computer – in July!

As she hadn't had time to make her usual sandwiches this morning, no wonder, she strolled down to the local sandwich shop for her lunch. As the weather was beautiful, which was so welcome after all the recent storms, she sat on a bench by the canal, which meandered through the town, to eat her prawn sandwich and drink her bottle of spring water. It was so nice to be able to relax and soak up the warm sun for a change. 'Life always seems so much better in nice weather' she thought. Katy was determined to make the most of it as it wasn't likely to last long, although tomorrow was forecast to be just as nice thankfully.

After she had finished her lunch and thrown her rubbish in the nearby bin she got her mobile phone out of her pocket to ring Sarah. It was easier to ring here than in the busy office. Katy only had Sarah's mobile number but she knew she always carried that with her. She dialled the number and fully expected her to respond with her usual cheery 'Hello'. This time, however, it went straight to voicemail. She waited a few minutes to ring Sarah again, assuming she was speaking to someone else, but the same thing happened when she rang a second time, and a third and a fourth. Katy thought this was strange but reasoned that Sarah could be busy doing anything. 'I'll ring again in my break' she thought.

Katy rang Sarah again during her break but was put straight through to voicemail again. The same happened again when she rang after work, while she was waiting for Steve to pick her up. He would be late tonight as he ran an after school club today. Katy was beginning to feel concerned about Sarah, especially as she hadn't responded to any of the messages Katy had left. She still thought there must be a logical explanation, everything had a logical explanation, but she was beginning to get a little worried. Sarah always responded to messages.

The day was still warm so she sat on the small wall that surrounded the flower bed outside reception whilst she waited for Steve. It was better than having to put up with the noise of the cleaners hoovering the reception carpet.

She was daydreaming about their holiday to Cyprus later in the year. She hated being away from Cuddles but knew he would be well cared for by Sarah. She was so engrossed in her thoughts that she didn't see the grey Kia C'eed pull up next to her.

"Taxi for Mrs Mills." She snapped back to the real world to see a smiling Steve holding the door open for her. She loved that smile. How could she stay mad with him for long?

She got into the car and threw her bag onto the back seat.

"Steve we need to go to Sarah's house."

"Why what's wrong with Cuddles?"

"Nothing. At least I don't think so."

Although Sarah picked Cuddles up and dropped him off each day they had visited Sarah's house once when they first took Cuddles to meet her. She explained her phone calls to Steve on the way. She also tried to ring Sarah one more time but with the same result.

Sarah lived in the back part of a back to back house. This type of property were not uncommon in the local villages. One family lived in the front of the house and another in the back. Sarah was glad that she had the back as it gave her a view over her beloved moors. It was also free of traffic noise. It didn't take long to get to Sarah's and they were pleased to see her car parked behind the house. Whilst during the day this was no indication that Sarah was home, because it was only a short walk from here to the moors, at this time of day if the car was here Sarah should be. They climbed the steps to the door and knocked.

"What a beautiful place to live," said Katy.

"Yes and it's not overlooked by workmen," Steve giggled.

There was no answer. They knocked again. No answer. They knocked a third time. No answer. Where was Sarah?

They knocked on the neighbour's door to ask if they had seen Sarah. The door was opened by a frail old lady for whom it had clearly been an effort to get to the door.

"I'm really sorry to trouble you," said Katy, "but we wondered if you had seen Sarah from next door today."

"I haven't seen her for a few days. She sometimes goes to stay with her auntie. She's not well you know, her auntie I mean, not Sarah. If she's going to her auntie's though she always lets me know. You see she does my shopping for me, I can't get to the shops these days. She's really kind to me. If she is going to her auntie's she always makes sure I have enough food to last me until she gets back. She makes me meals and puts them in my freezer so I only have to warm them up in my microwave."

"She is so kind," she added with a trembling lip, "I'm worried about her. She's never away for more than the weekend as she looks after peoples' dogs in the week time."

"Yes she looks after our dog. That's why we are here because we don't think she picked our dog up yesterday. Please don't get upset. I'm sure everything is fine. Maybe she went to her auntie's and couldn't leave her if she was ill," Katy said.

"Do you have a phone number for Sarah's auntie?" Steve asked.

"No love I don't. I don't have a phone you see. I don't know where she lives either but I know it's not too far away."

"I'm sure everything is fine. Has anyone else been asking about her?" Steve enquired.

"Not that I know of. I'm very deaf you see and usually spend my day sat in my chair watching television. Its good company you know but I have to have it on really loud, Sarah never complains bless her, so I don't usually hear people knocking at the door. I only knew you were here because I was at the sink making a cup of tea and saw you through the window. Would you like a brew?"

They really needed to get back to Cuddles, particularly if he hadn't been out all day, but they felt so sorry for the old lady. The least they could do was to give her a few minutes company.

Katy offered to make the tea but Mrs Evans insisted she did it. "You're my guests," she said, "So I will look after you."

They introduced themselves whilst drinking their tea and when they had finished they explained that they were sorry they couldn't stay any longer but they had to get back to Cuddles. Mrs Evans knew Cuddles.

"Sarah has brought him round a few times. He's a lovely little dog and I love having him sat on my knee. I must confess to giving him the odd biscuit or two, I hope that's alright."

"Of course it is, I'm glad you like him," Katy replied.

"It's a nice name you've given him; it really suits." Katy smiled, Steve tutted quietly.

They both felt sorry for Mrs Evans but they must get back to Cuddles. "We will call around tomorrow evening if you like," Katy offered, "We could bring Cuddles with us if you like."

"Oh yes please. If I don't answer the door just walk in, the door's always open."

"Do you need anything bringing from the shops when we come tomorrow?" Steve asked.

"No love, I'm fine for now and Sarah will be back soon I'm sure."

They said their goodbyes and set off on their short journey home. "What can we do Steve? What should we do? I'm worried."

"I'm sure there is an explanation and I'm not sure Sarah would thank us for sticking our noses into her affairs. The school is closed for the next two days. Tomorrow the boiler is being repaired and the following day it is the election, it's used as a polling station. So I will be working at home. If Sarah doesn't collect Cuddles in the morning I will call the police and ask for their advice. I'm not sure if they will want to get involved though, after all Sarah is an adult and hasn't been missing long but I'll try."

Chapter Eleven

The first thing Sarah did in the bathroom was to push the cupboard that contained the towels up behind the door to stop anyone getting in. She didn't think that John would hurt her but nothing in life is certain.

It was wonderful to take off the clothes she had now been wearing for several days. She guessed it was four days but couldn't be certain. She held her breath as she took off the boot from her damaged foot. She expected the ankle to hurt a lot but she only felt a little discomfort. This was encouraging, maybe John was right when he said it was only bruised.

She removed the rest of her outer clothing without too much trouble. Getting her sweatshirt off over her head was the worst. She tried her best to avoid it catching the wound on her head but her arms ached so much as she lifted them up that the inevitable happened. She let out a cry of pain as her sweatshirt dragged over the wound. 'How bad is it?' she wondered.

She scoured the room for any hidden cameras or any peep holes and checked that no one could see through the window before she removed her underwear. Now who was being illogical? She unfastened her bra, with some difficulty, and dropped it to the floor. Oh the relief! Finally, she removed her soaked and stinking panties knowing that none of her clothes would ever be fit to wear again. The bin would be the destination for them.

"Oh what a lovely aroma you have Sarah. Eau de Sweat and Terra Firma. Well actually Eau de Sweat and Terra Not-so-firma," she whispered.

Suddenly a thought brightened her up a little. If only she could persuade John to put her dirty clothes in his dust bin there was a chance, just a chance that whoever collected the rubbish would wonder what ladies' clothes were doing in his bin. Then as quickly as the thought had come it was replaced by her realisation that no one would collect dust bins in this remote location. John must take his rubbish to a collection point, or burn it. Disappointment followed elation, how often would this happen?

Looking at herself in the discoloured mirror she saw the full extent of the damage to her front. It didn't seem as bad as she expected. She assumed her back would be similar from the pain she felt. In a couple of weeks there should be no outward sign of the trauma she had suffered. Her ankle may take a little longer for the bruising to go as it obviously took her full weight when she landed on the ledge making the bruising worse than it appeared on other parts of her body. The damage to her mind and her emotions would probably take much longer to heal.

She couldn't see the back of her head in the mirror no matter how she contorted her body. She felt this may be the worst damage she had suffered.

It hurt like hell getting in to the hot bath. Every little scratch stung like she was being attacked by a swarm of bees. Slowly, oh so slowly, she lowered herself into the water. Slowly, oh so slowly, the water eased her aches little by little.

As Sarah soaked her aching body in the bath her thoughts turned to the search that surely must be underway to find her. Someone must have raised the alarm. How long would it take them to find her? They would be certain to find her; it was only a matter of time she thought.

She looked down at Betty who was laid by the bath. "Not long now Betty, they'll soon find us."

Sarah had argued with John about Betty going into the bathroom. He said it was unhygienic but she refused to let her out of her sight.

Wherever Sarah went, Betty went – and she meant everywhere. She still didn't completely trust her notion that John wasn't a physical danger to them. Betty would be sleeping with her tonight no matter how much it upset John.

Yes, the search party would be out by now. She hoped they would soon find her but it wouldn't be easy in this remote moorland. Like looking for a needle in a haystack she imagined. They would come though, eventually, she was sure. Until then she would play John's game, her survival game.

Time had no meaning at the moment so Sarah was determined to spend as long as possible in the bath. Time to soak away her aches and ease her memories and her fears.

She thought of John's peculiar habits. Why did he check the door was locked so often when he knew he had locked it only minutes before? She thought of how often she checked the door in her under stairs cell at her parents' home to see if they had opened it signalling her temporary release. Was that any different to what John was doing?

Why did he walk his circuitous paths, appearing to avoid the cracks? She had no answer to this. She giggled as she thought of playing hopscotch at primary school, avoiding the lines. She was rubbish at it she thought but couldn't really remember. She could clearly recall Colin Thomas pushing her over as often as he could just so he could get a quick glimpse of her knickers as she fell. Who would be turned on by navy blue school knickers? The last she heard of Colin he was the manager of one of the banks in Manchester. She laughed as she wondered if he remembered his infant voyeurism. Maybe one day they would meet and she could remind him. If she ever got out of this place.

Why did John stand up and sit down constantly? She hoped that one day he would explain, but did she really want to know? Her curiosity said yes, her fear said no.

She had wallowed in the bath so long that the water had gone cold. She couldn't stay in there any longer. Betty desperately needed a bath but she daren't risk putting her in John's bath. She didn't want to risk raising his anger, at least until she knew more about him. She'd only known him a few hours after all.

She wrapped the bath towel tightly around herself before she moved the cupboard from behind the door. She then popped her head outside the door to make sure the path between the bathroom and her bedroom was clear. It was.

She walked to the bedroom as quickly as she could. It was a pretty if old fashioned room. Just a double bed, which looked to have clean bedding on. Mind you there was no sign of a continental quilt, just sheets, blankets and a bedspread. There was one set of drawers and a small wardrobe. Both were old and showed the signs of many, many years of service.

There was just one small window covered with plain heavy gold curtains which had been drawn together. The curtains certainly blocked out the dull end of day light. Sarah opened the curtains to look at the view and jumped back in horror. Tears welled up in her eyes as she realised the windows had been painted with black paint. The paint was almost dry but still a little bit tacky, indicating that it had only been applied today. Had John done this when he came back for the rope ladder? She was terrified. John obviously had no intention of anyone seeing her through the window. What was he planning?

It took her a few minutes to regain her composure. She was determined not to let John see she was frightened of him. She looked at the bulge under the bedclothes and guessed these were the clothes he had found her. She assumed he had put them under the covers to warm up as she guessed they hadn't been worn for a while.

As she pulled back the covers to reveal the pile of clothes she burst out into roaring laughter. She was sure that Betty was thinking that she had gone mad. She laughed and laughed and laughed, tears rolling down her cheeks. Happy tears for a change.

There was a thick plaid skirt several sizes too big. It must be fifty years old at least she thought. There was no way that would stay up without several safety pins. She moved the skirt to reveal a pair of bloomers. New bloomers mind you, still in their packet. They cost 10 pence – old pence. My god how old were they?

It just got better and better. A blouse that her grandma wouldn't have been seen dead in, an old fashioned, old ladies top that must have been Marks and Spencer circa 1950.

She noticed that the bra was huge. She thought she would have to put both her boobs in one cup to even half fill it. "They must have made them big back in those days," she giggled.

She realised that her laughter was nervous laughter. She certainly didn't feel amused. In fact looking at the pile of clothes made her feel worse about her situation. Is this what the future held?

The only other item of clothing was a floor length pink flannelette nightdress. She thought of Nora Batty. No even Nora Batty was much more modern than these clothes. She guessed these were his mum's clothes and wondered how long she had been dead. She must be dead as she hadn't seen her and although she had never met her and knew almost nothing about her, for some reason she guessed that she wouldn't be the type to go on holiday.

She had no option but to wear the nightdress. She slid it over her head and let it fall over her body. She looked like a walking advert for Rent a Tent! At least John's passion wouldn't be aroused by this. If he had any passion that was.

She sat on the edge of the bed and sobbed. The situation was really depressing her. She was trapped in a strange house, with a strange man, wearing horrible clothes. "Is this my life from now on? Is this who I am now?" she asked herself. She had no answer.

She had managed to soak the dried blood off her hair by lying flat in the bath for a long time but she decided against trying to brush it with the brush that was on the top of the set of drawers, at least for now. She was afraid it would be too painful yet. The wound needed dressing anyway.

It was late when she made her way back downstairs but John was still there in his chair.

"Thank you for the clothes John," she said. She thought it better to please John than antagonise him. John seemed uncomfortable when she came down wearing the nightdress and tried his best to keep his eyes averted.

"You need to bind your ankle and bandage your head wound," John said without looking at her.

"I can't do it John. Not without you helping me. I can't see the wound on my head so how can I bandage it?"

"I can't help you Sarah."

"Why not. I've just had a bath so I'm clean."

"But I might not be."

"You look very clean to me. You wash your hands so many times and for so long that they are red raw. You must be clean."

"You can't be certain of that."

"Oh God help me. I am sure there is nothing wrong with you John. Why are you so paranoid about disease and contamination? Just snap out of it."

"I've said before, you don't understand."

"I sure as hell don't, so tell me."

"I can't tell you. The devil would claim someone I cared for if I did."

Sarah's eyes opened wide. She was lost for words. She was really terrified now. She took the bandages and plasters John had put on the small table and went to her bedroom without another word. Betty followed her as Betty always did. As she went upstairs she could hear John sobbing.

She had never had such mixed emotions for anyone before. He was kind yet crazy. Helpful yet obstructive. Emotional yet apathetic. "Betty we have to get through this somehow." She had no idea how.

Chapter Twelve

Like all old furniture the chest of drawers in Sarah's bedroom was built to last and very heavy. She had no option though, she had to push it behind the door.

Inch by inch, pushing and pulling, straining muscles that were already suffering, she managed to move the drawers close enough to the door to at least stop him pushing it open enough to get in. He would be able to open the door a little and therefore could watch her while she slept if he wanted but that was a minor inconvenience compared to the problems that her rescue had thrown at her. She certainly didn't look her sexiest so if he wanted to look, let him. She hoped he wasn't strong enough to push the door and the drawers together.

His comment about the Devil really freaked her out. What did he mean? Sarah wasn't religious nor was she an atheist. Agnostic was perhaps the best word to describe her. If someone or something proved beyond doubt that God existed, she would believe in God. Likewise, if someone or something proved beyond doubt that the Devil existed she would believe in the Devil. She hoped that the something wasn't her meeting the Devil.

She supposed she was looking for certainty but she knew that nothing in life, or death for that matter, could be 100% certain.

John had said that the Devil would take someone he cared for. Who did he care for? He'd never mentioned anyone in the few hours she had known him.

"Oh my god, does he mean me?"

~~~~~~~~~~

John heard the drawers being dragged across the floor in Sarah's room and knew his comment about the Devil had terrified her.

It had terrified him as well. Why had his thoughts about deals with the Devil resurfaced after so long? He wasn't sure he had made a deal with the Devil, but he might have. He might have made it when his father was dying, that sounded logical – to him. He remembered experiencing a fear of being left alone, so that might have been when he made the deal – if there was a deal. He wanted his parents, both of them, to live forever.

He had heard people talking on the radio about devil deals. Was it true or were they cranks? Until he knew with absolute certainty then there was a possibility he had made a deal with the Devil at some point and that put someone he cared for in danger.

It was an almost daily concern whilst his mother was still alive but since then it had stayed at the back of his mind. None of his bad thoughts ever disappear completely. They were always there suppressed but waiting to spring to the surface when they could do most harm. But why now?

"Is it possible to care for someone you only met a few hours ago?" he whispered.

~~~~~~~~~

Sarah knew it would hurt like hell but she decided that she really had to try and brush her hair. Its current state added to a night of tossing and turning would make it much more difficult to get through the tangles and knots in the morning.

She searched the chest of drawers in the hope of finding something she could use as a mirror and found an old hand mirror in the bottom drawer, which was the last drawer she checked. It was one of those old fashioned hand mirrors she had seen her grandma use. A thin black plastic frame surrounded the glass. The glass had lost its mirror backing around the edges leaving just a small round section in the centre that she could see herself through. Hardly enough but it would have to do.

She put her pillow on top of the chest of drawers to prop the mirror against. She knew she would need to use both hands on her hair to avoid it pulling too much. She held the brush in her right hand and used her left hand to hold her hair as she gently and very slowly eased the brush through her shoulder length blond hair. Tiny bit by tiny bit.

'This will take a long time', she thought, but that wasn't a problem because she knew sleep wouldn't come easy tonight. She was saddened to see that her hair had lost its usual bounce and shine. It was dull and lifeless. Her brown eyes, she noticed, were also dull and without their usual full of life twinkle. She hoped that those were the only parts of her anatomy that she would need to refer to as lifeless at the end of her ordeal.

~~~~~~~~~~

John lay in bed unable to sleep. He had finally got to bed about one o'clock in the morning after his long and repetitive checking and rechecking ritual. He hated his rituals but he had to do them. He daren't miss them out for fear of what would happen.

He lay awake with his two angels bombarding him with questions and commands. The good angel was on his left shoulder as usual and the bad angel on his right shoulder, his dominant side.

"Let her go John," he could hear in his mind the good angel say.

"But she might be contaminated John," countered the bad angel.

"How can she be John? There's no way you can be contaminated so how can you contaminate her?"

"Remember John when you trod on that used condom near the reservoir? You might be infected with HIV. That's deadly. You might have passed it on to her."

"That's not how you get HIV John. You don't catch it through your boots. It's five years ago anyway. You have never had sex with anyone so you can't have HIV."

"You might have John. There might be other ways to catch it. You can't be sure. Don't take any chances."

John put his head under the covers and screamed, "Stop it! Stop it! Please." He was shaking and tears were rolling down his cheeks.

"What have I done? What should I do?"

~~~~~~~~~~

Sarah lay in bed unable to sleep. Snuggling up to Betty gave her the only tiny bit of comfort she could get. Betty didn't normally sleep in her room let alone on her bed but she needed to keep her close now and keep her as far away from John as possible. They were in this together and they would battle through it together.

"Oh Betty how did I get us into this mess? Why us?"

What little sleep Sarah did get that night was punctuated by nightmares.

She saw all the dogs she looked after running wild through the village because she wasn't there to care for them. Cars were having to swerve to avoid hitting them. Parents were having to drag their

57

children out of the way of the wayward cars. She held her breath because she knew it was only a matter of time before one of the cars would plough through a group of people killing them all.

She was hyperventilating when she woke with a start. It seemed ages before she slipped into a shallow slumber once more.

She saw Mrs Evans being carried out of her home in a coffin. She'd had nothing to eat for days because Sarah wasn't there to do her shopping. Her prescriptions would have run out as well. Mrs Evans would have had a slow painful death. She would have starved to death, and been in pain whilst doing so. How long had it been before someone had found her? She couldn't even be at her funeral to say goodbye. Sarah would never forgive herself for that for as long as she lived, however long that may be.

Betty's snoring woke her up. At least one of them was getting a good sleep. More tossing, more turning. She had no idea how long it was before sleep returned again. She didn't want to sleep, she wanted to stay awake to plan their escape but fatigue forced her to submit to what little sleep she could get.

She saw the casket containing Betty's ashes on her mantelpiece. She remembered Betty becoming weaker and weaker because she had nothing to feed her with. She would never forget Betty wagging her tail as she lay on the floor too weak to get up. She knew Betty didn't want her to worry about her. She wagged her tail to try and say "I'm alright Mum."

Sarah was wakened by the sensation that someone was prodding her shoulder. She kept her eyes closed for fear of seeing John in bed with her. The prodding turned into licks on her face. That tongue was too long to be a human tongue. "Betty," she shouted, "You're alive, you're alive." She hugged Betty as though her life depended on it. Perhaps it did.

Betty continued to wriggle which she didn't normally do when she was snuggled up to Sarah.

"What's wrong Betty?"

"Oh my god you didn't have a wee last night." Sarah had been so keen to get away from John that she had completely forgotten Betty's pre bed toilet visit.

She knew Betty would never wee in the house no matter how long she had to hold on. Sarah had to get Betty outside.

"Come on Betty," she whispered, "Be very quiet." She hoped John would still be asleep and certainly didn't want to wake him.

Sarah managed to move the chest of drawers just enough to squeeze through. To avoid making a noise she eased the edge of the drawers up and placed her undamaged foot underneath. This way she managed to move the bulky piece of furniture away from the door bit by bit without making a sound. It hurt like hell but it was the only way.

Betty was too big to carry but Sarah had no doubt that she would follow her and hopefully wouldn't bark. Sarah's hope was that somewhere downstairs she would find a spare door key. Getting downstairs would be the easy bit she thought.

Slowly, tentative step by tentative step they made their way down the staircase. Sarah froze when one step creaked at a high volume but thankfully she heard no stirrings from John's room.

They reached the door at the bottom of the stairs and slowly she started to turn the handle. It wouldn't open. The door was locked. He had her contained just like her parents used to do. She would be let out when he felt it was right, and not a moment before.

Sarah slumped down on to a step and sobbed. Betty put her paw on Sarah's lap. Betty knew something serious was wrong and tried to lick away Sarah's tears.

"Oh Betty I'm so sorry," she whispered.

"What the fuck is wrong with him?" she whispered for fear of waking him up. "He needs locking up." In the deathly dark silence that surrounded her whispers sounded like screams to Sarah. Then she did scream like a banshee. Louder and louder as the waves of fear filled her body.

~~~~~~~~~~~

John was startled awake by the sound of a piercing screech, followed by another and another. The screech was joined by a frantic banging that grew louder and louder. Accompanied by the screeching it was building to the crescendo of a musical score of despair. He had to stop it. The constant noise coupled with all the thoughts going round his head was unbearable.

He saw Sarah hammering on the door at the bottom of the stairs trying to break it down. He knew he couldn't make her understand why he was acting the way he was. He didn't want to keep her a prisoner but he had to.

"What's wrong with me?" he screamed inside.

"I need help but no one can help me. No one understands. I don't understand."

Betty started to growl. Betty never growled. Sarah sensed a presence behind her and turned to see John looming at the top of the stairs, his form silhouetted against the small moonlit window behind him. Her heated blood turned to icy cold and the rage which had comforted her only a moment before deserted her. Defeat and despair took its place.

"Come on my dear," let me help you back to bed he said.

He seemed agitated which worried Sarah. She knew there was no escape as he led her submissively back to her room.

Chapter 13

Wednesday 5am. Mrs Evans woke up and sat on the edge of her bed taking her morning tablets, twelve in all. She thought about how much it must be costing the country to keep her alive. Was it worth it she wondered? Sarah sorted out her tablets for her each week into a pill box so that she knew just what to take and when.

Mrs Evans woke at 5am every day. It was the time she woke up when she was working in the local cotton mill and the habit stayed with her. She remembered the cotton mills with affection. Although the place was very noisy and very dusty, contributing she was sure to the deafness and asthma she now had to deal with, she made lots of friends there. Sadly, most had now passed away. The only one she had any contact with, and that was rare, was Ethel Johnson.

It was hard tiring work, six days a week, so they were shattered at the end of their shifts. Before and after work each day, however, she was still expected to help her mother with a lot of the housework, except for Sunday afternoon. After lunch on a Sunday she was allowed to go into the village to meet her friends. Her mother didn't know for years that when she got older she only met one friend, a male friend at that. If her parents had found out they would have stopped her going out even though she was twenty.

The atmosphere in the mills was kept hot and humid to stop the thread from breaking. The weavers used to imagine they were in some hot foreign country lazing in the sun. None of them would ever be likely to see a foreign country mind you. It was horrible in winter when you came out of the heat of the mill to freezing temperatures and snow. Their clothes were never warm enough for a northern winter.

They learned to lip read so that they could converse above the din of the weaving machines. They talked about men mainly, in a context they would never dare talk at home. She met her husband Tommy in the mill. Tommy was a cardroom operative and she smiled when she thought about the day when he asked her dad for permission to marry her. That was the norm in those days. She had listened with her mother through the closed kitchen door, both stifling their giggles. She remembered her dad saying, "Aye lad you can marry our lass if you can promise to keep her in the manner she's used to."

"Well that won't take much doing," she whispered to her mother.

Tommy was a good man and they were inseparable throughout their married life. They never spent a night apart in nearly fifty years. She had missed his company terribly since he passed away from cancer ten years ago, just six months short of their golden wedding.

"Come on Ellen," she said to herself, "no time to waste reminiscing." In reality she had all the time in the world.

She sat at her dressing table brushing her hair. Every day she saw more wrinkles and any remaining brown hairs had long since been replaced by grey but she chuckled as she thought 'not bad for 88 my dear'. It was true, you could see just how beautiful she must have been when she was young. She was still slim as she always had been but she could no longer keep her five foot eight inches frame perfectly upright.

"Early to bed, early to rise makes a man healthy, wealthy and wise," her mother always used to say. She still did the early to bed, early to rise bit but had lost the healthy bit and never found the wealthy and wise. She started to get ready for bed at 8pm except for Mondays and Fridays. She had a nice television but never found much she liked to watch on it. The only programme that she never missed was Coronation Street, which she had watched from the days when Ena, Minnie and Martha used to sit round the snug table drinking their milk stout. When Coronation Street first started she thought it was real but never admitted that to anyone. Coronation Street was the reason she went to bed later on Mondays and Fridays.

Ellen and Tommy had two children, Richard and Angela, but she rarely heard from either of them. Richard and his wife Barbara had gone to live down south to be near her parents and Angela lived in America where she was some high powered executive and didn't really have time to contact her mother now. She didn't even come to her father's funeral. Mrs Evans didn't mind that because it would have cost her a lot of money but she dreamed that one day she may see her again before it was too late. Occasionally Richard telephoned her on Sarah's phone. Sarah had a cordless phone, a walk about phone Mrs Evans called it, and she ran around with it so Mrs Evans could have a chat with Richard. He never chatted for long mind you.

Mrs Evans had her usual breakfast of Weetabix and a cup of tea and then shuffled around doing a little bit of dusting. She couldn't do much but liked to keep a tiny bit of independence. Sarah was like the daughter everyone would want but she couldn't let her do everything for her. Sarah never complained and had never mentioned the fact that Mrs Evans' real son and daughter never did anything for her.

'Where was Sarah?' she thought. She was really worried something had happened to her. Did that nice young couple say they were calling round again tonight? She couldn't remember. Her memory wasn't what it used to be. Oh she could remember every detail from 60, 70, even 80 years ago but most days couldn't remember what she had for dinner an hour earlier. Sarah kept her appointment diary for her. Hospitals, doctors, prescription dates. 'How will I cope without Sarah?' she thought.

She looked out of the window and saw it was another lovely day weather wise. "Two nice days in a row," she said to herself, "that's very unusual around here but we deserve it after all the rain and wind we have had recently." Although her short term memory was very poor it was amazing that Mrs Evans could usually, but not always, remember certain things. They tended to be the big things in her life, like Sarah's visits, like the weather. She certainly knew that she hadn't seen Sarah for at least a couple of days, maybe more.

Determined to make the most of the warm sunny weather she shuffled out of the door, a bit of a struggle with her Zimmer frame, and sat at the table in her garden. Oh how she enjoyed the fresh air and looking up onto the moors. She loved seeing the cows and sheep in the distance on the hillside farms and watching the birds swooping across the sky although she had no idea what kind of birds they were. The mysterious moors her mother had always said. Mrs Evans wondered just what tales they could tell, just what mysteries they held.

She was dozing off when suddenly she was jolted awake by something jumping on her knee. It made her jump but then she saw that it was only the cat from up the road. She didn't know who it belonged to but it was a regular visitor when Mrs Evans sat outside and always sat on her knee and curled up to go to sleep. Mrs Evans loved having some company even though it wasn't human company. In some ways that was better because she could say the silliest of things and the cat wouldn't mind at all. Both fell asleep in the mid-day sun.

"Good afternoon Mrs E, are you well today."

This startled her and she woke up to find Frank the local postman standing there.

"Sorry if I startled you," he said.

"No don't worry. I must have dozed off. You're late today."

"Oh I brought the letters this morning but I've got a parcel now for Sarah next door. Can I leave it with you, I know she calls in on you regularly?"

Mrs Evans started to cry.

"What's the matter Mrs E? Are you unwell?"

"No I'm fine, it's Sarah."

"What on earth is the matter?"

"That's the trouble I don't know. I haven't seen her for a few days."

"Maybe she has gone to visit her auntie."

"Perhaps but she hasn't let the people whose dogs she looks after know. I had a couple round last night, nice couple, to see if I knew where she was. She hadn't told them that she wouldn't be picking up their dog. Poor thing had done a wee in their kitchen it was that desperate. I wish I did know where she was."

"That doesn't sound like the Sarah I know."

"There never goes a day that I don't see her. She always pops in to see how I am and she does all my shopping for me, and a lot of other things as well. She always tells me when she is going away. I won't survive without Sarah."

"Don't worry Mrs E I'm sure everything will be fine. She's a tough cookie. I'm sure she'll come cheerily walking down the lane soon as though nothing has happened. Maybe there was some misunderstanding with the people who came to see you. Maybe Sarah didn't know she was supposed to pick their dog up."

"Maybe."

64

"Have any other dog owners asked you if you have seen Sarah."

"No."

"There you go then. If anything was wrong you'd have had other people round."

"I guess so but why hasn't she been to see me?"

"Maybe she has a cold or something that she doesn't want to pass on to you. She would know you would be alright for a few days."

This made sense and cheered Mrs Evans up a bit. Perhaps Frank was right. Yes he must be right.

When Frank had gone Mrs Evans ate the sandwich she had made for lunch. She made it before she came out to save herself having to struggle back inside unnecessarily. Well perhaps it was more correct to say that Mrs Evans shared the sandwich she had made for lunch. She couldn't resist having a piece herself and giving a piece to the cat, then another piece for herself and a piece for the cat. "Here you are Mr No Name. Here's your lunch." The cat purred a loud thank you.

The more she thought about it, whilst eating her lunch, the more she was sure that Frank was right.

After lunch both lady and cat fell asleep in the afternoon sun. Mrs Evans had no idea how long she had been asleep when she heard someone saying "Excuse me."

Standing at her gate was a very attractive young lady. Slim with long auburn hair and a cheery smile.

"Sorry to disturb you. My name is Natasha. I wondered if you had seen your next door neighbour Sarah recently. She looks after my dog but hasn't picked him up this week so far. I wondered if she was ill but she usually telephones me if she is ill or can't pick Henry up for some other reason. I just wondered if you knew anything."

"No my dear I don't. You're the second lot that have asked about her. I haven't seen her for a few days myself. I'm sure there will be some logical explanation."

"Thank you very much. I'm really sorry to disturb you. I'll call round again next week if I don't hear from Sarah."

"That's no problem. Good bye."

"Mrs Evans now knew there was no logical explanation. She knew Frank was wrong."

She gently pushed the cat off her knee and shuffled back inside the house. She hadn't the heart to look at the moors any more, Sarah's moors.

Chapter 14

Wednesday 6am. John woke as he always did at this time. It was milking time and even though he no longer had cows to look after he couldn't get out of the habit.

He hadn't slept well and his head was in a whirl. He realised that his world had been turned upside down in less than 24 hours. He now had someone living with him and that fact brought horrendous problems. Problems that had faded since his parents died. Life was much easier on his own. Now all the old thoughts were back and back with a vengeance. He had no idea what to do and no one to help him decide.

He didn't think he would harm Sarah even though his head told him differently. He'd never actually harmed anyone before but he thought there may be a first time. He did everything else his mind told him but not that. If she didn't fight against him she would be fine. He had to make her understand, for her sake and the world's sake.

He knew they would come looking for her sometime although he didn't know who they were. What if the police came? What if they arrested him? The thought of ending up in prison terrified him. How would his mind cope with being locked in a cell with criminals? He knew it wouldn't. The criminals may have diseases. They could be drug addicts and have shared needles. The bedding may be contaminated. The cell may be crawling with germs. There would be no cleanliness. He would have no personal space, no confidentiality. It would be hell. He wondered if he would have the courage to kill himself. He'd never had the courage before even when his mind had told him that if he didn't those around him would be in danger. Something terrible would happen to one or all of them. He had even driven into Manchester once and walked the streets at 3am hoping someone would stab him. Sometimes death seemed so much easier than life.

He had to confess, but he couldn't confess. He didn't know what he had done to confess to but he was sure there was something. He was only caring for a woman with a damaged ankle, and her dog.

He went into the bathroom for his bath. He always took a very long time to try and get as clean as he could but this morning's was much longer than usual. He scrubbed at his whole body but particularly his hands. The hands were after all what had contact with things that other people may then use. By the time he had finished his hands were red raw and on the point of bleeding. He wanted to scrub them more but he had to stop before they bled. He couldn't risk his blood coming into contact with anything else, things were bad enough as they were.

Eventually he made his way downstairs. He didn't feel at all like eating but he had to make breakfast, it was part of the routine. He would make his breakfast soon and make Sarah's breakfast later. It was too early to wake her now. He hoped that she would begin to feel better today. He so wanted her to trust him.

He began the day with his early morning cup of tea, which he drank outside as usual. It looked like it was going to be another warm sunny day. As he drank he walked around the yard to look for an appropriate place for Betty to use as a toilet. He wasn't really bothered about her fouling anywhere as he could hose it down. He was bothered however about anyone seeing her. Remote as the chances of this were he couldn't risk it. He had to make his plans before he took any chances. He had to be ready for them, whoever they were.

When he had finished his reconnaissance he went indoors to cook his breakfast, bacon, eggs and fried bread as always. His mind just wasn't on the task at hand and as a result he burnt his bacon and almost cremated the fried bread. He hurled them both into the bin in a mixture of frustration and anger. His life was so simple before Sarah. Why did that bloody dog have to wander into his farmyard out of all the farms on these moors? Why was Sarah not more careful? He spends his life being careful and then other people carelessly mess everything up.

Only the egg was edible but he sat just picking at it. He couldn't stomach eating anything, not until he knew if Sarah was alright. He

68

knew he wanted to care for her but he didn't know the right way to do it. The egg followed the bacon and fried bread into the bin. He left the plate to wash up later. He hated washing up and usually only did it when he had run out of plates, cups and cutlery. In his more logical moments he wondered why he was so particularly about cleanliness but yet left his washing up for days. It was just another thing that didn't make sense. Nothing made sense, yet everything made sense. Life was full of confusion.

John decided to wait until about 8am before taking Sarah breakfast in bed. Wasn't that what men did? He would have to take Betty something to eat too. Why had he thrown his breakfast away, she could have had that. The more he thought about Betty the more he realised that she greatly complicated the situation. Without her to deal with he was sure he would be able to more clearly see what to do but she was an added problem. Living on a farm he was used to no animal being for ever. When they became a problem they had to go. Betty was a problem.

He sat down in his chair to listen to the radio as he usually did in the morning. He suddenly realised he was listening to the local radio station instead of his usual Radio 4. He didn't remember tuning into that station but he must have done without thinking. He listened to the early morning news and was relieved not to hear any mention of Sarah. They obviously weren't looking for her yet. They would come though; it was only a matter of time. Would they be searching for her by Friday when he paid his weekly shopping visit to the village? If they were he couldn't miss going because that would look suspicious. He would have to have his answers ready. He would rehearse what questions he may get asked or what comments would be made by the people he met. He would really have to fight his compulsion to confess. It was too soon to confess. He had work to do first to protect the people around here from contamination. What was he confessing to anyway? Had he done anything wrong? He was doing the best he could in a no win situation but he knew that others wouldn't agree.

If they started to look for Sarah he would have to contain her upstairs. Upstairs she only had access to her bedroom where the windows were painted over with black paint and the bathroom where the windows were frosted. For now he was safe letting her come downstairs. In any case he needed to get Sarah to trust him and that wouldn't happen if he locked her upstairs 24 hours a day.

Sarah would have to trust him to take Betty out to go to the toilet. She would have to trust him enough to eat the food he made. He would have to trust himself enough to let Sarah eat the food he made. He made a mental note to buy some disposable gloves when he went to the village on Friday to use when he was cooking, in fact when he was doing anything that may affect Sarah. For now he would wrap his hands in cling film. He knew that may make it difficult to pick things up but he had to do it.

He needed help and advice. There was somewhere he needed to go. He had time before he made Sarah's breakfast.

He put on his coat and flat cap. Although it was shaping up to be a warm day there was still an early morning chill in the air. He put his boots on in the porch and set off to walk up the hillside behind the house. It was a steep climb but not too far. He got there in about ten minutes and knelt on the ground. This piece of land was sacred to him. It was where both his mother's and his father's ashes had been scattered. They had lived their lives on these moors so it seemed appropriate that they spent their after life here too. Religion scared John because no one could tell him for definite what happened after you died. Everyone told him that God forgives your sins and lets you into heaven but they couldn't guarantee that. John wanted a 100% guarantee. He didn't know if he had ever sinned but his parents always told him that no one was perfect therefore he must have sinned. He placed his hands on the ground and looked up to the sky. "Help me Mum, help me Dad."

He had no idea how long he was up with his parents but he had to get back to make his visitor's breakfast. He had no idea what Sarah would want for breakfast but he guessed at the same as he had. Bacon, egg and fried bread. To be honest he didn't have anything else in the house that was suitable. He would make sure he cooked it properly this time. He would have to make the same for Betty as he had no dog food. Again he made a mental note to get some on Friday if Betty was still here.

He wrapped the cling film around his hands. The first hand was easy to do but it was difficult to do the second hand when his other hand was effectively wearing a mitten. He did it and checked and double checked that there were no gaps or tears. He then took great care to cook the breakfast to perfection. He wanted to please Sarah. More than anything he wanted to please Sarah.

He placed the food and drink, tea of course, on a tray he had found in one of the kitchen cupboards. He added a bluebell that he had found on his way back to the house, placing it carefully in a vase.

He set off up the stairs. "I am on my way my dear," he whispered, "please like what I am bringing you."

Chapter 15

Wednesday 7am. Katy and Steve got up. They usually got up at this time during the week but allowed themselves a bit of a lie in on Saturday and Sunday. Well as long a lie in as Cuddles would let them have.

There were none of the antics of yesterday morning. They were both worried about Sarah, which made the atmosphere very subdued.

There were no arguments as to who made breakfast today. It was on the table waiting for Katy when she came out of the shower. After breakfast Steve took Katy to work. Normally when he was working at home she would take the car but not today. They had decided that Steve should keep the car just in case he needed it to go to the police station.

The journey to Katy's work was silent. Not the type of silence that follows an argument but a worried silence. Neither of them felt like making small talk.

He got out of the car when he dropped Katy off and gave her a big hug. He loved her with all his heart and couldn't imagine life without her. Like Mrs Evans couldn't imagine life without Sarah.

"Steve, let go I have to go in now." They gave each other a lingering kiss and then he watched her until she was out of view. He didn't relish the thought of a day at home with only silence and his own thoughts for company. Steve didn't like being alone at the best of times and especially not at times like this. He knew he could talk to Cuddles but it wasn't the same. He felt silly talking to a little fluffy dog, even though no one could see or hear him. It was like talking to a fluffy duster, a moving yapping fluffy duster. That reminded him that the car needed washing. How he wished he had a manly dog to talk to. That would be much better. Man to man.

Steve made a coffee when he arrived back home. He then sat down at the kitchen table to attack the pile of assignments he had to mark. He hated marking assignments. The same subject at least 30 times over. The good ones were interesting to read but sadly they were in the minority. He wondered if that was indicative that he wasn't a good teacher but thought it more likely that the students couldn't be bothered to put the effort in. He tried to encourage them but you got to a point that those you realised would never work could go to hell. He still had to mark their assignments though and give diplomatic feedback.

He decided that he would wait until 10:30am to see if Sarah arrived. She didn't and that really worried him. It also meant that he would have to walk Cuddles which annoyed him on two fronts. He resented the time this would take him away from his marking and would mean he would have to work later this evening. He had to meet the deadline. More than that he hated walking a fluffy duster on his own. He was convinced everyone would laugh at him. What man would have a dog like this? The only saving grace was that such a small dog needed less walking than a big manly dog would. He walked cuddles down into the village and along the canal bank. He thought he wouldn't meet many people with it being during working hours but how wrong could he be.

He met every man and his dog, so to speak. Yes men with manly dogs, except him. Oh god the embarrassment. It's the wife's dog he found himself saying to everyone who spoke to him without any great confidence that they believed him. He tried not to make eye contact with most people he met. He saw two men approaching him. They had a huge Alsatian with them.

"Oh my god," he said, "its Ben and Henry from the pool team. I'll never live this down. It will be all round the pub before I know it." He looked for a way to escape but he was too late. They had spotted him.

"Hi Steve," shouted Ben, "What's that cute little thing you've got there?"

"It's Katy's," muttered Steve.

"Are you sure?" Henry said through his chuckles, "We often thought you had a strong feminine side Steve."

"What's it called?" asked Ben.

Oh no. Why did they ask that? Why couldn't they mind their own business? He couldn't tell them Cuddles' name. The shame, the embarrassment.

"He's called Rambo," he said at which point Ben and Henry fell about laughing. Why had he said that name? He saw it on a poster in the shop window across the road and didn't think. The name just tumbled out of his mouth before he had time to engage his brain.

"Come here fluffy Rambo," Henry said. Just at that point Cuddles took a fancy to Ben's dog, a huge Alsatian. He was trying to mount it. 'The impossible dream', Steve thought, 'but you have to admire a trier.' It was definitely a one way love affair. Steve had visions of the Alsatian picking Cuddles up in its mouth and throwing him around. How would he tell Katy that her beloved dog was now mincemeat?

After a bit of a struggle Ben managed to pull Brutus away from Cuddles. Brutus by name, Brutus by nature Steve thought.

Steve picked up Cuddles and said, "Come on Cuddles time to go home. Oh shit!" Ben and Henry had tears rolling down their cheeks and kept saying Cuddles over and over as they walked away. Steve could feel his cheeks were red and very warm.

He was so glad when he got home and shut the door behind him. He made another coffee and then carried on with marking more of the assignments.

He became so engrossed in his work that without him realising it 4pm had arrived. He hadn't had lunch. It was too late to eat a meal now so he decided to have a piece of the wonderful banana cake that Katy made. With a good covering of real butter and another coffee it would see him through to his evening meal. He suddenly remembered that he hadn't phoned the police. Katy would be furious but he would tell her that he had tried to call but no one was available to talk to him so he thought they should call in at the police station on their way home from Katy's office. He hoped she wouldn't drop him in it at the police station by referring to the fact that no one could speak to him when he rang. He would just have to keep his fingers crossed.

At 4:30pm he put Cuddles into the small cage they kept in the back of their hatchback and set off to collect Katy. At least he had remembered that they had promised to visit Mrs Evans and take Cuddles to see her.

Katy waved as she approached the car and gave him a peck on the cheek when she was settled in the passenger seat.

"What did the police say?"

"We are going there now."

"What! You forgot to get in touch with them didn't you? How could you?"

Steve denied this and acted out his predetermined script. He was sure she didn't believe him but she didn't say anything.

They pulled on to the police station car park about 30 minutes later. There was no station in the village so they had to go to the nearest town. They approached the desk and the sergeant who was sat at the desk talking on the phone indicated that he would only be two minutes. When he had finished the call he walked over to the desk.

"What can I do to help you?"

"We want to report a missing person please. Well at least we think she is missing."

"Now make your minds up, is she or isn't she missing."

Steve felt this conversation was going in the same way as his meeting with Ben and Henry but at least the sergeant seemed to take them seriously when they told him all about Sarah and how they hadn't seen her all week and Mrs Evans hadn't seen her for about five days.

"She is an adult and that isn't too long to be away from home. Are you sure she isn't just visiting someone?"

"Sarah never lets her clients down. She would have told us if she was going to be away for more than the weekend and she certainly would have told Mrs Evans."

"Where does this Mrs Evans fit into this?"

"She is Sarah's next door neighbour and Sarah calls in every day to help her. She has no idea where Sarah is."

"With the greatest respect, if we are dealing with an old lady are you sure that Sarah hasn't told her and she has just forgotten."

"No we can't be sure but we really don't think so."

"Do you know any of her other clients? Have they not seen her either?"

"Sorry we don't know her other clients. Sarah picks our dog up at home so we never see anyone else."

"OK I've made a note of what you have told me and I'll pass them on to the person who is allocated the case. They will be in touch with you. Can you please give me your contact details?"

Katy found the anger boiling up inside her until she could hold it in no more. "You were very quick to book my husband last week when he was speeding, only by a little bit, yet you don't seem interested in looking for a missing woman. A woman who could be in danger."

"Madam speeding is speeding, no matter how little it is over the speed limit. I have already told you that someone will be assigned to the case and they will be in touch with you, probably tomorrow."

"Probably tomorrow," screamed Katy, "Only probably!"

"Come on Katy," Steve said quietly, "Let's go home. You shouting isn't doing any good."

Neither of them said a word until they were back in the car and had pulled out of the car park. "This is your fault Steve. If you had contacted the police this morning as you promised you would the search would already be under way."

"I didn't promise to ring this morning, I said I'd get in touch today and I did."

"Oh Steve you are useless. You can't do anything without me pushing you."

Katy heard Cuddles whimper in the back of the car. She had forgotten Steve was bringing her. "I bet he didn't take you for a walk either, did he Cuddles? You poor thing."

"Yes I did. You don't think I can do anything right. We had a lovely walk didn't we Rambo."

"What do you mean, Rambo?"

"Nothing. Just a joke."

By the time they reached Mrs Evans's house the tension had eased. Sarah never could stay mad with Steve for long. She loved him so much.

"Hello Mrs Evans," they both said in unison as she opened the door.

"We've brought a friend to see you."

Mrs Evans was really pleased to see Cuddles and immediately reached for the biscuit tin for a couple of biscuits to give Cuddles for a treat. She made sure that they didn't have chocolate or raisins in as Sarah had told her they were bad for dogs. She sat down in her chair opposite the television and broke the biscuits into little pieces to feed to the over excited canine. At that moment she was the dog's best friend. Once the biscuits had gone Cuddles jumped up onto Mrs Evans' lap, curled up and went to sleep.

"He's is such a lovely dog. Nice and small, not like these big ones that their owners can hardly hold on the lead. I bet you both love taking her for walks don't you."

"Oh yes we do," said Katy. Steve didn't say a word.

"How are you today Mrs Evans?"

"I'm fine, and please call me Ellen. How are you two? Have you heard anything about Sarah?"

"We are good Mrs Evans, sorry Ellen," replied Katy. She didn't feel comfortable calling an old lady by her Christian name but didn't want to upset her by ignoring her request to do so.

"We've just been to the police about Sarah," Steve said, "They say they will start to look for her tomorrow." That wasn't quite what they had said but he wanted to make Mrs Evans feel relaxed that something was happening. "The police may come to see you tomorrow to ask you a few questions."

"Could one of you be here when they do? I get very confused you see when someone asks me lots of questions."

They said that they would try their best to do so and that they would ask the police to let them know when they intended to visit Mrs Evans. Steve had no doubt that Katy would leave him a big note on the kitchen table and also put one in the middle of his marking pile so that he wouldn't forget.

"Is there anything you need us to do or to get for you for Ellen?" asked Katy.

"Oh that's kind of you dear. I think I am alright for food for a little while. Sarah always makes sure I am well stocked up. I'm not sure how many tablets I have left though. I only have enough left in my pill box for tomorrow morning. Would you mind checking for me please? They are in the cupboard by the door."

Katy looked in the cupboard and found enough tablets to last Mrs Evans another week. She also found a neat list that she presumed

Sarah had written that told her what tablets Mrs Evans took, how many and when, which was a great help as she filled up the spare pill box for next week. "You have enough for another week there Ellen."

"Oh thank you, thank you." She reached into the drawer next to her chair and pulled out a small box of chocolates. "Here you are dear, just a little something for doing my pill box for me."

"Oh don't be silly. I don't want anything for doing that, it only took me a few minutes," but Mrs Evans insisted.

"Shall we get your prescription for you tomorrow Ellen? Unless you have one of the other neighbours who usually gets it for you. We don't want to push our noses in."

"Oh would you do that for me? I hardly see any of the neighbours besides Sarah, except to say hello to as they pass. Most of them are computers you see. They live here but work long days in the city."

"I think you mean commuters."

"Oh silly me. I thought they were called computers," Ellen said with a cheeky grin, "What's a computer then?"

Katy realised that modern technology had hardly touched Mrs Evans' world. She genuinely had no idea what a computer was.

"Of course we will get your prescription. It's no trouble at all." Katy made a note of the chemist name on the bag that had contained the tablets she had just used.

They stayed with Mrs Evans for a further 30 minutes and then explained that they had to get Cuddles home to feed him and walk him, and to have their tea. "You can take him for a walk along the canal Steve while I make tea," Katy said. Steve gulped.

They wished Mrs Evans goodbye and promised to bring her prescription round sometime in the next couple of days.

"Don't worry about Sarah," Steve shouted as they waved goodbye, "I'm sure she will be fine." He was far from sure she would be fine but sometimes a little white lie served a good purpose.

They made sure Ellen locked her door before they drove off.

Chapter 16

Wednesday 8am. Sarah lay in bed delaying as long as possible the time she had to face John. She needed time to plan the way ahead. A plan to turn capture into freedom.

Betty had got off the bed during the night, which surprised Sarah, but as she rolled over to look where her best friend was she noticed a puddle on the floor and then saw Betty lay in the corner of the room with a sheepish look on her face. "Oh my darling, you must have been desperate," she said quietly and calmly with a smile on her face to try and reassure Betty that she wasn't in any trouble. "Trust me Betty, we will get out of this but I don't know how or when yet." Betty gave a little wag of her tail as if to say 'I do trust you." Sarah felt tears welling up in her eyes. It was alright to cry in private but she needed to be strong in front of John. She was sure that if he saw her upset he would try and care for her even more and that meant at best a delay in her release.

"OK Betty we need a plan."

Sarah had no idea what day it was. She was aware that it was her second day here at John's, the second of how many only time would tell. She had no idea how long she was in the sink hole. Lying here until it all goes away was the preferred option but that would do no good. Freedom wouldn't come of its own accord; it would have to be earned.

Just then there was a knock on her bedroom door. Betty gave a stifled bark from her corner shelter showing that she knew something was seriously wrong. Normally she would be barking very loud and wagging her tail in anticipation of what treats the visitor had brought.

"I've brought your breakfast my dear and some food for Betty." 'My dear' meant nothing romantic in John's vocabulary, it was just a greeting he had heard his parents use to anyone they met. Sarah, however, didn't read it this way.

"I'm not your dear and never will be," Sarah screamed, "I don't want any food you've made. Leave Betty's food outside then just GO AWAY."

Betty shouldn't suffer, this wasn't her fault. Well actually it was her fault. If she had gone to fetch her own ball none of this would have happened. "You stupid dog!"

As soon as the words left her mouth Sarah recoiled in shock. Her precious dog had never been shouted at before. What was happening? Guilt flooded over her as she saw Betty standing there wagging her tail. If only humans could show unconditional love in the way dogs did.

John was devastated by Sarah's reaction, he hated conflict of any kind. He was panicking and crying as he went downstairs again. Holding someone prisoner was just not in his nature, he hated what he was doing but he couldn't risk any possibility of other people becoming contaminated. Keeping Sarah here was the lesser of two very big evils.

Once she had heard John's footsteps on the stairs fading into the distance Sarah moved the drawers and opened the door a little to make sure that the coast was clear. The first thing on the agenda was to take Betty to the bathroom for a long overdue drink of water. The walk to the bathroom was delayed by the amount of time it took Betty to gobble down the food John had left her and Sarah's breakfast as well, which was still there. Typical Labrador. "Are you happy now you've eaten two breakfasts? Greedy."

Betty would also need a poo but that would have to wait. Sarah had to plan her approach to the day. Back in her sanctuary, the place she felt reasonably safe as long as she barricaded the door, Sarah sat on the edge of the bed and thought.

After what seemed like a long time with conflicting ideas whirling in all directions round her head Sarah had a plan. At least for today.

Still wearing the flannelette nightdress, she looked again at the clothes that John had given her. They were lying on the floor where they had been flung last night. Dispensing with the bra, which she had no intention of wearing, she put on the big beige blouse. Thankfully it was opaque enough to hide the fact she was bra less. She then pulled the green plaid skirt up her legs over the bloomers she had no option but to wear and then tucked the blouse into the waistband of the skirt tucking folds of it behind her back. The next problem was how to keep the skirt from falling down as soon as she let go of it. Suddenly she remembered Betty's lead that was in the pocket of the jeans she had been wearing yesterday. That would do the job.

Once the lead was tightened around her waist she looked in the small mirror she'd used to brush her hair last night and burst out laughing. There wasn't much that was visible in what remained of the mirror but it was so funny. "What a stunner you are Sarah Meadon."

She had nothing to wear on her feet other than her stinking wet trainers. She chose the barefoot option because she knew there was very little chance of being allowed to go outside. The stone flags on the floor downstairs would be cold but that was preferable to her trainers in the state they were in.

With the plan firmly in her head they made their way downstairs. There would be time to have a wash and clean her teeth later but there was no time to delay putting her plan into action.

John was in the kitchen when they got downstairs. Sarah said a cheery "Good morning. What a beautiful day." John looked pleased but surprised by her approach.

"Good morning Sarah. How are you today?"

"I am fine thank you."

John became more suspicious. Something didn't seem right but he hoped that Sarah had realised during the night that he really did want to help her and to be her friend. Yes that must be it.

"Betty needs to go out for a poo. Can I have the door key please?"

So that was why she was being nice John realised. She wanted the key so she could escape or send Betty off to run home. Had she put a note under Betty's collar?

"I'll take her out. You have to stay in so no one sees you. Where is her lead?"

Sarah pointed to her waist. John thought for a moment and then took his belt off and guided it under Betty's collar. He unlocked the door and Sarah welcomed the very brief waft of fresh air she felt. He closed the door behind him and Sarah heard the key turning in the lock. Her escape was going to be harder than she thought.

Remaining alert for the sound of the door opening Sarah had a look around the room. There was little worthy of noting. Just a couple of small photographs in silver frames. One of a man and one of a woman. Were these his parents? There were no photos of John as a child or indeed at any age. It was as though he had been hidden away from the world, just as she was now. Or had John hidden any photos that existed which related to a time when he wasn't crazy? How long had he been this way she wondered and what had caused it? Had he always been strange, even as a child?

She needed to know more about John. She needed to get him to talk, to open up and to do that she had to convince him that she was his friend and that she trusted him. That way maybe, just maybe, he would learn to trust her. Trust could lead to freedom eventually.

The door opened whilst she was deep in thought about Mrs Evans. She was sure her clients would have sorted out alternative arrangements for their dogs but there was no one to look after frail old Ellen. Worry consumed her but what could she do?

Betty bounded over to Sarah when she came back in and jumped up at her with the joy of discovering she was still there. "Did you have a good walk?" asked Sarah, more of Betty than John but John answered.

"Yes thank you, we did. We just walked around the farmyard. It isn't as easy for anyone to see her there as it is on the open moors."

"What are your plans today John?"

"Just to stay here and care for you."

"I desperately need some things from the shops. If you won't let me go could you go and get them for me please?"

"I go to the village shops every Friday so if you make a list I will get what I can. There is a pad and pen on the dresser over there." He couldn't change his routine.

Sarah began to make her list fairly certain that some of the things she needed would embarrass John therefore she was uncertain whether he would get them or not.

Whilst the list was being compiled John went into the kitchen to make them both a brew. Sarah heard what she thought was the sound of tablets being pushed out of blister packs. This sound was very familiar to her, one she heard every week at Mrs Evans'. What tablets did he take? Where did he keep them? The embryo of an idea crept into Sarah's mind. She stored it there for future use.

She gave John her shopping list when he sat down to drink his tea. He took a long time to go through the list item by item. Although the shops John went to were only in a village they were lucky that the village had an old fashioned general store that sold just about everything of a non-food nature, of course they didn't deal with prescription medicines but the chemist, bakers, butchers and grocery store covered all the items the general store didn't sell. She knew all the items on her list would be available.

She carefully looked at John whilst he perused her list. She needed to be able to describe him to the police when they found her. She guessed he was in his fifties but his lifetime exposure to the high moorland elements had probably weathered his skin beyond his actual years.

He had a good head of hair but it was too long for his age and unkempt, which indicated that his trips to the barber's shop were few and far between. It was dark brown speckled with grey. Perhaps she should offer to cut it for him. If he would trust her with scissors that is. Surely he would be pleased if she cut his hair. She had never cut a man's hair before but she couldn't make it any worse than it already was.

He was about 5 feet 10 inches tall she estimated and a little on the rotund side. No doubt when the farm was active the hard work would keep his waistline trim and his muscles firm but both had now gone in the opposite direction.

His clothes belonged to a time gone by just like her current outfit.

His nose was a little bent, perhaps, she thought, the result of a kick from a cow at some time in the past. His face was littered with worry lines. Of course they looked just like wrinkles but the permanent sad look in his brown eyes indicated that they were worry lines.

Spruced up and kitted out with new clothes she knew John could be a good looking man but all she saw now was a sad man. A permanently sad man.

John looked up at her when he had finished looking at her shopping list. "I can get most of those things but no mobile phone and no prescriptions."

"Why on earth not?"

"I can't have you able to contact anyone and although I've never had a mobile phone I believe that they work anywhere. If I got your prescription they would question me as to why you weren't getting it yourself. It might lead them here when they realise you are missing."

"They will already be searching John. It won't be long before they find me," she said more in hope than belief.

She noticed that John was very agitated as he said, "There was nothing on the radio this morning about you so I think you are here for longer than you think." This statement was like a kick in the guts to her but she couldn't show it. She had to make John believe that she was happy to be here. She hated lying but needs must.

"I am happy to stay here John. I am beginning to like it here and you are being so kind."

This swing from anger to happiness confused his already muddled mind. If she meant what she said he would be a very happy man but could he trust her. He had no idea.

"I am so sorry. I want this to be over as much as you do but I can't take the risk of letting you go yet. I feel so guilty and so scared of what may happen to us. You are welcome to stay here as long as you like. I promise you I will do you no harm. Maybe eventually we will be able to prove beyond doubt that neither of us are contaminated, then you can go home."

She could see he was in a state of panic however she grasped the sliver of hope that his last comment gave her but wondered how they were going to get the proof he needed. Somehow she had got a strong impression that he would want 100% unequivocal proof and nothing could be that certain. While there was even a tiny bit of doubt she knew that he would try and keep her here. She had asked him a number of times what he was supposed to be contaminated with but as soon as the question left her lips he switched to silence.

Sarah wasn't one for small talk but she felt her life depended on acquiring that skill, and quickly. She had to know all about John. At the moment she had no idea what was wrong with him and she feared neither did he.

She had a lot of unanswered questions, not least of which was 'Why could he go to the village, risking him spreading his contamination, yet she had to be locked away?' No doubt there

84

would a reason in his muddled head. Whether that reason was logical to her she doubted.

"John what have you contaminated me with?"

"HIV. I'm sorry but it's HIV."

Chapter 17

Sarah slumped in the old armchair stunned. Her mind racing. 'What have I done to deserve this?' she told herself. 'I can't die. What would happen to Mrs Evans? Who would look after Betty?' Her shock had bolted the door to her mind's logic compartment but slowly, second by second, millimetre by millimetre the bolt eased to an open position.

"I can't have HIV," she screamed at John. "I don't inject drugs and I sure as hell would never have sex with you. So tell me how the hell could I have caught HIV from you?"

Sarah's raised voice upset him. He was only trying to care for her yet here she was screaming at him. He remained calm. "There are more ways to catch aids."

Remaining agitated she spit out the words "How, tell me how?"

"You can catch HIV from contaminated blood."

"I've not had a blood transfusion using your blood, or anyone else's for that matter."

"When I pulled you out of the sinkhole I cut my finger on the chain and my blood may have dripped into the cuts on your hands and face."

"That's practically impossible."

"But there is a chance."

"What 1 in 500 million?"

"There is a chance. No one can guarantee 100% that it can't happen."

"There are no 100% guarantees in life. The sooner you get used to that the better."

"You think you are an expert on HIV but you know nothing," John said angrily

Sarah suddenly felt very sad as she said, "The only close friend I ever had in adult life died of aids. She was raped on a backpacking trip. She had travelled most of the world without any problems and then it happened, just before she was due to come back home.

"The sight of her in the hospital bed the last time I saw her will never leave me. It made me research HIV and aids in the forlorn hope that one day I could help to make people aware of the dangers and how to avoid them. That day never came but I do know more than most about HIV."

John was frustrated and angry with Sarah's reaction. How could she be so blasé?

Both of them sat in stony silence for a long time. He watched her the whole time but she couldn't bring herself to look at him and kept her eyes firmly on the stone floor. She counted the cracks to keep her mind occupied on something other than the crazy guy sat next to her, to keep her from going insane.

As John calmed down a little he saw a beautiful woman with long blonde hair tied back into a ponytail. He thought back to his time at primary school when he was friendly with Jenny Haworth. She always had a ponytail. They would be about seven at the time and spent all their time together; best of friends. Until his parents told him he shouldn't be friends with anyone. They told him he was different and bad things would happen to anyone he was friends with. He loved his parents unconditionally so did everything they said. The next day at school he told Jenny that he hated her. Seeing her tears was one of the worst experiences he had ever had. He had never had a friend since then.

He looked at Sarah and saw that she had beautiful blue eyes, a kind face, even in her current agitated state, and a nice slim figure. He could see her figure was slim even though she was wearing his mother's clothes. He decided that he would buy her some clothes at the charity shop in the village tomorrow. He would have to guess her size but he would try. He worried that she hadn't put any clothing on her shopping list. It was as though she didn't think she was staying long or she didn't trust his taste. He thought she would be pleased if he bought her some nice clothes.

Sarah slowly regained her composure a little. She realised that screaming at John wouldn't do any good at all. If she wanted to get out of this alive she would have to be nice to him no matter how much she hated him. He was clearly unstable mentally which made her wary of how he would react if she annoyed him.

"John we need to talk," she said quietly.

"I'm not used to chatting," he replied, "I spend most of my time alone. I don't even have the cows to talk to now."

"It's ok John we can take it very slowly. If we are living together we need to know about each other." She hated using that phrase 'living together'. It was the last thing she wanted to do.

He liked hearing her say 'living together' despite all the problems her being here brought.

"I'll ask you questions if you like?" Sarah offered. She knew he would never open up about his thoughts, HIV or otherwise, without her prodding him for information. She realised that going straight into questions about his HIV could scare him off. She needed to start with some more general questions first.

The sun was shining through the small windows of the farmhouse when Sarah began her questioning. She decided to start right at the beginning. She had no idea if John had been crazy all his life or if he had ever been free of the thoughts that appeared to torment and distress him so much.

"Tell me about your childhood please John."

He sat silently, deep in thought for a minute or two. Then very quietly he started to respond.

"I had a happy childhood. After morning milking each day mum and dad would take me for long walks over these moors. I loved running up and down the hills. Dad said I would be a marathon runner one day. We looked for birds' eggs but we always left them in the nest. My parents said that we should never hurt any living creature no matter how small."

"Did you have any sisters or brothers?"

"I did have a sister. She was called Christine. She was three years younger than me."

"Where is your sister now John?"

"She's dead."

"I'm sorry. What happened?"

"She died when she was nearly three years old. I had just turned six and I didn't understand what was going on. I looked at her in her cot one morning. The first thing I did every day was to go and say hello to Christine. I loved the way she smiled at me."

"Then one morning," he continued. Sarah could detect a faltering in his voice.

"One morning she had a rash all over her. I told mum that I thought she had nettle rash. I didn't know any other things that caused rashes. Mum covered Christine's rash with some lotion she had in the kitchen cupboard. It's still there. Dad said she would be better tomorrow.

"The lotion didn't work though and Christine got worse, much worse. Dad sent for the doctor who came a few hours later. Doctors always visited you at home in those days. The doctor said she was very sick and had to go to hospital quickly.

"Dad got the van out of the barn. He only used the van on special occasions. They dropped me at Mr and Mrs Green's farm up the valley on their way to hospital.

"They didn't come back for me until the day after. I cried when they told me Christine had died. I didn't understand how God could take such a young child. I never got the chance to say goodbye to her."

"I am so sorry," Sarah said, and she meant it.

"After that mum and dad seemed to watch me even more. They seemed scared that something would happen to me too."

"I can understand that. Do you think that was when you started to have concerns that bad things may happen to you and to people around you?"

"I don't know. I was only young but I seem to remember washing my hands a lot. I didn't want to get the germs that killed Christine. My hands used to get very sore; I remember that. Although it doesn't matter what happens to me, other people must be protected.

"I also think it was about then that I started wondering if there really was a God. If there was why did he take Christine? Was there a devil? Could there be both? I have always thought that I had to be perfect throughout my life to go to heaven. I had to care for everyone."

Sarah was terrified by John's apparent instability but at the same time she found herself beginning to feel sorry for him. She had to remind herself that he was still her captor. "What happened next John?"

"About a year later mum couldn't cope with me being out of her sight, even while I was at school, so she started to teach me at home. She made me tell my only friend that I hated her. Mum said I was different and bad things would happen to people I like."

'Nothing has changed then,' Sarah thought.

"Jenny was my only friend."

"Your only friend at primary school?"

"My only friend ever," replied John with a sad look in his eyes.

Sarah was shocked.

"I've never talked so much to anyone," John said, "Am I talking rubbish?"

"You are doing fine. Take your time."

John felt a surge of relief washing over him as he told his story. But then his mind quickly returned to the hopelessness of the current situation. He knew it wouldn't change anything but he wasn't bearing all the burden himself now.

After a short break he continued his tale. "I can't remember ever leaving the farm again after mum started to school me at home. All my teenage years were spent here. I didn't know it wasn't normal.

"I don't remember leaving the farm again until I went to my father's funeral and then again to my mother's funeral. Once both my parents were gone I knew I had to start going to the village; I was scared but I had to eat. Gradually I got used to my weekly visits to the shops and I even had the courage to say hello to people. Now I don't mind going but I am always glad to get back here."

"You seemed confident when you were rescuing me, you didn't seem nervous at all," Sarah said.

"That was because I had to care for you. Somehow when I have someone to care for, someone who is in trouble and I'm the only one who can help, I can fight my concerns a little better. They are still there but I manage to push them to the back of my mind temporarily. If there is someone else who can help however I turn my back and go the other way, I can't get involved."

Sarah felt the time was right.

"John you said you had never had a friend since Jenny but yet you think you have HIV. There must have been a lady in your life at some point."

"No."

"You don't strike me as being the type of person that would take drugs. Have you ever taken drugs?"

"No."

"Have you ever had a blood transfusion?"

"No."

"Then how the hell have you caught HIV?" she snapped. She instantly regretted losing her patience. It wasn't anger, it was just frustration. What the hell was she dealing with here? Taking a deep breath she risked carrying on.

"John you can't have HIV."

"Why?"

"Because you haven't done anything that can cause HIV."

"You can't be sure."

'Oh my god' she thought 'is he gay?' She realised that she had asked if there had ever been a lady in his life. How the hell was she going to approach this?

"John I don't really know how to ask this but has there ever been a special man in your life?"

"No."

She was worried by the way his answers had reverted to staccato. She decided to wait a few minutes before continuing. She looked at John whose turn it was now to look at the floor. She saw a strange look in his eyes. It was almost as though his mind was elsewhere.

She had to carry on though. She had to know more about John to be able to plot her escape from this prison.

"Honestly John you can't have HIV."

"My medical book doesn't say you can't catch it in other ways. What if you touch a toilet seat? What if you touch a door handle with blood on it? I'm always careful to cover my hands when I am closing a door so I do everything I can not to pass anything on but I can't be sure that other people will be as careful, I can't be sure you'll be as careful."

"But if there is any chance of catching it in those ways the chances must be so miniscule as to not be worth thinking about."

"Unless you can give me a 100% guarantee then there is a chance and if that chance materialises the effects could be so bad. I can see in my mind a picture of a crying child as her mum passes away from the HIV I let you spread. No matter how small that chance is it has to be given consideration. Can you give me that guarantee?"

"No one can give you a 100% guarantee about anything in life John. These are just silly thoughts you are having."

"It could be real."

The more Sarah heard, the more it troubled her. What was this monster she was dealing with? She would love to run through the door and leave John to his habits and stupid thoughts but he had the key. She had to press on.

"Tell me then how you think you caught HIV?" This would be interesting she thought sarcastically.

"I was walking by the reservoir several years ago. I often used to walk up there very early in the morning before anyone else got there. I love the sound of the water."

"Tell me what happened," she said impatiently.

"I trod on a used condom. At least I think it was a condom. I've never seen one. I didn't see it and I trod on it."

"How on earth can that give you HIV?"

"I may have touched the soles of my boots when I was taking them off or any time I put them on or took them off after that."

"That's stupid."

"There is a chance."

"Hundreds of people may have been contaminated by it."

"How?" This was getting more fantasy by the minute.

"I was scared when I first trod on the condom so I ran off and left it there. I went back later the same day to collect it and throw it away but it had gone."

"So what?"

"What if a dog had eaten it then licked its owners? What if it had stuck to the bottom of someone's boots? They may have been a teacher and all their pupils could have been contaminated? Worse still what if the condom had fallen into the water; the whole of the water supply could be contaminated."

Sarah could see that telling this story had put John in a state of emotional turmoil again. There were tears rolling down his cheeks, he was trembling and the pained look on his face upset her. It was as though he had brought this situation back to life, it had become today's problem after lying semi-dormant for some time.

"Just forget it John. It can't happen. The virus can't live outside the body."

"You can't be sure Sarah. It could live for some period of time. It's unlikely to die instantly."

"So you think it lives for a short time…"

"I didn't say a short time. I said a period of time. Who knows how long? Do you know how long?"

"I'm not a medical expert John, I'm just using my common sense. That's something you obviously don't have."

John ignored that remark and continued, "The following day I went to the water board offices to tell them that my negligence may have risked causing hundreds of deaths. I should have taken the condom away and burnt it. I asked them to drain the reservoir to look for the condom and then once they had found it to then fill the reservoir up with clean water."

"Did it make you feel relieved to tell them this?"

"I felt incredibly embarrassed and I suspected they would think my idea was stupid but I had to tell them."

"What did they say?"

"At first they were very attentive. I think they thought I had put poison in the reservoir. I would never do that. I would never do anything to hurt anyone. When I told them my story though they just laughed. I was horrified. So many lives at risk and they laughed. I'm still very worried about it but I don't know what to do."

"Why are you still worried? You say this was years ago. Even if you had got HIV germs on your boots, and I know you didn't, those germs would have died long ago."

"You can't guarantee that. There is a chance."

"John if you think you have HIV why don't you go and have a test? That would put your mind at ease."

"I have had."

"And?"

"It was clear."

"There you go then. Everything is fine."

"No its not."

93

"How can it not be fine if your test was clear?"

"Because I might have caught HIV in the clinic waiting room. The doctor didn't wear gloves either."

"This is getting ridiculous. Get into the real world."

"Lots of people who go into these clinics have HIV so there is a good chance they will leave some of their germs behind. Don't you understand that?" John was getting very frustrated at Sarah's attitude, at her lack of understanding.

"No I don't," she shouted in frustration, "It's not logical." 'Calm down Sarah' she told herself. It was easy to get frustrated at his intransigence.

John continued as though Sarah hadn't even spoken. "I go to a private clinic in Manchester. It's expensive but it means nothing goes on my medical records. It's the only times I have been further than the village. It's really scary in the city. There so much noise and people dashing around. I have to wait three hours for the results. It's hell."

"You said it's the only times you have been to the city. How many tests have you had John?"

"Five."

"What! Let me guess, they were all clear."

"Yes but I might have caught HIV in the clinic the last time I went."

"That's ridiculous. Just pull yourself together."

"Why can't you understand that there is a chance I did? It is so logical that if the doctor didn't wear gloves and he had a cut on finger there was a danger. After he tapped at my vein the needle would have pushed his blood into me. If he is so careless he could well have caught HIV from one of his patients. It's so obvious, why can't you see it? It's as plain and clear as it could be. If only that idiot had been more careful."

John was very frustrated and shouted at Sarah, "If only you hadn't been so stupid falling down that sinkhole. Why can't people be more careful? It's so frustrating."

"I think you are just an attention seeker, that's what you are. Your life is so dull and boring that you try and add some excitement by dreaming up these stupid stories."

"You are wrong Sarah. I'm not worried if I have HIV I'm just worried about passing it on. I don't care if I die. In fact I want to die. The world would be a better place without me."

"Attention seeker," she shouted.

"I don't want attention at all. I just need to make sure everyone is safe."

"Who is everyone?" Sarah said exasperated.

"Everyone in the world."

"Who do you think you are? God? You are not responsible for everyone in the world. What makes you think you are so special?"

"Sarah I need to explain something."

"Oh here we go. I must confess something then you will feel sorry for me. Well it won't work," She felt herself getting more frustrated with every word he spoke.

He carried on regardless. "I said I had only been to the city when I had HIV tests but that's not true."

"Let me guess. You went to seek out some comfort from the ladies of the night. Is that how you really caught HIV?"

"No ladies. I went to walk the streets in the middle of the night. I went in dangerous areas. I wanted someone to stab me, to end my life, but no one did. I went several times but I never got my wish. That's an explanation, not a confession. I need you to understand how hard things are for me."

"John why do you keep standing up and sitting down repetitively, over and over?"

"I have to get to a good number so nothing bad will happen."

"What the hell do you mean? It's just a stupid habit. Like the crazy way you walked from the kitchen. Why did you do that?"

"I have to avoid the cracks or bad things will happen to people I care for."

"Who, who do you care for? Who would have you as a friend," she shouted right into his face.

Sarah was confused and frightened. All this talk about good numbers and bad numbers, of bad things happening, of people he cared for, what was he on about? She did her best to regain her composure, or at least to hide her fear.

"John I have no idea what is wrong with you but you need help."

"Will you help me?"

"No way. You kidnap me and hold me prisoner. Why the hell should I help you?" She wasn't sure she really meant that though.

Sarah had heard enough. She bent down to cuddle Betty knowing she would be lay by her feet. She wasn't. "Where the hell is Betty?" she screamed.

They had been so engrossed in their conversation that they hadn't noticed Betty walk away. They found her in the kitchen lying in pools of vomit and diarrhoea. On the floor surrounding Betty were mounds of chocolate bar wrappers. Sarah had never seen so much chocolate in her life, or at least the evidence that there had been huge quantities of chocolate; now it was gone.

"Oh my god she's eaten loads of chocolate. You stupid man leaving that where she could reach it. Chocolate can kill dogs."

Sarah dropped to her knees by Betty's side. Tears flooded down her cheeks as she held Betty's head in her arms. Betty looked up at her as though to say 'Sorry."

Sarah panicked. "Get help you fool, she shouted at John, "She needs to go to the vets NOW."

"Don't worry, she'll be fine. The cows were often sick but they soon recovered."

"They hadn't eaten chocolate."

"She'll be better by tomorrow."

"That's what your dad said about Christine."

She saw the look of shock that this comment brought about but it didn't lessen his resolve.

"Please help her. Do what you want to me but please help Betty. She doesn't deserve to suffer."

"If she is no better by tomorrow I will take her to the vets when I go to the shops. Tomorrow is my day for going out." John felt really guilty about not helping Betty straight away. He hated to see her suffer and he was very concerned for her. However, he had to have time to consider all the options and all the possible outcomes. He had to be careful because everyone knew he didn't have a dog.

"Your bloody routines."

He held out his hand to help Sarah up off the floor. "Let me help you up to your bedroom. You look tired."

"Don't touch me." She had no intention of leaving Betty.

"She looked John straight in the eyes and spit out, "Fuck off you creep." John didn't argue and went upstairs. Being already very down because of his HIV fears Sarah's reaction was like the proverbial last straw. Every step felt like quick sand, he sobbed as he struggled to survive, as he struggled to progress from one step to the next. He knew his concern for the germs that now lay on his kitchen floor would trouble him all night. He wanted to clean the floor right now but Sarah scared him when she was in this mood. Sleep would be hard to find tonight.

Sarah sat on the kitchen floor all night softly talking to Betty. "Everything will be alright my girl," she tried to reassure her but she could see Betty getting weaker and weaker as the night progressed. She tried to get her to drink water. She hoped this would dilute the chocolate but Betty was too weak to drink it. Sarah soaked a cloth in water and dabbed it around Betty's lips and on her tongue. Betty gave a little wag of her tail.

"Please don't die. I need you."

Any thoughts she had of perhaps helping John had disappeared. She hated him.

"Betty I love you." Betty moved her eyes to look up and Sarah knew she was saying "I love you too."

Chapter 18

Sarah watched as Betty's condition worsened overnight. The vomiting and diarrhoea had stopped eventually but this was most likely due to the fact that there was nothing left to come out. She alternated between gently stroking Betty's head and cleaning up the mess. It definitely wasn't being cleaned to satisfy John's hygiene issues, that didn't enter the equation. Sarah knew there was very little she could do but if Betty was going to die she would sure as hell die on a clean floor.

She found several cloths on her search of the kitchen cupboards. She also found more chocolate which she smashed into small pieces and then threw in the bin. Chocolate was the only enemy she could attack and destroy. She carefully fastened the bin lid. Betty was in no fit state to open the bin at the moment but Sarah had to make sure.

When looking into the drawer beneath the sink to try and find a clean sponge to cool Betty down her eyes fell on a small knife at the back of the drawer. Without thinking she grabbed the knife and slid it into her skirt pocket. It may come in useful later.

The metronomic clicks of the kitchen clock tortured her all through the night. Each click disturbing the multitude of thoughts whirling around her head. So much had happened in the last few days to adversely affect her life; she had to conjure up an end.

Her bottom and legs no longer had any feeling from hours sitting on the hard cold floor. It was like she was being punished, but for what?

The first light of dawn shone round the edges of the blind covering the small window. "Hold on Betty. Morning's here, John promised to help you today. You'll be ok soon." The words coming out of her mouth didn't match the thoughts in her head.

~~~~~~~~~~

The first light of dawn shone through the thin blue curtains covering John's bedroom window. He hadn't slept all night but he knew he had to get up and follow his routine. He had spent all night desperately wanting to go downstairs and care for Sarah. His logic however, making a very rare appearance, told him that would only make matters worse. This constant shall I, shan't I battle had left him with a bad headache and feeling weak. Life had to go on though. If he didn't go to the village today people may worry about him and come to the farm to see if he was alright. He couldn't let that happen. They didn't know exactly where he lived but it wouldn't take them long to find the farm.

The shop keepers would expect him about 10am and he needed to work out how he could keep to that time when he now had the inconvenience of taking a dog to the vets. He couldn't go to the vets on Manchester Road, they knew him and knew he didn't have animals anymore. They would be suspicious. He would have to drive to a vets where no one knew him, somewhere he had never been before. He would tell them he was visiting the area.

John liked to look good when he went to the village so took his time having a long shower and choosing which clothes to wear. He didn't have many clothes but choosing an outfit always seemed difficult. Making any decision was never easy for him. He had to consider all the possible consequences of his decision, and then consider them again. He liked to be sure, although he never could be.

He felt excruciatingly nervous as he walked down the stairs. Unsure of what he would find.

~~~~~~~~~~

Sarah heard footsteps coming down the stairs. The thought of facing John again was repulsive but he held her future in his hands. The devil and the deep blue sea.

Her captor came into the kitchen. She didn't turn to look at him.

"How's Betty?"

Betty hadn't opened her eyes for the last hour but she was still breathing albeit very shallow. There wasn't much time.

"You need to take her to the vets now!"

"Oh good she's ok then. I told you she would be."

"No she's not alright."

"I will take her to the vets after my breakfast, as I promised."

She turned to face him with rage in her eyes. She couldn't believe what he had just said. She stood up on her aching legs and moved towards John. She slapped him across the face – hard.

"She needs help NOW! Not in half an hour – NOW," she screamed.

John touched his stinging cheek. No one had ever hit him before, this was new territory. He knew breakfast would have to wait. He didn't know how he would cope with this change of routine but he knew somehow he had to.

Sarah hadn't finished. "I want to go with her to the vets."

"I can't let you."

"Why can you go out and I can't?"

"I am careful. I don't know for certain that you will be."

There was no way she was getting away from the farm. She put her hand in her pocket and gripped the knife handle. She knew that wasn't the answer though, at least not yet. She kissed Betty as John gently carried her out to the van. He had to use the van to keep Betty hidden. He hoped it would start after all this time. It did.

Sarah slumped into the armchair with tears rolling down her face and butterflies floating around her stomach. She wasn't religious but she silently said a prayer for Betty. She knew she had no option but to wait.

~~~~~~~~~~

Detective Brian Wilkinson entered the incident room to brief everyone present.

He explained that they had had a report of a missing person yesterday. A woman in her early forties. Long blonde hair, about 5 feet 6 inches tall, blue eyes, average build, no distinguishing marks.

Miss Meadon hadn't been seen since last Saturday morning. She was a dog carer looking after the dogs of several local people but their dogs have not been collected so far this week. The report was made by a Mr Steve Mills. He hadn't reported her missing until yesterday because he initially thought she was just unwell.

Detective Wilkinson passed around a photograph of Sarah, explaining that it had been taken a few years ago. They had obtained it from a Mrs Evans who is Miss Meadon's next door neighbour and she was the last person to see her.

"I suggest that we start by interviewing people in the village centre and then the walkers up at the car parks at the bottom of the moors," he said, "Apparently she still walks her own dog on the moors at

100

weekend even though she doesn't look after any of her clients' dogs then."

He continued, "Take the photograph and ask everyone, and I mean everyone, if they recognise her and, if they did, when they last saw her. Make sure you get their contact details in case we need to follow up with them later.

"I also want an appeal put out on the radio today and in the next edition of the local newspaper which I think goes out on Tuesday. We need any possible sightings. We also need to hear from all her clients. We need to find out who they are first.

"Thank you ladies and gentlemen. Off you go. We'll reconvene at 10am tomorrow."

Chapter 19

John drove as carefully but as quickly as he could. He knew Betty was really ill and he needed to get her to the vets as soon as possible. He knew she would be alright though; it was amazing what they could do these days. He'd seen his cows in terrible conditions but all of them had recovered, except for poor old Daisy. Giving birth had put an end to her. They tried everything they could to save her but she had passed away as they pulled the calf out. Luckily another cow took the calf as her own and it thrived, a constant reminder of Daisy.

Betty would be treated in a sterile room not a draughty old corner of a barn, as Daisy had been, so everything would be fine.

He carried Betty into the reception and explained that he was visiting the area and his dog had eaten a large amount of chocolate while they were visiting his family.

The receptionist took one look at Betty and immediately called for a vet. She knew it was urgent. John helped the vet to carry Betty into a treatment room and lay her on the floor.

"When did this happen?" the vet asked.

"Last night," replied John.

"Why didn't you bring her in then?"

"I thought she would be alright."

"Does she look alright," the vet said exasperated. He wondered about the suitability of some people to have animals. He knew that many pets didn't lead the pampered life that his dogs did. It wasn't his job to judge though, it was his job to do everything possible to save sick animals.

"She is very dehydrated and needs medicines to try and counter the effects of the chocolate. We may need to flush out her stomach and she will definitely need intravenous fluids to counter the dehydration and also medication to control her heart rate and blood pressure. You will need to leave her with us. We will ring you later in the day when we have any news."

"I don't have a phone," explained John.

"Then I suggest that you call late this afternoon. Are you happy for us to go ahead and give any treatment we feel is necessary? We would normally ask your permission when we know what we need to do but as we can't contact you."

"Yes of course. Do what you feel you need to do. The cost doesn't matter."

John gave Betty a few strokes before he left and set off to drive back to the village. Back to his routine. It was only ten minutes later than normal when he parked on the car park by the railway station. It was free to park there and he liked the walk down the hill into the centre of the village. Mind you he wasn't as keen on the walk back up the hill and was always thankful when the old ladies' shopping lists didn't include anything too heavy.

He was armed with his and Sarah's shopping lists, together with those he had collected from the old farm widows as he made his way to the village centre. Today was different though, today his worries made his eyes constantly flick from scene to scene to make sure he would spot any danger before it was too late. He had to make sure his visit to the village was incident free.

He always did the shopping for the three old ladies who were stranded on the remote farms since their husbands passed away. He wondered why farmers' wives always seemed to outlive the farmers. Perhaps it was because they didn't have women to put up with he chuckled to himself. Not that he knew much about living with women.

His first stop as always was the bakers for the two loaves he bought each week. 'Better get three today', he thought, 'I have a guest.'

"Morning John," the baker greeted him warmly, "Usual two home baked unsliced?"

"Better make it three please."

"Are you entertaining John?"

"No I thought I would start to feed the ducks on the reservoir again while the weather is nice."

"I believe it's going to rain later today. I think we've had our summer, all two days of it, if you believe the forecasters. Three it is though."

John bade farewell to the baker. 'That was close,' he thought, 'I need to be more careful'.

He took his lists to the general store next. They would make up his order while he went to the chemist, for Ada Clement's prescription, and the butchers for some steak mince for himself and all the widows. There were no more scares at these shops.

As he went back into the general store Carly gave him a wink. Carly was only in her twenties but had worked in the general store since leaving school. She always had a big smile and a cheeky comment or two to make to all her customers.

"Now John. What have you been up to?"

"Nothing," he spluttered. He could feel his cheeks beginning to burn, and the cause wasn't Sarah's slap this time.

"I think you've got a lady living with you. Good on you John."

"I don't know what you mean," he said trying to keep his composure. How did she know?

"Don't be silly Carly. You know I live alone. Stop being so cheeky." He was sure she was just making all this up as a joke.

"We don't recognise the writing on one of the lists and there are some things on it that your farm ladies wouldn't use at their age. You secretive old devil. There's life in the old dog yet it appears. Come on John spill the beans."

He had to control his overwhelming urge to confess about Sarah and his part in her disappearance. He couldn't confess, not yet. He had to think quickly, very quickly. "Oh that must be Mrs Clements' daughter Ann. Ada isn't well and her daughter is staying with her for a while. She has decided that she will need to stay longer than she planned. That's who did that list."

He knew he must sound flustered but hoped they didn't suspect anything. Why didn't he ask Sarah what the thing was on her list that he hadn't heard of? He didn't want to seem stupid that's why. There was only one thing he had no idea what it was and that was at the bottom of the list. Sarah had written Tampax with applicator. He had no idea what it was but he knew from reading his history books that the word Pax meant 'a period of peace that has been forced on a large area'. He assumed therefore that it was some kind of ointment that you applied, using the applicator, to a large area of skin to cool down the irritation of a rash maybe. It would bring peace to the person using it. Didn't all women use the same things though? 'Why are women so complicated?' he thought.

He left the general store as quickly as he could.

"See you next week John," shouted Carly as she winked again. "Don't do anything I wouldn't do."

What did she mean? He could think of a lot of things Carly did that he wouldn't do but how was he meant to know what she wouldn't do. That sounded very personal. She went dancing in Manchester she told him. He wouldn't do that. She liked raw fish which apparently costs a lot of money in posh restaurants in the city centre. He wouldn't eat raw fish if someone offered him a million pounds. She wore makeup. No he wouldn't do that. John was confused. He had no idea what she meant.

His next stop was the corner café where he ordered his usual ham sandwich, with a cup of tea of course.

"Lots of police around today John," said the sandwich lady. He had never asked her name. "I wonder what's wrong?" she asked.

John felt his heart skip a beat. He probably knew what was wrong but he had to control his panic which was at the very top end of the scale and in danger of going off the scale completely. In his mind death seemed to be the only way to end this situation, his death. He had to battle hard to seem normal however. "Oh just an exercise I guess," he said.

John sat in silence not able to concentrate on the newspaper he had taken from the rack by the door. They were there for customers to read when they were having their food and drink. It was a popular place for the locals to pass away an hour or so. He looked at the headlines in the paper and was pleased to see that none of them could relate to Sarah. No news is good news he thought or did he? Why had he taken a newspaper from the rack, he never had before for fear of the germs they might hold, he had no idea who had held those papers before. Why had he picked up a paper today? Maybe part of him wished that Sarah would be in the newspaper and that would lead the police to finding her and therefore taking the responsibility for the whole situation out of his hands.

He became increasingly concerned about the lies he had told in the last few minutes. He wanted to confess but that would only make matters worse. He knew he would confess some time and he knew by then he might confess to things he hadn't done. His mind never remembered the exact facts. It always told him that he might have done things. He was worried. Who was going to suffer because of his lies?

After lunch he still had two more places to visit before he left the village. These weren't normal stops for him but today they were important.

He left the café and took a circuitous route along the back streets. It was only a hundred yards down the road to his next stop but he didn't want to make eye contact with a policeman. He knew that if he did his overwhelming guilt would make him confess. Part of him was desperate to confess but the turmoil and confusion in his mind left him unsure as to if that was the right thing to do or not. He needed to be 100% sure.

He had noticed that the police were stopping people and seemed to be showing them a photograph. He knew who the photograph was likely to be. Things had taken a worrying turn. He needed someone to tell him what to do but nobody knew about Sarah. In any case he wouldn't believe anyone's advice unless they gave him 100% unequivocal proof. If there was the slightest doubt he had to wait.

He emerged down a narrow alleyway right by the greengrocers.

"Good morning sir, can I help you?"

"I need two grapefruits but they need to be nice ones."

"Go ahead sir, take your time choosing the ones you want. They are all beautiful grapefruits they are."

John eventually chose two grapefruits that he thought were perfect. He paid the greengrocers his 60 pence and left the shop.

"Do call again sometime Sir."

John was out of the shop before the greengrocer finished his sentence. Now how to get to the last place he had to visit without being stopped. If he was asked if he knew the lady in the photograph could he lie? His life was based on being scrupulously honest. He had already told lies today, could he tell one more? He didn't know if he would be allowed to.

He found his way to the charity shop without incident. He explained to the ladies about Mrs Clements daughter and her extended stay. "She needs some clothes you see," he told them, "she only came prepared for a couple of days but Mrs Clements isn't fit to leave."

"What does she want?" asked the matronly lady behind the counter.

"I don't know. Could you just make up a couple of outfits? You'll know better than me."

"What age is she?"

"I'm not sure but I would guess at early forties."

"One more thing. What size is she?"

"I forgot to ask I'm afraid." He bent down and reached into his bag. He pulled out the two ripe grapefruits and held them in front of his chest.

"About this size I think."

The lady serving him was trying very hard to stifle her giggles. "Fine sir. I'm sure we can put something together for you."

John kept his eyes on the shop window watching for any approach by the police officers. He wished the lady would hurry up. He didn't want anything that matched perfectly. He just wanted clothes, any clothes.

After about 10 minutes the lady said "How about these sir?" He swung back to face the counter. "Yes fine," he said.

"But you haven't looked at them."

"They'll be fine. You look like a lady with good taste. How much do I owe you?"

"There are two complete outfits. One based on a skirt and one on trousers. I included both thin and thick tops; you can never be sure of the weather."

"How much do I owe you?"

"I've also put some shoes in. You didn't say if you wanted shoes or not but I took the liberty of putting some in. I hope they are the right size. I've included two sizes to be sure. You can bring the ones that don't fit back next time you are in the village, no hurry."

"Does £20 cover it?"

"Oh yes sir. It's less than that. Now let me add up. There's a skirt at £2, some trousers at £1.50 and….."

John slammed a £20 note on the counter, grabbed the pile of clothes and stuffed them in one of his bags.

"Don't forget your change sir." But he had already gone.

John wished he had parked his van closer but at least he could see that the police were at the end of the village away from where he had to go. They only seemed to be stopping people on the street and didn't seem to be going into the shops to speak to the shop keepers; at least not yet.

Shutting his van door gave a feeling of security. No one could touch him now. He pulled out the choke and turned the key in the ignition. He heard the whir of the engine, on and on, but the van didn't start. His heart began to pound. He tried again and to his relief the engine started.

He remembered that he had to go back to the vets to see how Betty was. He knew the net was closing and felt that Betty was becoming more of a liability, just a complication he could do without. He wondered how he would stop Betty barking when he dropped off the shopping at the other farms on his way home. If she barked he would have no way to explain her away.

The vet's car park was busy when John arrived and he had to manoeuvre into the last remaining space at the far end of the car park. It was a tight space too. He had never been good at parking, he didn't need to do it often.

Parking successfully negotiated he walked towards the modern building. 'Must be money in being a vet' he thought. He pushed open one side of the glass double doors and walked into the crowded waiting room. It took a good fifteen minutes before it was his turn to be attended to.

"I left my dog this morning. It had eaten chocolate."

"What was the dog's name?"

Questions, always questions. The more questions you were asked the more chance you had of saying the wrong thing. Of saying the one thing that would lead them to Sarah.

"Betty. It's Betty."

The receptionist tapped away at her computer keyboard. John was fascinated. He had never used a computer.

"Ah yes Mr Whittle. The vet would like a word with you. Please take a seat."

He had no time to wait but wait he had to. He fiddled with his fingers whilst he sat there for what seemed like an age. He saw two young girls and what he assumed to be their mother crying as they came out of a treatment room. Why were they crying? He had never been emotional about an animal. He had only known cows and they were there to earn a living. He looked upon them more as machines than animals. He liked them of course but when they died they died; part of the natural life cycle.

"Betty's owner please," the vet shouted.

John sat for a few seconds before he realised they meant him. He jumped up and followed the vet into the treatment room. The vet seemed very young but John assumed he knew what he was doing.

"Please sit down. I am sorry but I have bad news for you. Betty is very ill I'm afraid. Please let me explain."

The vet went on to tell John how eating chocolate in large quantities can poison a dog. He explained that chocolate contains an ingredient called theobromine which is also found in tea, coca cola and some other foodstuffs.

"Humans metabolise theobromine at a fast enough rate that its toxic properties are negated and not harmful," the vet continued, "Dogs, however, metabolise it at a much slower rate leading to the dog effectively being poisoned. To result in irreversible damage the dog has to eat a large quantity of chocolate. I am afraid Betty has eaten a very large quantity."

He paused to let John take in what he said. John said nothing.

"I am afraid that there is no more we can do for her. She is in a lot of pain and the kindest thing to do is to put her to sleep. I'm sorry."

There was no response from John.

"Do you understand what I am saying sir?"

"Yes that's fine, do it."

"Would you like to see Betty to say your goodbyes? You can take as long as you want. Would you like to hold her whilst we administer the pentobarbital? It will be painless but it may be nice for someone to be with her."

"Just do it," John snapped as he ran out of the room.

The vet thought this was a strange reaction but over the years he had seen people react to the loss of a pet in many different ways.

It appeared that Betty was to die alone.

Chapter 20

The noise startled Sarah back from her slumbers. She had no idea how long she had been asleep but she must have nodded off after John left. It wasn't surprising as she hadn't slept a wink all night.

What was the noise? It was in the distance but the sound was familiar. It took her brain a minute to focus and realise that it was a helicopter, she could hear a helicopter. They were coming for her. But Betty wasn't here, they couldn't come before Betty was back. She looked through the window in the living room but couldn't see anything. 'Why are all the windows so damn small' she said to herself.

It was about 5 minutes before the helicopter came into view in the distance. It was weaving back and forth across the moors. "I'm here," she shouted "Betty come home, they're here." She watched intently as her rescue craft edged closer and closer. She waved her arms frantically although she knew they couldn't see her. Her excitement grew minute by minute as the distance between her and her rescuers reduced – until she saw the liquid being sprayed from the back of the helicopter. She was devastated. They weren't looking for her at all, they were spraying the moors. She should have known. She had seen them spray the moors hundreds of times. She should have known it was the wrong colour for a police helicopter or one of the mountain rescue craft. She still maintained a constant watch until the helicopter turned and returned in the direction it had approached from. She was still a prisoner.

Maybe John had left the door open for her. He wouldn't want her trapped if there was a fire would he. He said he didn't want to harm her. Was this why John hadn't taken Betty to the vets last night? Maybe he thought it was too dangerous to leave Sarah locked in the house in the night. In Sarah's logical mind it was no more dangerous night or day, but John's mind wasn't logical.

She ran to the door and grabbed the handle but the door wouldn't move. In frustration she hammered on the door until her hands hurt. She went to smash a window but snapped back to reality before it was too late. The windows panes were far too small to climb through and there was no one within hearing distance if she shouted through a broken window pane. All she risked doing was damaging her hand and wrist, possibly fatally. It was hopeless. "Someone help me," she screamed in vain and then sank to the floor whimpering "Help me, help me, help me."

Sarah could honestly say that she had never even come close to hating anyone in her life before but she really hated John. He had turned from her rescuer into an unpredictable monster. He didn't care if she burnt to death should there be a fire while he was out. It was more important to him to keep her away from the outside world. She instinctively bent down to stroke Betty but realised her companion wasn't there. "Be strong Betty," she whispered.

There had to be a way out. She had the knife in her pocket but really couldn't see herself even hurting someone let alone killing them, even in these circumstances. She knew she just couldn't do it.

Slowly she pushed herself up off the floor. She had to look around but she had no idea what she was looking for. Everything in this place looked like it belonged in a 1960s museum. She was even dressed in ancient clothes. Clothes that were beginning to feel like they were in need of a wash but she had no alternative. At least she had put some knickers on her shopping list. Oh how she longed to get out of these bloomers. Would John be brave enough to buy knickers she wondered?

She turned on the radio. She wasn't really listening to it but the background noise made her feel less alone. She wanted to try and tune into the local radio station but how the hell did you retune this ancient contraption. It didn't appear to have an FM waveband at all but she knew Radio Moors also broadcast on medium wave. She wanted to find it, more in hope than expectation of hearing some news of the search to find her. They must be searching by now surely. After several minutes of turning dials and shaking the contraption she heard what she had been searching for. 'Good morning. This is Andy King welcoming you to the mid-morning show on Radio Moors. I hope you are all well and having fun this morning.'

"Sod off," was her reply.

She didn't know how long John would be in the village so she had to look around quickly. She should hear the old van spluttering back into the yard but couldn't be sure.

There wasn't much of interest in any of the drawers. There were a few photos of a little girl who she assumed was Christine. Why didn't John have these on display she wondered?

She found a letter sent to John's parents by his teacher in the last year he attended school before his home tuition.

It read:-

'John could do very well at school if he kept his mind on his work. Instead he appears to be in a world of his own and is becoming more reluctant to join in with class discussions. He also appears very reluctant to accept any point of view that differs from his own, being adamant that he is right. We needn't be concerned at this stage as he is still very young and will hopefully develop out of these negative behaviours in the next year or two. I just wanted to bring this to your attention and would ask that you keep watch over John's interaction with others when at home. It would be useful to determine if this behaviour occurs at all times or if it is just a school problem.'

So John has had introverted behaviour from an early age Sarah realised. Perhaps Christine's death was the catalyst.

She continued her search, finding, in one of the cupboards, a large biscuit tin full of bills dating from recently back to before John's birth. There was an invoice for the tractor which was bought in 1955. She was impressed that it was still running. It cost £715.14sh.10d, which she guessed was a lot of money in those days but they had certainly had their monies worth out of it.

Also in the tin were some newspaper cuttings. Two were dated 1953 and covered the coronation of Queen Elizabeth II and the other was about Edmund Hillary and Sherpa Tenzing being the first people to reach the summit of Mount Everest.

There was also a ration book. The first unused coupon being dated 1954. She guessed that must have been when rationing finally ended. Fascinating as this tin was though she forced herself to close it and put it back in the cupboard. She still hadn't found anything that she could use to gain her freedom. She didn't know what she was looking for and logically she knew she wouldn't find anything but at least the search occupied her. She couldn't just sit doing nothing worrying about Betty. She had to be busy.

".....and now it's time to hand you over to the news room for the latest local news headlines."

On hearing this she paused her search and focused her attention on the radio. She sat and listened as if her life depended on it. 'Please let them know I'm missing' she thought.

"The planning committee last night approved controversial plans to build a supermarket in the valley citing job creation as the main reason for approval. Opponents of the plan say they will lodge an appeal.

"The local health authority have announced the closure of all A & E facilities at the Valley Hospital. People will in future have to travel 15 miles to the nearest facility.

"Police have been out in numbers this morning to begin to ask shoppers in the local villages if they had seen missing dog walker Sarah Meadon who has not been seen since last Saturday. A police spokesman told Radio Moors that they are not unduly concerned at this stage. They think that Miss Meadon may have gone to visit relatives and forgotten to tell anyone but they will continue their enquiries."

Third behind a supermarket and a hospital closure but at least she was mentioned. The phrase 'not unduly concerned' frustrated her. They should be concerned, very concerned.

"………… and now for the weather forecast."

Sarah went back to her search. There was nothing more of particular interest in the living room until she looked in the final drawer. Pushed right at the back was an envelope 'To Christine' written on it. The writing on the envelope was very neat, obviously written by an adult, but the writing on the small piece of paper inside the envelope was obviously that of a young child.

It was a poem:-

My Sister
I loved my little sister
Christine was her name
Now she's been taken from me
Life will never be the same

By John Whittle Aged 6

Sarah guessed this had been written by John. She felt sad by what she read. She really felt the poignant message from a child's heart. Poor little John. How prophetic. His life obviously had never been the same again. She wondered if he was ever able to tell his parents how he felt or had he shouldered the burden of his feelings alone. Could this explain his introverted nature? A troubled young boy who had, in her mind, turned into a monster adult.

She lost any desire to search any other rooms. It was unlikely that she would find anything useful.

She cleaned the kitchen to remove the lingering odours of Betty's little accidents last night. She scrubbed and scrubbed with the brush she had found under the kitchen sink until there couldn't possibly be any germs left on the floor. She still wasn't doing this for John's sake. She wanted Betty to come back to a nice clean floor. For the same reason she cleaned the carpet in the living room. She had never used a vacuum cleaner as heavy as John's. By the time she had finished she felt shattered.

She sat in the chair, her chair as John called it, to wait for Betty's return. The radio was doing an interview with some professor at the local university. She only half listened as he droned on.

"It can manifest itself in many ways. These range from cleanliness, security, religion, confession and so on. They try and counter these obsessions by doing compulsions but these often increase the anxiety because they have to repeat the compulsion until they reach a 'good' number of repetitions."

"John mentioned good numbers," Sarah thought. She gave the radio her full attention.

"The problem is that they usually don't know which are 'good' numbers. If someone interrupts the compulsion they have to start all over again."

"This must be dreadful for the OCD sufferer," the presenter commented.

"It certainly is. To them their OCD thoughts are real, no matter how anyone tries to convince them otherwise. They can end up doing a compulsion for hours on end. For example they can wash their hands so often and so much that their hands bleed. They avoid

contact with people for fear of passing on some disease. Even though they never have the disease their OCD convinces them beyond any doubt that they have. They will not move from that thought until they are given a 100% cast iron guarantee that what they are thinking is wrong. That never happens of course because in this world nothing is 100% certain.

"Their concern is always for other people. An HIV fear, for example, is linked to a fear of dying but even so an OCD sufferer would prefer to die themselves rather than being responsible, in their opinion, for someone else's death..

"In the religious manifestation the sufferer often thinks they are a bad person and will be punished by God. People can tell them until they are blue in the face that God loves everyone and forgives everyone for their sins but they want unequivocal proof. They can always find a counter argument even if their argument is based on an incorrect interpretation of something they have heard or read.

"Often they fear they will cause harm to someone through being violent. It is not uncommon for this person to be someone very close to them, a parent or sibling for example. This feels so real to them but thankfully OCD sufferers never carry out any acts of violence. They are actually incredibly caring peaceful people.

"Some sufferers only have to cope with one aspect of OCD but the more unfortunate have multi aspect OCD. In other words they suffer from many different forms of OCD. For these people life can be constant hell twenty four hours a day. It can wear them down so much that they may want to die as that seems easier than living through all their worries."

"I'm sorry Professor Jones but we must go to the traffic now but we will return to this subject right after hearing about which roads to avoid today. Don't go away listeners."

"Get on with it," Sarah muttered, "Who cares if there is a traffic jam on the M62. Come on."

"Welcome back to the programme. You are listening to Professor Jones telling us about OCD which sounds a horrendous illness. Professor Jones can I ask how can we tell if someone is suffering from Obsessive Compulsive Disorder?"

116

"By looking at them you can't. You may notice that their hands look chapped but that could be for any number of reasons. You can work with an OCD sufferer for years, for example, and never have any suspicions that they are anything but healthy intelligent people. They are excellent at hiding their problems if they need to. OCD is a horrible condition for the sufferers' nearest and dearest as well but obviously nowhere near as bad as it is for the sufferer themselves. Some people find it difficult to help a sufferer because OCD scares them. It's an illness like any other. Just because it comes under the umbrella of mental illnesses shouldn't make any difference."

"What can we do to help OCD sufferers Professor?"

"Very few people know anything about OCD when they first realise that is what the problem is. They can go for years thinking that the sufferer has some stupid and annoying habits. They tell them to pull themselves together, which is the worst thing they can do. It is easy to lose your temper with an OCD sufferer out of frustration at what you perceive as their lack of effort to make themselves better.

"OCD is more in the open recently than it used to be thankfully but it is still very misunderstood and consequently trivialised and we need to change that. Sadly most times you hear about OCD on television and radio or in social media it is the subject of a comedian's joke. Let me tell you that OCD is not funny at all, as any sufferer will tell you. But the jokes have at least increased the number of people who have heard of Obsessive Compulsive Disorder, even if they don't fully understand what it is. It's not the completely dark mystery that it used to be.

"If someone you know is showing any of the symptoms I have mentioned they should try and persuade them to get professional help as quickly as possible. There is no cure, but sufferers can learn to manage their condition. It is a long, slow and painful shared journey and there will be many ups and downs along the way."

"Thank you Professor we must finish there. If you would like to know more about OCD please contact our help line for our fact sheet.

"Now for a bit of Joe Cocker singing 'With A Little Help From My Friends'. Very appropriate I'm sure you will agree."

"Oh my God that sounds like John," Sarah gasped. "Has John got OCD? No one deserves to suffer like that." He couldn't help what he was doing to her. Despite her situation she felt sorry for John. Could she help him? Should she help him or should she accept that he isn't her responsibility? She was still his prisoner after all. How could she help him, she had no real understanding of OCD and how it affects the sufferer. But who else will help him?

"Poor John," she said, and she meant it.

She couldn't begin to comprehend the strength of the hold OCD had on John, if it was OCD. How could she? She had only know him a short time, she knew that she had to do much more research and even then she felt that only living with an OCD sufferer for an extended period would bring her even remotely close to having an adequate understanding.

Just then she heard the van drive into the yard. "Betty's here," she cried. She couldn't wait for the door to open so she could see Betty's wagging tale.

John unlocked the door and walked in carrying his shopping. She presumed he was bringing that in first and then would go back out for Betty. She wasn't surprised that she needed carrying in. When the shopping was placed on the kitchen worktop John started putting each item away carefully. In its correct place, in perfectly straight rows, labels facing to the front. Like any work of art it took an age to complete.

Sarah was desperate for him to go out and get Betty but the knowledge she had just gained from the radio made her frightened of disturbing his routines. She knew she would have to wait.

After he had placed the tins in the cupboard next to the window, cleaning materials in the cupboard under the sink, biscuits in the yellow tin with a cockerel on, his cereals in the top cupboard near the living room door and his fruit in the fruit bowl, making sure that the bananas didn't touch the other fruit, he turned to Sarah and handed her two carrier bags.

"Here's your shopping and I bought you some clothes. You can't be wearing my mother's clothes for ever. I hope you like them."

She felt like throwing the clothes back at him but she knew that it wouldn't have been easy for him to go into a shop and buy ladies clothes. How she wished her feelings for John were singular. She wanted to hate him, to really hate him and did so almost all of the time. Just occasionally though he did something that made her heart soften towards him ever so slightly. Sarah looked at the items he had bought her and held them up against herself to try them for size. They seemed roughly the correct fit and although they weren't necessarily what she would chose for herself they were considerably better than what she was wearing now, and clean. It was a lovely thought.

She couldn't wait any longer. "John, please bring Betty in."

He came towards her and took her left hand in his. She let him.

"Betty was very ill Sarah. I had to agree to her being put to sleep."

Sarah pulled her hand away and screamed "NO." He had never heard any living creature scream like that. It scared him.

"I thought you would be pleased that I had ended Betty's suffering. I thought it was what you would have wanted me to do."

"How the hell do you know what I want?"

"She was suffering."

"And whose bloody fault was that? Why did you have enough chocolate in to open a sweet shop? Why didn't you put it out of reach? You are so stupid."

"I like eating chocolate."

"I wish it had poisoned you."

"Why didn't you take her to the vets last night?"

"Because I had to care for you. I couldn't leave you locked in here all night, what if there had been a fire."

"Then you should have taken me with you, you knew I wanted to go with Betty," Sarah shouted, "Taking her last night might have saved her."

John was too upset to respond.

There was silence for a minute or so while Sarah tried to comprehend the shocking news she had just had.

"I want to go and say my goodbyes."

"It's too late Sarah."

Sarah grabbed the knife from her pocket and lunged towards John.

Chapter 21

It was an understatement to say that Anna's parents were surprised when she came home from college and said she was taking the dog for a walk. Absolute shock would be a better description. They had bought the dog for Anna when she was thirteen and going through a stage in her life when she thought that the world was totally against her. She dashed off to school eating her breakfast, a slice of toast, on the way and then went straight to her room when she came home from school each day. Other than sitting at the table to eat the evening meal with her family she withdrew from any contact with them.

She seemed so unhappy and any effort they made to find out what was wrong met with stony silence. Was it bullying or was she struggling with her work they wondered. She'd always been a chatty, happy and bright child until her second year at secondary school. Then their daughter just wasn't the same person.

During the Easter holidays they decided that maybe getting her a dog would be a good idea. Something to take her mind off what was bothering her. Anna seemed excited for the first time in months when they approached her with the idea. She immediately searched the internet for puppies for sale, she insisted it had to be a puppy, much to her parents' horror. They knew the disaster that a puppy can bring to a house but they agreed for Anna's sake. The dog would be her responsibility they said and she eagerly agreed. Three hours later Anna sat on her bed looking at the photo on her phone of her cute fluffy little Husky cross. Only six weeks to wait before it would be sat on her bed with her, snuggling up.

"What the hell have we done," her dad said to her mother. "She doesn't seem to realise that the cute little fluffy bundle will quickly turn into a destruction machine."

"A Husky too," said her mother "hardly a young girl's dog."

The arrival of Harry, named after the One Direction star, certainly seemed to improve Anna's frame of mind. She loved to cuddle Harry and to play with him in the garden. She was even keen to feed him and take him for walks. Well, for the first two weeks. Then it was just the cuddles and occasional garden play sessions, if it wasn't raining of course.

So now, almost four years later, she walked in from college just after lunch and announced she was taking Harry for a walk. A proper walk involving going further than the garden. Her parents were speechless, which was very rare for her mother.

"I'll be back for tea. I'm meeting some friends up by the reservoir," Anna said. "Where's the dog's lead?" They weren't surprised that she didn't know.

After Anna had closed the door her parents looked at each other with a mix of amazement and concern on their faces.

"She's seventeen. We have to trust her," they both said in unison. They couldn't help but worry though.

Anna had told them the truth about what she was doing, well apart from the fact that she had used the plural of the word friend when she should have used the singular form. She couldn't tell them she was meeting Mark because she knew they didn't like him at all and would do everything they could to stop her seeing him. They didn't understand him. True he had been in trouble with the police when he was younger but he had changed. He told her he loved her and that made her happy. He told her that she was different to all the other girls he had been with and that made her feel special. He was also her first boyfriend.

Anna lived in a stone terraced house on a steep cobbled street that wouldn't be out of place in the Hovis adverts. It was only a short walk to the car park at the start of the moors but it was a tough climb to get there. That was why most people drove to the car park and started their walks from there. She had arranged to meet Mark a short distance beyond the car park, where the tracks went off in three directions. One of the tracks was far less worn than the other two, in fact hardly worn at all. Almost no one went that way because it was very remote indeed if you got into any trouble. That was the path she would take with Mark. They couldn't risk being seen by anyone who knew her parents.

Mark was waiting for her as arranged. Anna rushed into his arms and they exchanged a quick kiss. "Wait until we are out of sight

Mark," Anna instructed with a cheeky grin on her face. Harry growled at Mark.

The path they took lost its definition after about half a mile but they continued walking across the tufted grass surface, not a care in the world. Anna had met Mark when he was waiting outside college for his now ex-girlfriend. He had approached Anna and told her how beautiful she looked. She was embarrassed but flattered. He told her that he was only meeting his current girlfriend because he felt sorry for her. The following week he was at the college gates again, this time waiting for Anna. Her friends had told her not to get involved. They said that Mark used girls and then dumped them when he became fed up with them. They were just jealous she told herself.

They had been walking for well over half an hour when Mark said, "Let's sit down here for a while." They sat on the damp ground and talked about the strange man that was rumoured to live further over the moors from where they were. Beyond the next hill or two, very remote. Anna had never seen him but people said that he was odd and she was warned to keep away from his farm. There were all sorts of rumours about what went on there. She had no wish to go there but Mark said, "Let's go and find his farm. Maybe we will see him." Anna told him she was scared to go there and Mark let the matter drop, for now. He intended to suggest it again when he had done what he came here to do. Anna thought she would do anything for Mark but the thought of the strange man scared her.

Mark put his coat down on the grass so they could have somewhere dry to lay. Very chivalrous Anna thought. Harry lay nearby all the time keeping a close watch on Mark.

"Go and play Harry," said Anna. Harry didn't move.

Mark pulled Anna close to him and she loved the warmth she felt from Mark hugging her. They kissed. She was very naïve in such matters so followed Mark's lead. The more they kissed the more the butterflies in her stomach danced around. Mark pushed his tongue into her mouth. She didn't like that at all but wanted to make him happy.

He put his hand under her top and slowly and gently walked his fingers up to her breasts. She knew from the chatter of the girls at college that this was normal so she let him continue. She had never felt the sensation that was all over her at the moment. He pushed her bra up and massaged her young firm breasts before he took hold of her nipples between his thumb and first finger. Anna thought she was going to explode.

She floated off into a world of dreams, very relaxed with what was happening to her. She wasn't thinking about what Mark was doing, she was just enjoying the pleasure. She felt Marks fingers get hold of the fastener on the zip of her jeans and slowly pull the zip down. He pushed his hands inside and started to move his finger up to the top of her panties and started to pull them down.

"Stop," she shouted as she pulled away from him. Suddenly she had returned to the real world and knew this was wrong. She didn't want to do this anymore. She knew Mark would understand.

"What the fucking hell is wrong with you?" he said angrily. "You bring me up here, play the teasing game and then turn into Miss Goody Two Shoes. What the hell did you think we were going to do, bird watch?"

Anna was shocked. "I thought we were just going for a walk."

"Get real you bitch. Fuck off and find you own way home." At this point he stormed off leaving her with tears rolling down her face.

"I love you she shouted."

"Well I don't fucking love you."

Harry snuggled up to Anna as if to try and comfort her. Anna sat there awhile staring out into space and then started to put her bra back in position, fastened up her zip and generally tidied her clothes. "Mum and Dad were right," she whispered into Harry's neck.

She had no idea how to get home. It all looked the same up here. She had spent all the time looking up at Mark. She knew she could rely on him to find their way home. How wrong could she be? Her Mum had always said you could never trust men. Anna had thought she was joking. Surely her mum trusted her dad, or did she?

Just as she was pushing herself up she notice a small circular piece of metal tucked under a tuft of grass. She reached across and picked it up. She saw it was a dog disc with the name Betty on it.

'Betty. Wasn't that the name of the dog that was with the missing lady I heard about on the radio?' she thought. She had obviously been up here. What had happened to her here? Had someone kidnapped her? Was it the strange man? Was he still around? Anna was terrified. She pushed the disc into her pocket and ran as fast as the terrain would let her. She was in a valley therefore couldn't see the car park. She didn't even know if it was near enough to see anyway. She was lost.

"Harry take me home please," she sobbed.

Harry led the way and they eventually reached the track she thought they had taken at the start of their walk. Not long after that they reached the car park. She wasn't surprised to see a lot of cars there, they would be people walking their dogs after work, but she was surprised to see several police men and women there. They were talking to people. What would she say if they spoke to her? She couldn't tell the truth. Her parents would find out. She didn't see any signs of Mark, perhaps he had found another way off the moors. She was sure now that he would have done his best to avoid the police. 'How could I have been so stupid?' she thought.

She used a tissue to try and wipe away any trace of her tears. As she walked onto the car park a kind looking policewoman approached her.

"Hello do you mind if I ask you some questions?"

"No."

After the preliminaries of giving her name and address she was asked just where on the moors she had been. She tried her best to explain.

"That doesn't seem a sensible area for a young girl to walk alone."

"I wasn't alone. I was with some of my friends but we had an argument and they all ran off and left me." She couldn't contain her tears any longer.

"Are you alright?"

"Yes I'm fine. I'm just upset because I thought I could trust my friends and I was wrong."

The policewoman handed a photo of Sarah to Anna. "I'm sorry but I need to ask you if you saw this lady while you were on the moors. Or anything else that might help in our search for her."

"No I didn't see her," Anna replied. She reached into her pocket and pulled out the dog disc. "But I did find this in the grass." She passed the disc to the policewoman. "It said on the radio that her dog was called Betty. Could it belong to the lady's dog? Do you think something may have happened to her up there?" Anna shivered at the thought that she had just been up there alone.

"It's too early to say what has happened yet but it looks like that may be her dog's tag. That's very useful. Where exactly did you find it?"

"I'm not sure. We took the track to the left just up there and I guess we had been walking for between half an hour and an hour. I'm sorry I can't be more helpful."

"You have been very helpful Anna. Can we give you a lift home?"

"No thank you. I only live at the bottom of this road so I can walk there in a few minutes." She didn't want to get home yet.

The policewoman gave the dog disc to the sergeant in charge of the car park team.

"At last we have something but I think we are still looking for a needle in a haystack," he said.

Chapter 22

Sarah stood there, her eyes wide but looking at nothing. What had she done? Never in her life before had she shown violence to any living creature. She wouldn't even hurt a fly. John had killed her best friend though. He didn't even give her a chance to say goodbye.

She hated this man, no, man was too kind a word, she hated, really hated this creature standing before her. The creature she had just attacked with a knife. The fight drained out of her with that one action, she now felt the overwhelming urge to fly. She had to get away from here. She had to get away now.

Without thinking she ran to the door. She tried the handle not remembering that John always made sure that it was locked, it wasn't. She paused a moment, was this a trap. She flung the door open and ran, with no aim and no direction. In her mind Betty was running beside her, the wind sweeping up her ears. Sarah always found that amusing. Freedom, just two best friends together. Nothing could stop the tears that flooded down Sarah's cheeks. She realised at that point that dogs were far more important to her than humans. "That bastard can rot in hell," she screamed in her mind.

An early evening mist had descended on the high moors, disorientating her. Which way should she go? She had no idea. Anywhere away from John would do.

Her pace seemed slow motion to her. Her heart was pounding louder than a pneumatic drill. She was cold yet sweating. How far behind was John? Panic was setting in but she must keep going.

~~~~~~~~~~~~

John had been shocked when Sarah lunged at him with the knife. Where had she found the knife? He had obviously not been careful enough to protect her. That raised his anxiety levels. He would have to do better next time. He was relieved that she had used the knife on him and not herself. The knowledge that he could have been responsible for injuring her or worse still, possibly causing her death would be unbearable. He had tried so hard to care for her and he had failed.

He cursed himself for not locking the door. He had meant to lock it after he had brought the shopping in but Sarah's reaction to his news about Betty had been foremost in his mind. He couldn't understand why she was so angry. He had stopped Betty's suffering. Why wasn't Sarah pleased? He was confused. Had he done wrong when he thought he was doing right?

He held a towel against his arm to stem the flow of blood. The knife had luckily glanced across his arm rather than stabbing into it. The cut was never the less quite deep and it was bleeding a lot. He had to stop the blood contaminating the house even more than it already was. Sarah might come back, no, she would come back, and he had to make sure his house was safe for her just in case she didn't have HIV yet.

He wanted to run after Sarah to stop her getting away but that wasn't possible. He was bleeding. He couldn't risk his blood falling on to her. That was how this situation had started. "Damned blood," he shouted as a sense of overwhelming frustration shot through him. He was also worried about getting blood on the grass in case any walkers pass by in the future. It was very rare that that walkers came this far into the moors but John couldn't be certain that they wouldn't.

~~~~~~~~~~

Sarah had no idea how long or how far she had run but she knew she couldn't go much further. Darkness was falling fast and that would bring plummeting temperatures. She had to find shelter. "You fool," she cried, "Where the hell are you going to find shelter in this god forsaken place?"

She would have thought by now that she should have reached the track that led to the road down to the village but there was no sign of it. She must have gone in the wrong direction into territory where even she hadn't ventured before. Betty would have known which way to go. Without her she had no direction in life. She flopped to the ground and sobbed for her lost companion. Could she go on without Betty? Did she want to go on without her? She knew Betty would want her to go on with life therefore she eased herself up off the ground and summoned up all her energy to take the next step towards the future.

127

She was getting increasingly cold by the minute thanks to the dropping temperatures that the mist and darkness brought. She was still wearing John's mother's antique outfit which didn't include anything of great warmth. Could she survive the night out here? She had no choice.

Most of her injuries were healing well including her ankle. A couple of days ago this escape attempt wouldn't have been possible. The only concern remained the injuries to her head. She still hadn't been able to see the damage and John had refused to look for fear of contaminating her. She had tried time and time again to convince him that he could not have HIV but his mind was firmly closed to any thoughts but his own. It still hurt if she touched the back of her head or when she brushed her hair, no matter how gentle she was. She hoped the wounds weren't infected. No time to think about that now though.

Her progress across the rough surface had slowed to an amble. Still John hadn't caught up. Just then a hazy shape appeared on the horizon.

~~~~~~~~~~

Every member of the team working on operation 'Dog Walker', as it was now called, were gathered in the briefing room waiting for Detective Wilkinson to update them on the day's activities. They had all been working since early morning and now more than twelve hours later they still had not been able to go home to their loved ones but their dedication meant that not one of them complained. It was part and parcel of the job that they had to have understanding families. Three of the team had tickets to watch the United match tonight but that wasn't going to happen now. "They'll lose anyway," one of them whispered.

Detective Brian Wilkinson walked into the room accompanied by Sergeant Lou Smith. Lou had been christened Louisa but she hated that name so Lou it was, at least to everyone except her parents. Lou had worked closely with Brian for several years and understood him more than most. She could sense something was bothering him but finding out what would have to wait until later.

128

"Good evening," began Detective Wilkinson, "Thank you all for your hard work today. I appreciate you all staying late, please give my apologies to your families."

He continued, "As you all know, we have had teams working in the village and up on the moors car parks today. I have met with the leader of each team and would now like to summarise what we have found."

He went on to explain that in the village they had started by interviewing shoppers but that had returned nothing of use. Once the shopper footfall diminished they turned to interviewing the shop keepers.

"The assistant in the general store, a Carly Shepherd, informed us that a regular customer, a John Whittle, had purchased items that wouldn't normally be on his shopping lists. She told us that he comes into the village on the same day every week and as well as his own things he does shopping for the old ladies who live in the isolated farms. This morning though he bought female items that would be more appropriate for a younger lady. He explained that one of the farm widows had her daughter staying with her and because her mother was ill she was having to stay longer than anticipated. Hence the reason Mr Whittle was buying the items he did. She teased him that she thought he must have a woman living with him but he didn't react in any suspicious way. Miss Shepherd said that he was a really nice kind man."

Detective Wilkinson took a drink from the tumbler of water on the desk in front of him. He hated these plastic tumblers but health and safety dictated that real glasses were a hazard in a police station. He couldn't remember a single attack in this building involving a glass of water in his 30 years on the force but the overzealous health and safety officers said that it might happen so he had to put up with this objectionable drinking utensil.

Once his throat was quenched he continued.

"Also the manageress of the charity shop told us that a man, who she did not know, had gone into her shop and asked her to put together two ladies outfits for someone in their early forties. When she asked him about the size he held two grapefruit up in front of him and said that big."

A titter went around the room.

"Gentlemen, ladies, please," said the detective.

"When she put together some clothes he didn't even want to look at them before he paid. He gave the same reason for this purchase as John Whittle did in the general store therefore we can assume that it was the same person."

He paused while everyone wrote down this information.

~~~~~~~~~

John was worried about Sarah. She was his responsibility now and he had failed her. If any harm came to her he would have to confess to the police that he was to blame and he was sure he wouldn't be able to bear going to prison.

The blood had stopped flowing although there was still obviously a deep wound on his arm. He looked into the medicine cupboard in his kitchen. From the neat rows of various medical items, all with labels facing to the front, he picked out a box of antibacterial fabric plasters. He preferred the fabric type because they stayed in place better he thought but still rubbish though in his opinion. Surely they could create something better in this day and age he thought.

Once the plaster was firmly in place he took the bloodied towel out into the yard and burnt it in an old incinerator he kept in the barn. The towel could do no harm now. He tried desperately not to engage with the thought that the flying ash may be contaminated.

Going back into the house he decided to leave the door unlocked in case Sarah came back. This lack of security heightened his anxiety to levels he hadn't experienced for some time. Even higher than his anxiety during the last few days whilst Sarah had been living with him. He would have to spend the night in his chair downstairs, facing the door. Logic said that leaving the door unlocked overnight in this remote area would not be a problem at all but to John leaving the door unlocked was a huge security risk. He had to be on guard but it would be worth the discomfort to avoid her being locked out if she came back to him.

"If she doesn't come back I will find her tomorrow," he said to himself.

~~~~~~~~~

Sarah walked towards the eerie shape. She was sure the shape wasn't a human being and therefore thought she had nothing to lose by finding out what it was. When the shape became clear she discovered that it was an old shepherds hut. She knew about these huts but had never seen one before. Very few still existed.

These huts were used in the late 19th and early 20th centuries mainly during the lambing season. Shepherds lived in them to watch over the sheep before modern technology and the spread of electricity to remoter areas almost eliminated the need for them, although she had heard that a few still remained in use in Cumbria and Northumberland.

This hut was made from corrugated iron in common with most huts made before the Second World War. It was no longer held up by its iron wheels, which lay nearby, and the iron cladding had many holes in it as a result of sitting for the best part of a century in the harsh weather experienced on the high moors. For Sarah though it was shelter for the night. As welcome as any five star hotel. There was no such luxury as anything to sit on so her bed was the metal floor of the hut. It was interspersed with tufts of rough grass that had, in many places, won the battle with the iron and claimed its place as an integral part of the floor. She used one of the tufts as her pillow.

Her lack of sleep over the last 24 hours meant that even her rough hard bed couldn't keep her awake. As she drifted to sleep she promised herself, "Tomorrow I will find my way home."

~~~~~~~~~~

"Now for the report from the moors car park team. I will keep it brief as I am sure you would like to get home. Several people we spoke to knew Miss Meadon. It appears she was a familiar face on the moors but it seems that she walked in the remoter areas as no one seemed to see her once they had reached the three tracks. No one had seen her in the last few days.

"One item of interest was given to us by a young girl called Anna Hudson. She had been walking on the moors away from the main tracks with a group of friends but they had become separated. As she set off from the high moors to return home she found a dog tag that we believe belonged to Miss Meadon's dog.

"Finally the radio appeal has resulted in several of Miss Meadon clients coming forward but other than confirming that their dogs hadn't been collected any day this week and that they hadn't seen Miss Meadon in that time there was nothing useful they could add. We don't know at this stage how many clients she had so there may be others who haven't contacted us yet.

"So to summarise, we have a gentleman buying suspicious items, at least for him, and we know he lives in one of the remote farms but we don't know which one yet. We also have a dog tag found in a remote area of the moors but we don't know exactly where. No one has had any contact from Miss Meadon since early last Saturday morning when she called in on her neighbour. From what we have heard this is totally out of character.

"Her neighbour also told us that Miss Meadon always carries her mobile phone with her, even to the toilet we are told, so if she had an accident whilst walking on the moors surely she would have contacted someone. We have her mobile number now and have tried to ring it several times but it goes straight to voice mail every time.

"I feel we may be looking at a containment here. Tomorrow we will visit the moorland farms at first light. Go home and get some rest now. Tomorrow will be a long day."

~~~~~~~~~

Sarah had a bad night. She dreamt she was running to catch up with two hearses. One held her auntie and one carried Mrs Evans. Just as she was getting fairly close one hearse signalled left and the other signalled right. Which should she follow? She decided left, then right, then left, then right. "Make up your stupid mind," she screamed.

Her auntie, her dad's sister, was her only remaining relative. They weren't close but Sarah felt a familial responsibility to visit her occasionally, very occasionally.

Sarah woke up confused. Where was she? What was happening? How had she got here from the funerals? Had there been funerals or had she just had a nightmare? Was both her auntie and Mrs Evans dead? Was it her mind playing tricks? She had no idea. She needed to get home quickly to find out.

~~~~~~~~~

John had a bad night. He dreamt he had gone to the local pub for a pint or two. John never drank alcohol but tonight he just fancied it. He was really missing Sarah. Was he here in the hope he would see her enjoying a night out?

As he walked through the pub door everyone's eyes turned to him. The attention was on him. He wasn't being passed by with just a cursory hello as was normally the case. They no longer saw him as the odd guy from the moors. They were interested in him. He felt happy for the first time since Christine died.

At the bar he ordered a beer. He hoped they didn't ask him what sort of beer because he had no idea. Luckily they automatically gave him a pint of the local best bitter. He took a mouthful and nearly spit it right out again. He hated it but he wanted to belong here so he had to swallow it. He had had enough of being a loner. He wanted friends.

He looked around and saw several people covered in red. It must be blood was his instinctive reaction. Everything red meant danger. What had he done to these people? He knew it must all be his fault. He was weary of trying to protect everyone but now he had a lot more people to worry about.

He hadn't seen the small child at the table near the window shake a tomato ketchup bottle much too hard sending the sticky red sauce over several people on his and adjoining tables. Their cries of outrage at being sprayed emphasised the horror scene playing in John's mind. He was certain the red was blood and blood may be contaminated. He hated the colour red, it made him anxious.

He had to get away and think how he was going to protect them. He was running back to the safety of his farm when he woke up soaked in sweat.

How could he have friends? He couldn't cope with any more responsibility.

At this point John knew that he was destined to be alone until the end. Even then there would be no one at his funeral. "God why didn't you take me instead of Christine?" he asked.

He knew he was missing Sarah more than he had ever missed anyone before, except maybe his little sister. She was his only hope. It was time to take action.

Chapter 23

The team was all assembled by 5am to enable them to be up on the moors before first light.

Lou grabbed Brian's arm. "Are you alright?" she said with concern in her voice. After the briefing last night she had followed Brian back to his office and closed the office door behind her. "Is it bothering you again?" she asked.

This was Detective Wilkinson's first case for six months. He had only returned to work the previous week after sick leave for stress. Stress brought on by the disastrous end to his last case, also a containment. Brian had been in charge then as well. A young girl was held captive in a warehouse just off the Manchester Road. Brian was trained in hostage negotiation therefore he was always top of the list to lead such cases. Now here he was responsible for another person's life. How he hoped they could find Sarah safe and well, and free.

"Ok ladies and gentlemen here is our plan of action for today."

He laid a large map on the table at the front of the room. It showed where all the outlying farms were located. They had identified one farm as the prime suspect location because it was the nearest to the area were Anna thought she had found the dog disc. Also no one knew much about the occupant.

They drove to within half a mile of the farm using the force Land Rovers and then continued on foot, in silence, to avoid giving advanced warning of their arrival. Everything progressed well and just as the very first signs of dawn began to rise over the horizon ten policemen were positioned surrounding the farm but crouched out of view.

Detective Wilkinson and Sergeant Smith were positioned nearest to and in a direct line with the door. Every other member of the team knew exactly what to do on Brian's signal. How he hoped he wouldn't have to give the signal to charge into the house, especially after last time. He would only give that signal as a very last resort.

They waited out of view just behind the corner of the barn. Brian preferred to wait until the man came out into the yard if possible. That way he would be separated from the captive. If, that is, the captive was here.

Luckily Lou Smith's mind was fully on the job. She glanced at Brian and the vacant look in his eyes told her his mind wasn't focused on the here and now. She knew exactly where his mind was.

It was six months previously when he was looking up at the face at the window. She was so young. He thought he recognised her despite the tormented look on her face. The eyes confirmed that he knew her. Despite staring in sheer fear and being blood red from the tears that had accompanied her pleas for mercy the irises still shone a vivid blue. He only knew one person with eyes like that. He had to set her free.

Negotiations went on for hours with no progress being made. He had no choice but to give the signal to storm the building. It was risky but his men were well trained. He didn't think the captor was armed so the risk would be minimal. Just as his men rushed into the warehouse he heard the shot and Nicola Martin disappeared from view.

He had failed. The sight of the 16 years old's slim youthful body being carried out to the police ambulance, make up replaced by blood, would torment him forever.

Lou had been talking to Brian for a minute or two with no response. She shook him. "Sir what's the matter. Are you seeing her again?"

"She was so young Lou."

"You did everything you could."

"She was my daughter," he said softly, "You are the first person I have ever told. Even Nicola never knew I was her dad."

Just then both their minds were focussed back on today's action when they heard the farm house door opening. 'Does his wife know?' Lou wondered but there was no time to discuss Brian's revelation now.

Brain knew that this exercise was another risk. They had no firm evidence that the occupant of this farm was involved in Sarah's disappearance. All they knew was that they thought he was the

135

person the shop keepers had mentioned. If so then he was shopping in the village at the time of the strange purchase of ladies clothes. Also this farm was the nearest to, although still quite a distance from, where Betty's disc was found.

John came out of the door and was walking straight towards their hiding place. The slightest of signals from John and the rest of the team knew exactly what to do. The two men hiding just round the corner of the farmhouse rushed John from behind and in one precise move placed the handcuffs on his wrists. His mind went into overdrive. Had these handcuffs been worn by a HIV sufferer in the past? Had they dug into their wrists and drawn blood? Yet another thing for him to worry about.

John tried to turn to look at his captors but they held him in such a position that he could only look forward towards where Detective Wilkinson and Sergeant Smith were walking towards him. When they reached him they introduced themselves and showed him their ID cards.

"I am leading the search for a missing woman, a Miss Meadon and our evidence leads us to believe that you may be holding her captive here," Detective Wilkinson said.

John couldn't believe his luck. Sarah's escape had played into his hands. This would buy him more time with her when she came back.

"I live alone here." He was surprised how calm he was. Mind you he wasn't having to tell lies so he didn't need to worry about that. He hoped they didn't ask him if he had seen Sarah because he would have to lie then. They didn't. How remiss of them he thought.

"We are aware that you normally reside on your own but do you have anyone staying with you at the moment."

"No."

"We have a warrant to search your house sir. We would like to do that now."

"Go ahead. I have nothing to hide."

Brian signalled for all his team to enter the house. Once inside they moved around the house in a well-rehearsed choreography.

John felt himself stiffen at the thought of strangers becoming contaminated by his house and the things in it. He dreaded that he may find things no longer perfectly in place or worse still out of order after they had left. In John's world everything had its place and that could never be changed or bad things might happen.

He had been allowed back into the house to sit and wait whilst the search was completed. He was still handcuffed. He felt violated as every part of his private world was intimately disturbed. He knew though that they would find nothing. He had made sure of that.

Once the house search was over the police moved on to the outbuildings and went through those with the same precision.

After what seemed like a lifetime to John he could see through the open door that several police officers, obviously not including the policeman who was guarding him, were deep in discussion. They were obviously discussing their findings. This shouldn't take long John hoped but yet he was wracked with worry in case despite all his efforts he had left a clue.

After a few minutes Detective Wilkinson came back into the house and sat in the chair next to John's. Sarah's chair.

"Sir could you please tell me why the window in one of the bedrooms is painted over with black paint?"

"That's my darkroom. My father liked photography and I have carried on the hobby. It is wonderful up here for taking shots of wildlife. Would you like to see some of my work?" He hoped they would say no.

"No that won't be necessary sir. I am glad to say that our search was clear. You are free to go. Thank you for your cooperation and I am sorry we have disturbed you."

John hoped they were careful when they took the handcuffs off.

He knew what he had to do next. After he had returned everything to its rightful place of course. The fact that he had put everything back in place quickly made him anxious but he knew he had no time to waste.

Chapter 24

It was very dim in the shepherds' hut and it took some time for Sarah's eyes to adjust to the lack of light. Then she saw the figure in the corner. She screamed.

How had the person got into the hut without her hearing them? Were they real or was her mind playing tricks on her? 'Am I going crazy?' she thought.

"Don't be afraid my dear," the figure said. The voice told her that the figure was male but she still couldn't see his features clearly. The figure was crouched down as far into the corner as possible with his head down. He was between Sarah and the door.

"Who are you?" she shouted, "Get out." How she needed Betty now to protect her. She missed her in so many ways. She wanted to sob for her friend but she had to appear strong in front of the stranger.

The figure slowly lifted his head. "Please don't be afraid, I won't hurt you," it said. The visitor's features slowly became clear. Her heart sank and yet also jumped with panic at the same time. It was John.

"What do you want you creep?"

"We have to make a decision." At this point he lifted his right hand and she saw he held a knife. She shivered at the thought of what he was going to do with it. Was this the knife she attacked him with? Was he going to have revenge? She was scared, really scared, despite his assurances that he wouldn't hurt her.

She stared at him from the place that had been her bed for the night. Two tormented people sat on the rotting floor of a shepherds' hut jousting for survival.

There was a long silence before John spoke again. "Meeting you has taught me that I can't go on leading a recluse's life. My parents, and briefly Christine, have been the only people who I have ever had close to me. Since my parents died I have been alone, completely alone. My only break from the isolation of the farm is my weekly shopping trips to the village. Other than that the only living things I have contact with are the birds who visit me and they are only interested in the food I give them. They eat and fly away.

"I choose not to see the farm widows I shop for. I ask them to leave their shopping lists outside and I deliver the goods to the same place. They leave me their money the following week. This avoids the dangers that contact with them could bring.

"No one wants to be friends with John Whittle and I used to like it that way. Since I met you I know I want a friend. Who will be my friend though? I realise that no one will be my friend. Will you be my friend? No of course you won't."

Sarah remained silent.

"The shopkeepers see the jovial friendly façade I display for just a few hours each week but even they don't want to be my friend. Happy, strange John they think but they don't know what is wrong with me. No one knows what is wrong with me. I don't even know myself."

"I know," whispered Sarah.

John slowly looked up. He said nothing.

"I know what is wrong with you John."

"How can you?" he snapped "I just have a crazy mind that's all."

"No John. You have OCD. Obsessive Compulsive Disorder. It's a medical condition."

"You are talking rubbish. Are you a doctor all of a sudden?"

"I heard it on the radio when you went to the village. When you ……….. killed Betty." she said. She could feel the tears welling up in her eyes and did her best to keep them from surfacing. It was no good, her body was wracked with her sobbing for her departed friend."

It took some time for her to control her anguish before she could continue to speak.

"You have a medical condition. A condition of the brain."

"You mean I'm nuts?" he spit at her.

"No you aren't nuts. You can't help what is happening to you. You need help."

"Will you help me?"

"No. I can't"

Both sat silently in their own little worlds.

Neither knew how long had passed before John slowly raised his left hand. He held a key.

"I have the key to your freedom," he said softly.

She looked at the key. It looked like his door key.

John continued, "If you will help me I will give you this key now. If you won't I must use the knife to end my life. The decision is yours."

Her mind was in a whirl. Knife, key, knife, key. It was like following the hearses again. Knife, key, knife key. Her mind was in a whirl, she didn't know what to do. She wanted to be free of John and all his problems but she couldn't be responsible for his death, not even indirectly. Would he carry out his threat to kill himself? She had no idea but she decided that she couldn't take the risk. She slowly reached out and took hold of the key.

Now it was John's body wracked with sobbing. But his were sobs of hope.

Chapter 25

Late night working and the added burden of having to walk Cuddles meant that Steve and Katy hadn't visited Mrs Evans for a couple of days. They decided they would remedy that on their way home from work tonight. They both hated the thought of her being alone without her regular visits from Sarah. No one should be alone, especially when they get older.

Steve thought of his own grandma. It was only after she was gone that he knew he should have visited her more. He was a teenager though so he was too busy having fun to visit old people. Then she was gone. His young mind thought she would be there forever. She died without him telling her he loved her.

"Hello Mrs Evans," they shouted through the door which was open slightly. There was no reply. They shouted again but with the same result. They looked at each other and both knew the thoughts going through each other's mind. 'Please Lord let her be alright', they both thought.

"Should we go in," asked Katy.

"I don't know. I don't like just walking into someone's house."

"But what if she's fallen or something. She could have been lying there for ages. Why the hell didn't we come before?"

They opened the door a little more and saw the side of Mrs Evans in her chair facing the television. Her head was slumped forward.

~~~~~~~~~~

Detective Wilkinson was in his office despairing at the complete lack of evidence that they had managed to gather so far. It was as though Sarah Meadon had simply vanished. It was as though she had been abducted by aliens.

As always at times like this Sergeant Smith sat on the other side of his desk. Normally two minds were better than one but not on this occasion.

"We have visited every farm on the high moors, we have had increased coverage in the media, we have interviewed people in the surrounding villages, we have talked to all of Sarah's clients that we are aware of and we have even visited local vets and pet shops but no one has seen her. What do we do next Lou?" They dispensed with formalities when they were alone, it was Brian and Lou then but formal titles when others were around.

"I have no idea," said Lou, "Let's go through it all again."

They re-read every word of every interview that had been conducted. Most of them were so dull they would be a good remedy for an insomniac. They were both looking for that proverbial needle in a haystack. The only clue they had so far was the dog tag and that was a weak clue. They needed a lucky break.

Until then the search must go on.

~~~~~~~~~~~

"You go and see if she is alright," Steve said as he pushed Katy forward.

"Why me?"

"Because you are a woman."

She wondered why in a difficult situation such as this it's always the men who are the cowards. They like to give this air of bravado but really they are wimps. She remembered when the people next door had a fish pond in the garden. Yes next door had a garden whilst they didn't, which was always a bone of contention to Katy. Steve was terrified of little fish, poor thing. One day next door's cat kindly brought them a present – of one of the fish from the pond. The cat came in through the open door and proudly deposited its gift right in front of Steve's feet. He had a panic attack, Steve not the cat, and if she hadn't descended the stairs like an Olympic sprint champion the poor fish would have gulped its last breath. There it was flipping and flopping a piscine ballet, seeming magnetically attracted to Steve's feet as he jumped out of the way. Super woman to the rescue. She ran next door and returned the fish to the pond in the nick of time. The fish recovered well only to be eaten by a heron later the same day.

She knew there was no way that Steve would touch Mrs Evans, just in case she was dead. He seemed to think that people were more dangerous dead than alive. She knew she would have to do it.

Katy carefully approached the chair, talking softly all the time to hopefully lessen the shock for Mrs Evans, if she wasn't already the late Mrs Evans. Still no movement. Little by little she edged closer to the chair and was now within touching distance. She reached out her hand to gently shake the arm nearest to her when suddenly there was an almighty sneeze. The two visitors had never jumped so high or moved so quickly in their lives.

"Oh hello dears. I didn't hear you come in. It's nice to see you. Are you alright? You look pasty." Her own sneeze had shaken her out of the shallow sleep she was enjoying.

"We are fine Mrs Evans," they laughed.

"I told you to call me Ellen."

"Sorry Mrs Evans, I mean Ellen. We thought we would call in to see if you needed anything."

"I'm fine thank you. The postman has been very kind and brought me some bits and pieces from the supermarket. Easy things I can just heat up. He's a really nice man."

"He seems it. Is there anything we can get for you?"

"Well there is one thing if you don't mind. Could you bring me a bottle of brandy? I like a tipple now and again; only for medicinal purposes of course. I ran out last night."

They smiled. "You little tinker Ellen. A secret boozer eh?" said Steve. Ellen giggled.

"Will you stay for a cup of tea and a biscuit?"

They really could do with getting home but how could they refuse this dear old lady. They were probably the only people she had seen today or even longer. "Of course we will. I'll make the drink if you like," Sarah offered.

"That's very kind of you. Do you know where everything is? If you can't find something just have a root around. I don't have any secrets, well not in the cupboards," she said with a chuckle. They imagined that Ellen had experienced quite a colourful life.

"I was just watching The Chase. I love it but don't get many questions right. Mind you I didn't actually see much of it tonight; I was resting my eyes."

Just then Mrs Evans began to cry quietly. Katy left her tea making and went and sat on the floor next to her. "What's the matter Ellen? Are you ill?" she asked gently.

"I was thinking about Sarah," she said between her tears, "Have you heard anything about her? It's been a long time now."

"I'm sorry, we haven't heard anything. The police are searching for her and I am sure they will find her soon. Don't worry." Katy realised that was a ridiculous thing to say to someone who feared for the wellbeing of her closest, maybe her only, friend. She could tell that Ellen was concerned she would never see Sarah again.

~~~~~~~~~

"Would you mind calling all the team together please Lou? In one hour in the meeting room. We need some new ideas."

Without a word Sergeant Smith set about her task.

Detective Wilkinson sat at his desk head in hands. "I can't fail again," he said to himself, "I can't lose another one."

One hour later Sergeant Smith put her head around his door. "We are ready for you sir."

She heard his sigh as he pushed himself up from his chair. They both knew this wasn't going well.

After he had outlined the current information, or lack of it, he asked for ideas from the floor. He knew his team was one of the brightest but even they had little to suggest. They had done so much already.

One constable stood at the back of the room suggested they widened the area for farm searches. This was agreed and would be undertaken later that day.

Detective Wilkinson then added his own ideas. "I know we have no hard evidence that Miss Meadon is being held in one of the moors' farmhouses but we can't afford to wait for concrete proof. If we have nothing better than we already have by this time tomorrow I want a team up on the moors overnight. Not a pleasant task I know but it may be that the captive is being moved under cover of darkness."

Brian sat long after the others had left the room and held his head in his hands, deep in thought. "Where am I going wrong?" he whispered.

Chapter 26

They walked back to the farm in silence, John leading the way. Sarah followed a few paces behind with a heavy heart and leaden feet. She was battling her thoughts. She knew she had only agreed to help John to avoid his death being on her conscience for the rest of her life. Was that selfish? If she was honest she didn't really care if he lived or died, which was totally out of character. What had she let herself in for? He was emotionally blackmailing her and this made her hate him even more.

John had a spring in his step and hope in his heart, neither of which had been there for a very long time. He had a friend, he thought. A friend who was going to help him, he thought. Would that still be the case when she discovered the truth?

Half her life was spent walking on these moors and she felt alive when surrounded by nature's wonderful creations and when she heard the cheery sounds of the birds. This morning none of it registered in her mind.

John heard nature's calls clearer than he had since Christine's death. The world seemed alive and happy. A new dawn.

"Welcome home," he said as they reached the farm. She knew she needed to make sure he was completely clear about the arrangement. True she had agreed to help him but this was most definitely not her home. She would visit to support him but her bed would be at 28 Spring Road, every night. She had mixed emotions about returning there. She was excited about seeing Mrs Evans again but she knew that the house would seem very empty without Betty. The tears came again. She could not think of Betty without crying. For now it was just crying, she could grieve properly when she returned to her home. Not long now.

John held the door open in true gentlemanly fashion to allow Sarah to enter the house. She wasn't surprised that he locked the door behind them. She realised things wouldn't change overnight. She clutched the key to her freedom and realised that it must have been a huge challenge for John to give it to her. To let her come and go as she pleased. It went against the whole reason he was refusing her the freedom she craved. Why had he had the sudden change of heart? It didn't make sense to her at all but never the less she clung tightly to the little ray of hope that the key gave her.

She was very hungry and eagerly devoured the food that John prepared for them both. Fried eggs on toast had never tasted so good. She even made sure she licked the dribbles of yolk from round her mouth; mustn't waste any. She began to relax a little. John had shown he trusted her and she needed to trust him. This would only work with mutual trust. He couldn't control his thoughts; she knew that now and would always take that into consideration she hoped.

Sarah was desperate to get home but something told her not to rush it. This arrangement was very embryonic so needed the rules establishing.

The meal over she desperately wanted to feel human again. "Do you mind if I have a bath and change into some of those clothes you bought me, and then we can talk?" she asked.

"Of course my dear." How she wished he wouldn't use that term.

She was puzzled when John knelt on the floor and rolled back the rug that was lay in front of the wood burning stove. He then proceeded to lift a trap door that was set into the stone floor. He pulled out two parcels and handed them to her.

"I had to make sure the police didn't know you had been here."

"Wait a minute," she snapped, "You mean the police have been here and you didn't tell them about me." Was there no end to this man's stupidity and insensitivity? She grabbed the parcels without a word of thanks and ran upstairs. She kept the key with her all the time.

It took an age to fill the large bath with the poor water pressure in this area. She closed the toilet seat and sat down to wait. She thought of how Betty loved to play in water. It didn't matter whether it was clean or absolutely filthy, she didn't mind. She would stand for ages in the river chewing at fallen tree branches or trying to retrieve her ball that had lodged under the river bank. She never gave up. At times Sarah would plead with her to have a different ball but Betty would have nothing of it, she wanted her ball. "I'm sorry Betty," Sarah sobbed.

There were no toiletries here that were made for women so she had to make do with 'Forest for Men' bath gel. She suspected it had come from the bargain shelf. 50p a bottle no doubt but it would have to do. At least it hid the scum floating on top of the water.

Lingering in the bath soaking away the aches and pains of last night's adventure, not to mention the dirt and grime, her thoughts turned to her home, to Mrs Evans and to her auntie. 'I must visit auntie', she thought.' She would never forget her childhood horrors but she thought she could forgive and her auntie wasn't really involved directly in her punishments anyway. In Sarah's eyes she was just guilty by association.

There was a need to contact her clients. That is if she still had any. She felt sure they would all have had to make alternative arrangements for their dogs but hoped these would be temporary and that they would come back to her. She thought of ironing in the kitchen watching the sunset slowly disappear behind the moors. She hated ironing but she loved that time when she could reflect on the joys of the day about to end.

She had no idea how much time had passed but suddenly she became aware that the water was cold. She dried herself on the pale blue bath towel which had certainly seen better days. At least it was very clean, which was more than she could say for the bath water now. The idea of putting on some clothes more appropriate to her age was very appealing. She just hoped they had been chosen well. Mind you anything was better than the outfit she had just discarded; well almost anything.

Once she was dry and safely back in her bedroom she tipped the clothes out onto the bed. 'Could have been worse', she thought. Apart from the clothes John had also got everything she asked for on her shopping list. Oh the joy of putting on clean knickers, especially knickers that fit. Bliss. She would continue to go bra less for now until she got home. John had done alright with the clothes and she could happily wear any of them. For today she chose a white short sleeved tee-shirt, blue denim jeans and a dark blue sweatshirt. She felt more like herself now. She couldn't find a hair dryer so for that reason, and to avoid disturbing her head wounds, she roughly scrunched her hair and let it dry naturally.

The simple fact of wearing reasonable clothes made her feel much better. A tête-à-tête with John was now within her capabilities. She noticed that he had changed her bedding. Another indication of his caring side. She sat for a while on the edge of the bed planning her opening gambit before going downstairs to agree the rules.

She knew that she needed to empathise more with him in order for her to coerce him into talking more openly with her. Above all else there had to be mutual trust. He had shown trust in her by giving her the door key now she must show trust in him.

There could be no more procrastination therefore she slowly, and somewhat nervously, descended the stairs. When she opened the door into the living room John was sat in his chair listening to the radio, in accordance with his routine. Sarah wondered if his routine and his habits could ever be changed but by the simple action of taking hold of his door key she had committed to helping him.

"John we need to talk," she said as she eased herself down into the chair next to him, her chair. "I obviously don't know for certain that it is OCD you are suffering from but it sounds likely enough to need to investigate more. To be honest we don't really know what OCD truly is yet. I need to know more about how you feel. I have no knowledge about OCD other than the brief bit I heard on the radio so we need to talk. Please tell me more about how you feel."

There was a long tense silence before John looked into her eyes.

"Where do I start? I have never spoken to anyone about it before other than mum and dad and they just told me to pull myself together but I couldn't control my thoughts, I couldn't do what they told me to do. I tried Sarah, I really tried." John was very overcome with emotion and continued through frequent sobbing and with broken speech. "My thoughts are very real to me. I feel that I have to be perfect otherwise I will go to hell, the devil will take me or worse still he will take someone close to me. I have to do everything my mind tells me or someone will die. I have to be a perfect person or I will never go to heaven. I'm not even sure there is a heaven but I can't take the risk of not going there if there is.

"I think that I am contaminated and must protect everyone else from becoming contaminated themselves. It doesn't matter whether I think they will become contaminated from me, or from someone or something else, I have to protect them.

"I know that I must confess to things I have done that may affect other people. Often I am not sure that I have actually done the thing in question but I might have therefore I must confess."

"Why have you not confessed to keeping me here?" Sarah asked. John had no idea how to answer this, he couldn't explain it to himself, so he ignored Sarah's question.

"Soon after my father died I did once apply for a job. Only working in a warehouse but I would have loved it. I didn't need to work for the money, Mum and Dad had left me enough to live on providing I live a simple life, which suits me. I just wanted to do something rather than sit here all day every day. I got the job but that's when the problems started. My mind told me that if I accepted the job someone close to me would die. That someone had to be my mother. I couldn't risk it so I turned the job down. I knew then I could never work.

"That is only a small part of what I think and feel. My mind is constantly on alert 24 hours a day, 7 days a week, 52 weeks a year. It makes me weary and the more tired I get the worse the problems are. I have to do everything in a certain way or bad may befall someone.

"I am tired Sarah but just knowing there may be a reason that I am the way I am is wonderful. I'm tired but I feel really elated just hearing what you've said yet I'm also very frightened that it may not be true. I am relieved to have you to help me, I know I couldn't do it alone. Thank you."

Whilst John was talking Sarah began to realise just what a terrible burden he was bearing every minute of every day. She knew now that he was trapped just as much by his OCD as she had been by him, until he gave her the key that is.

Sarah sat in silence whilst he was talking. She guessed that it must be very difficult for him to tell his story. She was absolutely sure that there was a whole lot more to tell.

"I am not an expert on OCD John. Indeed I don't know much at all but I am pretty sure that is what is causing your problems." Sarah said when John had finished talking "You need professional help."

In the last few minutes Sarah lost all the anger and hatred she felt towards John. She felt sympathy for him. No one deserved to suffer the way he was obviously suffering. She still felt angry at Betty's death and at her own imprisonment but she was beginning to realise that John may have had no control over what he did. It didn't make it right but it was pointless blaming someone who was forced to take the actions they did, forced by OCD.

She turned to look at John face to face. She saw tears running down his cheeks. "I know you have taken your first tiny step along your journey by trusting me enough to give me the door key. I will try and hold your hand as much as I am able along the rest of the journey. Tomorrow I will try and find out more about OCD and how you can get help."

Seeing how upset he was she felt she couldn't leave him tonight. One more night here wouldn't harm her. "John I will stay tonight if you would like that."

"I would like that very much. Thank you Sarah. You are very kind."

She found listening to John's story, albeit a very brief synopsis, stressful. Goodness knows what lay ahead. "I am just going out for a bit of fresh air for a few minutes. I will come back I promise."

"Please don't go out Sarah. I don't feel strong enough at the moment to cope with the risks it would involve. Please wait until tomorrow."

"Sorry but at the moment I don't feel strong enough to face the tasks that may lie ahead. It's difficult for me too. You are not the only one suffering. I need some fresh air."

She saw John put his head in his hands as she pushed herself up out of her chair and slowly walked towards the door. She looked back at John. 'Poor man', she thought. She felt into the pocket on the right hand side of her jeans and took out the key. The key that must have caused John to battle hard with the demons in his mind. She felt proud of him.

She slid the key into the lock and began to turn it. Nothing. She tried again and again but the lock didn't turn. She turned, walked across to John's chair and slapped him across his face, very hard.

All her hate and anger returned. He had tricked her. He had given her the wrong key. She was still his prisoner. She ran upstairs to the sanctuary of her bedroom.

"I couldn't risk you contaminating anyone," John said very quietly.

Chapter 27

Sarah lay on the bed furious with herself for being so foolish. She trusted a man and he let her down big time. That brought back memories of her father.

She had escaped and then been naïve enough to walk right back into her prison of her own free will. 'How stupid', she thought. "Now what do I do?" she said to herself. She knew her captor wouldn't make the same mistake again. Her chances of a second escape were practically nil. 'At least Betty is free God rest her soul', Sarah said in her mind. The thought of Betty brought the usual flood of tears. The pain wasn't lessening at all. If time is a great healer then in this case it would take a huge amount of time.

She lay on her bed fully clothed as dusk turned to night. She was oblivious to the transformation of course due to the blacked out windows. Sarah had no idea why she had put the useless key back into her pocket but as she felt the shape of it through the thick material an idea came to her. It was a very long shot but maybe, just maybe it would work. What had she to lose?

She pushed the drawers tight against the back of the door. She certainly didn't want to be disturbed whilst she completed her work. It would be slow, it may be painful, but she began. Tiny bit by tiny bit the creation took shape. After an hour there was little to show for her effort but determination drove her on. Her fingers were very sore but there was no time to feel sorry for herself. She was getting the hang of the job now so hopefully the rate of progress would increase.

~~~~~~~~~~

Detective Wilkinson addressed his team as the last light of day faded away.

"Good evening ladies and gentlemen. As you are aware despite all our best efforts we have gathered very little information in our search for Miss Meadon. Searches of the moorland farms have all been clear even though we extended our search area."

He looked around the room and saw nothing but eagerness on the faces of his team. Not one of them seemed unhappy to be taking part in the night time exercise. He knew how lucky he was to be heading such a committed team. They all wanted a successful end to this case just as much as he did.

"We will set off from here in 30 minutes. The van will transport you to the three tracks but I am afraid that to avoid announcing our presence it must be on foot from there, and in silence please. If the captor, if indeed there is a captor, gets wind of our presence any potential movement planned for tonight will be cancelled.

I hope you have all got your long johns on and your waterproofs, it is going to be cold and damp up there."

The whole team knew exactly where they were to be positioned. They also knew that it was important to keep a very low profile and that meant laying on the wet grass all night. It had to be done though.

"Be very careful where you lay," said Brian, "especially you Keith." He directed the remark towards a young constable sat on the third row back. Laughter came from every occupied seat in the room as they remembered the last time they had done a night exercise on the moors. Keith Haworth, a rookie in his first year with the force, had lowered himself into a face down prone position when he heard a squelching sound. He knew immediately what it was but if he needed confirmation it was provided by the strong smell that drifted up his nostrils. At least the cow pat provided some warmth on what was a very cold night.

"Good luck team. Please report in anything you see that may be suspicious, anything at all no matter how insignificant it seems."

~~~~~~~~~~~

Sarah worked on until her arms, hands and fingers just couldn't take any more. It wasn't as she would have liked it to be but it would have to do. She was certain that John would have been in bed for hours but she listened at her bedroom door to make sure she couldn't hear him walking around. There was no sound.

The work had been completed in darkness to avoid any chance of John becoming aware on his late night wander round the farm yard. John had told her that he sometimes, on nice nights, walked around the yard whilst he drank his pre-bedtime brew. It would just be her luck that he would do that tonight.

Anyway she felt it was safe now. She flicked the light switch to illuminate her creation to anyone out on the moors tonight. 'Please someone see it before John', she thought. If John saw it first she knew she would never escape.

~~~~~~~~~~

Despite what happened last time, Keith Haworth wanted to create a good impression in his work. He was ambitious and worked hard to gain promotion as soon as possible. He saw the light go on out of the corner of his eye and turned his head in its direction. He unpacked his binoculars from the case attached to his belt and raised them to his eyes. Focusing on the light he knew he had something special.

"Detective Wilkinson, this is Constable Haworth. Over."

"Receiving. Go ahead please. Over."

"I can see a small amount of light in an upstairs window of the farm about 500 metres ahead of me at a bearing of 2 o'clock. The light is coming through illuminating a word. The word is HELP. Over."

"Ok constable stay in position. I should be with you in 10 minutes. Keep watching the window."

Detective Wilkinson wasn't far away but daren't use a vehicle for fear of alerting the captor. Walking was the only way.

~~~~~~~~~~

Although she had been awake most of the previous night, sleep still wouldn't come for Sarah. She was fatigued but her mind was constantly active and that, combined with the need to leave the light on, kept sleep at bay. She prayed that someone would see her sign before John did. What would John do to her when he saw it? Her tired mind really didn't care; she just wanted relief from this hellish situation, one way or another.

She closed her eyes to wait for fate to take its course.

~~~~~~~~~~

John was exhausted from all the stress and had therefore slept well despite the events of last night. He knew Sarah would be annoyed at his trick but it had been necessary. He hoped she would understand but doubted she would. Somehow her discovery of the truth had relaxed his mind. There were no secrets to worry him. Telling Sarah his story had also been a relaxant. It had felt like a weight being lifted from his shoulders just to share his problems. His mother always said that a problem shared was a problem halved but he felt the equation was even more weighted in his favour.

He had no idea what would happen next. He had no plans other than the need to stop Sarah spreading her contamination; if she had one. It was too early even for John to get up so he lay in bed with his eyes closed trying to work out what the next move would be.

There was no way that he would get back to sleep. He was finding this whole situation incredibly stressful which had a significant effect on his mood, he felt very low indeed. The situation he found himself in could not be described as anything but hopeless, the only likely outcomes, in his mind, being prison or Sarah spreading contaminations.

~~~~~~~~~~

They both became aware of the hammering on the door at the same time. Loud hammering. Sarah hoped her work had borne fruit. It had been hard labour but maybe it had worked. She remained lying on the quilted bed cover.

John immediately sat bolt upright. Who could be knocking at his door so early? John feared it would be the police which scared him, he was terrified of going to prison. He knew, however, that he had no option but to make his way downstairs. He unlocked the door at the bottom of the stairs listening to the continuing banging. It had been joined in a cacophony of sound by loud shouting.

"Come out with your hands in the air."

He knew who it was now but had no idea what had brought them back here so soon. He had been so careful.

As soon as he opened the door he was grabbed and handcuffed. Detective Wilkinson stood in front of him.

"I am arresting you on suspicion of the unlawful detention of Miss Sarah Meadon. You do not need to say anything but anything you do say will be taken down and may be used in evidence against you."

John only half listened to what Detective Wilkinson was saying. He was too preoccupied with the potential contamination on the handcuffs, but even this preoccupation couldn't lessen his fear of prison.

The detective continued, "Do you have anything you wish to say?"

John slowly moved his head from side to side. He knew what faced him but doubted he could cope with it.

"Take him away."

Sarah saw John's face at the window of the police car as it drove out of the yard. Surprisingly she felt a pang of guilt and a great deal of sorrow. If only he could have trusted her enough to give her the correct key.

'What will happen to him', she wondered, 'will he be able to cope with it?'

~~~~~~~~~~

Sarah didn't see John again after he was driven out of the yard. She couldn't stop thinking about how he was. She knew she would have helped him all she could if only he hadn't tricked her.

By the time the policeman dropped her off at her door it was 10pm. She had been at the station all day being interviewed and re-interviewed, being photographed and been taken to hospital to have her injuries checked and treated. The doctor said that there was nothing serious. Her head wound amazingly wasn't infected. Everything should heal well in time.

Now she was home for the first time in several days. Was it really only a few days, it seemed much longer? She looked towards Mrs Evan's house as she walked up her short garden path. It was too late to disturb Ellen tonight. Her house was in darkness, she would be in bed. She would call in on her first thing in the morning.

She opened her door and momentarily expected Betty to come bounding up to her. Then her mind focused and realised that was never going to happen again. On entering the house she saw that everything was in place. In fact it looked like she had only left a short time ago.

Her eyes fell on Betty's bed, and her dishes, and her toys. Betty was everywhere yet nowhere. Sarah sat on the chair next to the small round glass kitchen table and cried. Cried for Betty and cried for her own freedom.

~~~~~~~~~~

John sat in his cell at the end of a tormenting day. His anxiety level was off the Richter scale.

There was potential contamination everywhere. Who had been in this cell before? There must have been people who took drugs. There must have been people who had slept around. There must have been people who slept on the streets; he knew it wasn't their fault but it wasn't hygienic.

He could see red everywhere. On the floor, on the walls, on the bed. No way could he lie on that bed. There was no chair so he would have to stand all night, there was no option.

He was also really scared of being bullied and beaten in prison. He imagined he would be a prime target for the tough characters that he felt sure he would encounter. He was consumed with fear and lack of hope. Tears constantly welled up in his eyes ready for the slightest trigger to start the flow down his cheeks.

He had confessed to everything the police accused him of. He had no option; he couldn't be 100% sure he hadn't done those things so he had to agree with them. John hated the interrogation. He felt so scared that he couldn't think clearly. His mind was even more confused than it normally was. They sat in the small sparse interview room while Detective Wilkinson pressed John for answers to numerous questions including:-

"Did you kidnap Miss Meadon whilst she was walking on the moors?"

"I'm not sure but I may have done." Of course he hadn't but the police suggested that he had so he may have done.

"Did you keep Miss Meadon imprisoned against her will?"

"Yes." That he was sure off.

"Did you harm Miss Meadon?"

"I don't think so. I'm not sure. I killed her dog."

"You must know if you harmed her. Don't play games with us?"

"If you say I harmed her I must have done."

And so the questioning went on and on. John was terrified, a nervous wreck, he didn't know how much more he could take. All the time he could hear the hum of the tape recorder preserving his every word. He could see the flicker of the light bulb above the table. A light bulb about to die, a light bulb that would no longer have to struggle on against the odds. John envied that light bulb.

He had only wanted to care for people, including Sarah, but now he knew he was in a lot of trouble. He was sure he wasn't going home for a long time. He knew he was likely to end up in a cell with other prisoners. He knew he couldn't survive that. He looked around for something, anything to put an end to this hell he found himself in.

~~~~~~~~~~

Sarah knew she had so much to be grateful for. She was free, she was in her own home, she could wear her own clothes and she could sleep in her own bed. Tomorrow she could see Mrs Evans and begin to contact her clients.

Why then didn't she feel happy?

She hadn't eaten all day but couldn't face anything. She poured a glass of water and made her way to bed. Her bed was much more comfortable than the one she had been using in the last few days. Her room was bright and cheerful and she could see through her windows. Her lack of sleep last night and the stress of the last few days had left her absolutely shattered.

Why then wouldn't sleep come?

She fought hard to remove the images in her mind. Every time she closed her eyes she saw John in a tiny squalid cell. She saw the anxious look on his face. She saw him keeping his hands in his pockets to avoid touching anything. She felt sorry for him.

The same John that had held her captive. The one who had refused her freedom. The man who had tricked her when she trusted him.

The same John who had treated her with kindness. The man who had risked severe embarrassment to buy her clothes when she hadn't even asked him to.

The same John who had sanctioned Betty's death.

The same John who had rescued her from the sink hole almost certainly saving her life.

The same John who couldn't help what he did.

Sarah tossed and turned until well into the night .... until she made her decision.

"Be strong John. I will help you, I promise. Tomorrow we will start our journey," she said to no one but herself. She meant every word.

Chapter 28

Several days had passed since John's arrest. Every day had been a whirlwind in Sarah's life both in terms of activity and emotions. John's arrest had hit Sarah hard. After all he had never harmed her, he cared for her in his own strange way. It was true that he had taken away her freedom but she knew now that he did that for the best, in his mind. Freedom is precious to anyone but the more she had researched OCD on the internet since returning home the more she knew he wasn't containing her for any evil reasons. If only it hadn't been so hard to convince the police of that.

Sarah had visited the police station almost every day trying to convince them that John couldn't help what he had done, that it was his OCD manipulating his mind.

It didn't help that no one in the local police force seemed to have any knowledge of OCD. They'd heard the jokes of course but didn't think it was a real illness. OCD sufferers were just weird in their opinion and weird people had to be kept away from the public for safety reasons. Sarah felt so angry at this ignorant attitude.

It didn't help her that she had written HELP on her bedroom window. Why had she done that if she was in no danger? They suggested that she could be guilty of wasting police time and came very close to giving Sarah her own criminal record. She explained again and again in minute detail the story of her accident in the sinkhole, of John releasing her, of her containment. Damn the bloody containment! She understood why the police found it hard to take her seriously when after all she had been held captive and was desperate to be free from that captivity. She knew that she looked relieved and grateful when the police released her and now she was begging them to release her captor. It even sounded crazy to herself.

It certainly didn't help that John was admitting guilt to everything the police accused him of. In his mind of course he wasn't sure whether he had done the things they said he had or not, but he may have. If there was any chance at all that he had done them then he had to assume that he had and plead guilty. Sarah was sure that if the police had told John he had attempted to assassinate the Queen he would have agreed even though she was alive and fit and well and no such attempt had been made. His OCD said that he couldn't be 100% certain that he hadn't, so he might have and so he assumed he was guilty. She so wanted to tell him to keep his mouth shut but they wouldn't let her see him. Accused and accuser must never meet until all criminal proceedings were complete. It certainly wasn't unknown for the accused, or their associates, to put pressure on an accuser to change their story, but this was the other way round. The police didn't really know how to react.

There had been good times in the last few days of course. The sheer joy on Mrs Evans' face when Sarah walked through her door the morning after her release was a picture to behold. Mrs Evans held Sarah's hand tight and for so long that Sarah thought she would never let her go for fear of her disappearing again.

The cheery "Good morning Ellen," was by far the best thing that Mrs Evans had ever heard. She turned her head towards the voice and had she been able to she would have jumped out of her chair and into Sarah's arms.

"Oh my dear I never thought I'd see you again," Mrs Evans said through her tears. "I thought something had happened to you, something terrible." I prayed every night for you. I don't normally pray but I was desperate. Is it a sin to only pray when you want something?"

"No of course not Ellen. God says 'For I am the LORD your God who takes hold of your right hand and says to you, do not fear; I will help you.' Isaiah 41:13"

"My word who is the religious one all of a sudden?"

Sarah chuckled. "It's the only bit of the bible I know and that's because my grandma had it on a sampler on her bedroom wall. I've always remembered it."

"Well someone helped this time. You are back and I couldn't be more pleased. You're like a daughter to me Sarah. In fact you are better than my own daughter."

Now it was Sarah's turn to shed tears.

They talked and talked both enjoying each other's company. Sarah told her everything about her adventure. About the sinkhole, about her rescue by John, about how he had cared for her and about how he had kindly let her stay at his house until she felt strong enough to look after herself.

"He sounds a really nice man. You'll have to bring him round to see me some time. How about tonight for tea? Only if he would like to of course." It's strange how older people seem to think that everything can be organised in an instant Sarah thought.

"I am sure he would love to come but not tonight. He has gone away for a few days on business. He delayed his trip until I was better."

Sarah felt a little guilty about telling Mrs Evans a toned down version of the truth. Lies in fact, they were lies plain and simple but little white lies never hurt anyone. Sarah decided this was the version of the story that she would tell everyone in the future, well everyone except the police or they really would charge her with wasting police time. Yes this was the story everyone else would hear and she realised that the main reason was that she wanted people to like John. She didn't know why but she wanted John to be liked.

"How is that lovely dog of yours Sarah? The little scamp refusing to get her own ball and letting you fall into the hole. I bet you didn't even tell her off did you? Please go and bring her round so I can say hello."

Sarah had been dreading this question. She realised that she couldn't hide what had happened to Betty, she had to tell the truth. "I'm sorry Ellen but Betty passed away."

Mrs Evans was shocked. Her face looked like she had just been told a close relative had died. Her lips wobbled as she asked "What happened?"

Both ladies were in tears as Sarah explained how Betty had found some liquid fertiliser on the farm and thinking it was water had drunk some. "John did everything he could for her. He rushed her to the vets but they couldn't save her." More lies but Sarah wanted people to like John.

Some time passed before either felt composed enough to speak.

"How did you manage for food and your medicines Ellen?"

"Oh Frank the postman brought me some things from the supermarket and a lovely couple, I can't remember their name, visited me a few times and brought my medicines and a bottle of brandy."

"Tut, tut Ellen."

"It was only for medicinal purposes of course. I was depressed about you."

"I'll believe you, thousands wouldn't."

"You look after their dog, you know Cuddles. They brought it to see me." Sarah made a note to thank Steve and Katy when she visited them.

Sarah looked at the time on the new mobile phone she had bought and was shocked to see that it was afternoon. They had been talking for over four hours.

"I'm sorry Ellen but I must be going. I need to visit my clients to see if they will bring their dogs back to me. My old mobile phone got smashed and I've lost all their phone numbers. I'll be back to see you later."

Sarah knew that most of her clients wouldn't be in during the day. If they were why would they need her to look after their dogs, unless they were just very lazy of course? Those type of clients annoyed Sarah. She couldn't understand why people bought dogs if they weren't prepared to put the effort in that dog ownership involved. In her opinion there was nothing better than walking your dog over the moors. Sadness suddenly returned to Sarah as she remembered that she no longer had a dog to call her own. She would visit her clients this evening but there was one visit she needed to make before then.

~~~~~~~~~~

John wasn't sure how many days he had been in the police cell. It was easy to lose count since every day was a Ground Hog day of almost total inactivity. He was very relieved that they hadn't increased the occupancy of the cell but he assumed that this was because he was still in the cells at the police station. He realised that they would move him at some point and then he knew he wouldn't be alone, he would have company and not of his own choosing.

He had no idea how he would cope with that but he guessed he wouldn't cope well. For now the euphoria of discovering that he wasn't to blame for all the strange things he did, well not directly, it was his illness, helped him to cope. Yes he had an illness just like someone having measles except you couldn't see it.

The highlights of every day were the breaks from monotony when his meals arrived, if that's what you could call them. How he longed for one of his own breakfasts but he thought that it would be a long time before he ate one of those judging by the questioning he'd had.

The once daily walk to the interview room was the only other relief from monotony, and his only exercise. In a strange way he looked forward to it as a distraction from staring at the blank walls of his cells. He sat there hour after hour listening for any sounds that would indicate another guest was being brought in. When that happened he panicked that they may end up in his cell but none had yet. He noticed that other guests usually only stayed one night so why was he still here? He guessed that his crime must be more heinous.

Every day in the interview room the police told him what he had done. He didn't remember doing those things but if they said he had then he might have. If there was the slightest possibility then he had to confess.

He thought Sarah may have visited him but she hadn't. She would be able to tell the police exactly what he had done, that he had cared for her. That's all, he had cared for her. But Sarah never came. She was obviously not grateful for what he had done and had deserted him. He was upset to think that she probably hated him and was glad that he was where he was.

He was fighting this on his own but how could he fight if he had done those things they told him he had? The police had a duty to protect the public therefore they couldn't release him – ever.

If he did end up in a shared prison cell he knew that he couldn't possibly cope. There was only one way out in his mind..........but would he have the courage?

"Sarah please help me," he screamed silently. He knew she wouldn't hear him. The future was bleak, very bleak for John Whittle.

~~~~~~~~~~

Sarah knew nothing about the occupants of the house as she knocked on the door. The door was opened by smart looking lady who Sarah thought might be dressed for going out. She suddenly felt very scruffy in her jeans and sweatshirt. "Hello I'm Sarah Meadon. I wonder if Anna is in please?"

"She is in her room. May I ask what you want her for?" Sarah explained who she was and how the police had told her about Anna finding Betty's disc which had been a big help to the police in finding her. I would just like to say thank you if I may .... but if you are going out I could come back another time."

"No I'm just about to do some gardening but to be honest I'd love a reason for not doing it. Please do come in. I'm Judith, Judith Hudson, Anna's mother."

Sarah followed Judith through the door, along the hall and into what she assumed was the lounge. She noticed that the house was just as smart as Mrs Hudson.

"Please sit down. Would you like a drink?"

"No I'm fine," replied Sarah. She doubted that the cream suite had ever had clothes as scruffy as hers sat on it and she sure as hell wasn't going to risk spilling a drink on it.

"I am just making a coffee for my husband, David. He is in his office talking to a client on the phone. Are you sure that you wouldn't like one?"

"No honestly. I had one just before I left home."

"OK. I'll just take this to David and then go up and let Anna know you are here. If I just shout up she never hears. She always has her music on so loud she wouldn't hear even if a bomb dropped. I won't be long."

Sarah used her time alone to look around the room. She noted how everything exuded class, and money. She doubted they would agree with her plan. It appeared that they would have no reason to.

Shortly afterwards Judith Hudson reappeared closely followed by a young girl whom Sarah assumed to be Anna. She noted that Anna didn't share her mother's dress sense. Anna wore ripped knee jeans, a sloppy sweatshirt and had flip flops on her feet. She was about 5 foot 9 inches tall Sarah estimated with a slightly tomboyish look and ever so slightly on the plump side. She didn't seem to be the type of girl who went all out to attract the boys, which was good for what Sarah was going to suggest.

"Hello Anna, I'm Sarah. I wanted to thank you for giving Betty's tag to the police. It was a great help to them and I'm sure they wouldn't have found me as quickly without it."

"That's ok," replied Anna in a shy way, eyes facing the ground as many teenagers tended to do in Sarah's experience.

"It's a good job you like walking your dog on the moors or the tag may never have been found."

Anna's mother gave a quick tut. "Actually that's the first time she's walked that dog for months. I think she was meeting a boy."

"Mum!" Anna didn't like being shown up in front of other people and Sarah could understand that.

"Ah well that's a pity because I need some help with my dog walking business over the summer. I thought you would be starting your holidays soon and would like something to help occupy some of your time – and earn a bit of money too."

"I would love to," Anna said without hesitation.

"Now don't rush into things Anna. Think about it before you commit yourself. You don't even like dog walking and you don't know this woman."

"Sarah." Sarah reminded Judith of her name. She objected to being called 'this woman'. She could tell that Judith was very controlling over her daughter and felt sure that a bit of independence would be good for her. "I will take very good care of her I can assure you."

"What if you send her up on the moors and she meets a man like you apparently did. She might not be as lucky as you have been."

This comment made Sarah angry. She took it as a slur on her character. "I had an accident Mrs Hudson and John found me, rescued me and cared for me." She was finding it easier and easier to give her 'official' version of events but she still wasn't sure why she wanted people to like John. Something in her heart told her that was how it should be.

"Mum I want to do it. It will be nice having some independence and having some of my own money."

"You don't need money dear, we will give you everything you want."

"That's part of the problem Mum. I'm 16 and I don't want to be totally reliant on you and I certainly don't want to be controlled by you any longer."

The more she heard the more Sarah liked Anna and respected her for what she said. In Anna she could see herself of nearly 30 years ago although their reasons for wanting to break the ties to their parents were quite different.

Sarah thought she had to prevent the argument between mother and daughter getting any more heated. "Why don't you have a think about it and if you are still interested when your summer holidays start come round to my house and we can have a chat to go over the details." She handed Anna her business card.

"I will be there for sure," Anna said and then turned and went back to her room. Sarah wasn't so sure that she would see Anna again. There was one hell of a battle ahead she thought.

Just then a tall bearded man came into the room. "Hello I'm David and you are?"

Sarah again explained who she was and why she was there.

"That will be a great experience for Anna. Thank you for giving her the opportunity. It will do her good to get out of her room more." Sarah knew the balance of power had just shifted in Anna's favour but the outcome of the battle was still far from certain.

"David how can you say that? She has no idea how to cope without us."

This comment took Sarah's mind back to John. She realised that he had no idea how to cope with his new found knowledge about OCD without someone to support him. He had no one except herself.

Sarah bade her farewells and knew she was leaving behind a fraught Hudson household.

~~~~~~~~~~

John had his daily visit to the interview room but he didn't recognise the person who followed him into the room this time, an unexpected visitor. Today wasn't Groundhog Day after all.

"Hello John. I'm Doctor Kowalski, I am a psychiatrist. I just want to have a little chat with you."

John didn't know what was going on. His routine was being broken and he didn't like it.

"I'm not mad, I've got an illness."

"No one said you were mad John. I just want to have a chat about these thoughts you have."

John was puzzled. He hadn't mentioned the things that go on in his head. Only Sarah knew about those so how could this man know?

Doctor Kowalski mentioned OCD but how did he know about OCD? Only Sarah had ever mentioned it, it had been her discovery. He knew Sarah hated him though, he knew Sarah hadn't been anywhere near him since his arrest. She was obviously glad to be rid of him and he couldn't blame her. John didn't know what was going on. His mind couldn't work out any sensible answer.

The psychiatrist talked to John for over two hours and asked him question after question. When they had finished John was very tired. He just wanted to sleep but his mind couldn't rest. Why had this man come to see him?

~~~~~~~~~~~

Sarah's business was small scale. She only had six clients therefore it didn't take long to call on them all that evening. By 8:30pm she only had one more client to visit, Steve and Kate Mills. Of the five clients she had visited so far four had agreed to bring their dogs back to her the following Monday. That gave her three days to sort everything out, if it could be sorted out. The fifth client had decided to give up their dog, a beautiful springer spaniel. It was mad, as a lot of springer spaniels are, but Sarah had a soft spot for it. Now it was gone and effectively it was her fault. Sarah had rung the rescue home immediately she had left their house but the dog had already been rehomed.

Sarah would have readily taken the dog and that would have given it at least some continuity. Now the poor dog would be going to a strange home with strange people. How could people do that? They had had the dog for four years and because of one little problem they gave the dog away. Why didn't they find another dog walker? It made Sarah think that the dog was more like a fashion accessory that they had become bored with, not the living family member who had given them four years of unconditional love. It really made her angry.

Sarah realised that she hadn't eaten since breakfast she had been so busy but her hunger would have to wait until she had made the last visit of the day.

~~~~~~~~~~

Steve and Katy wondered who could be knocking on their door. They never had evening visitors. In fact they rarely got visitors at all. Their families lived away and they didn't seem to have had the time or the inclination to make any close friends here.

Katy answered the door and her face was a mixture of shock and elation. "Sarah," she screamed. Steve heard Katy and immediately dashed to the door.

"Come in, come in. Where have you been? Are you ok? Are you going to take Cuddles again?" Steve and Katy alternated the questions.

Sarah laughed. "Wow what's this, the Spanish inquisition?"

"Sorry," said Steve "We are just so excited to see you. Come in. Coffee?"

Sarah sat drinking her black coffee and told them the full story, well her official version. They were shocked and upset at what she had gone through. If only they knew the truth.

"Thank you for visiting Ellen while I was away. It was very kind of you."

"No problem at all," said Katy, "In fact we enjoyed her company, she seems a real character."

"Oh she certainly is. She has a wicked sense of humour at times. She was really pleased you'd called round and so am I because I don't know what she would have done without you."

"We were wondering," Steve said, "if you would mind if we carried on visiting her. We don't want to intrude into your territory but we really did enjoy her company."

"Of course you can. She would be delighted. The more company she gets the better as far as I am concerned. I'll tell her tonight that you'll be calling round sometime. By the way don't worry if she doesn't remember your names sometimes. She can tell you everything in minute detail from 50, 60 or 70 years ago but ask her what she had for dinner half an hour ago and she'll struggle, bless her."

"She remembered that she liked brandy," Katy chuckled.

"Oh yes, she never forgets that."

"One other thing," Sarah said rather nervously, "I wondered if you would consider letting me look after Cuddles again."

"Oh yes please," Katy said excitedly, "We did find someone else to look after him but, well, they are just not like you. Can we bring him back tomorrow?"

"It's only fair that you give your current person some notice so how about we say Monday."

Ever the considerate Sarah they both thought.

Steve knew he had to ask the next question but had hesitated for fear of hearing bad news. "You've not mentioned Betty at all. Is she alright?"

They were both so sad to hear of Betty's death. Sarah noticed a little tear rolling down Katy's face as she told them and was touched by this display of emotion.

"Anyway I have taken up too much of your time, I must be going. I'll pick Cuddles up on Monday morning. I'm sorry for all the trouble I've caused you."

They both watched as Sarah drove away in her blue van. The van was kitted out with dog cages in the back to ensure that her charges travelled safely. There was no advertising on the van, typical Sarah just getting on with the job quietly and in an understated manner.

As Sarah drove home she reminded herself that she still hadn't eaten since breakfast. She loved to cook for herself but she was very tired so for once decided that a visit to the village chippy was justified. Although she didn't frequent the chip shop she knew she still risked being questioned about her disappearance due to all the publicity there had been. She knew she would just have to get used to that, at least for the first time she visited every shop where she was known. 'Remember to tell the official story' she told herself. They had to like John.

Sarah opened the door to her silent and empty house. She still half expected to see Betty's excited wagging tail greeting her. Before she ate her supper she went round to Mrs Evans and made sure she was well and had everything she needed for the night. Typical Sarah, always putting other people first.

Only after returning from Mrs Evans' did she allow herself to sit and eat her supper. Fish and chips, warmed up in the microwave, not cordon bleu gastronomy but food, very welcome food.

Just as the first chip was on route to her mouth her phone tinged to signal the arrival of a text. 'Who can that be at this time of night?' she wondered. She was momentarily tempted to ignore it but she knew a text so late would probably contain unwelcome news so she reached for the phone in her bag and flipped open the black leather cover.

The text was from the police. *'Please call Detective Brian Wilkinson at your earliest convenience'* the message read. Late texts usually contain unwelcome news she reminded herself. No more time for fish and chips now.

Chapter 29

Sarah had a good idea that the phone call to Detective Wilkinson would be conclusive one way or the other. They would either be formally prosecuting John and moving him to a penal institution or they would be releasing him. Her head said it would be the former, her heart hoped it would be the latter.

She was still unsure about why she cared about him. He wasn't her responsibility, not a relative, not a close friend so why did she care what happened to him. If she had angels on her shoulders the bad one would be saying forget him, let him rot in hell and the good one would be telling her that he had no one else therefore she should help him all she could. She didn't believe in angels but this was exactly the battle that was going on in her head.

Detective Wilkinson had left the station when she rang which at least gave her the opportunity to finish her chippy supper. The food was very welcome even though it was almost stone cold by the time she ate it. The duty sergeant had told her that he would be back in his office at 8am the following day.

At 8:01 Sarah was on the phone to the police station again. 'Why such eagerness when John shouldn't matter to me?' she thought to herself. The phone was answered on its second ring. After explaining who she was and what she wanted the call was connected through to Detective Wilkinson's office.

"Good Morning, Brian Wilkinson. How may I help you?"

"Hello its Sarah Meadon. You asked me to call you."

"Ah yes. Good morning. I wondered if you could get down to the station to see me please? As soon as possible."

"Yes of course." She didn't think to ask why. Maybe she didn't want to know really.

After quickly making sure that Mrs Evans was alright and had something to eat for her breakfast Sarah was walking through the police station doors before 9am. The police station was typical of village stations, built of stone and about the size of a domestic dwelling. It was likely that one day it would indeed become a domestic dwelling again as more and more of these village police stations were closing down.

Detective Wilkinson came to meet her in reception. "Please follow me, we will talk in my office." This relaxed Sarah somewhat as she knew it would be more informal. No tape machine meant that every word was not being recorded therefore it couldn't be a formal interview.

They walked down the narrow corridor and through the black door at the end. "Please take a seat. Would you like a drink, tea or coffee?"

She hadn't had time for her morning cuppa therefore she eagerly accepted his offer, asking for a black coffee, no sugar. He picked up the phone and asked someone, his secretary she assumed, to bring her black coffee and a tea for himself. She had assumed it was his secretary but did detectives have secretaries? She had no idea.

"Please call me Brian," he said as they waited for the drinks. This relaxed Sarah even more. This was going to be very informal. They passed pleasantries about the weather, last night's television and so on until the drinks had arrived. He obviously didn't want the main subject to be interrupted.

"Now Sarah, may I call you Sarah?"

"Yes." She realised that sounded a bit abrupt but she was now eager to know what he had to say.

"Thank you. We have listened to what you have told us and taken the advice of a mental health expert and we must say that we still have concerns about releasing John. We would prefer to continue to prosecution. I must ask you again Sarah would you be willing to testify in court against him?"

She didn't need to think about her answer. "No I will not testify against him. Although at times during my time at his house I was concerned, indeed scared, but I realise now that his underlying intention was just to care for me, and everyone else for that matter. He doesn't have control over some of the crazy things he does, it is all down to his OCD."

"I must say that your decision is far from helpful."

"Let me ask you Brian, would you lock away a man with cancer rather than get him treatment for his illness?"

172

"No of course not but you can't compare the two things."

"I think you can. Cancer eats away at the sufferers body, OCD eats away at the sufferers mind. In both cases urgent treatment is required."

"If you are not prepared to change your mind you leave us with no option but to let John go. He will be a free man. I must stress though that it does concern us greatly. John is very unstable in our opinion."

Sarah was silent for a while before she spoke again. "I would like to see John for a few minutes if that is possible please."

"Of course. I will arrange to have him taken to the interview room and you can speak to him there. There would, of course, be a member of my team with you all the time but not myself. After all John is still a suspected criminal until we complete the paperwork for his release."

Following a quick phone call a female officer entered the office. "Sergeant Smith will escort you to the interview room and then bring you back here when you have finished. May I ask that you don't let the accused know of our decision please?"

'Why are they still referring to John as the accused' she thought. She didn't like that.

Sarah knew she had just two questions to ask John. His answers would guide her decisions.

Ten minutes later Sarah was back in Detective Wilkinson's office.

Sarah sat down again and looked directly at Brian. "I will try to help John to find professional help. I will also visit him regularly to do what I can to help on a day to day basis. I am not an OCD expert but I do know someone who needs help when I see them."

"If that is what you wish to do who am I am to try and stop you. I must say that I think you are starting out on a long tough road."

"I'm under no illusions." She had no idea just how tough it would turn out to be.

"Are you not concerned about entering John's house again, alone with him?"

"I am prepared to take my chances if it helps John."

"You are taking on a huge commitment which is very brave of you Sarah. As John lives so remotely we will of course drive him home. We would prefer that rather than just releasing him out onto the streets. Would you like to be informed when we have taken him home?"

The comment 'rather than just releasing him out on to the streets' really annoyed Sarah. What the hell did they think John would do?

"There is no need for you to take him home," she said, "I will do that."

"It will take us several hours to complete the paperwork and go through all the formalities so John will be available for collection any time after 9am tomorrow."

"Ready for collection! It sounds like I am picking up some goods I've ordered. John is a human being. A kind human being who needs help," Sarah snapped.

As she drove home the thought of entering John's house again played on her mind. Even though John had given her the answers she wanted to her questions, the answers that should have pacified her, the more she thought about it the more she knew she certainly couldn't 'live' in his house again, even if she could bring herself to just enter the house for a short period. In John's house he would be in control.

There was only one solution.

Chapter 30

Again and again Sarah's mind asked her 'Why?' She couldn't answer.

Why had she said she would help a man she had only known for a few days and a man with mental health problems as well? Was she the one going mad?

No she wasn't going mad, neither was John. Throughout her life she had always cared for sick and injured birds and animals she had found on the moors. Some didn't make it but many recovered and went on to live a normal life. If she could care so much for birds and animals she certainly wasn't going to refuse to help a human being. A human being who was suffering considerably and constantly and had been for a very long time.

She remembered one robin a few years ago that had a broken wing. She found it in her own garden, thankfully before the local cats did. She had no idea what to do for it therefore she took it to the vets. They told her that it wouldn't survive and suggested that they should euthanize it before it suffered any more. Sarah refused to give in without a fight. Whilst there was a slight chance the robin might survive she had to help it and she would go on helping it until it took its last breath.

Armed with the advice on what to feed it she placed the bird back in the cardboard box she had carried it to the vets in and took it back home. "Come on my little friend, together we can win the battle. She made a makeshift splint for its wing using a lolly stick and tied it in place against the bird's body using some soft material she found in her bits and pieces drawer. She was amazed how still the bird had kept whilst she completed her medical work, it was as though the bird knew it could trust her.

That bird was cared for as though it was Sarah's child and after several weeks it's wing was healed and it had regained full strength. It had survived against the odds. The day of its release back in to the wild brought mixed emotions of sadness and joy for Sarah. She had a tear in her eye as it flew into the nearest tree then turned and looked at her as if to say 'thank you' before flying away into the distance.

Since that day she has had her daily visit from a robin. Sometimes two or three would appear on her window sill each morning. She knew after all this time that it wouldn't be the original bird but she liked to think that her current visitor was a descendant of her robin.

If she could put that amount of time and effort into bringing a small bird back to good health she sure as hell couldn't refuse to do the same for a human being. She realised though that her latest challenge would need more than a lolly stick and a piece of soft material.

To occupy her mind Sarah spent the evening cleaning her house from top to bottom. She wanted to make it as easy as possible for John to visit, if he ever did. She didn't want to put any unnecessary OCD problems in his way. There would be enough challenges for him as it was. She had spent all her spare time in recent days researching OCD on the internet. As with everything there were contradictory versions of how to help an OCD sufferer. The majority view seemed to be to refuse to help, to not get involved in the sufferers thoughts and anxieties. She really didn't think she could do that, she couldn't stand back and watch someone suffer. On the other hand though she had no experience of what to say or do to help. She imagined it would be like walking on glass most of the time, trying to help but being afraid of saying or doing the wrong thing and making matters worse. She had read about CBT, Cognitive Behavioural Therapy, and how it was used to make people face their fears head on. She couldn't even begin to imagine how difficult that would be for an OCD sufferer, but if it helped it was worth the battle she thought.

She thought long and very hard about what to do with Betty's things. They were still exactly as they had been when Sarah and Betty set off for their walk on the moors that fateful day. Somehow it had helped the grieving process a little by being able to see Betty's bed and toys. She had found it comforting on difficult days to be able to sit and snuggle Betty's blanket. Was this the time, however, to move on. She imagined it wouldn't help John to be reminded of Betty any more than necessary. She made the decision to put all

Betty's belongings away in the large cupboard in her bedroom. That would be the one room that John would have no reason to go into and Sarah could still feel that Betty was near to her.

Sarah led a very busy life as it was therefore she knew that her added responsibility would necessitate the need to have help with her day to day responsibilities. Earlier in the day she had received a text from Anna to confirm that she would love to help her and would be available in two weeks. Sarah rang Anna to ask if she could come and meet her after college on Friday to discuss the details. John may be there of course but she knew she couldn't hide him. He would have to meet her friends, starting with Ellen who would no doubt get the wrong idea and be dusting off the hat she had worn for previous weddings. Sarah smiled at this ludicrous thought. She had some feelings for John but they were of pity and certainly not love. Persuading Ellen that John and she were most definitely not an item romantically would be difficult she knew.

She really thought that she should tell her tonight to avoid any embarrassing moments in front of John. She would no doubt have to remind her again in the morning but the more she repeated the warning the more Ellen had a chance of remembering it.

Before that she needed to make one more phone call.

"Hello Steve speaking."

"Oh hi, this is Sarah."

"Hi Sarah, is something wrong?"

"No absolutely not but I am going to ask you a huge favour. I feel awful but I need some help."

"Anything if we can."

She explained about John, her official version of course, and how she was going to help him.

"So I wondered, as you are going to keep visiting Mrs Evans, if you would mind helping a little. I wondered if you would mind doing things like picking up her prescription once a month. I feel awful asking but I am going to be very busy for a few weeks and it would be a real help." Little did she know that a few weeks was a huge understatement. "Please don't worry if you can't. I understand. Look sorry I shouldn't have asked. I hope you're not annoyed that I did."

"Whoa slow down Sarah. Of course we will help. We'd be delighted to. It's about time we got a bit more involved with other people round here." He knew he didn't need to ask Katy before he said they would help, she'd be more than happy to.

"Oh thank you Steve. Why don't you come over for a bite to eat early evening on Friday if that's ok? Feel free to bring Cuddles. I'm going to invite Ellen as well and she would love to see Cuddles again. Mind you it is no use inviting her until the actual day or she will forget."

"We'll be there. What time?"

"About 6pm?"

'What am I doing?' she asked herself silently. She had now arranged for Anna, Steve and Katy to come on Friday evening. How would John react if he was there, she wondered?

Now to go next door.

"Hello Ellen, how are you?"

"I'm fine Sarah and you?"

"I'm ok thanks. Look I've got something to tell you. I may have a man coming to visit me from tomorrow." She knew right away that wasn't the best way to break the news.

"Oh how exciting. You kept that quiet. When did you meet him? What's his name? Where is he from? What does he do for a living?"

Sarah laughed at this inquisition.

"It's nothing like that."

"That's what you tell me. Shall I get my hat down from the top shelf of the cupboard and brush it off ready for the wedding," Ellen said with a cheeky grin on her face.

"Listen to me you little tinker. John is just a friend."

"John. Wasn't that the name of the man who cared for you recently?"

"Yes, it's the same man. Now he needs a bit of care and I have agreed to help him. It's nothing more than that."

"Not at the moment!" Ellen said with a glint in her eye.

"Oh you are impossible. I can assure you that you can leave your hat in the cupboard. You know me, I much prefer dogs to men."

Back in her own house Sarah completed the cleaning and tidying.

Sarah knew she couldn't help John alone and would need to find professional help for him. The first place would be John's GP but she had no idea who that was so that would have to wait until John was free.

She took one last look around the house. Everything seemed to be in place.

She had her supper, two digestive biscuits and a cup of coffee, and thought about the journey that lay ahead. A journey largely into the unknown. After supper she made her way to bed. Following her usual bathroom routine, teeth clean, face wash and moisturiser application she sat on the side of the bed to take her medication. Finally she got into bed and pulled the continental quilt tightly up around her. She read one chapter of her book as usual and then put out the light and settled down to sleep.

After a few minutes a sudden thought made her sit bolt upright. She thought back to Brian's comments.

She knew that she would have to take John to his house. She knew that she would have to be very careful not to fall into a trap again. That made her very nervous and added to her anxiety about what lay ahead. Once home would he agree to leave his house again to get help? Once home would he try and confine her again? John had answered yes to both the questions she had asked him in the police station but could she trust him?

Sleep didn't come easily that night.

Chapter 31

Sarah was awake at 1am, 2am, 3am and every other hour during the night. What little sleep she had was in infrequent very brief fitful spells of a few minutes at a time. She gave up at 5am, got out of bed and sleepily went downstairs. She was so tired that her brain just wasn't functioning. She made herself a black coffee on auto pilot and sat at the kitchen table to drink it. She had hoped to start the day well rested but she would just have to cope with the trials of the day in the condition she found herself. She was concerned that she was far less tolerant when she was very tired but she knew she would have to try very hard to put her brain in gear before opening her mouth.

She shivered as she suddenly realised how cold the house was. The heating didn't come on until 6am. She hated being up so early today, it gave her far too much time to think about the times ahead. Far too much time to argue with herself as to whether she was doing the right thing or not.

Sarah sat staring into space looking at nothing in particular. Every minute seemed like an hour. She made herself wait for what she guessed would be at least 15 minutes before she looked at the clock again, only to find that less than five minutes had passed. The tick, tick of the old wall clock was metronomic torture.

Even though it was still not 6am Sarah knew the only way to pass the time until she had to pick up John would be to walk on the moors. This would be the first time since her accident and the first time without Betty. She put on her warmest coat and walking shoes and stepped out into the cold early morning chill.

Sarah walked briskly listening to the dawn chorus sung by an eclectic choir of birds. She could normally identify one or two individual calls but today to her confused mind it was just noise, albeit pleasant noise. After walking for over an hour she decided it was time to help Mrs Evans with her breakfast. As Sarah had taken a circuitous route it didn't take long to get back home.

"Morning Ellen. How are you today?"

"I'm not bad for an old un. You know at my age every day is a bonus Sarah."

"Don't be so morbid Ellen. You'll be teasing me for a long time yet. You'll probably outlive me." Sarah thought back to a few days ago when she thought that might not be too far from the truth.

The two ladies worked together to make Ellen's breakfast. Weetabix with the milk warmed in the microwave for exactly one minute, one slice of white toast with orange marmalade and a cup of tea with lots of milk. Sarah always joked that Ellen had half a cow in her cup of tea. Ellen always laughed at this comment although she must have heard it hundreds of times.

Once the old lady was sorted Sarah gulped down a slice of toast and a few mouthfuls of coffee before setting off to the police station. She knew traffic would be heavy at this time of morning and wanted to make sure she wasn't late. She didn't want there to be any chance that the police would take John home themselves.

On the journey to the police station every traffic light seemed to be on red and the traffic slower than she'd hoped. She was desperate to be there waiting for John when he was released. As time passed her anxiety levels increased which wasn't helpful, she needed to be calm and clear headed when John appeared.

Sarah had been sat in the waiting room for just five minutes when John appeared. They both seemed nervous as they greeted each other.

"Hello John," she said quietly.

"Thank you for helping me," he replied, "I thought you would hate me. You never came to see me, but then why should you?" The police had informed John about Sarah's offer to help before they released him.

"They wouldn't let me see you. Don't forget you were accused of containing me.

"I have agreed to help you because I dread to think what the alternative may be. Please don't misinterpret my offer of help, don't get any wrong impressions about my feelings for you. To make things absolutely clear, my feelings for you are neutral, not hate but certainly not affection."

181

As they settled themselves in Sarah's van the rain started to fall heavily. So hard that the windscreen wipers struggled to keep the screen clear as they started the journey home. 'Stormy times ahead' Sarah feared.

For several minutes the journey was silent until John very softly said, "I really am sorry for what I did. I never wanted to upset you, even less hurt you."

"I know John. I understand."

Again silence. After a further 10 minutes they were approaching the junction where John knew they would turn right to go up Moorland Road towards the three lane junction where they would turn left towards his farm. Not long before he would be home now. He knew he owed Sarah a great deal of gratitude because without her help who knows what would have happened. Now soon he would be sat in his chair drinking a cup of tea made just the way he liked it. No one can make you a cup of tea like you can make it yourself.

As they drove on John wondered what the people in the shops he visited every week had heard. He would ask Sarah later. John allowed a bit of excitement to creep into his feelings. He waited for the indicator to signal the right turn but Sarah signalled left. What was going on? Where was she taking him?

As if reading his thoughts Sarah said, "We are going to my house first. We need to talk. I promise that I will take you home later." John got a feeling of déjà vu. He was worried. Was Sarah seeking revenge?

It wasn't long before they were walking up the short path to Sarah's door. She took the key out of her handbag. It was too big to have on her key ring. That was the trouble with old mortice locks. She had never had the lock changed because she felt mortice locks were more secure.

Sarah's hand was shaking a little as she opened the brown door, nervous of what lay ahead. She gestured for John to enter which he did nervously. Was she going to contain him now? He didn't think she was that kind of person but to be honest he hardly knew her. This time last month he didn't even know that Sarah Meadon existed.

"Please take a seat and I will make a brew. Then we can talk. Are you hungry? Have you eaten this morning?"

182

"I'm fine thank you." He hadn't eaten but didn't want to impose on her hospitality.

John noticed that Sarah hadn't locked the door which was both encouraging and worrying. Encouraging that he could walk out if he wanted and worrying that anyone could walk in. He would have to talk to Sarah about this lack of security but that would have to wait until after he had heard what she had to say to him.

Sarah placed the drinks down on the small round glass kitchen table, in fact the only table in her small house, and sat on the chair opposite John. Butterflies performed the fastest ballet ever in John's stomach as he sat nervously believing deep down that he didn't deserve Sarah's help. He thanked her for his drink and waited nervously for her to start the conversation. He didn't have long to wait.

"John I have spent a long time researching OCD on the internet since I got home. We have a long hard battle ahead of us, a battle we can only win if you want to win it. You have to have the desire to change your life."

"I am desperate to change my life. Please help me." He really meant it even though his eyes almost automatically scanned Sarah's hands to check that there were no cuts that could spell danger to others. He realised that whatever they did wouldn't be, couldn't be a quick fix. It was impossible for all his thoughts and fears to just disappear, there was a very long and very difficult road ahead.

"I have already said I will help you and I promise I will but you have to help me. The first thing we need to do is to make an appointment for you to see your doctor. Who is your doctor?"

"I don't know."

"What do you mean you don't know?"

"I haven't been to a doctor since I was a child and that doctor is dead. Where his surgery was there is now a betting shop."

"Have you never been ill?"

"Once or twice but I usually find something in the cupboard that makes me better. I've never wanted to go to a doctor in case they told me I was mad and locked me away. I couldn't cope with being locked away. I thought the police were going to lock me away, I couldn't have survived that."

"Okay I will ring Doctor Warburton, he's my doctor, and see if he will take you on. He's really nice." Sarah picked up her mobile phone and pressed the button to call the surgery. John heard Sarah tell the receptionist what she wanted and then silence while she listened to the person on the other end of the phone.

"Right John, that's good news. The surgery will take you on as a patient and you have an appointment at 9:15 tomorrow morning. It is with Doctor Warburton which is really helpful.

"Also John I think it is really important that you get a mobile phone so that we can contact each other any time we need to. We can sort that out tomorrow after we have been to the doctor."

"Thank you," was all John could say as he racked his brain to wonder why she was doing this for him. Her kindness only added to the intense guilt he had felt and still felt about keeping her at his farm. 'How frightened she must have been all because of me', he thought. His chin wobbled. How would he ever overcome this guilt?

"I've not finished yet. I think it would be helpful for you to mix more with other people, I think it will help to occupy your mind with things other than your OCD thoughts. I have some people I want you to meet over the next few days." She decided not to tell him about Friday's get together yet, she didn't want to scare him too much. The next thing she had to say would be a huge thing for him to accept. She would let him finish his drink before she mentioned her idea.

They sat in silence while they both finished their drinks. Sarah looked out of the kitchen window at the moors knowing that in a few days she would be back up there with her client's dogs. Back to normality, well at least as far as her business was concerned. She wondered if she could cope with John but it was too late to change her mind. She had promised and she had never in her life broken a promise.

John was the one to break the silence. "Will you be taking me home soon?"

Sarah couldn't delay her announcement any longer. "John I have one more thing I need to discuss with you." She hesitated, not knowing quite how to approach her suggestion. She paused again.

"You are worrying me Sarah. What is it? You're not going to change your mind are you? Without you I have no future."

184

"No it's not that. I just think that if we are going to achieve some improvement in your condition you need as fresh a start as possible. We need to minimise your exposure to things that worry you if we can. I still don't know much about OCD but I think it would help if you felt that someone else was responsible for the cleanliness and security of your surroundings and also I think someone needs to be with you most of the time, at least initially."

"I don't understand. Are you suggesting that I go in a mental institution somewhere?" John's face displayed significant worry as he asked that question.

"No I'm not. No I'm definitely not saying that. I don't think that would help at all. I'm suggesting that you live here."

Chapter 32

John was stunned by Sarah's suggestion. His mind was a whirl of questions and concerns. Would she try and contain him? What if he contaminated her house? What if she wasn't security conscious? What if, what if.........................

He wanted help but he was scared to move out of his familiar surroundings. At his house he was in control, at least as much as his OCD would let him be, but here things would have to be on Sarah's terms. If he lived here he would have to tell her all the things she was doing wrong of course. That would probably annoy her.

Sarah closely studied John's face and she knew her proposal was causing him great concern. She knew he didn't know what to do. It was time to get tough, totally contrary to her normal character.

"John it's my way or no way. I will accept responsibility for anything bad that happens, not that anything will happen of course."

"But you can't be sure."

"Oh don't go there again. It's your choice. Do you want to try and get better or do you want to go back to your miserable existence for the rest of your life?"

There was silence for several minutes. Sarah was getting quite annoyed that she was making what she thought was a very generous offer and he seemed not to appreciate it. 'Calm down', she said to herself silently. She worried that she was getting frustrated already. Not a good start.

"Well?" she said.

"I have no choice."

"Does that mean you will move in?"

"Yes. But it won't be easy for me."

"Are you for real? Do you think it's going to be a bundle of fun for me? Have you no idea what I am offering to do for you?" She had read that OCD was a very selfish illness. On the one hand sufferers were concerned for the welfare of everyone but on the other hand they could be very self-centred. But she knew deep down that she was also being self-centred by offering to let him move in. Her overwhelming fear of returning to his farmhouse left her with no alternative.

"Sarah."

"Yes."

"You didn't lock the door when we came in."

"Who do you think is going to come in when we are sat here?"

"I don't know but someone could. Someone could come in and steal something."

Sarah put her head in her hands in frustration. This was going to be even harder than she had imagined. She took a deep breath before she continued.

"Here is your key," she said as she handed him the new key she had had cut at the village cobblers especially for him. "And it is the right key," she added sarcastically.

He didn't thank her. He just stared at the key as though it was a dangerous weapon. Maybe to his OCD it was. After all it gave him access to Sarah's house and all the problems and concerns that would bring.

"Right now I will take you to your house to get some clothes and any other bits and pieces you may need." The memories of her time at the farm meant she wasn't looking forward to this at all but she intended to stay in the car while John went in alone. That way she would be fine she thought.

~~~~~~~~~~

Sarah became increasingly tense the nearer they got to John's farm. No matter how hard she tried to push the memories of her time there out of her mind she couldn't erase them completely. She pulled her van up into the yard and parked right by the door. Subconsciously was she preparing for a quick escape?

She desperately wanted to wait for John in the van. In fact she really wanted to go and leave John to drive back to her house either in his van or on his tractor but that wasn't realistic because there was only room to park her van at home. The narrow lanes did not facilitate visitors' vehicles very well. In any case this arrangement had to be based on mutual trust therefore she had to show John she trusted him and going into his house with him would help to do that.

She fought her fears as she walked through the door, her ears waiting for the sound of John locking the door. The sound never came. John didn't lock the door. She knew at that moment he was really trying hard, he was doing his bit. She understood how difficult that simple action, or lack of action, would have been for him.

It didn't take long for John to gather what he needed. As they left the house he locked the door and tried the handle to make sure it was locked, and tried it again and again and again. She grew more and more frustrated as she sat in her van waiting for him to complete his ritual. When would he be convinced the door was locked? He then walked around the house to check all the windows were locked – three times – windows that had never been opened. The locking up routine was taking longer than the time they were in the house. Sarah knew that there would be many ups and downs, she just hoped that in time the good days would outnumber the bad days but realised there was a very long time to go before they reached that stage – if ever.

~~~~~~~~~

Back home Sarah showed John his bedroom and couldn't resist showing him the view from the window, no black paint here. She gave him a tour around the house pointing out that there were no locks on any of the internal doors, he was free to go wherever he wanted, except, of course, her bedroom.

As there was no lock on the bathroom door they agreed a system of hanging an item of clothing on the external door handle to show the room was in use. She also made a mental note not to wander between bedroom and bathroom in her underwear as was her habit. Not that the sight of her in her frumpy M&S underwear would excite anyone, she always put practicality and comfort before fashion.

This arrangement would mean changes for both of them. Neither was looking forward to the restrictions it would place on them.

Sarah ended the guided tour by showing John where things were in the kitchen cupboards. "Please just help yourself to anything you want. I'm certainly not going to wait on you hand and foot, if you don't help yourself you'll go hungry." She wanted to clarify the rules right at the start. "Of course we will eat our main meals together, there's no point making two separate things. I suggest that we work out a rota for cooking once you have settled in.

The thought of cooking in Sarah's kitchen terrified John, especially after noticing her cooker was gas. He would have to be certain the gas was completely turned off when not in use. That was a huge concern for him. There could be a fire or an explosion and Sarah may die. He was also worried that he may infect the food and in turn infect Sarah, if she wasn't already infected. The worries were mounting up.

"If you don't mind I'll just pop a couple of pizzas in the oven for tonight's tea. Will that be enough? You must be starving, we've hardly eaten all day, and we've been so busy."

"That will be fine. I'm not hungry really."

Sarah turned the gas on and put the Pizzas on wire trays in the oven. "I'm just popping round to make sure Ellen is alright while they are cooking. Why don't you come round and meet her."

"No," John said emphatically. "The gas is on, we can't both go out."

Sarah decided not to push things too far tonight. "OK, you can meet her in the morning. I will be back in a few minutes."

John was amazed that Sarah had been prepared to leave him alone in her house, trusting him to look after it. That confirmed that she completely trusted him, now he had to learn to trust her.

~~~~~~~~~~

"Hello Ellen. How are you?"

"I'm fine Sarah. Where's your boyfriend?"

"He is NOT my boyfriend you naughty woman. If you must know he is sat in my kitchen watching pizzas cook."

"Is your television broken again?" Despite her advancing years and the fact that her short term memory wasn't great her mind remained very sharp in thinking up humorous quips.

"Ah very funny. I'll bring him to meet you in the morning but watch what you say. He is ill and I am helping him to get better. There is nothing else to it, can you remember that?" Ellen gave a cheeky wink.

"If you are bringing him here in the morning I'll put a clean nightdress on tonight."

"What on earth for. You'll be dressed by the time he comes."

"You can't be certain of that."

You can't be certain would become a phrase that she would hear far more times than she wanted to before the night was out..

"Right Ellen your suppers on the tray and I've put your Horlicks in the cup ready for you to just pour water on it. If you need me for anything just ring my mobile, remember just press number one on your phone."

"I'll try not to disturb you. You might be otherwise occupied."

"You are impossible. I'm going."

~~~~~~~~~~

They ate their pizzas in front of the television whilst watching the evening news. John was fascinated by it. Of course he had seen a television before but not for several years. Sarah thought that he looked like a dog with a new toy, super excited. She decided that showing him the internet would be an overload tonight. That could be tomorrow's treat.

The rest of the evening passed with nothing more than infrequent small talk briefly interrupting the silence. At 10pm Sarah announced that she was going to bed.

"Have you checked the door?"

"No, I know I locked it when I came back from Ellen's."

"But can you be certain? Have you checked that the gas to the cooker is switched off?"

"I switched it off when the pizzas were cooked."

"But one of us may have caught the knobs since then."

"We've been nowhere near."

"Can you be certain? Have you checked that all the windows are closed?"

"They haven't been open. Oh let me guess, a bird may have tapped on the window and shaken it open."

"It's possible. Have you pulled all the electric plugs out of the sockets?"

"Oh my goodness. No I haven't, I never do."

"But what if some condensation runs down the window and drips onto one of the sockets while it is still switched on. That could cause a fire."

"Would you like me to unplug the fridge/freezer as well?"

"Of course not, all the food would spoil."

190

"So how can that one stay on when everything else has to be switched off? That's just not rational."

"I'm sorry if it annoys you but I am being serious. You have to be careful."

"You're not being serious, you are just being irrational. I'm going to bed." Already she could feel the onset of a headache.

"Don't forget that we will need to be leaving here at 8:45 in the morning to get to the doctors on time," Sarah reminded him. How she hoped the doctor could suggest something that would help. She couldn't do it all alone.

When Sarah had finished in the bathroom she lay in bed listening to John trying the front door handle over and over. It wouldn't be long before she would need to buy a new handle at this rate. She imagined that she would go downstairs in the morning to find all the electrical items unplugged, except the fridge/freezer of course.

Chapter 33

Both Sarah and John woke knowing today was going to be a testing day in more ways than one. Sarah had got up especially early to make sure that the bathroom was free for John to use when he got up.

"Wish me luck today Betty," she whispered. She still 'spoke' to Betty when times were stressful and she was sure that her best friend was still there looking after her. Sarah sat in the kitchen drinking a cup of coffee and pondering on whether she had been foolish to plan the evening get together on the same day as John's visit to the doctors. Actually she hadn't really planned it, it had just happened but it probably wasn't the best situation. On the other hand it would keep John's mind occupied all day, but could he cope with all the new experiences.

She heard John coming down the stairs and she suddenly became very nervous. It was going to be a tough day, she decided that the only way to approach it was to be cheerful.

"Good morning John. How are you today? Did you sleep well? What would you like for breakfast?" She knew she was gabbling as she always did when she was nervous. What would he think?

"Hello." A man of many words as usual.

"Did you sleep well?"

"Not too bad."

"Are you ready for the day ahead?"

"Maybe."

"What would you like for breakfast? I'll make it today."

"Anything."

"Oh for goodness sake John, talk to me. I am trying to help you but it doesn't help when you won't talk to me."

"I am talking."

"You know what I mean. You are going to meet some people I know today, are you going to give them one word answers."

"Two answers had three words."

She shook her head slowly whilst looking at John all the time. She was frustrated with John for not saying much and annoyed with herself for getting frustrated. She had to be patient. John had had very little contact with other people for years, he wasn't used to talking.

'Count to 10 Sarah', she said in her mind.

"John I'm sorry if I'm expecting too much too soon. I know this is all strange for you and must be difficult."

"I am trying Sarah."

"I know."

Sarah knew she had to try and remain upbeat. There was no other way to tackle this first day in her opinion. John had to face new challenges.

"I'm going to check on Ellen next door before we have breakfast and you're coming with me."

"No I can't."

"Why not?"

"What if I…. you know?"

"No I don't know but I can guess, what if you contaminate her. John when will you get it into your head that you are not going to contaminate anyone? You don't have anything wrong with you."

"You can't be sure."

"No I can't be 100% sure but I think there is more chance of Betty walking through that door right now than of you having HIV." As soon as she said that she regretted it. She needed to get John to buy into her ideas and that wasn't going to happen if she kept reminding him of the bad things that had happened just a few days ago. "I'm sorry I shouldn't have said that."

"Come on let's go and see Ellen," Sarah said even though she could tell that it was the last thing John wanted to do.

As they left the house he was panicking that she hadn't checked that the gas cooker was definitely turned off but he thought better of saying something. When she didn't lock the door as they set off for next door that was another matter.

"Sarah you haven't locked the door."

"I never do when I pop round to Ellen's."

"How can you do that? Your house could be burgled."

"John I've been leaving the door open for years and nothing has happened."

"But it might have and you just never realised. Maybe people have been secretly sneaking in and stealing information about you for years. Maybe they will steal your identity. Is there any information about me in there that they could get?"

"OK I'll lock the door," she said in frustration. She knew she shouldn't have given in to his thoughts, the internet said that was the completely wrong thing to do. They didn't have time to argue this morning though, they had to get to the doctors on time, so she gave in and cursed herself for doing so.

"You've not checked it's locked."

Sarah didn't respond. She quickly walked next door without a glance behind at her reluctant companion.

"Morning Ellen. How are you?"

"I'm fine Sar.........................now who is this handsome man?" Ellen said as she noticed John behind Sarah. "Hello young man." Sarah wouldn't use either of the words handsome or young in relation to John but to Ellen he probably was, well young at least."

"This is John. I told you about him yesterday."

"Hello John."

"Hello Mrs Evans," he said very quietly.

"What did he say Sarah?"

"He said hello.

"You will have to speak up John, Ellen is a bit deaf."

"Have you had your breakfast Ellen?"

"No not yet, I was just going to make some toast."

"You just sit there, John will make it for you, won't you."

John looked like he had just had the biggest shock of his life. He was sure he was contaminated and he was being asked to make an old lady her breakfast. He couldn't do it, yet he knew he had to do it. If he didn't he would have to explain his OCD to Mrs Evan's and he didn't want anyone to know besides Sarah and the doctor.

"I'll just go to wash my hands first." He was gone for over ten minutes and when he returned his hands were red and looked very sore. He had obviously washed them over and over again, much more than was necessary. They had already looked so sore that he had obviously been washing them over and over in the police station to try and eliminate any germs. He would have no access to moisturiser there either. She still couldn't understand why anyone, even an OCD sufferer, would excessively scrub their hands to such an extent that they became almost raw. Why didn't they realise that just one good wash would be sufficient?

John minutely examined his hands for signs of cuts. It was a catch 22 situation, contaminated if he didn't wash them so much, cuts if he did. He couldn't win.

He looked around the kitchen and spotted a roll of kitchen towel. He covered his fingers with his shirt sleeve and pulled off a couple of pieces and used these to pick up two slices of bread which he placed in the toaster. He used the same protection to take the bread out of the toaster when it was finished. He managed to butter the toast without touching it, again using the kitchen roll, so mission completed successfully. He worried however in case some of the kitchen towel had fallen into the toaster and would set on fire.

"Could you please pass the toast to Mrs Evans Sarah?"

"No sorry I'm busy." She wasn't but she knew that he needed to face challenges. Although her knowledge of OCD was very limited that much she did know. John knew exactly what she was doing and he didn't like it one bit. He knew Sarah was trying to help him but right at that moment he wished he'd never met her.

His shirt sleeve again protected the plate as her carried it and placed it on the table next to Mrs Evans. At last he could relax a little, well as much as any OCD sufferer is ever able to relax.

Sarah noticed that John was a picture of complete discomfort, she decided it was time to release him from this anguish.

Back at Sarah's house they had a quick bowl of cereals and then it was time to set off for the doctors.

Traffic was light therefore they drove at a leisurely pace and still arrived at the doctors fifteen minutes early. They sat in the van on the car park for a few minutes.

"John, Doctor Warburton will try his best to help you but you need to honest with him. You need to tell him everything, leave nothing out."

"Will you come into the doctor with me please? I'm never sure if I have remembered what people say to me or if my mind has twisted things. It would be better if you were there to remember things for me."

"If that's what you want then of course I will."

The time came to go into the surgery. Sarah took the lead. She hoped that John wouldn't turn and run at the last minute.

"John you check in on this screen."

"I can't do that. Just imagine how many sick people have touched that screen. It will be full of all sorts of germs. I'm worried about catching something myself but I am much more worried in case I add my contamination to the screen and then lots of people may become infected. Hundreds of people could catch HIV because of me."

"John don't be so ridiculous."

"I can't do it."

"OK I'll do it for you. Why is it ok for me to do it but not for you? Is it alright for me to catch a disease?"

"You are less likely to be contaminated than me."

"But you said you may have contaminated me when I was at your house. You said that was why you couldn't let me go. Now you are saying that I'm not contaminated when it suits you. I give up." She didn't mean the bit about giving up of course.

Check in completed John waited for Sarah to open the door.

John carefully checked every available seat before deciding which were safe to sit on. The ones with any kind of mark on, no matter how small the mark, were rejected. John couldn't be sure what the marks were. Could they be dangerous bodily fluid? Could part of a needle from a syringe be underneath the marks?

They sat and waited in silence.

Chapter 34

It didn't go unnoticed by her parents that Anna was in a much better mood than usual before she left for college this morning."

"My word what on earth has happened to Grumpy," her mother said to her father when Anna had gone upstairs to collect her school bag, "There must be another boy on the scene."

Her father knew very well that the cheerfulness wasn't due to a boy. "It's not a boy at all Judith, it's a dog, in fact several dogs. You are so wrapped up in your social scene that you have forgotten that she is going to Sarah Meadon's this evening. She is cheerful because she has something to look forward to. It will do her good to have something to occupy her during summer, and she will appreciate being able to earn some money of her own rather than asking us every time she wants to buy something."

"She doesn't need to work for money and she has her own dog here which she hardly gives any attention to."

"Oh you really have no idea do you?"

Anna came skipping back down stairs.

"Hello love."

"Hi Dad. Daaaad." She drawled out the 'a's like children do when they want something.

"Yes."

"You don't know what I'm going to ask you."

"It's irrelevant really. I don't really have the option to say no do I?"

"Suppose not. So you will give me a lift to Sarah's tonight – and back again. Thank you daddy."

"Go away, you cheeky madam."

Anna left for school knowing that even double French couldn't dampen her spirits today. She knew it was going to be a good day.

~~~~~~~~~~

Steve and Katy were also full of the joys of spring today. It was the last day that Cuddles had to go to his temporary carer. As far as

197

they knew Mel had been fine with Cuddles but, well she just wasn't Sarah. No one was as good as Sarah in their opinion.

"Katy do you have a £5 note in your purse. I need to leave Mel's money."

"I think so, help yourself."

"Why don't we have a day out this weekend Steve, the weather is supposed to be nice? We could go somewhere where we can take Cuddles."

"That's a great idea. Hey what about asking Mrs Evans if she would like to come. We could go somewhere where she can sit in the car and look at the scenery. Then we could call in at a little tearoom somewhere. We should check with Sarah first to make sure that Ellen is fit enough to cope."

They spent the journey to work trying to decide where to go for their day out. They were getting nowhere.

"You decide Steve."

"Everywhere I suggest you find something wrong with."

"I don't. It's just that places you suggest aren't suitable."

"See you are agreeing with me now. You do find fault with my suggestions."

"If you suggested sensible places I wouldn't find fault."

"Women!"

Steve gave Katy a half-hearted kiss when he dropped her off at work.

"Oh and don't forget to buy some decent wine to take to Sarah's tonight, and some flowers for Ellen."

"Yes boss." 'It's a good job I love her' he thought.

After dropping Katy at her office he drove on to his school. Even the heavy traffic couldn't dampen his spirits today. He knew it was going to be a good day.

~~~~~~~~~

Every time they heard the bleep that signalled a new name on the electronic notice board their eyes moved in unison to see if their turn to go into the doctor had arrived. In between bleeps they half watched the board as it scrolled various bits of information. Topics covered included how many appointments had been missed last

198

week, how the surgery was temporarily trying Saturday opening, how Doctor Warburton had a student working with him this week.

"Sarah look. Student. I can't talk in front of a student."

"What are you on about?"

"Look at the notice board, quick."

She quickly averted her attention away from the couple at the reception desk who were informing the receptionist that the man's urine sample they were bringing in for testing had leaked in his wife's shopping bag, all over the fish she had just bought at the market. "The fish will be fine, it will add a bit of flavour, but he can't possibly go again yet, can we scoop it out of the bag?" Sarah realised that doctors' receptionists must have an interesting job. By the time her attention had been focused on the notice board the message had disappeared. There was no option but to sit watching the board until the message came around again. She was amazed how many varied screen transitions could be built into such a basic small electronic information board. Obviously someone had tried to be clever but it hadn't quite worked, no matter how flashy the transitions they can't overcome silly errors in the information. Sarah was amused by the message that it was Mr Brown's turn to go to 'Sister Back Treatment Room'. 'What a strange name she thought and what if it wasn't his back that was troubling him' she thought sarcastically. Why couldn't it just say Sister Brown? At least it gave Sarah a momentary slice of humour in her difficult world, albeit almost childish humour, any humour would do at the moment.

After what seemed like hours, although in reality was probably only a couple of minutes the message appeared again. 'Doctor Warburton has a student working with him this week. If you wish to talk to the doctor in confidence please mention this when you enter his surgery.'

"So we can ask the student leave if that's what you want John."

"I can't do that, they'll think I am being difficult."

"They will understand but to be honest the student doesn't know you and to them it is just a job. They probably won't see another OCD patient during their time here so it will be interesting."

"They will think I am mad though and what if they talk about me in the pub tonight, all the village could know by tonight."

"Oh don't be ridiculous. Either they stay in or we ask them to leave, it's your decision. You can make a decision can you?" John didn't answer. He knew he could make a decision but he had to weigh up all the angles, all the pros and cons of every variation before reaching a decision he thought was the safest. He had no chance, therefore, to make that decision before it was his turn to see the doctor.

"Sarah you decide please."

"Oh my goodness. OK then. I think that they should stay in the room."

"I'm not sure that is the right decision Sarah."

"Then make your own bloody decision." She realised that the people sat near to them were staring at her. She had tried to keep her voice very low but obviously had failed.

"Why are you shouting at me? Shouting doesn't help. Perhaps we should go, maybe this is a bad idea."

"No way. I got you this appointment and you are going in there whether you like it or not."

Sarah sat frustrated through another period of silence.

At last they saw the words 'John Whittle for Doctor Warburton. "Here we go John, the start of our journey."

Sarah hoped that this would go well. She hoped what they would hear would raise both their spirits but she wasn't convinced that it would be a good day.

John was just pleased that she had said 'our journey'.

Chapter 35

Sarah tapped on the doctor's room door with John following behind like a little helpless lap dog. She realised he must be very nervous, after all this could be the start of a better future for him, but would it be?

"Come in."

Sarah pushed the door open and they walked into the room.

"Please sit down," Doctor Warburton said addressing John, "I have Natasha, a final year student, observing me today. Are you happy for her to remain in the room?"

"Y-y-yes," stuttered John. He wasn't sure that was the right answer.

"Thank you. What can I do for you today?"

John sat nervously on the chair next to the doctor's desk whilst Sarah perched her bottom on the edge of the examination couch.

"I'm not well," said John.

"Most people aren't when they come to see me," the doctor replied trying to lighten the mood and put John more at ease.

John sat in silence.

"He, sorry we, think he is suffering from OCD," interrupted Sarah.

"Really. That's not something I come across every day. What makes you think you have OCD?"

John explained how he had thoughts in his mind that make him worry about almost everything and make him think he is responsible for other people.

"Please give me a couple of examples if you can."

John thought for a while before answering. "One day I took the train to Manchester to visit someone." He didn't explain that the 'someone' was an HIV clinic. "Everything was alright until about 10pm that evening. I was having my supper at the time when I was convinced that I had left contamination on the door handle of the place I had visited and also on the train handle."

"And what did you do."

"I had to go back to Manchester to wipe the handles. You see if I hadn't hundreds of people could catch HIV and die and it would be my fault. I would be responsible."

"Did you feel better when you had wiped the handle?"

"No. Wiping the handle at the place I had visited was easy but I couldn't be sure which train I had been on. I went up and down all the platforms at the railway station and wiped as many handles as I could but how could I be sure any of them were my train. That train could be anywhere by now. It could be in York, or Liverpool or any of a hundred places. That made everything much, much worse. It could now be millions of people who may be contaminated. How could I live with that?"

"This place you visited, what was it?"

"Not one of those places if that is what you are thinking." He couldn't bring himself to actually say the word brothel. "I would never go to one of those, there are too many risks. I went to an HIV clinic for a test. I've had five tests so far."

"Have any of the tests been positive?"

"No they have all been negative."

"So why are you still concerned?"

"Because I may have caught HIV in the clinic waiting room and it would be too soon for that to show up on the test. It takes at least four weeks for infection to show up in the tests you see, it can be up to three months. Also the doctor didn't wear gloves when he took my blood sample, that's dangerous. Maybe the test result was wrong. The tests are only 99.9% accurate so one in a thousand are wrong. "

"The chance of you contracting HIV in the clinic are miniscule so you don't need to worry at all."

"But there is a chance. Can you give me a 100% guarantee that I couldn't catch it there?"

"I cannot give you a 100% guarantee about anything in life Mr Whittle. I can say, however, that the chances are so tiny as to not be worth thinking about."

"But there is a chance and the consequences could be enormous. How can I not think about it? People could die if I ignore it! I would essentially be a murderer."

"Is it just contamination that bothers you?" the doctor continued.

"Oh no. Security bothers me, and religion, and I feel the need to confess all the time."

"Confess to what? Something you have done?"

"Something that I may have done, I'm not always sure if I have or haven't."

"Have you ever suffered from depression? OCD and depression often go hand in hand."

"I'm not sure. I have felt very low at times but whether it was depression I don't know. I think people say they are depressed when they are just fed up."

"That's true. How is your appetite John?"

"It's ok I think."

"Do you sleep well?"

"Most nights."

"Is there anything you do that gives you pleasure?"

"No."

"If you don't mind me asking you, have you ever felt like killing yourself?"

John considered the question before answering. "I have felt like the world would be a better place if I died but I don't have the courage to kill myself. I have often hoped, in fact wished, that someone else would kill me."

John went on to explain about walking the streets in the rough areas of the city hoping someone would stab him.

"Ok Mr Whittle, from what you have told me I don't think there is any doubt that you are suffering from some degree of OCD. I must tell you that there is no cure for OCD."

Sarah noticed the look of despair on John' face.

The doctor went on, "However, there is support you can get to help you to manage your condition better which will make your life much more bearable.

"There are a few things that can cause OCD but the most common is an imbalance of serotonin in the brain. Serotonin is a chemical the brain uses to transmit information from one brain cell to another. I will prescribe a tablet called Fluoxetine for you. This can help with correcting the serotonin imbalance to some degree.

"I must warn you that there can be side effects, particularly during the initial period before the drug begins to have an effect. This can be up to 4 or 5 weeks. During this time it is possible you may feel depressed. Do you live alone?"

For the first time Sarah felt it appropriate to join the conversation. "He is living with me at the moment."

"Are you a relative?"

"No I'm………….um." What was she? She didn't know how to describe herself.

"John helped me recently when I had a few problems so it's my turn now to repay his kindness and support."

John fought back the smile he could feel about to break out right across his face. It would be inappropriate just now. Sarah's comment did please him though – a lot. It sounded like she really cared for him and she did appreciate what he had done for her, despite some of the things she had said at the time, but that couldn't be the case. He couldn't believe that.

"That's very kind of you. I really hope that you appreciate the big sacrifice Miss Meadon is making to help you Mr Whittle. Living with an OCD sufferer can be very stressful for both the sufferer and the carer.

"You take the tablets twice a day. It is likely that you have had your OCD for many years and therefore it will be very deep rooted, for that reason I am putting you on a high dose of Fluoxetine although gradually I hope that we can reduce the dose.

I also think you would benefit from some CBT treatment."

"What's that," asked Sarah. Sarah had read about CBT on the internet but wanted to hear the doctor's explanation. It seemed like she had taken over the discussion with the doctor. John was seeming to listen but his stare into the distance indicated to her that what the doctor was saying wasn't really registering in his memory. He wouldn't be sure later what the doctor had said she feared.

"CBT, Cognitive Behavioural Therapy, consists of talking to a therapist to identify ways that can help you manage your problems by making adjustments to the way you think and behave. In simple terms it tries to make you face your fears and to keep your anxiety levels low whilst doing so.

CBT cannot remove your problems, but it can help you deal with them in a more positive way. It also deals with your current problems rather than dwelling on issues from your past. That way you will hopefully be able to make some improvements fairly quickly, albeit they are likely to be very small improvements but any improvement should give you the encouragement to carry on."

"How do we get this CBT?" Sarah asked. By now John had totally switched off. He appeared to be concentrating but somehow Sarah knew he wasn't.

"I will refer you to a consultant. They will discuss your situation with you and decide the most appropriate treatment. Unfortunately there is a 6 month waiting time in this area."

"That is ridiculous. We can't wait six months. John needs help now," Sarah almost shouted. At least her raised voice snapped John back into the real world.

"What if I pay?" said John quietly.

"Then I can probably get you an appointment next week."

"Bloody ridiculous," snapped Sarah. She hated the fact that people like her who had paid her taxes and National Insurance all their lives had to wait for treatment yet the landed gentry, her description, could get treatment tomorrow.

"I will pay," John said.

Sarah suddenly remembered Natasha who had sat in the corner all the time, eyes looking down, without contributing one comment. She guessed that in normal cases the doctor would have asked her opinion but this wasn't your run of the mill cough and cold. Poor Natasha, she must have been dreading the doctor turning to her for her opinion. She probably hadn't covered OCD in her course so far.

"If you are sure that is what you want to do I will ring the clinic when you have left and you will probably get a phone call from them either later today or tomorrow morning."

"Thank you doctor." John seemed to have regained his role in the discussion.

"I really do hope everything goes well for you. Please don't hesitate to make another appointment with me if I can do anything to help. Here's your prescription."

They left the room without another word being said. Sarah was still annoyed at the lack of fairness in obtaining treatment. John was elated that it had been confirmed that his problems were medical, albeit a mental illness, and that he couldn't help the things he thought and did. He was determined to work very hard to succeed. This could be the start of a new life for him.

Sarah was under no illusions that they were both about to embark on the most difficult journey either of them ever had been on. She realised that the climb up to the moors was nothing more than a tiny mound compared to the mountain they now both had to climb.

"Let's go home John."

Chapter 36

After a quick lunch of cheese on toast Sarah had managed to reduce the levels of angst and anxiety she felt when leaving the doctor's surgery. She decided it would be alright now to broach the subject of this morning's visit to the doctors.

"How do you feel after your visit to the doctors John?"

"I feel really elated that I now know I have an illness and that something can be done to help me. Thank you Sarah, without you I would never have known that. I also feel very nervous though, nervous about whether I have the strength to go through with the treatment. I promise that I will try hard though."

"I have no doubt about that. John I have some friends coming round for tea tonight. I thought it would be good for you to meet them. It should take your mind off your OCD for a while, hopefully."

"My mind is never completely free of OCD, as I now know it to be. I am never totally relaxed. The best I can hope for is a day nearer the lower levels of my anxiety scale now and again."

That comment made her feel really sad for John. At times like this she found him very vulnerable and this attracted her to him.

"They are all nice people, and you already know Ellen from next door."

"I am sure they are nice but I find meeting people very hard, what if I contaminate them?"

"John did you not listen to a thing the doctor said this morning? He said you can't have HIV."

"No he didn't. He said there was a miniscule chance."

"Grrrrr!" was all she could say.

This comment made her feel really angry towards John. At times like this she wondered if she was completely wasting her time trying to help him. There was no point her trying to help him if he wasn't prepared to help himself.

She forced herself to calm down again. This was a skill she would have to hone and use many times over the coming weeks and months. She was conscious that her feelings for John swung

207

dramatically and frequently from one end of the scale to the other, from sadness to anger and back again. She had to try and get her feelings on a more even keel.

"Right John. We need to go to the supermarket to get some food for this evening and we need to get your prescription."

"OK see you when you get back."

"I said we! I thought you could come with me. It will stop you sitting here moping. You can't lock yourself away." Reluctantly he agreed to go.

"I've never been in one before," John said on the way to the supermarket.

"You're joking."

"No I always go to the shops in the village. They serve you there which is easier."

"And more expensive," Sarah added.

John couldn't believe his eyes when they went through the doors. It was huge, and so many things to choose from. "How do you decide what to buy?" he asked.

"You just do. Sometimes you see things advertised on television that you fancy trying, sometimes you just buy what you have always bought and sometimes you buy what is on offer."

They started in the fruit and vegetable aisles. "Right I'll have some of those potatoes for making baked potatoes tonight. No I won't I'll have those, I have just noticed that they are two packs for the price of one."

John stood there deep in thought. "Don't get those."

"Why on earth not?"

"Because the ones you were originally going to get are better value."

"These are two packs for the price of one."

"Yes but per 100 grams the others work out cheaper."

She really couldn't be bothered arguing about it, she was sure John would never back down, so she slammed a pack of the original potatoes in her trolley. She wondered if she could cope with him constantly weighing up all aspects of something before making a decision.

John hated conflict and certainly didn't like making Sarah angry but he had to stop her taking all the risks that it became apparent she was taking. He had to protect her.

They continued the shopping. Lettuce, strawberries, cucumber and tomatoes were added to the trolley before John froze, routed to the spot.

"Sarah look."

"What?"

"Over there. The lady in the red dress."

"Do you know her?"

"No. Look what she's doing."

"She appears to be buying pears to me."

"She is but she is touching them and putting them back on the display."

"So what?"

"Well she may have contaminated them. She can't touch them and then put them back."

"John everyone feels fruit to see if it's ripe. I do it all the time."

"You can't. You mustn't. Should we go and tell the manager?"

"Tell them what. That someone has touched a pear to see if it is ripe?"

"Yes. They should remove the whole display and destroy it because they can't be sure which one she touched. If we don't tell them we could be responsible if someone became ill from eating the contaminated pear. They may die. It might be a child."

"You can't go and tell them. They'll think you're crazy. Come on, forget about it."

"He knew they would think he was crazy which really made him not want to confess but he had to in order to protect people. He wished that Sarah would go and tell the manager while he was in another part of the store to avoid him the embarrassment but he knew that wasn't going to happen.

"Come on John, forget about it." Easier said than done. John really wanted to tell the store staff what had happened. Not confess as such, he knew he hadn't done anything, just subtly let them know that they may have a problem. That way if they did nothing any consequences were their fault, he had passed on the responsibility.

They completed the shop without further incident but with the potentially contaminated pear still foremost in John's mind. Sarah was relieved when they got to the checkout. She started to put her items on to the conveyor belt but hadn't finished when it was her turn to be served. "John can you finish putting things onto the belt while I go and start packing?"

There was no answer. She turned around and John wasn't there. She scanned her eyes around the area and after a few seconds she spotted him – at customer services speaking to one of the people manning the desk. She knew he was reporting the 'contaminated' pear. "Oh my God. How am I going to cope with this?" she whispered to herself.

Once she had paid for her goods she strode purposely to customer services. She grabbed John's arm. "Come on. We're going – now."

He followed like a scalded child.

"What on earth did you tell them?"

"I told them what had happened, or what I think happened."

"What did they say?"

"They were very nice but they said not to worry it happens all the time and that they have had no reports of anyone becoming ill. That's not good enough though is it?"

"Yes it is. Let's get your prescription before we leave here."

The visit to the pharmacy passed without incident and they made their way back to the van.

"Sarah, there's a nail on the floor there."

"So? I can't see one anyway."

"There right in the middle of the road between the parking spaces. I need to pick it up. It may get into someone's tyre and then when they are taking their children to school next week they could get a puncture and the car could swerve into the oncoming traffic. They could all be killed and it would be my fault because I didn't pick the nail up."

"Don't be ridiculous. It's so small it wouldn't go through a tyre anyway. Come on, leave it. You need to try not to engage with your thoughts, as the doctor said, remember."

Reluctantly he followed her back to the car and they headed home.

After about ten minutes John said, "Sarah I'm really sorry but I have forgotten to get something at the supermarket. Can we go back please?"

"What have you forgotten?"

"I'd like to get Mrs Evans some flowers. She seemed a lovely old lady and was very nice to me this morning. I just want to say thank you."

Here was the caring John back again. She thought his idea was wonderful and didn't hesitate to turn around and go back to the supermarket.

"I'll wait in the car. It will be good for you to go in on your own."

She watched John walk towards the entrance but before he went in he turned and walked down between the parked cars. "Why was I so gullible?" she muttered.

John returned to the car a few minutes later.

"Where are the flowers?"

"They didn't have any nice enough. I'll get some another day."

"Open you hand."

"What?"

"Open your hand." John opened his left hand. "Not that one. The other hand."

Slowly he opened his right hand to reveal a small nail.

Sarah held her head in despair.

"What's wrong Sarah?" John asked.

"You really have no idea have you?"

Chapter 37

The rest of the afternoon passed with Sarah making the salads and rice for the evening's get together while John sat in the living room listening to cricket on the radio. She was glad of the time on her own.

Anna's dad dropped her off at 5:45pm. "I'll ring you when I need picking up dad," she said as she turned towards Sarah's house.

Sarah saw her through the kitchen window and went out to meet her.

"Hi Anna. Come in."

Anna had really made an effort and was dressed more for a posh restaurant than a back garden barbeque. She wore a loose fitting short sleeved lemon top with a short pleated pale grey skirt. Sarah really hoped these clothes could survive a barbeque or more particularly the barbeque sauces.

"You look gorgeous Anna."

"Ah thank you." She looked genuinely pleased with Sarah's comment.

"John, Anna is here," Sarah shouted in to the house. There was no response and no one appeared. She suddenly wondered if tonight would be a huge disaster. She had intended it as some entertainment for John but was he going to even appear.

"He must be upstairs. I'm sure he'll be down in a minute," Sarah said to Anna.

"You've got a lovely house here Sarah."

"Thank you, it's not a patch on your house though."

"I hate my house. It's just a house, not a home. Yours looks like a home."

Sarah thought back to her younger years and knew exactly what Anna meant.

"Anna some other people will be arriving soon so we had better sort out the details of you working with me. When can you start?"

"I can do after school next week and then after that I finish for summer so can do any time."

"That's great. Can you be here for about 4pm on Monday? Don't dress as nice as you have today though, you will be dealing with dogs after all. We'll sort out your pay on Monday. I can't afford to pay a lot but I promise I will be as fair as I can."

"That's fine. To be honest whilst the money will be really good to have the most important thing is that this job gets me away from my family for a while. Well from my mum mainly. Dad's lovely but Mum's a real pain."

'At least she has one nice parent' Sarah thought to herself. "I'm sure they both think the world of you Anna."

"Maybe."

Just then Steve and Katy pulled up. They both shouted "Hi" as they got out of the car. Katy opened the back door of the car and released the dynamic fluffy ball. Cuddles ran straight to Sarah.

"She loves Sarah," Katy said to Anna. "Hi I'm Katy and this is Steve, and that is Cuddles. Sarah looks after our dog."

"Hi I'm Anna. I'm going to start helping Sarah with the dogs."

"That's great. Do you think you can cope with that?" Katy said pointing to Cuddles.

"Of course," Anna replied with a little giggle.

Still no sign of John.

"I'm just going round for Ellen," Sarah said.

"Would you like me to go?" Steve asked.

"That would be great if you don't mind."

Steve went next door. "Hello Ellen, its Steve. Remember me?"

"I never forget a handsome man," Ellen replied.

"Come on its party time."

"Ooh are you taking me clubbing. That's what they call it isn't it?"

"Well not quite. I'm taking you to a barbeque next door."

"I'm not dressed up. Why didn't Sarah tell me this morning? I could have got ready then."

"You're fine. Come on."

Steve slowly walked Ellen back to Sarah's garden and sat her in one of the white garden chairs. "Will you be comfortable there?"

"I'd be more comfortable on your knee," Ellen said.

"Hey Mrs E, I'll be getting jealous," Katy said, joking of course.

Still no sign of John.

"Excuse me a moment," Sarah said as she headed back into the house. She found John still sat listening to the cricket.

"What the hell is wrong with you?"

"I can't do it."

"You can and you bloody well will. Now come on. I'm sick of you sitting here feeling sorry for yourself." Sarah hated herself for saying that but she wanted to spur John into action. Early signs for their journey weren't good so it was time to get tough. It worked. John followed her into the garden. Sarah had no idea how difficult this was for him. Was the problem nerves, or his OCD, or both.

Sarah completed the introductions.

"So this is your new man Sarah," Ellen said. Ellen had forgotten that she had met John earlier.

"He is not my man, he's just a friend. Now who is cooking, isn't a barbeque a man's job."

There was no reaction from John but Steve said "I'll do it."

"That's fine if you want everything burnt."

"Thank you Katy," Steve said sarcastically.

The next hour or so passed with everyone seeming to enjoy the evening. Even John appeared to be relaxing and talking to the other guests. Well answering their questions at least. The food went down a treat with everyone except John. He couldn't accept that food cooked on a barbeque, which probably hadn't been cleaned to his standard since it was last used, could be hygienic. He couldn't accept that food cooked outside could be hygienic. Also he had seen an old cut on Steve's hand. John ate just a little salad. Sarah made a note to make him something when the others had gone. He was at least putting an effort in and that pleased Sarah.

When the food was finished Steve said, "Right what do we do now? How about us all telling about our most embarrassing moment. That should be hilarious." Everyone thought that was a great idea, except John. He thought it was silly and couldn't think of an embarrassing moment. Well not one he would want to talk about anyway. He would have to make something up but that was difficult because it would mean he was lying.

"I'll start," offered Ellen. "One day many years ago my daughter was taking me out for a day, which was very rare. She decided we

214

would go to Blackpool. I hate Blackpool but I was so pleased to be taken out for a day. Anyway my daughter is a mad driver and was driving far too fast on the motorway, and weaving in and out of the lanes.

"I started to feel really sick but daren't ask her to stop. I held on until she had to slam on her brakes to avoid running into the back of another car. I flew forward and whilst I managed to keep the sick down, my teeth flew out of my mouth and right into Angela's hair. Her hair was bushy so somehow they just stuck there, she had no idea. I couldn't stop giggling long enough to tell her, anyway she deserved to be shown up the stuck up madam.

"They stayed in her hair all the time we were walking round Blackpool until we went into a little café for a drink. The waitress there said 'Your hair slide is very unusual.' Angela didn't wear a hair slide so she felt the back of her head and her hand landed on my teeth, complete with bits of sick between the teeth. She wasn't happy. In fact she has never taken me out since then."

They all gave Ellen a well-deserved round of applause.

"I'll go next," said Anna. "It was my first day at secondary school and my dad dropped me off near the entrance. As I got out of the car I saw my best friend standing in the foyer. I was so pleased to see someone I knew that I ran at full speed towards the open door and went smack into a closed plate glass window. It wasn't an open door at all. I was so embarrassed."

Katy told about the time she had walked out of a shop changing room with her dress tucked into her knickers. She didn't find out for a good half an hour.

Sarah recalled when she was walking in the park one day and a young boy was having trouble riding on his skateboard. 'Would you like me to show you how?' she had asked him. 'Yes please', he replied. She confidently put one foot on the skateboard and it immediately tipped up and sent her rolling into the pond, right onto the back of a very startled swan. The young boy picked his skateboard up and ran away from the mad woman.

"That leaves John and Steve," Katy said.

"Have you anything to tell us John?"

"No not really."

"Ok that's fine. Your turn Steve tell them about your classic."

"Oh no not that one. Alright. One day I was driving to work and stopped for petrol. The garage I went to had an offer of a free car wash with £20 of petrol so as I had time to spare I couldn't refuse the offer.

"I drove into the car wash, wound my window down and pressed the start button. Just then I noticed that I hadn't put my aerial down. The car wash would break it off. The brush was a long way off the car so I decided that I had plenty time to get out of the car, push the aerial down and get back in the car before the brush arrived. That would all have been fine except I forgot that the start button was on the end of a long V shaped metal construction which got wider as it got nearer the brush.

"After pushing down the aerial I turned round to see the V shape had gone through my open window and was slowly ripping my car door off. I ran into the garage shop and shouted 'stop your car wash it's ripping my door off'. The place was packed, it was rush hour.

"Feeling very embarrassed I went back to the car to discover the door wouldn't shut. I had to go back into the garage and ask if they had anything to tie my door up with. All they had was a length of plastic clothes line.

"So I completed my journey to work with a door tied up with clothes line and a car that was soaking – inside. By the time I got to work, via the local body repair shop, I was soaking wet. I had to sit in my office all day until my suit dried out. No one at work ever found out what had happened."

"I think that one wins," said Sarah.

It was getting quite late. Sarah asked if anyone would like a coffee.

"I'd better ring my dad to come and pick me up," Anna said.

"That's OK Anna, we'll take you home," Steve said, "It's no trouble at all."

"Thank you. If that's ok it will be great."

"Come on Ellen, I'll take you home first."

"Oh thank you handsome man. It might not be your wedding I'm brushing my hat off for Sarah."

"Ellen behave. He's a married man," Katy pointed out.

Everyone bade their farewells and said what a fantastic evening they'd had.

"We must do it again soon," Steve added, "At our place next time."

They picked Cuddles up from under John's chair and carried him to their car. He was fast asleep from the excitement of all the attention he'd had, not to mention all the meat he had eaten.

When everyone had gone John helped Sarah to tidy everything away.

"How was the evening for you John? I realise it wouldn't have been easy for you but I wanted to show you what you could enjoy if you can learn to manage your OCD better."

"It was good, honestly. I felt a bit silly that I couldn't think of an embarrassing moment."

"No one thought anything about it John. Don't even think about it."

"I bet they thought I was dull and boring."

"Not at all. I'm just going round to make sure Ellen is alright for the night. Could you make us a brew before I come back? I'm shattered."

"It will be a pleasure Sarah. Thank you for this evening. I really appreciate it. I am trying hard you know. The contamination dangers were significant but I managed to cope. It was hard Sarah."

"I know, and it's very, very early days yet."

Sarah really liked this version of John.

Chapter 38

It was well past her usual time of waking up when Sarah opened her eyes on the morning after the barbeque. She had really enjoyed it and thought that John had too. At least he said he had.

John was pottering in the garden when Sarah came downstairs. He had opened the door and gone outside but hadn't run off. "That's a good sign," Sarah whispered to herself, "At least last night hasn't frightened him away."

She popped her head out of the door. "Morning John. How are you?"

"I feel good today."

"Don't count your chickens Sarah", she mumbled, knowing John wouldn't hear her.

"I hope you don't mind me doing a bit of gardening. I'm only pulling up some weeds."

"Be my guest. I don't get much time to do anything in the garden and to be honest I have no idea what the plants are. I am really grateful for your help."

"Can I be your unofficial gardener then?"

"With pleasure." 'Another good sign' Sarah thought. It was only 24 hours since John saw the doctors but she could already see improvements. Tiny improvements. She knew John was trying and that was all she could ask.

Just then her mobile phone rang. She took it out of her jeans pocket and pressed the green button to answer. "Hello."

"Hi Sarah, its Katy. I just wanted to say how much we enjoyed last night. We had a great time."

"So did I. Its years since I did anything like that."

"Well we must do something again soon. Anna seems a lovely girl, I think she will be a big help to you. I thought she may have felt out of place with us wrinklys."

"Hey if you are a wrinkly what does that make me? I know what you mean though. She doesn't seem to have many, if any, friends her own age. I think her mother is quite controlling so it was probably something new for her too. I can't wait for her to start work with me on Monday evening. I've only known her a few days but I really like her."

"Does the same go for John? He seems really nice too."

"Have you been listening to Ellen? She already has us married off you know Katy. He is a friend, nothing more. I hardly know him but he helped me when I had my accident in the sinkhole, now he needs a bit of help and support so how can I refuse?"

"What's wrong with him Sarah? He seemed fine to me. A little shy maybe but otherwise nothing seemed wrong with him."

The question she had been dreading. "Oh it's nothing serious, nothing to worry about." Thankfully Katy accepted that answer, vague thought it was, and didn't ask any more about John.

"Hey Sarah, was that story about Ellen's false teeth true. It was hilarious."

"Who knows? I have no doubt that the bit about her teeth falling out of her mouth was true but as for the rest, well older people do tend to embellish stories. She enjoyed telling it though and it made us laugh so no harm done. We will probably never know the true story."

"Yes I really like Ellen. Do you think she would come out for a ride with me and Steve sometime? We often take Cuddles to the river at weekends. We park the car right next to the river so she wouldn't have to walk. That's if it's alright with you."

"Oh of course it's alright. I would be delighted and Ellen would love it."

"Speaking of stories Katy was Steve's tale of the car wash true?"

"Oh yes, every little detail. I love him to bits but he is a bit of a dimwit at times. He acts before he thinks."

Just as Sarah ended her call with Katy her phone bleeped to signal a text had arrived. She opened it to discover it was from Anna.

'Thank you for a great time last night. I loved it. Everyone was so nice. See you on Monday.'

Yes last night had been a great success all round.

She looked over at John who was still deep in thought about his gardening task.

Sarah's phone rang again.

"What a morning!" she said before she pressed to answer.

"Hello."

"Hello I would like to speak to a Mr John Whittle if possible."

"Hold on a minute please. John it's for you."

He seemed very nervous as he picked up the phone.

"Hello," he said very hesitantly.

"Hello this is Doctor Kaur's secretary. I am ringing about your appointment to discuss your OCD issues. Doctor Kaur could see you at 7pm on Monday if that is convenient."

He put his hand, covered by his sweater sleeve of course, over the phone and turned to Sarah as he whispered "Is 7pm on Monday alright?"

She guessed he meant for his appointment. "Yes that's fine."

"That time is ok thank you," he relayed to the doctor's secretary.

"That's good. We'll see you then." She gave John the directions before ending the call. John hoped he would remember what she had said. "Have you got a pen and paper please?" he asked Sarah. Sarah went into the kitchen and came out with a black biro and a small note pad which she handed to John.

"John I think we should go and get you a mobile phone today." She expected him to say it wasn't necessary.

"That would be good."

Sarah was surprised. This was going too well, too soon. She couldn't help thinking that there was a shock waiting around the corner.

Chapter 39

The rest of the weekend passed relatively straight forward. There were no major successes with John's attempts to manage his OCD but no major failures either. Well except perhaps the visit to the mobile phone shop. 'Good morning Sir, how may I help you?' must have been words that the salesman who approached John regretted for the rest of the day.

John just wanted a phone that he could use to make calls and maybe send texts, nothing more. The assistant spent ages extolling the virtues of 4G, Wi-Fi, 15 megapixels cameras, unlimited media etc., etc. but John wanted a phone just to make phone calls. He didn't understand all the other things the salesman had mentioned, they were like a foreign language to him. Being connected to the rest of the World, the words the salesman used, seemed fraught with danger in his opinion and he wanted no part of it.

He did eventually acquire the most basic handset the shop had, with a lot of persuasion from Sarah, but it still did a lot of fancy things though, which John was far from happy about.

Sarah was excited about the arrival of Monday morning, it was back to work day. She was up and ready by 5:30am and now realised just how much she had missed her walks on the moors with her canine friends. John had declined the invitation to accompany her but in a way she was glad he had. Strange as it may seem she didn't want his mind taking off his OCD today otherwise he may omit to tell the consultant the full story. He needed to be able to relay the full extent of his suffering to ensure that he received the treatment he needed.

Once all her clients, the canine ones, were safely in the cages in the back of her van she set off on the climb up to the moors car park. The higher they climbed the more Sarah's excitement levels rose. The dogs looked as eager as she was when they were released from the van. Off they went in front of Sarah, twirling, twisting, chasing balls and sniffing up the multitude of scents that rode on the clean moorland air. In fact just having a generally good time. They took a different route from normal, the memory of the sinkhole still sat heavily in Sarah's mind. She knew she would go there again, but not just yet. She had also remembered to bring more than enough tennis balls. If the dogs refused to fetch one she sure as hell wasn't going to go for it herself.

Sarah returned home after the morning walk to find a subdued John sat at the kitchen table picking at a slice of toast that had long ago gone cold. "Are you ok?"

"I guess so."

"What's the matter?"

"I'm worried Sarah. What if the consultant says he can't help me?"

"Of course he will try and help you."

"You said try. That means he may fail."

"Oh for goodness sake John stop picking up on every word I say and twisting them to suit your negative views."

"There are no guarantees he can help."

"Don't go there again," she snapped.

"But you can't guarantee me that he will be able to make me better, can you?"

"No of course I can't but neither can I guarantee that I won't hit you round the head."

"What have I done?"

"You have no idea have you? It's not just you who is suffering with this." As soon as she had said that she regretted it. She knew that her suffering wasn't even close to being on the same scale as what John was having to put up with, but it wasn't easy for her.

"I feel like I am walking on egg shells all the time, trying not to say the wrong thing, trying not do the wrong thing. We are only three days into our journey, only three days since you saw the doctor and I'm not sure I can cope."

"You really have no comprehension what I go through Sarah." She had to admit to herself that she didn't but was disappointed with John's complete lack of acknowledgement of the fact that this was difficult for her as well.

The atmosphere was somewhat strained during the early afternoon, until Sarah took the dogs on the second walk of the day. Sarah chose to hold conversations with the dogs rather than with John.

222

Sarah completed the dog walks, with the help of Anna who had now arrived, and then took her doggy friends home a little earlier than usual to allow enough time for her to cook and eat tea. She wanted John to be well fed before his appointment, she wanted him to feel comfortable. Normally she would grab anything for her tea, whatever was to hand and easy to make, but she felt she had to cook a proper meal while John was here. She remembered that they still needed to work out a cooking rota but that would have to wait until another day. John had been hoping that she wouldn't remember the rota. How would he deal with the contamination risks? He wasn't sure that he could.

John readily tucked into the pork steaks, boiled new potatoes and carrots like he hadn't eaten for a month. Sarah noted that his OCD didn't seem to affect his appetite.

~~~~~~~~~~~

The journey to the clinic would take about half an hour Sarah thought so she suggested to John that they leave at 6:15pm to allow for any delays. They arrived with plenty time to spare.

John walked behind Sarah as they approached the clinic entrance.

"Hey it's your appointment, you go first."

He did as he was told. He covered his hand with his sleeve before he pressed the buzzer on the intercom to the right of the red door.

"Hello Reflections Clinic."

"I – I –I have an app – appointment. Doctor Kaur" John stuttered.

"Come in please." They both heard the buzz of the door lock being released and walked into the clinic reception. Sarah noticed that the place exuded money and wondered just how much this would cost John.

"Hello. You must be John," the kind looking middle aged lady behind the reception desk said. She handed John a clip board. "Could you please complete this before you go into the therapist? The waiting room is right behind you."

They went into the cheerfully decorated waiting room which was lit by the natural light coming through a huge bay window. Beyond the window was a well-tended garden complete with colourful flower borders. There were several small birds dashing backwards and forwards between the bird feeders and the nearby trees. Sarah noted that the clinic had done everything it possibly could to make patients feel relaxed.

There was a coffee pot and a stack of plastic cups on a small wooden table in the corner of the room.

"Would you like a coffee John," Sarah asked.

"No thank you. You don't know who may have touched those cups before."

Sarah poured herself one.

The questionnaire John had been given to complete consisted of several statements about how the patient had been feeling over the last two weeks. John had to answer most by selecting from a scale of 1 to 5, with 1 being effectively 'I feel fairly good' to 5 being 'I am really struggling'.

"I don't know what to put Sarah," John said, "The way I feel is normal to me so how do I know where it fits on the scale."

"I suggest that you put 5 for all of them. If you don't they may think you are better than you actually are."

"But 5 may not be right."

"Does it matter? The main point is that you get the treatment you need."

"I have to fill it in correctly. I can't lie."

"It is only an indication to the therapist of how you are feeling. Please put 5s."

"I'll put 4s for some and 3s for others."

Sarah shook her head in despair.

The few questions that required a narrative answer, for example *'List the three things you have worried about most recently and why?'* caused him even more concern. How could he choose just three things? How could he say why? That required a degree of logic and that was rare in John's mind.

John was only part way through the questionnaire, reading every word of every sentence several times to make sure he put the correct answer, correct in his opinion, when a young attractive lady wearing a white overall walked into the room.

"Hello," she said looking at John. There was no one else in the waiting room other than John and Sarah.

"You must be John," she cheerfully said. I'm Doctor Kaur, Manpreet but please call me Mandy. Would you like to follow me please?"

John looked at Sarah as if to say *'come on then'* but Sarah stayed firmly in her chair. The consultant therapist gave no indication that she would like Sarah to join them. In any case she really felt that the actual therapy sessions should be private, between John and his therapist. He would tell her what he wanted her to know later.

She sat nervously waiting for John's return. She wondered how he was feeling. When she had asked during the journey there he had said he felt excited, relieved and nervous. She wondered which of those was at the forefront now.

Time went so slowly. The metronomic click of the clock seemed so fast but every time Sarah looked at the clock only another minute or so had passed. She tried to play a game on her mobile phone but she couldn't concentrate. She tried to read a magazine but could do no more than skim through the headlines. She tried to text Anna to apologise for having to cut her time so short tonight, her first night of helping Sarah too, but the words wouldn't come. She hoped Anna wasn't too upset or annoyed. She made a mental note to call her when they got home if it wasn't too late.

After what seemed like several hours to Sarah, but was actually less than one hour, John and his therapist reappeared.

"Ok then John. From now on you will be seeing Miss Rackham, Melanie. Your first session with her will be next Monday at 1pm."

"Ok thank you." Doctor Kaur shook John's hand before leaving the room.

"How did it go?" Sarah asked eagerly. All the waiting had made her even more eager to know what had happened.

"It was ok."

"Is that all you have to say? It was ok!"

"Well it was ok."

"What did she say, what did you do."

"We talked."

Sarah's frustration grew. "Talked about what?"

"Me and my thoughts. Then she put her hands on a toilet seat and ate a biscuit without washing her hands."

"That's good. Did you do it too?"

"She made me."

"And how did that make you feel?"

"Very anxious. Please take me home."

Nothing more was said on the journey home but Sarah was determined to find out more, later in the evening.

~~~~~~~~~~~

It was almost 10pm before Sarah had washed up the pots from tea time and got everything ready for tomorrow's dog walking. She had managed to find the time to quickly ring Anna and was satisfied that she wasn't upset at all about this evening. She was, she told Sarah, really looking forward to coming again tomorrow.

"I'm going to bed Sarah."

"Not just yet please John. I'd like to talk to you about your session with your therapist."

"I've told you everything."

"I'm not convinced you have."

"Did she give any opinion on your OCD? Did she think there was something they could do for you?"

"I think she said they could help, that's what I think she said."

"Can't you remember?"

"I think that's what she said. She told me I would have to work very hard, that no one could put in the effort for me."

"Are you prepared to put the effort in?"

"Yes."

"You don't sound convincing."

"Well I don't know if what she told me was correct or not. She was very young so how can she know enough to help me?"

"What! She is a trained medical professional, she must know all there is to know."

"No one knows everything."

"True, but you know what I mean. Stop taking every word literally. Why do you really have a doubt about what she said? It's not just because she is young is it?"

"Because what she said wasn't the same as I thought."

"What makes you an expert all of a sudden? John you have to listen to these people and do what they ask you to do. Did she ask you to do anything before you go again next week?"

"She asked me not to wash my hands so much. To only wash them after I have been to the toilet and before I make food."

"That's a good challenge for you."

"Maybe."

"Oh John. I'm going to bed. See you tomorrow."

"Have you locked the doors and checked the gas is off?"

"Yes!"

"Are you sure?"

"Goodnight John."

Chapter 40

It was just over six weeks since John's first therapy appointment and he had now had four sessions. Sarah could clearly see changes in his behaviour. Only tiny steps forward but never the less movement in the right direction. Even then it had been two steps forward and one back but John was trying. 'Very trying at times' Sarah thought.

Sarah had got used to living with someone else in the house and to be honest most of the time she welcomed the company.

John was doing more about the house but did take significantly longer than Sarah to do any task by the time he had ensured cleanliness, safety and security. At least it was pleasing that toilet rolls and hand soap were both lasting a reasonable amount of time, not as long as they should but better than when John first moved in. He could be very wasteful though. On more than one occasion Sarah had found almost a full toilet roll unwound in the waste bin in John's bedroom. The reason, he said, was that he had touched it and therefore it may be contaminated so he had to throw it away. Alternatively she had found the toilet bowl holding a huge amount of unused toilet roll because, as John told her, he had to make sure his contamination didn't escape from the toilet.

He would take his turn at cooking now and indeed his efforts were very palatable. He could, however, also be very wasteful with food. There was the time that Mrs Evans went into her kitchen to get a banana to have with her lunch. She couldn't find any even though she was sure Sarah had brought her some in her shopping only a couple of days before.

"I know my memory isn't what it used to be," she said to Sarah, who was paying one of her multiple daily visits, "but I can't find any bananas. I'm sure I haven't eaten all that bunch you got me the other day."

"You must have put them somewhere strange Ellen, you know what you're like."

Ellen chuckled long and loud. "You are probably right Sarah. Do you remember the time when I couldn't find the present I bought for

Mrs Green's granddaughter when she was born. We both searched for it and couldn't find it anywhere – until Christmas when you opened your present to find the baby's present wrapped in the middle of it. What am I like?"

It was only later when Sarah tidied the kitchen up for Ellen and lifted the lid of the pedal bin to throw some rubbish in that she saw them – the bananas.

"They are in the bin Ellen."

"Oh I'm a silly old woman. I must have thrown them away instead of putting them in the fruit bowl."

Then Sarah saw it. "You didn't throw them away Ellen," she said very quietly to herself. She saw red.

~~~~~~~~~~~

"John why did you throw Ellen's bananas in the bin?"

"They weren't fit to eat."

"Don't be so flaming ridiculous. I know why you did it. I saw one tiny spot of red on one of the bananas."

"That's why they weren't fit to eat."

"I fear I know what your stupid answer will be but please tell me why a tiny spot of red on a banana makes the whole bunch unfit for human consumption."

"Not just humans."

"God give me strength." Sarah screamed, "What did you think the red was John?"

"It might have been blood. Contaminated blood."

"Or it might have been red marker pen."

"But you can't be sure Sarah and if it was blood the consequences could be terrible so we can't take the chance. The cost of a small bunch of bananas seems a small price to pay for avoiding contaminating Mrs Evans."

"Even if it was blood, which it wasn't, you peel a banana before you eat it so it still wouldn't be a problem."

"But it might have soaked through the banana skin."

"What and jumped onto the other four bananas and soaked through their skins as well."

"It's possible."

"No it's not possible. Why can't you see that? You drive me mad. I am trying to help you and I am proud of the progress you have made so far but then you do and say such stupid things and I don't know if I can really help you anymore."

"Or the skin might have been touched as someone was peeling the banana and then touched the banana itself, therefore passing on the contamination. Sarah wouldn't you spend £1.50 to avoid Mrs Evans becoming seriously ill?"

"Just don't say any more. I just don't want to listen to you."

"Sorry," John said very quietly.

"Maybe you are sorry, maybe you aren't," she said as she turned her back, "Don't forget you have another therapy session this afternoon. I will be back in plenty time to take you."

Sarah gathered up the dogs from the garden ready for their early afternoon walk. She was really grateful for the help Anna gave her now she was working full time for her. She didn't know how she would manage without her.

~~~~~~~~~

Watching her six charges get more and more excited at the prospect of running free over the moors brought a smile to Sarah's face. Anna's youthful company made sure she couldn't wallow in her annoyance and frustration for long.

"Anna thank you for your help," Sarah said when they were on the moors, "I don't know how I would manage without you."

"I love working here. To be honest I would do it even if you didn't pay me."

Sarah laughed at that. "Drat, why did I offer you money then?"

"I feel so trapped at home. Dad is great and I know Mum loves me but she is so controlling. She worries if her little girl goes out of her sight. It's as though she doesn't trust me. I wouldn't do anything silly, I'm sensible."

"I know you are sensible. It's only because she cares for you."

"Yes I know but I want some freedom and that's what you are giving me. It's nice to have some money I have earned, I don't feel I need to ask Mum's permission to spend it and on what. Thank you Sarah."

"It's a pleasure. I love having you around to be honest. I have been walking these moors for years and I never realised before just how much nicer it is having company, human company that is." Sarah realised that had there been someone with her on that fateful sinkhole day she would never have met John. Would that have been a good or a bad thing, only time will tell?

"Anna, Steve and Katy have invited us all to go to the beach with them on Saturday and then back to their house for a bit of tea. Do you think you will be able to come?"

"Oh yes please."

"Don't you think you had better ask your mum first?"

"No I don't. I will tell her where I am going of course, but I'm not asking her permission. I can't wait."

They walked along quietly, admiring the beauty of their surroundings and watching the dogs enjoying life without a care. A few minutes later Anna spoke again. "Aren't dogs wonderful? They just love people unconditionally and all they ask for is food, water and a walk. I wish humans were like that."

Sarah thought that was a very profound statement for someone so young.

"Sarah can I tell you something in confidence please?"

"Of course you can."

Anna hesitated awhile before continuing. "The day I found your dog's tag."

"Betty."

"Yes Betty. I told the police and my parents that I was up on the moors with some friends and we got separated."

"And that wasn't what you were doing?"

"Well technically yes but I wasn't with friends plural, I was with one friend, a boy. Mum would go mad if she knew, please don't tell her."

"Oh course I won't tell her. I promise you that anything you say to me remains secret."

"I was with a boy called Mark. I thought I liked him a lot and I also thought that he had finished with his girlfriend because he liked me but I was wrong. He took me up on the moors just to try and have sex with me. I guess that's why he took me to such a remote area, so no one would see us. I didn't let him of course but then he started saying horrible things to me and left me there alone. I knew then that he didn't care for me at all. I had no idea how to get home but he wasn't bothered about that. I waited awhile hoping that he would come back for me, but he didn't. Should I have let him do what he wanted?"

"Oh Anna, of course you shouldn't have let him. You did exactly the right thing. People like him aren't worth bothering about. One day you will meet a lovely boy who will want to be with you for all the right reasons."

"Sarah I'm scared in case he comes to find me again. My friends have told me he hates it when a girl says no and he usually gets revenge. Apparently he's used to getting his own way. If he goes to my house Mum will go ballistic. Dad won't be happy either to be honest."

"Anna you are a lovely girl. Perhaps you should tell your parents though. Come on it's time we turned this lot around and headed home."

~~~~~~~~~~

"Come on John, it's time we were going."

The drive to the therapist was completed free of any conversation. Despite her walk on the moors Sarah was still frustrated at John over the bananas and he was frightened of saying anything that may annoy her more.

In the clinic John completed the usual questionnaire. He didn't ask Sarah's opinions this time, he didn't dare. Miss Rackham, Melanie, came to the waiting room to meet him as usual and they had then both walked upstairs to her office.

She spent the first couple of minutes reading the questionnaire then looked up at John. "I see you are progressing really well."

"Yes I feel much more capable of controlling my OCD than I did when I first met you." Sarah certainly wouldn't agree with that.

"Talk me through what you have done since our last session."

"Well I am washing my hands a lot less and not throwing toilet rolls away because I have touched them so I think my cleanliness issues are much better."

~~~~~~~~~~

232

Sarah sat in the waiting room as usual. When anyone else came in she gave a courteous nod and sometimes a quiet hello but no conversations were ever struck up. She would try and work out who were patients and who weren't. It was so difficult to tell. It's not like someone having a broken leg, where their condition is obvious. No, with many mental illnesses you can't tell anything is wrong with the sufferer. They suffered inside and usually silently. She had come to learn that this was particularly so with OCD sufferers. In general they don't want people to know they have OCD therefore they become expert at covering up their illness. Only the sufferer, their immediate family and their doctor and therapist generally know.

This at times was so frustrating. Sarah felt that John would benefit from talking to more people about his problems, a problem shared is a problem halved they say, but he wouldn't. He said anyone who knew about his OCD wouldn't like him, that they would think he was weird.

"But I like you John and I know about your OCD," she would say in an attempt to convince him that his theory was incorrect.

"Yes but you are special Sarah," was all he could say. OCD and logic make very poor partners.

So John covered his illness very well indeed when other people were around. He was very careful of course not to put himself in a position that caused him too much anxiety. John insisted that no one should know except Sarah. So here she was again, sat in this waiting room waiting for a man she was growing to like very much but also a man who caused her a great deal of heartache and frustration.

Yes here she was again wondering how John was going on in his therapy session.

~~~~~~~~~~

"OK John so now you are showing some control over your cleanliness issues, from what you tell me, do you feel able and strong enough to move on to another area of your concerns now?"

"Yes I think so." Was he being too optimistic?

"I think we should move on to your confession compulsions now. Is that alright with you?"

"Yes."

233

"Why don't you tell me an example of a time you have felt you needed to confess."

John thought for a while before continuing.

"A few years ago, a year or so before my father died, my uncle came to visit us. It was very rare for him to visit but it was always nice to see him.

My uncle worked in a hospital in Birmingham, he was a consultant. Anyway one day, while my uncle was with us, he was having a telephone call with someone at the hospital. I think they were discussing a patient."

"So why did that bother you John?"

I was horrified for two reasons. First of all he was talking about the medical details of the patient and anyone in the house could have heard him. Also he had the patient's file open on the table. I could have read it, I could have taken it."

"You thought that was a problem did you? Your Uncle was in your house and obviously trusted you all. He obviously didn't think there was a problem."

"Yes, but what if he was as careless in the hospital. He could leave files lying around everywhere."

"And would that be a problem John?"

"Of course it would. Why can't you see that?"

Melanie could see that John was getting agitated but decided that she should carry on with the conversation.

"What did you think the problem was John?"

"Not what did I think, but what do I think. I still think there is a problem. I still think that something bad may happen. Criminals may use a file if they find it to gain information that would enable them to use other people's identities for criminal activities. It could be horrendous. People could end up going to jail for something they hadn't done, they could end up losing their life savings, their houses could be broken into because the criminals knew they were in hospital and if anyone was still living in the house, a partner or a child, they could be killed. It would all be my fault.

I would be responsible for their deaths. It would be like I committed murder. It would all be my fault you see. I should have contacted the hospital and confessed that I had seen the file. I should have told them to remind staff not to leave files lying around. But I did nothing."

"The chances of any of this happening are miniscule John."

"But there is a chance."

"Right John I definitely agree this is part of your OCD that we should deal with next."

Miss Rackham drew John's thoughts, obsessions and compulsions onto an OCD diagram. She went through this slowly with John before issuing the next challenge. "Here is a letter from my bank. You can see that it has my name and address on, and my card number. Please take it down stairs and leave it on the table in reception."

"I can't do that. You must understand."

"We will leave it there for five minutes and then you can go and bring it back up."

"Yes, but what if it isn't still there?"

"You can't spend your life constantly thinking of the 'what ifs'."

John was in a distressed state but did as she asked.

"It will be fine," she said.

"No it won't. Why did you ask me to do that? I need to ring your bank to tell them that you may have lost your card details. Can I use your phone please?"

"No. There is no need."

"But if I don't it will be my fault if anything bad happens."

Every one of the five minutes seemed like an hour to John. He couldn't think of anything except a criminal picking up Melanie's letter, just like his uncle's file. Why was she so careless? She was probably careless with everything. She probably didn't check that her doors were locked or that her gas was turned off properly.

Melanie observed John's increasing anxiety as the minutes passed. "Ok John times up. Let's go down and collect the letter."

John was down the stairs before Melanie had closed her office door. When she caught up with him in reception he was tightly gripping the letter.

"There you are John, the letter is still there."

"Yes, but what if someone has read the letter, written down the information and then put the letter back so you would think everything was alright."

"That won't have happened. In any case the 'criminal', as you put it, doesn't have my card so they don't know my PIN number or the security code on the back of the card. The information in the letter is useless without these things."

"But what if they have contact with someone who knew how to find those details from your card number. Someone must be able to. The police must be able to."

"So now you think that the police would help the criminal. The chances of that are miniscule John."

"But there is a chance."

"I need to go to the cash machine. It's nice and sunny out there. I'd like you to come with me please." She hoped that the walk would help to reduce his anxiety but wasn't confident that it would.

John knew that the urge to go into the bank and tell them that someone may have Melanie's bank details would be immense. He knew he should tell them. If he didn't then it would be his fault if anything bad did happen. He also knew that Melanie would never let him go into the bank."

~~~~~~~~~~

Sarah was puzzled when she saw John and his therapist walk out of the main door of the clinic. What was going on? Surely he hadn't forgotten she had brought him here.

She pondered whether to go and ask the receptionist if John had left but as she hadn't seen the therapist come back either she thought she had better wait for a while. Maybe they had gone out for lunch together, do therapist do that? Maybe she was testing John.

Sarah returned to the crossword puzzle she had been doing in a magazine she had picked up from the table where the coffee pot was. Normally she didn't pass her spare time with crosswords, what little spare time she had, but she was bored. She was always bored in this waiting room but that was a small price to pay to be able to support John in his recovery.

The crossword was one of those that had two sets of clues, cryptic and easy, or supposedly easy. Sarah did the easy option but had still been trying to work out one clue for several minutes. 1 down - 'A large seabird who likes to eat a lot' – 6 letters. She knew the third letter was an 'N' from the answer to 4 across.

Before she got the answer she heard the door to the clinic open and saw John, in a rather distressed state, come back in with his therapist walking behind him. She wondered what had happened and was really worried about how John appeared. Melanie Rackham said goodbye to John. His time was up so no matter how distressed John was the therapist had to move on to her next client.

John looked down at the floor all the time and didn't acknowledge Sarah. He just stood there in the reception area appearing to gaze into an empty space. Sarah could see him through the glass door, should she go to him or was his therapist coming back. John didn't move. He didn't enter the waiting room or signal through the glass that he was ready to go.

Sarah couldn't wait there any longer. She had to go and find out what was happening and how John was. She was very apprehensive.

"Have you finished your session John?" she nervously said.

"Yes."

"Are you alright?"

"Yes."

His monotone single word answers were not a good sign.

They walked back to Sarah's car in silence. She drove to the local McDonalds as usual. They had been to McDonalds after each session so far. It was Sarah's treat for John for the effort he was putting in, like treating a child for trying hard at school. Sarah's parents hadn't done that for her of course but the other children used to tell her about their 'rewards'. It had been John's idea after his first session and Sarah had been happy to go along with it. They always used the drive through and then sat on the car park to eat their meal, usually fillet of fish with a bottle of water for Sarah and a milk shake for John. John didn't want to eat inside and Sarah never asked why. The answer would only be another crazy OCD reason and she had heard enough of those already.

As Sarah pulled into the McDonalds car park John quietly said "Not today."

"What?"

"Not today, please take me home."

"John, just what went on in your session?"

"Not now Sarah. I want to go home." By home he of course meant Sarah's house. He hadn't mentioned returning to his own house even once since he moved in with Sarah. She often wondered if she would ever return to living alone but for now she was prepared to let things stay as they were – for John's sake.

Sarah did as John asked. The journey home was tense with a very heavy atmosphere.

Once inside her kitchen she knew she had to ask again what had gone on. She didn't like seeing John like this.

"What went on today John? Please tell me, I'm worried about you."

"I'm not going again," was the bombshell he dropped.

Sarah went to her bedroom and cried. She knew she couldn't take much more.

Chapter 41

The day after his therapy session John had calmed down enough to tell Sarah everything, including why he had made the decision not to go again.

"I just couldn't do what she asked me to do Sarah," he said, "It was too far too soon. I was frightened that if I did use her bank card my anxiety would go sky high, which in turn could trigger my depression again. I would rather die than have to try and deal with depression again. The therapist said she thought I had suffered from depression after my parents had died judging from how I told her I felt then. It was horrible Sarah, I don't want to feel like that again."

"I do understand, I think."

"No you don't," he snapped, "You have absolutely no idea how bad having OCD is. It is with me 24 hours a day, 365 days a year. And before you crack a joke about me getting one day's relief on the 366th day of a leap year just don't."

"I wouldn't do that John and you know I wouldn't."

"I don't know what I am thinking anymore. Are my thoughts real or just my OCD, I can never be sure? I am so tired, so weary. I'm not sure I want to go on."

"You mean go on with your therapy."

"No, with life."

"Please don't say that John." A surprising bolt of panic shot through her that caught her off guard. She realised at that point that she would really miss him if he wasn't here.

"Do you know what I would give to have just one worry free hour? No of course you don't, how can you know? I can't expect you to know. No one who hasn't got OCD can possibly know." Sarah could see the tears in his eyes and his trembling chin as clearly as she could hear the cracks in his voice.

"I am trying to understand but I am sure you are suffering much more than I can ever imagine. It's not easy for me either."

"I know you get frustrated but your suffering is not in the same league as the torment I have to deal with. I'm never allowed to be happy, I don't know what it's like to have fun. Would you like to swop with me for a day?

"I'm sorry Sarah, I should never have said that. I wouldn't want you, or anyone for that matter, to go through what I go through constantly."

Sarah felt desperately sorry for John. She put her arms around him and gave him a comforting hug. John felt so low and so emotional that he accepted but didn't reciprocate the hug. He was scared of the contamination the hug could lead to but he needed it right now.

After a brief time he pushed Sarah away.

"Don't Sarah, you might become contaminated."

She wondered if they had actually made any progress at all.

"John why are you not going to therapy anymore?"

"Because I don't agree with the way she is doing things. It's not right for me."

"Do you remember the two questions I asked you in the police station? You promised me you would do what the medical experts told you to do."

"I will."

"But you're not."

"I will when I find the right medical expert."

"Right in whose opinion? Yours?"

"Yes."

"Where are you going to find this expert?"

"The NHS."

"But that will take at least three months before you are able to see someone. What are you going to do in the meantime?"

"That's fine. I will make an appointment with my doctor on Monday morning, I should be able to see him next week sometime, to set the process rolling. In the meantime I would like you to set me challenges every day. Will you do that for me please?"

"Of course I will try but how am I going to think up so many new challenges? I'm really just here to hold your hand and support you, not to treat you. Sometimes you expect too much of me."

"I am sure you will do a great job."

His comment made Sarah's blood boil. He had lived with her rent free for about two months now, using her food, her electricity, her gas, her telephone, her everything and now he expected her to be his therapist as well. She decided now was the time he had to start contributing.

She took her time to calm down a little before she spoke again.

"John I've been thinking."

"What about?"

"I think you should get a part time job. I think it would do you good to be forced to cope in a different environment with people who would just know you as John, not John the OCD sufferer. I would also like you to contribute some of your wages to the cost of you living here. I don't earn much money with my doggy day care business, not enough to support two of us."

John burst into tears. Sarah was shocked.

"What's the matter John? I'm sorry. What have I done?"

"You've done nothing except make me realise what pressure all this is putting on you."

"Oh it's ok, I just feel particularly down today."

"No it's not ok Sarah. It's not ok at all. Since you met me your life has been horrible and it's all my fault. I think it would be better if I went away. Out of your life for ever and then you can get on with a normal life."

Sarah fought away the tears that were threatening to flood down her cheeks. She couldn't, wouldn't let John go. She thought too much of him to let him go out into the world to battle his demons alone.

"I'll go and pack now. Thank you for all the things you've done for me. I really do appreciate what you do for me, although I know I don't show it. I have spent so many years hiding my emotions that I find it hard now to be open about anything. I am so sorry for everything I have put you through. I'll be out of your life in a few minutes, it's for the best."

Sarah could tell that he really meant what he was saying. He wasn't saying it for attention or sympathy.

'Sarah say something', she screamed in her head, 'Make him stay.'

Tears rolling down her cheeks she looked directly at John's face and said very quietly, "Please don't go – I'm begging you, for my sake."

"For your sake. What do you mean? Your life as changed dramatically since you met me and all the change is bad, very bad. Why on earth are you begging me to stay? I'm confused."

Sarah didn't respond. After a few minutes John asked again, "Why do you want me to stay?"

"Because I'm not a quitter. I said I would help you and I meant it. I really want you to get better. I couldn't stand you being out there somewhere and not knowing what was happening to you, not knowing whether you were alive or dead. If anything happened to you it would be my fault."

This last comment shocked John. He realised that it wasn't just him shouldering the responsibility for everything. It wasn't just him responsible for the whole world.

"......... and because I have grown to like you very much," Sarah said very quietly.

John wasn't sure if he was really hearing this correctly but he certainly didn't want to ask her to repeat it, he liked what he had heard. Someone cared for him. He was scared that it was just his OCD playing tricks on his mind again.

"Will you please stay John? Together we can get through this. Please don't push me away."

This time it was John who gave Sarah a hug but she noticed he kept his hands turned outward to avoid his palms touching her.

Chapter 42

Saturday arrived with no further major traumas. Sarah was pleased to see that the weather was fine, she was really looking forward to the short term relief that the day out would bring. She wished Betty was still here, she would have loved the beach. It was really kind of Katy and Steve to arrange this she thought.

She had agreed to share the picnic making so set about boiling the eggs for egg mayonnaise sandwiches and slicing the ham and corned beef. The next task was to wash the salad.

"Good morning Sarah," John said as he entered the kitchen, "Let me do that," he said as he took the salad drainer from her. She was shocked, but delighted.

"And good day to you too kind Sir." They both laughed.

"I'm really looking forward to today," John said as he chopped the lettuce into small pieces.

Sarah pinched herself to make sure this wasn't just a dream.

When he had finished the salad he asked, "Is there anything else I can do for you?"

"Not really. There is only the eggs mayonnaise sandwiches to make now when the eggs have boiled."

"Right you go and sit over there, I'll make a brew and while you are drinking it I will make the egg mayo."

Sarah smiled. It was so nice to see John so upbeat. Sadly she was under no illusion that it would last for more than a few hours, if that. She only hoped he wouldn't suddenly snatch the egg mayo sandwiches out of people's mouths when he remembered he had made them. Nothing could be certain with John. One minute he could be fine and then, as if a switch had been flicked, he changed. It was like walking on a knife edge all the time.

"What time are we going Sarah?"

"Anna is coming here about 10am and then we will set off as soon as Steve and Katy get here. As my van only has two seats Anna and Ellen are going in Steve's car." Sarah felt it would be better if John travelled with her, just in case.

"Here you are Mrs Evans sit on this chair."

"I'll never get out of that again Steve."

"Don't worry we'll get a crane if we can't get you up again."

"Don't you be so cheeky? Here give me your hand." Steve got hold of both of Ellen's hands and eased her down into one of the folding chairs they had brought with them.

"Steady Mrs Evans. Slowly does it. Nearly there."

Just as Ellen's weight hit the chair it sank into the soft sand. Both chair and Ellen fell over backwards. The smiles disappeared from everyone's faces, they were all concerned for Ellen's safety.

They needn't have worried. There she was on her back, legs in the air, bloomers in full view, laughing her head off.

"It's a long time since I lay on my back and opened my legs for a man Steve," she said.

"Ellen!" Sarah said sternly, "We have a youngster with us."

"Sorry Anna," said Mrs E, "Now you two strong men lift me up again, and make sure the chair is safe this time."

With the seating of Mrs E successfully achieved they opened up the other chairs and all sat down, very cautiously.

"I'm taking Cuddles to the sea," Steve said, "Anyone coming with me?"

"Yes please," said Anna and surprisingly so did John.

"That's great. We'll leave the three old ladies here for a good old natter."

"Less of your old," said Ellen.

Steve, John, Anna and Cuddles walked to the sea which was a long way out today. Cuddles ran between his three human friends time and time again begging for their attention, he was having a whale of a time. Eventually they reached the sea and Steve threw a tennis ball into the water for Cuddles to fetch.

"Is he alright going into the sea?" John asked, "Will the water not make him sick?"

"No he'll be fine John."

"Don't throw the ball too far in. You don't want him to drown."

"Don't worry, I won't. Katy would throw me out if anything happened to Cuddles."

John was conscious of the worries going round in his head, only two of which he had voiced so far. He needed to control himself, he was doing so well. He needed to try and behave normally, well as normally as he could.

"I wish I had brought my dog," Anna said, "but I thought he may have been a bit too big and boisterous for Cuddles. He's a bit mad and just charges through anything in his way as if it wasn't there."

"You should have brought him," said Steve. "Cuddles can look after himself. In fact he would probably have bullied your dog."

They stayed at the edge of the sea for over half an hour. Steve was reluctant to drag Cuddles away and Anna and John for that matter. All four of them were having a great time but they were beginning to feel hungry.

John found it hard to admit it but he was really enjoying himself. He couldn't tell them he was enjoying himself though so he quickly supressed the thought. If he was enjoying something, or looking forward to something, his OCD usually gave him a worry of such magnitude that he couldn't enjoy whatever it was. He felt sure that something would happen today if he allowed himself to enjoy the day so it was better not to. He wasn't safe, his OCD could attack at any time.

When they had almost made it back to the ladies Cuddles started running back to Sarah. "Aren't you worried he may run off Steve," John asked.

"Absolutely not. He knows which side his bread is buttered."

By the time they reached the ladies Cuddles was lay by Katy's feet, exhausted.

"Well you two have obviously been riveting company," Steve said, "Look at Mrs E."

Mrs E was fast asleep, her mouth wide open, snoring softly. Steve got his handkerchief out of his trouser pocket and rolled it tightly up.

"No," shouted Katy, "Don't you dare."

"Dare what," asked John.

"He was going to tickle Ellen's nose with the tip of his handkerchief John. You could give her a heart attack Steve," she added

"No I wouldn't. She's a tough old boot."

Just then Mrs Evans woke suddenly, as though something had startled her. She certainly startled everyone else.

"Oh my goodness Ellen you gave us all a fright."

"Who wants a fight?"

"No Mrs E, I said fright."

"No I've never been on a flight. Have you?"

"Ellen is your hearing aid alright?"

"Pardon."

"HEARING AID," Sarah shouted as she pointed to her ear.

Ellen felt in her pockets and pulled out two hearing aids. She put them carefully in her ears.

"What on earth are your hearing aids doing in your pocket?" Sarah asked.

"Well when the boys, and Anna of course, had gone to the sea you two were making so much racket nattering that I couldn't get to sleep. I took my hearing aids out and then I dropped off in no time."

"Why didn't you join in our conversation?"

"Because you were talking a load of twaddle."

"Nothing new there then," Steve said.

"Time for lunch?" Sarah asked.

"Yes please," they all shouted.

Sarah and Katy rolled out the blanket they had brought on the sand and then laid out the boxes and bags that contained the various delights. Between them they had put on a great spread everyone agreed.

"What would you like Ellen," Sarah asked, "There's egg mayonnaise, ham and corned beef."

"I don't want corned beef. I had enough of that in the war to last me a lifetime, when we couldn't get much fresh meat. Egg mayonnaise gives me wind so I'll have ham please."

Cuddles sat patiently looking to see who would be most likely to give him the next titbit. He selected his target and went to sit in front of them looking up with his pleading eyes, eyes he knew no one could resist.

"He behaves very nicely when food is around," John said.

"That's all down to Sarah's training. She's kind but tough as I'm sure you have found out. We are too soft with Cuddles, he knows he can get away with murder when he is at home."

"Whose been murdered?" Mrs E asked.

"No one Ellen. Go back to eating your lunch," Sarah shouted to her.

They sat there eating, talking and listening to the distant sound of the sea and the noise of the gulls flying overhead. Then it happened. Plop! Right on John's nose, the biggest Seagull poo you have ever seen. A sloppy one that ran down his nose and on to his top lip. Everyone except Sarah began to laugh but soon stopped when John seemed to panic and ran off in the direction of the public toilets.

"Oh no," Sarah said very quietly under her breath, "not now, not here. Why does this have to happen to John of all people?"

She feared the worst. She knew John would be in the toilets now scrubbing his nose with all his might to try and get every bit of poo off, to eliminate every molecule of potential contamination.

"Is John alright?" Katy asked.

"Yes I'm sure he will be fine," Sarah replied. "He hates being dirty, that's all."

Fifteen minutes later John hadn't returned.

"I'll go and see if I can find John," Sarah said.

She found him fairly quickly, sat on a bench by the bowling greens.

"John are you alright. It was only bird poo. The seagulls do that to loads of people every day."

"It was my OCD. I was enjoying myself so my OCD had to stop me having fun. It always does."

"It wasn't your OCD at all. It was just an accident."

"No Sarah, trust me it was my OCD. It rules my life. I know that my OCD didn't remotely control the seagull so it flew right over me and dropped its load but it did determine that something bad would happen. It always does. It is possible that I may catch bird flu now."

Sarah could see that John was extremely anxious and clearly suffering from emotional toil. She knew it was pointless, indeed maybe even heartless, to argue against his latest worry, at least for now.

"You were doing really well today John. Don't let this spoil it."

"I have no choice. OCD is the boss."

Sarah took her phone out of her pocket and dialled Katy's number.

"Hi Sarah. Did you find John?"

"Yes but I'm ringing to tell you we are going home now. I presume you are happy to take Anna home and make sure Ellen is safely in her house when you get back."

"Yes of course. Is there anything else we can do?"

"I'm afraid not. I'm sorry I can't help to tidy up the food containers."

"That's no problem. Take care."

"Come on John, let's go home."

John looked up at her through the saddest eyes she had ever seen. She was gutted for him. He had tried so hard today but in the end his OCD had won.

"Damn you OCD, I am determined to beat you" Sarah whispered.

Chapter 43

Following the trip to the beach, life for Sarah and John fell into a bland routine. Sarah would always be up first and after a quick breakfast she would go and collect her canine clients for the day from their homes. By the time she returned home Anna would have arrived and be chatting to John at the kitchen table.

The dogs would then be taken on their morning walks by Anna and Sarah. John was always invited to join them but never did. Sarah really enjoyed the walks, it was the only relief she got from John, relief that was very necessary for her sanity. She had never felt such a mix of emotions over one person. It was like a whirlwind in her heart and head.

Lunch was always a snack affair, outside if it was nice weather, in the kitchen if it wasn't. John always joined them for lunch but the vast majority of the conversation took place between Sarah and Anna, John rarely offering any input.

The afternoon walks completed all too soon, in Sarah's opinion, it was time to take the dogs, and Anna, home. Then came the part of the day that Sarah dreaded now.

John sat listening to the radio for hours on end. It seemed to be almost all he did now. Since his therapy ended he had regressed with the management of his OCD. He was still better then when Sarah first met him but not as good as he had achieved. When she dared to broach the subject his response was always the same. "I need you to issue me with challenges every day. If you don't I have nothing to aim for." It was always her fault not his. She had issued him with challenges, like not checking the doors more than once when he went out. Some days he would do it, some days he wouldn't. Sarah couldn't understand why this was. To think of different challenges every day was impossible. She had seen him progress well in some aspects of his OCD but then not keep his success up. It was as though, at best, he had hit a plateau and had become comfortable with where he was or, at worst, he had given up. Sarah often wondered if his OCD was his equivalent of a comfort blanket. If his

OCD was telling him what to do he wasn't to blame or didn't need to take responsibility for deciding himself what to do.

Sarah tried to convince John that much of his OCD had become a habit, just like smoking. If he really wanted to he could manage it much better but like a smoker who gives up smoking it just takes one little thing to go wrong and the cigarette packet comes out again. She realised that being a habit made it more difficult for John to stop doing his compulsions. He completed them automatically almost without realising he was doing them.

The evenings were spent largely in silence. Like two strangers sharing a house. Occasionally Sarah would try and strike up a conversation of sorts but always the subject was one that John really didn't want to address. Subjects that annoyed him when Sarah dared to bring them up.

"John can I ask you something without you getting annoyed?"

"Of course you can." That wasn't exactly true. What he should have said was 'of course you can as long as you only say things I want to hear'.

"Do you really want to beat your OCD?"

"Of course I do," he snapped in reply.

"You seem to have given up trying. That's why I ask."

"Give me an example." Everything had to be proved to John.

"Remember when you first moved in here you only paid for things in the shops with notes. You said that as notes were in circulation for a much shorter period of time and they tended to be kept in wallets and not pockets they were much less likely to be contaminated than coins. You wouldn't use coins in case the person you gave them to became contaminated and then the coin would be given in change and the recipient would become contaminated and so on until, in your mind, half the population was doomed. Remember how I used to find huge piles of coins in your bedroom, on the window sill, on the floor?

You worked hard and started to use coins without thinking about it, just like the rest of us. I was really proud of you. I know it wasn't easy for you but the more you paid with coins the easier it became."

"Yes I remember. It was good."

"Then why have you gone right back to how you used to be? I cleaned your room last Saturday and there were piles of coins everywhere."

"I don't know. I think it's because I need someone to be pushing me all the time, I can't do it on my own. I have no therapist at the moment so it's harder to improve."

"We're not talking of improving, I am just talking about you maintaining the level you had worked so hard to achieve."

"I'll try hard again, I promise."

"I know you will."

She knew John had the ability to manage his OCD much better, if only he wanted to and he had the determination to battle on. His life would be so much better if only he could get through the pain he would inevitably face on the journey. She was sure he understood this.

Another evening she decided to approach the subject of jobs. Sarah was very nervous approaching any subject, not knowing how he would react. She was as certain as she could be that he wouldn't react aggressively, that wasn't in his nature, but he may get upset or defensive.

"There is a job here in the paper that may be good for you," she said one evening, "Have you seen it?" Sarah never used to get a newspaper but had started to have one delivered for John to read.

"Which job?" His tone wasn't encouraging.

John still wasn't working although he was helping out financially from his savings. It wasn't as though he hadn't had the opportunity to work, he had actually been offered two jobs and accepted them. In both cases though within a couple of days of being due to start work he had contacted the company to inform them that he couldn't work for them after all. He told them he had had a better offer. That in turn caused him a lot of anxiety because he had told a lie.

There was the job at the tourist information office. Sarah thought that it would have been ideal. He would be meeting the public and would have so much to occupy his mind, leaving less time for the OCD to attack, but the OCD won in the end. It had told John that if he took the job his deal with the devil would be activated and Sarah would suffer greatly, most likely she would die. John had to give the job up.

The same happened with the job delivering the local free newspaper. John was really looking forward to that one. He liked the idea that he would be on his own a lot of the time but would also have the opportunity to meet people. The devil said 'NO!' according to his OCD.

John was very frustrated, he believed that there were no jobs his OCD would allow him to do.

Sarah thought the job she had seen in today's newspaper would be ideal, if only he could stop his OCD putting a spanner in the works. The local steam railway wanted someone to collect tickets on the trains they ran each weekend. The fact that it was a weekend job really appealed to Sarah as it would give her some time alone, no dogs, no John at least two days a week. She had forgotten what it was like to be truly alone but she knew it was something that would be good for her.

John read the job and really seemed interested. Whilst his interest increased so did his anxiety. He knew his OCD would place thoughts in his mind that may lead him to having to refuse the job if he was offered it.

"My grandfather used to drive steam trains," he informed Sarah, "I will ring them in the morning."

Sarah wouldn't count her chickens before she actually saw him on the platform wearing his uniform. Nothing could be guaranteed until then. Even then no one knew how long his OCD would allow him to work there.

Sarah was living on her nerves all the time. Frightened of saying the wrong thing, frightened of doing something the wrong way. Words and actions that John could interpret incorrectly, to suit his point of view. She knew that John didn't have a violent tendency at all, quite the opposite, but riding the emotional rollercoaster they were both on had an awful effect on her nerves. Would the ride ever end, she had no idea but she prayed it would.

There was still no sign of a letter giving him an appointment with an NHS therapist but surely one should arrive soon.

There had been no more outings with Steve and Katy. John believed that they would hate him after the day at the beach therefore he said no to anything that was suggested. Sarah was left to make up an excuse, an excuse that could never include the letters OCD.

Sarah was tired both emotionally and physically, not that John noticed. His illness didn't give him time to notice. She desperately wanted to talk to someone about John but he didn't want anyone to know. She was weary from bottling all this up inside and pretending to everyone that life was good. She decided at that point that she was going to talk to someone. It couldn't be Mrs Evans of course but she knew who it could be.

Chapter 44

Life with OCD was like a rollercoaster. Full of ups and downs and twists and turns. You knew to cherish the better times, better but never good, as you never knew how long they would last.

Last night had been very tense. It was Friday evening, they had been sat in the living room, John listening to the radio and Sarah looking forward to her weekend, well as much as she ever looked forward to anything these days.

Suddenly John broke the silence, a rare event indeed.

"Did I kill Christine?" he asked.

Sarah was stunned. "No of course not."

"But I might have."

"You said she got a rash and that was what killed her. From what you said it sounds to me like meningitis. You said she died really quickly after getting the rash and that's what happens with meningitis."

"But could I have given her the meningitis?"

"No John you couldn't." She decided not to expand. She knew that meningitis could be contagious through coughs, sneezes and kissing as well as sharing toothbrushes and similar items but she sure as hell wasn't going to tell John that.

"I have always been worried that in some way I caused her death. Are you sure I couldn't have?"

"I'm absolutely certain John. You didn't get a rash did you so you couldn't have given it to Christine." Sometimes little lies were justified, and in this case they definitely were.

"John do you think that is when your OCD started?"

"I don't know but it might be."

"Did you like Christine?"

"I loved her more than anything. She's the only person I have felt so much love for."

"Then why don't you do something in Christine's memory. Something to show that you still love her." Sarah stopped short of saying 'I'm sure she still watches over you' because that might trigger the religious spectrum of John's OCD.

"Like what? Plant a tree?"

"No something much better than that. Show your OCD that you are the boss. That you are not going to listen to its nonsense anymore."

"Do you think Christine will like that?"

"I'm certain she will. What better reason can you have for beating your OCD? To do it in memory of your little sister."

"I will." Sarah knew he meant it but wasn't sure he could do it.

~~~~~~~~~~~

The weekend was really good. John had actually started his job on the steam train and his NHS appointment letter arrived. Sarah had never seen John so relaxed since the morning of the beach trip but look how that had ended! She had learnt never to relax too much, always to be alert for the next bombshell.

"How was the job today," Sarah asked when John came home.

"It was really good." This was a great sign, John never usually went beyond 'it was ok'.

"I've been really busy, there were loads of people on today," he added, "I even got to ride on the footplate on one trip. It was exhilarating but wow it was so noisy. You couldn't hear yourself think."

Sarah thought that was a good thing in John's case.

"What did you do?"

"I did a spell in the ticket office, some time on the platform oh and I served in the café."

John had served people with food and given them change. 'Please Lord let this last," Sarah whispered to herself.

"A letter came this morning just after you had gone out. I think it will be your therapy appointment. It's on' the worktop near the microwave."

John got the letter and eagerly opened it.

"I've got an appointment next Tuesday at 3pm at the clinic in town."

"That's great John."

"I know that's not a good time for you but I'll catch the bus. I will do it for Christine."

Sarah smiled. How wonderful to see John so upbeat.

"Let's go out for tea tonight Sarah. I'll spend my first day's wage on a treat for us."

"Are you sure?"

"Yes I'm sure. Why don't you ring Steve and Katy and see if they would like to come. It's only 4pm so presumably they won't have eaten yet. Mrs E could come too, and what about Anna? It's time I apologised for my behaviour at the beach."

"If you are absolutely sure, it would be good to get out."

If she didn't know better Sarah would have thought John had sent his twin brother home instead of himself. Except he didn't have a twin brother.

~~~~~~~~~~

By 8pm they were all sat around a table at the Green Man, a lovely pub in the village. It was incredibly busy but they were sat in the corner by the window, out of the main hustle and bustle, in their own little oasis.

"Hey John how was the job on the steam train today," Katy asked.

"Oh it was great. I really loved it."

"Which steam train is that John?" asked Anna.

"The Valley Railway."

"I'm going on that tomorrow with some friends from college. Will you be there?"

"Yep I'll be there. If you come in the café I'll give you any extra squirt of cream on your hot chocolate."

"Don't go mad John will you," Steve said sarcastically.

John was amazed that everyone still seemed to like him. No one had mentioned the disastrous trip to the beach. He couldn't understand why no one had asked what had happened that day. Little did he know that they had all been warned by Sarah not to mention it. She had told them simply that John was embarrassed about dashing off in the way he did. She didn't want his happiness shattered. One wrong word and this evening could become another disaster.

"Right what's everyone having to eat?" John asked, "By the way tonight is my treat. It's my way of saying thank you for your friendship and your help."

"No you can't do that," said Anna, a sentiment that was echoed by everyone else.

"No arguing. I'm paying. No ordering champagne mind you or you'll all be washing up to pay the bill."

"Champagne. I love champagne. We had some on VE Day, it made me giddy. Mind you I was held up by a gorgeous American GI before I passed out."

"Oh Ellen, what are we going to do with you?" John said.

"Are you ready to order?" the young waitress asked.

"I think so," replied John, "Ladies first. That way we'll get a nice rest from nagging while they decide what to have."

"Very true," agreed Steve.

"We'll ignore that," said Katy.

Sarah was so delighted to see John like this that she even dared to relax a little, partly helped by the red wine. She didn't need to worry about driving for once as the pub was in walking distance of home. A long walk but walking distance nevertheless.

"What are you eating Katy," Ellen asked.

"Chicken Madras."

"Oh I'm not having any of that foreign stuff, give me ham, egg and chips anytime. Yours looks like the dog's been sick."

"Thank you Ellen. I was enjoying it until you said that."

"Only saying what I think." Sarah had noticed that the older Ellen had got the more she spoke her mind no matter who could hear.

"Ellen do you remember that time in the shopping centre when we were sat listening to those two men playing guitar and singing?"

"No. I can't even remember what I had for dinner most days but I don't mind anymore."

Sarah related the story to everyone else.

"I had taken Ellen on a trip to the shopping centre one day. She needed a few items and I thought it would be a nice day out for her."

"I remember now. I needed some big knickers. I don't know how you youngsters can wear those G Springs."

"G Strings," Anna corrected her.

"Tell me dear, don't they get up your…."

"Ellen – enough!" Sarah said quickly to avoid any embarrassment for Anna in particular. Plus she was worried about the whole pub turning to look at them. Ellen certainly didn't need a microphone to be heard.

"Anyway," Sarah continued. "We sat at a little café in the rotunda having a coffee and listening to these guys sing. They were really good. They started to sing 'My Way' and after just a few bars madam here said, at the top of her voice, 'They're murdering that song. They're rubbish.' I have never been so embarrassed in my life."

"Well it was true. I was only saying what everyone thought but daren't say."

"They were good Ellen."

"My dear have you ever thought of getting hearing aids." Everyone had a good laugh at this story.

They talked and ate and drank through a fantastic evening. Before they knew it, it was nearly midnight.

"We'd better be going soon," Sarah said, "We are the only people left in here and you have to go to work tomorrow John. We'll walk you home Anna on our way."

"That's out of your way. I'll be fine on my own."

"Not a chance young lady," John said.

'Caring John', Sarah thought.

"Thank you so much for dinner John," everyone said.

"It's a pleasure. Thank you for a fantastic evening, I've really enjoyed it. We must do it again soon."

Sarah hoped for another good day tomorrow.

~~~~~~~~~~

John had gone to work before Sarah got up. She had allowed herself a lie in, partly fuelled by the red wine she had drunk last night. She knew John would have been ok this morning because he had only had one alcoholic drink. He told her later that alcohol has an effect on his OCD, it makes everything worse, especially with his medication as well.

She had a lazy day. No dogs, no John, just a massive hang over.

She felt someone shaking her.

258

"Are you OK Sarah?"

"Y-Yes I'm fine," she said drowsily, "I must have dozed off for a few minutes. Why are you home early?"

"I'm not. Its 4:30"

"Oh my goodness, I've been asleep for hours."

"It will do you good, especially that head of yours."

"I don't know what you mean."

"I think you do. There was young Anna drinking very sensibly and you more mature ladies putting it down your neck as though there was going to be a world shortage of wine."

"Anna is too young to drink. Oh shit, what will her mother say?"

"Not true. If you're 16 or 17 and accompanied by an adult, you can drink, but not buy, beer, wine or cider with a meal. She had one half of lager so she was fine."

"Who is the lawyer all of a sudden?"

"I listen to the radio. You find all sorts out that way. Not just what the latest drama is in EastEnders."

"Ha, ha. Anyway how was work today? You still seem chirpy."

"It was ok."

The alarm bells sounded in Sarah's head. 'OK', just 'OK'. What happened to 'Really Good'?

She didn't ask anymore. She daren't ask anymore. She wanted John to stay positive for his therapy on Tuesday.

"You sit down Sarah. You look like death warmed up. I'll make tea."

She didn't argue.

John made a very nice pork steak with roasted vegetables. It was delicious. His culinary skills were both improving and widening."

"It's Anna's last full time week with me this next week. After that she goes back to college. She has offered to still help in the evening but I am worried that it might harm her college work, and I don't want that. I don't want to hurt her by telling her not to come again, after all she has been a godsend over summer, but her college work is her future. I don't know what to do."

"Be honest with her. Why don't you tell her that you are delighted for her to continue working in the evenings but that you have concerns for her studies? Let her know that if she finds it a problem at all she should tell you straight away and that you will give her as much time off as she needs. That way she gets the best of both worlds, she still has a job but can take time off to do college work when she needs to."

"That sounds great but what about me? I am really going to miss her help. I don't know how I am going to cope on my own again."

"You won't be alone. I will help you in the morning and on any evening that Anna can't be here."

'What a nice man John is', she thought.

"Thank you. That would be a big help if you don't mind."

"It's the least I can do after all you have done for me."

John did the washing up after they had finished tea. He then took a coffee through to the lounge for Sarah and a tea for himself. John would like to try coffee but his therapist said that it wasn't a sensible drink for an OCD sufferer. Caffeine tends to have an adverse effect on their anxiety levels. He was told that even decaffeinated coffee could still have a bad effect.

For once they both decided to watch the same program on television but soon Sarah was nodding off again.

"Why don't you go to bed Sarah? I'm going myself soon, all this working takes it out of you."

"You've only been playing at trains," she joked.

"It's a huge responsibility keeping everything on track."

"Oh very funny," she groaned. John had a good sense of humour Sarah thought, at least on the very rare occasions his OCD would give him a break, so he was chirpy enough to use it on this occasion.

"OK you go up and use the bathroom first John while I tidy up a bit down here."

"I'll tidy up Sarah."

"No you have done more than enough. I'll do this, it will only take me a couple of minutes."

"Goodnight Sarah," John said as he gave her a little kiss on the cheek.

"Goodnight to you too. See you tomorrow." She was stunned by his show of affection but she didn't dislike it.

Sarah quickly tidied the living room. She hated coming down to a mess in the morning. She was just about to go upstairs when her phone vibrated in her pocket. She got the phone out and looked at the number on the screen. It wasn't one she recognised. She cautiously pressed to answer the call, phone calls so late at night usually mean trouble.

"Hello."

"Hello is that Sarah?"

"Yes."

"It's Judith, Anna's mother. We met when you came to our house."

"Yes I remember. How are you?"

"I'm fine but I'm afraid Anna won't be into work tomorrow."

"Oh is something wrong?"

"She's in hospital. Didn't your friend John tell you?"

"No he hasn't said anything."

"Well I suggest you ask him what happened today. I must go now, I'm sat by Anna's bed. Goodnight."

Mrs Hudson ended the call.

"What the hell has he done now?" Sarah said quietly.

It had been a good weekend – until now.

Chapter 45

The late night phone call didn't aid a good night's sleep. Sarah tossed and turned wondering what John had done. Surely he hadn't hurt Anna. He wouldn't would he? If it had been something good surely Judith would have told her the details.

"Good morning Ellen," Sarah said cheerfully on the first of her multiple visits that day. She was surprised, and a little alarmed to find her still in bed. "Are you ok?"

"I'm not too bright this morning Sarah. I feel a bit shivery and my head is mussy. I'll be fine though, it's just a little chill I suppose."

"Maybe but you can't be too careful. I'll ring your doctor and see if he will call round on you. I'll also get John to pop in and see how you are from time to time, it's his day off today. I'll make sure he is definitely here when the doctor comes. Unfortunately Anna isn't well today either, otherwise she would have walked the dogs and I could have stayed with you."

"Oh stop making such a fuss my dear. I'll just stay in bed a bit longer to sleep it off then I'll be fine. How are you and that young man of yours getting along? You make a lovely couple."

"Don't go there Mrs E. We are just friends."

"But you really like him don't you? I can see it in your eyes."

"Some days I like him, some days he really frustrates me."

"If he is going to make an honest woman of you you'd better get a move on before I pop my clogs. I want to wear my hat one more time before I go."

"We are just friends Mrs E and you aren't going anywhere. Now let's change the subject. Can I tempt you to eat something?"

"Just a cup of tea please. I'll eat later."

"OK I'm not going to force you. Keep yourself warm and I'll come again as soon as I finish the morning walks."

~~~~~~~~~

When she got back home Sarah quickly phoned the doctor's surgery. The receptionist said one of the doctors, she wasn't sure who it would be yet, would call on Mrs Evans after morning surgery, about 11:30am.

"Damn I'm not likely to be back by then."

She wrote John a note explaining about Ellen not being well and asking him to keep an eye on her, and to be there when the doctor came. Then she set off to collect her 'friends' for today. She looked after a couple of dogs every working day, the rest coming for one, two or three days a week.

Her work was a joy, not a chore. She loved looking after dogs and relished a challenge. Her approach was firm but fair. Her favourite canine at the moment was Jaguar the 2 year old black Labrador. When he first started with Sarah a year ago he was a boisterous big mischievous lovable rogue, nothing was safe near him, especially food, clothes and shoes. Gradually she had managed to turn him into a well behaved and trustworthy, not to mention handsome, dog. In fact he behaved much better for Sarah than he did for his owner, he knew he could wrap his owner round his little paw. For example he played nicely with Sarah's cats but nearly pulled his owner over trying to catch any cat he saw when he was at home.

Anna's bubbly character was missed today, even the dogs seemed more subdued. There was too much time to dwell on what John may have done the day before. The more she thought about it the more fanciful were her ideas.

"Oh my goodness I'm behaving as though I have OCD now." she shouted to the dogs. There were a couple of woofs in reply.

The walk took a longer route today than normal, Sarah had no desire to get back home, no desire to face John and ask what he had done. She saw John's farm in the distance and wondered if he would ever want to go back there. Instead of turning round when she had circumnavigated the reservoir, as she usually did, this morning she turned 90 degrees to the right and walked until she came to the stream that meandered across the moors. She sat for a while on the grass by the stream whilst the dogs splashed about in the water.

After half an hour of sitting there Sarah decided that she really must get back, partly because she didn't want to over tire the dogs but also because she wanted to check on Mrs Evans. She knew she would still be about an hour later back from this morning walk than was usually the case.

As Sarah drove through the centre of the village on her way home she had to stop to let an ambulance, blue lights flashing, go through. 'I hope whoever it is will be alright', she thought.

When she went into her house John was sat at the kitchen table looking very subdued. She knew immediately something was wrong, but what?

"What's the matter John? What's wrong?"

"It's Mrs Evans. They have taken her to the hospital. The doctor thinks she has pneumonia."

"I need to go and see her. Can you watch the dogs please until I get back? There's only three today and they are quiet ones. They've had a very long walk so should sleep for perhaps a couple of hours."

"Of course I will look after them but would they be alright on their own for an hour or so? I'd like to come with you."

"Yes I imagine they would but what if I am longer than an hour?"

"Then I'll drive back here to look after them and then come back for you when you are ready. I'll even walk them if you think they will be good for me."

She really liked it when John showed his caring and helpful side. If only this could be more often.

It didn't take long to get to the hospital but finding a parking space was another matter. They queued for fifteen minutes just to get on the car park and even then spaces were very difficult to find. Sarah was furious at the driver who had parked across two lanes. "If you can't reverse into a parking space catch the bus," she shouted in frustration.

After enquiring at reception they found Ellen in ward 3. John was very nervous about being in a hospital. He knew there had to be germs almost everywhere, after all people didn't come into hospital for a holiday.

The doctors were doing their rounds so there were curtains round a few of the beds including Mrs Evan's bed and also the bed next to hers, the one on the side nearest the ward door. They waited until the curtains were drawn back to unveil Mrs Evan's and the doctors and nurses came out. Sarah sat in the chair next to the bed and John perched on the side of the bed. He surreptitiously checked the chair Sarah used before she sat down to make sure there were no stains or other dangers.

"Now what are you doing - pretending to be ill just to get a free holiday?" John asked. Sarah looked at this chatty jokey John. Why couldn't this John turn up every day? Why did she have to have the daily mystery of 'Which John Will Turn Up Today?' That sounded like a quiz show she thought.

"Well I must admit the doctors make for attractive scenery, especially that tall blond one over there, he can take my pulse any time. The food though is another matter, I wouldn't feed it to the pigs."

"Sssh Ellen. Not so loud. Anyway you haven't been here long enough to eat yet so how do you know?"

"I just know it will be. It was when I was last in hospital."

"And when was that?"

"When Angela was born."

"Oh goodness that must be forty odd years ago. Anyway how are you feeling?"

"I'm fine. I told you this morning I would be fine. I'm going to miss Coronation Street tonight now."

Sarah knew that Ellen wasn't fine. It was only the medications she had been given since arriving in hospital that made her feel temporarily better, that and Mrs Evans' iron will.

"You can watch it on the television over your bed – there." Sarah said as she repositioned the television so that Mrs Evan could see it.

"I'm not watching that, it costs a fortune."

"I'll pay for it," offered John.

"Don't go wasting your money, you'll never know you might just need it one day. Isn't that right Sarah?"

Sarah glowered at Ellen. She knew exactly what she was getting at.

"What have the doctors said?" Sarah asked.

"I can't remember," Ellen admitted. Sarah made a note to ask one of the nurses on her way out.

"There's a lovely young girl in the next bed," Ellen said. "She seemed to know me but I've no idea who she is. Lovely girl though."

Just then the curtains around the next bed were pushed open.

"Anna!" John and Sarah said in unison.

"Your mother said you were in hospital but she gave me the impression you'd only be in for a few hours. What's the matter, why are you still here?" Sarah asked.

"I had a little accident, did John not tell you?" The same phrase that Anna's mother used last night. "He saved my life, he was very brave. Thank you John, I'll never be able to repay what you did. You put your life in danger to save me."

"Whoa," Sarah said. "Is anyone going to tell me what has been going on?"

Just then the bell went to signal the end of visiting. "Time to leave everyone," the ward sister shouted. "Now, not in five minutes. We are about to start the enemas, free to any visitor who is still here." It was amazing how quickly the visitors left.

As they were walking down the corridor towards the exit Sarah saw the OCD look suddenly appear on John's face. She had come to know when something was concerning him.

"What's the matter John?"

"Blood, too much blood. Blood everywhere."

Sarah could see no blood at all but she knew everything red could be blood in John's mind. His short phrase had put paid to any chance of questioning him about Anna's accident for the next few hours at least.

"John hospitals are very careful. There is no way you, or any of us, have become contaminated in there. Just forget it before you make a mountain out of a mole hill. I'm going back to see them both again tonight – you can stay at home."

"But I'd like…. "

"I don't care what you'd like. I'm not having any of your nonsense in hospital so that's that."

Chapter 46

Both John and Sarah had phone calls they needed to make before the evening visiting at the hospital.

Sarah dialled one of the numbers she had in the contact list on her mobile phone. After a few seconds she heard ringing and very quickly the phone was answered.

"Hi Sarah is something wrong with Cuddles."

"No Katy Cuddles is fine. It's Ellen and Anna, they are both in hospital. I thought you would like to know."

"Yes, of course. What's wrong, nothing serious I hope?"

"I don't think so. Ellen has a dose of pneumonia but she was fairly bright when I visited this afternoon, in fact she was eyeing up all the doctors, she said they made attractive scenery. As for Anna I'm not sure what is wrong yet." She went on to relay what both Judith and Anna had told her.

"How on earth is John involved?"

"I have no idea but it seems he has done something to help Anna when she had an accident. I hope to find out tonight when I visit again."

"It must be difficult visiting two people at the same time."

"Actually it's very easy, they are in adjacent beds. How's that for a coincidence?"

"Sarah would you mind if I came with you this evening? I've really grown to like both of them a lot. Or is John going with you?"

"No he's not. I banned him from coming this evening?" As soon as she had said that she regretted it. How would she explain that away?

"Banned him? That's a bit strong, why?"

"Oh I'll explain sometime. Probably me just being over sensitive."

"Are you alright Sarah?"

"Oh yes Katy. Things are pretty good at the moment."

"Hmm I wonder what that means," Katy replied in a cheeky tone. "Shall I pick you up about 6:30pm?"

"If you don't mind that would be great. That will give me plenty time to take the dogs home. I'll get changed before I take them. See you later."

Katy sat in deep thought when the call had ended. She felt there were a number of leading comments in what Sarah said. It was time to suggest they got together for a coffee soon.

Sarah was just very relieved that John hadn't heard what she said.

~~~~~~~~~~

John had to make sure that Sarah didn't overhear the call he was about to make. To be honest he wasn't sure if the call would be able to be answered, but he had to try. He knew the number would be in Sarah's phone but how would he get it without her knowing. Luck was on his side when she took the dogs on a short walk and very unusually left her phone on the kitchen worktop. The dogs would normally have a second long walk in the afternoon but there just wasn't time today. The fact that she wouldn't be going far had resulted in her not being as fastidious about making sure she had everything with her.

He picked up her phone thinking he had plenty time to find the number before Sarah returned.

"Damn there is a password. What do I do now?" he said in desperation.

~~~~~~~~~~

Sarah only walked the dogs along the canal as far as the old cotton mill. The mill would have been a hive of noisy activity during its heyday but now it was executive apartments that no locals could afford.

"Sorry dogs but we need to turn round now." They all looked up at her as though she was mad. 'We can't go home yet' they seemed to say with their eyes.

On her way home she met Frank, the postman, who was taking his young grandson for a walk.

"Is Mrs Evans alright? I didn't see her this morning when I delivered the mail. I usually pop my head round the door to say hello but the door was locked."

"She's in hospital Frank but she is doing fine. I would think she will be home in a couple of days at most."

"Oh that's good. Give her my love won't you."

"Oh course. You look like you've got your hands full there Frank."

"You're not kidding. Half a day with James and I could do with sleeping for a week. I love him to bits though."

~~~~~~~~~~

There was one other way John could try and make contact. It was a long shot but he had no other option.

He rang the main number and left a message for the person he needed to speak with to ring him back if possible, urgently. Then he waited, tapping his fingers on the kitchen table.

"Come on hurry up, Sarah will be back soon," he mumbled.

He jumped when his phone rang and answered it before the second ring.

"What's the matter John, I got a message to ring you urgently. Is something wrong?"

"No Anna, everything is fine. I just need a couple of favours from you please. Sorry to ask while you are in hospital."

"That's fine, what can I do for you."

John explained what his plans were and Anna agreed to help in both cases.

"Thank you Anna. By the way how are you?"

"I'm feeling fine. I expect to be going home maybe tomorrow, thanks to you."

~~~~~~~~~~

Katy and Sarah arrived at the hospital with just five minutes to spare before visiting started. By driving the wrong way round the one way hospital car park Katy managed to grab the last parking space just before the 4 x 4 that had been in front of them at the car park entrance.

"Katy, you little devil," Sarah said with a giggle.

As ward 3 wasn't far from the entrance they got there just as the doors were opened to let the visitors in.

"There they are, mid-way down on the right," Sarah said as she pointed in the general direction.

"Now I guess we'd better sit between you two to stop you scheming. How are you both?" asked Katy.

"I'm fine thank you," replied Anna, "and Ellen is leading them all a merry dance."

"Oi that's our secret little madam."

"I can see you are feeling better too Ellen," Sarah said sarcastically. "What have the doctors said today?"

"They said I'm as fit as someone half my age. I can come home tomorrow."

"That's fantastic news, and what about you Anna."

"Yeh it's all good. They are x-raying my wrist again in the morning and it may have to go into plaster if they find it's broken but once they've done that I can go home as well."

"That's great news. Now young lady spill the beans. I want to know what happened and exactly how John fits into the story."

Anna looked down avoiding eye contact with Sarah and Katy.

"Come on I'm waiting." Sarah said a little impatiently.

"I promised not to tell you."

"Promised who?"

"John."

"When did you promise John? It wasn't this afternoon when he was here with me."

"He rang me this afternoon."

"What! Now I am getting worried. I need to know Anna. I promise I won't tell him."

She took a while to start talking.

"It was at the steam train station. I was just watching the train coming into the station when I saw Mark and a gang of his friends coming onto the platform, you know the boy I told you about. They all started jeering at me and calling me a slag. Then they started to push me around. No one came to help. I could see the platform attendant at the opposite end of the platform, he had no idea what was going on. Why did no one else help me Sarah?"

"I don't know Anna, I really don't know."

"They were pushing me closer and closer to the platform edge, it was a game to them. Anyway I slipped on the wet platform and fell onto the track. They probably ran away then but I don't know. The next train wasn't due to stop at that station as it was a cream tea special. They start at the station go east on the track as far as they can

270

then turn round and go west to the other end of the track before turning round again to come back to the station. So on this run it wasn't due to stop and therefore wouldn't slow down.

"I remember falling and hitting my head on the track. Then I don't remember anything else until I woke up in the ambulance on my way to the hospital. The paramedic explained what had happened and told me that he had heard that the platform attendant had jumped on to the track and pushed me out of the way of the train. It turns out that the train just missed hitting him by a couple of inches. He put his life in danger to save mine."

"And the platform attendant was John I presume." Sarah said softly.

"Yes it was but he asked me not to tell you." Anna felt guilty at betraying her promise to John, but at least she had kept his other secret.

"That's typical John. He worries that if he has done something good then something bad may happen. Thank you for telling me Anna. I promise I won't tell him but I will try and get him to tell me himself. I won't say that we have spoken."

Katy looked at Sarah with questioning eyes all the time she was speaking. Katy felt sure that there was more to John than met the eye.

"I'm really scared about Mark," Anna softly said, tears running down her cheeks. "He's doing this just because I wouldn't have sex with him. He's not going to give up, I'm certain of that I'm sure he will try again."

"Why don't you tell the police?"

"That will only make it worse, I know it will. Sarah what can I do?"

"I think you need to start by telling your parents everything. They may be angry to start with but then I am certain they will do everything they can to help, as John and I will."

"And me and Steve," Katy added.

"You don't need to face this all alone Anna." Sarah added. "Are your parents not visiting you tonight? I would be happy to be with you when you tell them."

"Mum's got a bridge night and Dad has to pick her up as she always drinks too much Prosecco when she plays bridge, so they can't come tonight." Sarah was furious to hear what Anna said.

"I'm sure they would have caught what Mark did on CCTV, the police will find him without you telling them." Katy said.

"I hope not. I'm really scared."

"Don't worry, we will look after you," Sarah told Anna. She had no idea how she was going to look after her, she already had John and Ellen to care for.

They said goodnight to Ellen and Anna and gave each of them a kiss on the cheek. As Sarah bent to kiss Anna she whispered "Don't worry." Easy to say but hard to do. Sarah had lots of things she was worried about.

~~~~~~~~~~

Sarah had checked on Ellen's progress with the nurse on the nurses' station as they left the hospital. It seemed what Ellen had said about coming home was true. Sarah made a note to make sure Ellen's house was tidy and warm before she came home.

"Coffee?" Katy said.

"Where?"

"My place. Steve is out playing pool and won't be back until nearly midnight. I sense you need to talk."

"That would be good, thank you."

272

Chapter 47

Cuddles was fast asleep in his bed when Katy opened the door. Within seconds he was awake, out of his bed and wagging his tail so fast you suspected his rear end might fly off.

"He's certainly pleased to see you Katy."

Cuddles froze momentarily when he heard Sarah's voice, then he recognised it and suddenly he could only be described as an out of control canine pinball machine, running here, there and everywhere.

"I sometimes think he likes you more than me," Katy said "Please take a seat. Tea, coffee or something stronger, remember I'm driving you home."

"Just black coffee please. If I drink too much wine you may never get rid of me."

Katy went into the kitchen to make the coffee while Cuddles jumped onto Sarah's knee and snuggled down.

"Is it alright for him to come on the chair Katy?" The small size of Steve and Katy's house enable conversation to continue no matter which rooms the two parties were in.

"If you can keep him off you are a better person than me."

Katy returned with the coffee and a plate of homemade buttered banana loaf.

"Ok Sarah, I'm all ears."

"I don't know where to start."

"Well let me say what I see. You're a lovely person Sarah, perhaps too kind for your own good at times. You take a man who you have only known for a few days into your home because he needs a bit of help for a short time. What help? There doesn't appear to be anything wrong with him to me, and to Steve for that matter. A short time you said but he is still there and showing no signs of leaving.

"The only strange thing we have seen was when he ran off because a seagull dropped its load on him at the beach. We didn't see him for a few days after that.

"Then you ban him from visiting hospital with you. That's very strange. Anna has an accident and somehow John is involved in that but he doesn't want anyone to know.

"I know it's none of my business but I don't like seeing you the way you are, I'm worried about you. You seem anxious all the time, you have a lovely smile but we rarely see it now, except when you drank a bit too much when we went for that meal."

"Don't remind me about that."

"Look Sarah if you need any help both Steve and I are more than happy to do what we can."

They were both silent for a short while. Sarah needed to decide just how much to tell Katy. She decided to tell her everything.

Sarah began by recounting her accident in the sinkhole, her rescue by John and then her containment by him.

"I thought he was a weird individual at first although he showed a caring side most of the time. A split personality would probably be the best way to describe how I felt about him initially but yet I could see he wanted to care for me."

Katy was shocked and felt a little scared for Sarah still being alone with him.

"Why did he keep you prisoner?"

Sarah explained all about John's irrational contamination fears.

"He had never had sex or taken drugs but he thought he could have HIV. He had paid for several private tests. He thought because he cut his finger when he was rescuing me that his blood may have dripped on to me and I may have become contaminated as well. He said he had to protect everyone from me."

"He must have gone out to get food."

"Yes he did, he went to the village every week, always on the same day."

"Then why could he go out and you couldn't?"

"He said he was careful but he couldn't guarantee I would be. He wanted 100% unequivocal guarantees about everything. I tried to tell him that nothing in life can be subject to a 100% guarantee but he couldn't understand that. If there was a miniscule chance of something bad happening then it had to be protected against.

"He thought, and still thinks, that the world would be a better place without him but I know he is fundamentally a very kind man."

"Sure sounds it," Katy said sarcastically.

"Oh I hated him too at first and when Betty died I just wanted to kill him. I wouldn't have done of course, but I wanted to."

Sarah went on to explain the circumstances of Betty's death.

"He didn't even let me go and say goodbye to her."

"Was there no chance of you escaping? He couldn't watch you every minute."

"He used to lock the doors, even the one that led to upstairs, I was trapped but I did escape once." She told Katy about escaping to the shepherd's hut and her night there.

"When I woke up in the morning he was there in a dark corner of the hut. I was terrified. He said he couldn't go on without my help, that he would kill himself if I wouldn't help him. He held up a key in one hand and a knife in the other. He told me to choose. Katy I wouldn't let a sick animal die if I could do anything about it so I sure as hell couldn't abandon a human who was suffering so much. So I chose the key, the key to his door he told me. The key to my freedom, I could come and go as I pleased he said. Only it was the wrong key, he had tricked me.

"I thought by then that I knew what was wrong with him. I heard it on the radio when John was in the village. Now we know for sure."

"And what is wrong with him?"

"He has OCD."

"Isn't that just when people wash their hands a lot and like things to be neat?"

Sarah explained in detail about OCD and all the areas of the OCD spectrum John suffered from.

"Katy from what I have seen I wouldn't wish OCD on anyone, not even my worst enemy."

"I had no idea it could be so bad."

"Most people don't. I get angry every time I hear an OCD joke on television or see an OCD jibe on Facebook. It's nothing to joke about believe me. It's horrendous. The sufferer can never relax, OCD is there all the time chipping away at them, planting thoughts into their heads, irrational thoughts but they think they are real or at the very least that they could be real. OCD sufferers need support and understanding not to be the subject of jokes.

"It isn't just the jokes. People not understanding the severity of OCD, or trivialising it can be just as bad. The OCD sufferer can be going through an awful time and nobody knows, nobody is there to offer support, except of course the very few people who understand OCD. The sufferer has all this to put up with, has to try and battle alone, and then they hear or see someone else getting sympathy just because they have a cold.

"I try to put myself in John's position sometimes. What would I do? How would I feel? It's impossible to know because I understand that it's not real. Even John says that sometimes he struggles to comprehend OCD types that he doesn't have at that particular time. He wonders why they don't just stop doing the compulsions. That's how crazy OCD is."

"John dashed off from the beach because he thought the seagull poo may have contaminated him and he didn't want to pass on that contamination to the rest of you. He ran off to protect you."

"Oh Sarah, it must be horrendous for you living with this all the time."

She explained everything to Katy. Confession, Security, Religion, Cleanliness, every aspect of John's OCD was covered.

"The reason I banned him from going with me to the hospital was that when we went in the afternoon he had serious problems with the thought that there would be lots of blood around in a hospital, contaminated blood. I couldn't go through that all again in the evening."

"So was John there when Anna had her accident, did he see blood and that's why he doesn't want anyone to know."

"If only it was that easy.

"John believes that if he is looking forward to anything, if he is enjoying anything or if he has done anything good and is likely to get praise then his OCD may make someone close to him suffer, usually with the possibility of death. That's why he doesn't want anyone to know he had been a hero. He saved Anna's life Katy, as you know, but to him that may have put someone else in danger.

"While he has been with me he has turned down jobs because his OCD told him to. It told him that horrible things would happen to someone he cared for if he took the jobs.

"He is always protecting other people. OCD sufferers prefer something to happen to themselves than other people. This responsibility is enormous for the sufferer to bear. It can make them feel that being killed is easier than dealing with the responsibility, easier than dealing with their OCD. That's why John has walked rough city streets in the middle of the night hoping someone would kill him. He didn't have the courage to do it himself but he genuinely wanted someone to kill him.

"I couldn't abandon him Katy. I had to help him to try for a better future. Do you understand that?"

Katy took hold of Sarah's hands. "Yes I understand."

Sarah realised that she had been talking for almost two hours.

"I'm sorry Katy to burden you with all this. I'd better be going, John will wonder where I am. He worries that something bad has happened to me if I am one minute later than the time I told him I would be home. He won't let me go out without telling him when I will be back. If I tell him I don't know he just says 'approx.' over and over until I guess a time. Trouble is then he takes that time as a definite, to the minute."

"You are going nowhere yet. Phone him and tell him I insisted you came for a coffee. I'll fill our cups. Are you sure you don't want something stronger?"

"No honestly. I need to keep a clear mind."

"You must be living on your nerves all the time."

"I'm shattered."

"I don't know how you are managing to keep your business going with everything else you have to contend with."

"To be honest the dogs are my escape. When I am on the moors with them life seems better for an hour or so."

Katy went to make more coffee. Sarah sat wondering if she had said too much. What if John found out?

Katy returned and placed the coffee on the table next to Sarah. Sarah had to smile at the words on her mug 'Keep Calm and Stay Strong'. How appropriate she thought.

"So how are things at the moment Sarah?"

"At the moment things are great. John has his job at the steam railway and he starts his new therapy sessions tomorrow. He seems relatively relaxed at the moment, well as relaxed as an OCD sufferer can be. He is managing some aspects of his OCD really well. I'm proud of him. I think the future is looking much better for him."

"Thanks to you. Is proudness the only feeling you have for him?"

"Of course it is. You've been listening to Mrs Evans too much Katy." Even Sarah wasn't convinced that the words coming out of her own mouth were completely true.

"It was really good to see Ellen looking so well tonight," Katy said.

"It certainly was. I can't believe how quickly she has recovered, especially at her age. I'm sure she'll outlive me."

"Probably. She's a real character, I love her to bits."

Sarah felt the need to move away from the subject of John. She hadn't realised just how stressful it would be talking about him.

They spent the next half an hour in idle chit chat before they heard the door opening. It was Steve coming back from his pool match.

"Oh my goodness is it so late," Sarah said looking at her watch. "I really think I had better be heading home. Thank you for a lovely evening Katy, I really enjoyed it."

"I'll just get my coat and then take you home," Katy said. "I won't be long darling," she said to Steve.

On the way home Sarah asked Katy to keep the content of tonight's conversation a secret between the two of them.

"I think it would do you and John good to talk about this more but I will do as you ask." Sarah hoped Katy meant that.

When they were half way back to Sarah's house her mobile phone rang.

"Who on earth can this be at this time of night? It's after midnight. I bet its John checking up on me." Sarah said as she felt for her phone in her handbag.

She answered the phone without looking at the screen.

"Hello........Yes," was all Katy heard her say. The call lasted about two minutes, Sarah doing the listening rather than the talking.

"Of course," Sarah said as she ended the call.

Katy kept her eyes on the dark wet road but she could tell that the call hadn't been a good one. What had John done now?

"It's Ellen. She's taken a turn for the worse."

Katy turned right at the next traffic lights in the direction of the hospital. Sarah realised what she was doing.

"No Katy, you've done enough for me today. Please take me home to get my van."

"There is no time for that. Hold tight."

Katy drove as fast as the conditions allowed. They arrived at the hospital ten minutes later.

They were too late.

Chapter 48

Sarah hardly slept at all that night. Through her tears she saw visions of Mrs Evans. Happy, cheeky, loving Mrs Evans, her surrogate mother – gone.

Ellen gone, Betty gone – both of them leaving huge voids. Both of them died alone. Sarah was distraught that she had let them both down when they needed her most. Could she ever forgive herself?

John was in bed when Sarah got home so he was unaware of the sad news. The fact that he had gone to bed before she was home was a really good sign, he had never done so before he knew Sarah was home safely in the past. She decided not to wake him and she also made the decision to let Ellen's son and daughter know about her death in the morning. She couldn't face making the calls now.

Sarah was shocked to find that John was already up and out before she came downstairs the next morning. 'What was going on' she wondered. Just then she saw a note next to the kettle. Obviously John knew she would find it there. She picked up the folded piece of paper and apprehensively opened it. The message in John's easily recognisable hand writing read 'Gone to get my van. See you later.' She was puzzled and concerned. He had never given any indication that he wanted to go near his farm since he moved in with Sarah. When she had broached the subject he had cut her short every time. Now he was walking, she assumed he was walking, all the way up onto the moors to his farm to get his van. Very strange. Today was the first of John's NHS therapy sessions. Would he turn up? Sarah hoped he would.

Sarah made herself a coffee, she couldn't face any food. She sat at the kitchen table knowing she couldn't delay ringing Richard and Angela Evans. She took a deep breath and dialled the first number.

Richard's wife answered, "Hello Barbara Evans here."

"Hi it's Sarah Meadon, Mrs Evans neighbour. I am afraid I have some bad news for you. Ellen passed away during the night. It was all very sudden."

"Oh my goodness. Thank you for letting me know."

"Is Richard there please?"

"He's out playing golf at the moment. He started his round at 6am, madness in my opinion."

"Could you let him know please? I presume he will want to organise the funeral."

"The golf club won't let players take calls on the course, it's a very exclusive club you know."

"Snob," Sarah said under her breath.

Barbara continued, "Can't you sort the funeral out, it's not that difficult is it?"

Sarah was aghast. She couldn't believe what she had just heard.

"No I'm sorry I can't. Please ask Richard to ring me as soon as he gets home."

"He's a very busy man."

"Barbara his mother has just died." She ended the call forgetting to ask Barbara to let Angela know. No doubt she would have asked Sarah to do it anyway.

She dialled the second number and waited a short while before she heard the overseas ringing tone.

"Angela here," said the sleepy voice.

"Hello its Sarah Meadon. I am afraid I have some bad news."

"Do you realise it's the middle of the night here? Couldn't it have waited? You've woken me up."

"Angela I am afraid your mother passed away last night."

"Oh, well she'd had a good life."

Sarah was stunned. 'What a horrible pair of siblings' she thought.

"Do you know when the funeral is yet?" Angela asked.

"No she only died in the middle of the night and I am waiting for Richard to ring me back. He will need to make the arrangements."

"Good luck, he's useless at organising anything. Anyway my view is to keep the costs as low as possible. No use wasting money."

"This is your mother you are talking about," Sarah said in disgust. "I presume Richard will let you know when the funeral is."

"If he does he does, if he doesn't he doesn't. I won't be coming of course."

"What!"

"Oh no, I can't possibly come. It costs far too much for the flights, and for what? It's not as though Mum will know I am not there is it? No you'll do fine without me. I'll no doubt have to come over later to see the solicitor. I can't afford two fares."

For the second time this morning Sarah abruptly ended a call in anger.

Just then Sarah's door began to open. John must have forgotten to lock it when he went out. Very strange. Had he gone out in a hurry? The mystery deepens.

"Hi it's Katy. Anyone in?"

"What are you doing here?"

"I thought you might need some help today so I phoned into work and told them I needed an emergency day off. They are very good that way.

"Good grief you look like you've seen the end of the world, what on earth is the matter Sarah."

She told Katy about her phone calls.

Katy was just as shocked as Sarah. "They'll be here soon enough when the will is read."

"My thoughts too Katy."

"Anyway we have a doggy business to run, Ellen's house to tidy and a funeral to plan it seems. Let's get cracking – after a cup of coffee of course."

Katy always seemed to lighten Sarah's mood. She was particularly grateful for that today.

"…and a missing John to find," Sarah whispered.

~~~~~~~~~~

John knew he had to go to the farm alone. He wanted to see how he would react to being back there before he saw his new therapist later in the day. Plus he also needed to pick up his van to carry out his plans for the day.

It was a long walk but he didn't mind that. The solitude that the moors provided was very welcome. You could easily lose yourself in your thoughts and today John's thoughts were good. He thought he was managing his OCD very well but would the visit to the farm disprove this?

He opened the door with trepidation. Everything looked the same as when he was last here but with an extra layer of dust. He paused for a moment but he felt fine. He stepped into the living room, then the kitchen but he still felt alright, even when he got the flashbacks of Betty lay dying on the floor.

He went upstairs looking in each room one by one. The last room was Sarah's bedroom. Her 'HELP' message was still there scratched into the window. He sat on the edge of the bed to try and deal with the huge feeling of shame that engulfed him when the memories of what he had put Sarah through came flooding back. He could see clearly now what he had done, at the time it had been behind an OCD mist. He could now see what a strong hold the OCD had on him at the time. He knew he would always feel immense guilt for what he did to Sarah and Betty.

He just couldn't understand why Sarah had agreed to help him after all he had done. He knew she was a special lady and he owed it to her to try his best to manage his OCD much better.

"I will make it up to you Sarah I promise. Starting today," he said to himself.

He was delighted that he still felt fine. Had he finally won the battle? Maybe, but he knew he certainly hadn't won the war. He felt he had the strength to continue the fight however.

He knew it was time to leave to go to his therapy session. He surprised himself to discover he hadn't locked the door behind him when he came in. He smiled, the first genuine smile that had crossed his face for a very long time.

~~~~~~~~~~~

Amazingly, and luckily, the old van started first time therefore he arrived at the clinic in good time. Somehow he expected it to be run down and shabby compared to the private clinic but that wasn't the case. It was hard to tell the difference. He wondered if the private clinic put profit before patient comfort.

The procedure was exactly the same. He completed a questionnaire before a middle aged lady came to meet him in the waiting room. She was short and slightly overweight with brown hair in a rather old fashioned style. John liked what he saw, homely he thought.

"Hello I'm Ruth, Ruth Mason-Hart. I presume you are John."

283

"Yes."

"Pleased to meet you. Please follow me. Would you like to grab a coffee before we go to my office?"

"No thank you, I'm fine." Yes, John really liked this therapist. He felt that she would know what to do to help him.

They entered a neat pastel decorated room. There were pictures of the local countryside on the wall and a vase of flowers on the low table. John noted that there was no desk, everything was informal and very relaxing, just as it should be.

"OK John. Tell me a little bit about yourself."

They were sat in very comfortable chairs at the round table which took up most of the small room.

He told her all about his life, starting with childhood right up to his current situation.

"Sarah seems a lovely lady, especially after what you did to her."

"She certainly is. I'm not sure I would still be here if it wasn't for her. Now here I am managing my OCD well and looking forward to a better future. I also have friends now thanks to Sarah."

"That's great John but don't get carried away please. You must not relax your effort when times are good, the OCD is just waiting for you to do that. Whilst things are good at the moment there may be set backs and that is when you need to be even stronger in your battle. It is important that you don't let those setbacks weigh you down too much."

"Yes I know. Sarah will always support me through the tough times."

"Do you really realise what this lady is going through for you? Do you realise how tough it is for her too? OCD is a very selfish illness in that often all the sufferer sees is what they are going through. They usually don't see the full extent of the suffering experienced by those close to them."

John hung his head. Did he know just how much Sarah was suffering? He realised that he couldn't be sure of the answer to that.

"Right John I think you will definitely benefit from a course of therapy from us. We are allowed to give you 12 one hour sessions."

"What happens after that?"

"Hopefully you will be able to manage your OCD much better then."

"But what if I'm not?"

"I'm sorry John but that is all we are allowed to offer you."

"And then you leave me to try and continue the battle alone? What if I can't?"

Ruth didn't answer so John continued.

"I've heard there is an excellent clinic in London where you can go as an inpatient. I've read that they have an excellent track record. Can I be referred there after your sessions?"

"You mean the Eccleston Clinic. I could recommend that you go there but to be honest your chances are very slim indeed of getting a place. First of all you don't meet the criteria for admittance and even if you did the local NHS would be unlikely to fund your treatment there."

"I thought NHS stood for National Health Service but you are telling me, I think, that what treatment you get depends on where you live. A postcode lottery."

"I am afraid so. Please don't get so agitated John, don't upset yourself."

John felt a real mixture of emotions. He was really pleased that he was standing up for himself but he was also shocked and saddened, not to mention worried, about Ruth's bombshell. He knew he needed support, he couldn't do this alone. Sure Sarah supported him but she wasn't an expert.

They continued talking, Ruth trying to ease John's fears about life after therapy.

"OK John I think that is an appropriate time to end today's session. I will see you again next week, same time."

"I've only been here 50 minutes."

"Goodbye John. Don't forget to do the things I have asked you to do, every day please and keep a diary of how you are feeling."

He left the building in a bit of a daze. John knew he couldn't give in. He had to get the most possible out of the twelve sessions.

He knew Ruth had talked a lot of sense, she knew what she was doing and he guessed the twelve session limit wasn't her fault. It would be the managers in ivory towers who had dictated that. He decided he would work hard and do everything Ruth asked him to do.

He couldn't let this setback spoil his plans for the day.

~~~~~~~~~~

Sarah and Katy had worked like the dream team all day. The dogs had two long walks as usual and been played with in the garden.

They had tidied and cleaned Ellen's house. Sarah found it very upsetting when she had gone into the house. There was Mrs E's chair near the television – empty. There was her breakfast tea cup, half full. It didn't feel like a home any more, it was just an empty box. Sarah wondered who would move in next. Whoever it was she couldn't possibly think as much of them as she had of Ellen.

Sarah had even put a casserole, John's favourite meal, in the slow cooker. He would enjoy that, if he ever came home. She hadn't seen him all day and was getting very worried indeed. Just then she saw John walking up her garden path as if he hadn't got a care in the world.

"Where the hell have you been?" she asked when he came through the door.

He told her what he had been doing all day, well almost all of it, and how it had all gone. Sarah was furious to hear about the twelve session limit and wanted to march down to the clinic right away to tell them that it was a stupid rule in John's case.

"It's fine Sarah. I'm doing great at the moment and I'm sure after another twelve sessions I will be able to manage without a therapist." He was more relaxed now than during his therapy session.

"But you do have regressions John. You do so well for so long and then a tiny thing happens and you let it all slip, you know you do. Plus there are lots of aspects of your OCD that haven't been addressed yet. You have a hell of a long way to go.

"I know but I will just have to try harder. There's nothing I can do about the limit so that's it."

"We'll see about that." Sarah was worried about John's attitude. Whenever anything went in a way that he didn't like he tended to go into the depths of despair, but not this time. She really wished she could relax about John but she couldn't."

286

"Anyway sit down Sarah. I've got a surprise for you" John guided her to one of the chairs. "Come in," he shouted in the direction of the door.

"Anna," both Katy and Sarah shouted in surprise "You're out of hospital. That's wonderful."

Everyone laughed at the synchronised speaking.

"It's great to be back and to see you two."

Anna sat down and slowly opened her coat to reveal the most gorgeous yellow Labrador puppy. Sarah went all gooey eyed.

"Ah it's adorable Anna. What a surprise. When did you get him? Where did you get him? Can I have a cuddle please?"

"Oh course you can, here," Anna said as she handed over the wriggling bundle.

"What a stunner you are," Sarah said as she snuggled the dog tightly. Just then she felt the warm wet trickle run down her chest.

"I guess he likes you," John said. "What shall we call her?"

"That's not up to me. Anna should pick the name for her dog."

"Oh he's not my dog."

"He's yours Sarah," John said, "To say thank you."

Sarah looked from John to the puppy and burst into tears. Tears of joy.

She looked up at John and softly said, "Ellen is dead."

Chapter 49

Tomorrow was Sarah's birthday. Her first birthday for many years that she wouldn't celebrate with Mrs E but John had promised her it would be a day she would never forget. She sat in bed drinking a late night cup of hot chocolate and thinking back over the last few months since Mrs E's death.

The period following Ellen's death had been a particularly difficult one. It took a long and very difficult course of persuasion to even half convince John that he wasn't in some way responsible for her death.

"I might have touched some contaminated blood when I visited her in hospital and then passed the contamination on when I gave her the glass of water she asked for. She was well and yet just a few hours later she was dead, just like Christine. I killed them both." He said with more repetition than a small child wanting attention.

Sarah felt despair like she never had before. Here was a man she had grown very fond of, a man she wanted to help but a man who wouldn't listen to common sense. She had lost her patience a number of times through severe frustration, every time she had snapped at him guilt ate away at her.

Life with John was always like riding a roller coaster. There were a sequence of highs and lows. You learnt to make the most of the highs and deal with the lows.

The days immediately following Mrs Evans' death had been a particularly deep low. Like the first part of a roller coaster there was then the long slow climb to the first high point, progress was very slow.

The funeral had been a very sad affair. Sarah had given in and helped Richard to organise it. Well to be honest Richard had made the decisions, usually based on a least cost option, and then instructed Sarah to get on with it and put his decision into action. Sarah had a severe dislike of Richard but she wanted to do her best to give Ellen a good send off.

The day of the funeral was dull and wet. Richard attended but his wife and children couldn't make it, Sarah didn't ask why. It was no surprise that Angela didn't put in an appearance either. Sarah and John had secretly paid part of the cost, no way was Ellen going to have a penny pinching last day on earth.

Sarah imagined how difficult it must be for John to attend the funeral due to his OCD thoughts concerning religion. She imagined that would probably be the first time he had been in a church since his parents' funerals. It would also be difficult for him to meet people that he hadn't encountered before, particularly the difficult people that they were. She felt certain that this day would heighten his anxiety levels but despite this he was an absolute rock for Sarah on the funeral day. Sarah had noticed several times that when he had someone who needed his support his OCD concerns were pushed to the back of his mind, if only temporarily.

It was amazing that all of Mrs Evans' family, Richard, Angela, Barbara and the children had been able to attend the solicitors for the reading of the will. Well actually Sarah wasn't surprised at all. Sarah had received a letter asking her to attend but she declined the invitation. She wanted nothing from Ellen except the rose bush in her garden that she had admired for many years. She would like that in memory of her wonderful friend and neighbour. John had made sure that it was securely planted in Sarah's garden long before Richard arrived for the funeral.

She remembered the lynch mob almost knocking her door down on the day of the will reading, just as she and John were sitting down to tea. When she opened the door Richard and Angela burst in.

"You'll never get away with it you scheming bitch," Angela spat at her. Sarah was shocked by the venom in Angela's voice. She had no idea what this was all about but guessed that Mrs E had left her something in her will, something that they wanted.

John shot up from his seat and stood between Sarah and her accusers. "That's no way to speak to a lady, now just calm down and explain what it is you are on about," he said.

"She's no lady. Her twisted mind has worked on my mother for years to get what she wanted. A frail old woman whose mind was anything but alert and she has conned her."

"Right you can either explain clearly what has got you in this state or you can leave," John added.

"The house. My bloody mother has left her house to her, to that woman. After all we have done for mother and she gives her house to this bitch."

Sarah looked at John, her protector, and then turned her attention to Angela and Richard.

"I had no idea but I know you won't believe that. I do not want your mother's house, you can have it. If I need to sign anything for the solicitor I am happy to do so," Sarah softly said.

"Now you've heard the lady," John added, "I presume asking for an apology would be a waste of my breath so just get out before I throw you out."

They left but not before Richard had said "We'll make sure you hear from the solicitor before you change your mind."

Amazingly Angela's parting shot was to ask Sarah to show prospective buyers round next door.

"Get out now!" John screamed.

Sarah grabbed his arm. "I'll do it, I don't mind."

'What an amazing lady Sarah was', John thought.

'What a lovely man John was', Sarah thought. Despite his heightened state of anxiety he was still caring for her.

A part of her eagerness to show people round the house was personal selfishness. Her time next door to Ellen had been wonderful. They had never had a cross word. She was worried what life would be like with new neighbours. At least if she was showing prospective buyers round she could be more encouraging with people she thought would be good neighbours and more downbeat with the rest.

After about two months a nice young couple moved in. They had one young child aged two, a little girl called Amelia. They had moved up from Birmingham for work reasons. They were nice enough but it just wasn't the same as living next to Ellen. To be honest Sarah had very little contact with them other than saying hello if they passed in the lane. They had knocked on her door once to ask her to keep Lady quiet, the barking was keeping Amelia awake they said. Obviously not doggy people.

Lady, her canine present from John, was growing fast. It had taken Sarah a long time to decide on a name. She wanted to name her in memory of Mrs Evans but decided that Ellen wasn't really a suitable name for a dog. Eventually she decided on Lady. Ellen was a wonderful Lady.

Lady had certainly made an impression since she arrived. Hardly anything in Sarah's house didn't bear the damage caused by sharp puppy teeth. It was amazing that the coffee table was still standing, its legs looked like they had been attacked by a colony of beavers. Lady had a particular liking for shoes, much to Sarah and John's annoyance.

Lady would grab anything she could to initiate a chase. 'Come and get me – I might give it you back', her eyes would say. If they hadn't managed to win the tug of war when they caught her she would very quickly chew the item, whatever it was, beyond repair.

"She's just a puppy," Sarah would say when John indicated that getting Lady wasn't his brightest idea. Sarah loved Lady. To be able to walk the moors at weekend with her own dog again was wonderful. Sarah knew that Betty would understand.

Katy & Steve were still regular visitors. Sarah particularly remembered the day they had come round to announce they were expecting the patter of tiny feet. She was thrilled for them and couldn't wait to hold the new arrival in her arms in about five months' time. How would Cuddles accept Junior Mills Sarah wondered?

Anna continued to help Sarah in the evenings and during college holidays. There had been no more trouble with Mark since he and his gang tried to intimidate Anna again when she was walking from the railway station down the hill into the village. Luckily for Anna, but rather unluckily for Mark, John had been walking Lady at the time and saw what was happening when he turned the corner from Worthy Street into Station Road.

John told Lady to sit and stay, he knew she wouldn't move until he told her to. Sarah loved her dog but she was also firm and had trained Lady well. John slowly approached the bullying gang from behind without being noticed. He grabbed Mark by the collar, swung him round and pinned him up against the wall. Suddenly all of Mark's so called friends deserted him and ran off in various directions. John assumed they wouldn't want to risk adding to their existing criminal records. Mark look terrified.

"Not so brave now are we," John said, his face no more than an inch from Mark's. "Now I will only say this once so you had better listen carefully. If you or any of your so called friends ever, let me stress ever, even so much as insult this young lady again I promise you that you will suffer. Your suffering will be much greater that anything you subject Anna too, much, much worse. Am I making myself clear?"

"Y – y – yeh."

"Good. Now get out of my sight or I will march you down to the police station right now. I'm sure you'd like a nice holiday at her majesty's pleasure." He wasn't sure that Mark knew what he meant but he didn't care."

"Thank you John. If you hadn't come along…"

John hated conflict, it wasn't even on his agenda at the worst of times. The last few minutes had left him feeling very anxious but he knew he had to remain calm, at least outwardly, for Anna's sake.

"Sssh. Don't cry. Do you fancy a coffee at Sarah's before I walk you home."

"Yes please."

"You won't need to worry about any more problems with that lot," John said and so far they had left her alone. John called Lady who immediately came to them and they took the short walk to Sarah's.

Sarah knew she would be sad to see Anna go off to university next year. She had said that she wanted to go and study animal management. Sarah didn't really know what that meant.

As for John, well he had certainly had his ups and downs. There were times she was so proud of him when he had tried really hard and moved up another level in managing his OCD. Then there were other times she was frustrated when he slipped right back again. She accused him of having reached a plateau that he was happy at and therefore relaxing his effort. "You have stopped trying," she would say to him, "Why have you stopped trying?" He couldn't deny it but he always had an answer, it was never really his fault.

Sarah began to wonder if John was ever going to get to a stage when he could relax and be happy. She doubted it. She knew his OCD would never disappear, there was no cure, but she also knew that John could manage it to such an extent that his life could be as near to normal as was possible with his illness. He understood that life would be much better for him if he could gain the upper hand but somehow he just couldn't get there.

"When your OCD attacks with another problem why don't you tell it to get lost?" Sarah would ask him, "Don't engage with the thought at all."

"I try but you don't understand how hard it is," he would say and she had to admit that even after all this time she didn't understand, she never would understand what went on inside his head.

She could go weeks noticing that the hand soap and toilet rolls were lasting as long as they would normally be expected to do but then, soon after, she would find his waste bin full of toilet roll and the bottle of hand soap lasting no more than two days.

"Why, oh why have you let it win again? You had it beaten but you have gone right back to square one," she would say in a raised voice.

"I'll beat it again," was all he would say.

John's job at the steam train had finished at the end of the summer season. He had done well at that job and managed to not let his OCD spoil it. The same couldn't be said for the next job he got.

He succeeded in getting a job at the local supermarket. Sarah was really proud of him, he found the job, he applied for it and, after an interview, he got the job. Of course he had to declare his OCD so the completion of several medical forms was required before they would confirm the position. Nothing is ever straightforward for an OCD sufferer.

All went well for a while until they asked him to work in the bakery. Prior to that he was on meat and fish and Sarah was amazed at how well he had controlled his OCD during that time. That environment was a nightmare for someone with cleanliness and contamination concerns but John performed well and got good reviews.

His anxiety levels began to rise dramatically after just a few days in the bakery. John had to make sure every minute aspect of the task adhered to the rules. Everything had to be baked according to set procedures and to do that John had to read the procedures thoroughly and repetitively. He was fine until the manager began to ask why items were going onto display late. No matter how hard John tried, including going into work early, he just couldn't finish things in time. He knew this was largely due to the fact that he hadn't received sufficient training but management wouldn't accept this.

Sarah felt desperately sorry for him during this time. She was upset that there was nothing she could do for him. He helped her at the times when she needed support, now he needed support and she couldn't help.

John asked to be moved from the bakery, he never wanted to go there in the first place, but the management said they couldn't move him until they had found a replacement and that would take some time. John resigned. Since then he has helped Sarah with the doggy day care business and the arrangement was going really well. It wasn't without OCD problems but together they could cope with that. They had been able to take on three more clients, a white cockapoo, a bouncy boxer and a mad springer spaniel. They certainly had their hands full.

The NHS therapy sessions had ended two weeks ago. John felt that he had benefitted greatly from them, Sarah wasn't so sure. She saw them as his comfort blanket. While he had a therapist to see he was happier, he knew that there was someone he could call for help but now the therapist was gone, the twelve sessions were over. In time he could get more sessions of course but only if his condition deteriorated to levels that definitely warranted more help. The only other way he could get treatment was to become a danger to himself. Sarah was fairly certain that wouldn't happen. He didn't talk any more about the world being better without him. This in itself was a huge step forward.

Most times John had done what the therapist asked him to do but as he began to feel better his willingness to obey diminished.

Yes Sarah thought that the therapist was a comfort blanket but she did also wonder if the OCD itself was in a way a comfort blanket.

Having to deal with his OCD avoided him having to face the real problems that other people face, there wasn't time to do both. John, of course, said that he would prefer to deal with real everyday problems but Sarah wasn't convinced, not yet at least.

John was now visiting the farm fairly regularly and coping with the visits really well. He had even taken to staying overnight at the farm occasionally. He told Sarah it would give her a break. Sarah was really proud of him for doing this, she knew it indicated that he was much stronger in his battle with his nemesis. She really missed him when he stayed away overnight. She likened it to releasing an injured bird when you had nursed it back to health. You were happy to see it strong enough to be released but also sad to see it go.

All in all life was OK in Sarah's opinion, not great, just ok. John's bad days were now fewer than his better days, which was encouraging. Sarah could never describe days as good, only better. She hoped the truly good days would come in time. There were still the bad regressions but overall John was much better than he had been when he first moved in with Sarah. There was still a very long way to go though and she wondered if he had the determination to move any further along the journey. She prayed that he had – for his sake.

Anyway tomorrow was her birthday and her day to remember, according to John. Dear kind, considerate, caring John. She had grown very fond of him.

She turned out the light, closed her eyes and dreamt of a happy future, for them, together.

Chapter 50

Sarah was glad her birthday fell on a weekend otherwise she would have had to work. In previous years this hadn't bothered her since apart from Mrs Evans she'd had no one to celebrate with, but this year was different. She had no idea what John had planned but as she looked down at Lady in her basket in the corner of the bedroom she was reminded that he was very good at arranging things in secret. She guessed that Katy, Steve and Anna would be involved somewhere along the line. They had become a close knit group of friends, there to socialise with one another and there to support each other.

Many were the times that Sarah had used Katy's support over the last few months when John was having a particularly bad day. You never knew when the bad days were coming but she felt sure that today wasn't going to be one of them, as sure as you could be living with an OCD sufferer. She knew John wouldn't want to spoil her birthday. Even if he was struggling today she knew he would try his best to hide it, although she had become an expert in spotting the tiny tell-tale signs. Living with an OCD sufferer is never going to be easy. Sarah likened it to walking barefoot on broken glass and hot coals at the same time whilst holding your breath to make sure you didn't say or do anything that could upset the OCD sufferer.

Just then there was a knock on her bedroom door.

"Come in." Her relationship with John, although still platonic, was very close. Sarah therefore had no hesitation to invite John into her bedroom.

John walked in carrying a tray holding a full English breakfast, toast, orange juice and coffee. Then she saw in the corner of the tray a single red rose. No one had done anything like this for her before – ever.

"Good morning birthday girl."

Sarah was glad to hear the cheery tone in John's voice. That was a good sign.

"Oh thank you. You shouldn't have gone to all the trouble," she said whilst trying hard to hold back the tears, tears of happiness. Could life get any better for Sarah Meadon? She hoped it would get better in time, for both herself and John.

"Yes I should. Just remember all the things you have done for me. Enjoy your breakfast and then treat yourself to a lie in. When did you last have one of those? You'll need your strength for your birthday surprise," he added as he was leaving the room.

Sarah smiled. She ate her breakfast, delicious it was too, whilst thinking about the difference in John now compared to when she first met him. He had progressed significantly although he was still a million miles from leading a normal life, she doubted he would ever reach that milestone. If only he could be consistent in controlling his OCD.

She really couldn't understand why he would do so well in managing an aspect of his condition but then, often for no apparent reason, he would revert right back to the start. He knew he could do it, he knew his life was better when he did but still he slipped right back. She guessed that was how life would have to be, although she hoped he could, with her help, progress more. She kept dangling the happiness carrot to try and encourage him to try harder. Try harder was a harsh thing to say, she knew that. He had tried, he was trying so very hard.

Poor, poor John. What a dreadful illness OCD was. No one could see you were ill. No one understood what you were going through. To many people it was just the subject of jokes. If only they could experience OCD for a day but she wouldn't even wish that on her worst enemy, not even for one day.

She worried what may happen now John had no therapy sessions to support him but so far he seemed ok, although it was early days yet. Sarah suffered along with John and on his good days he realised that but on his bad days it was difficult for him to see beyond his current torment.

Neither sufferer or carer could ever relax, you never knew what was around the corner. In fact you never knew what even the next minute would bring.

Anyway today was her birthday. "Please let it be a good day for John," she said softly.

Sarah enjoyed her lie in, what a luxury. By the time she came downstairs John had gone out. No doubt out organising her surprise. Sarah took Lady out for a long walk over her favourite part of the moors. The sun was shining, cotton wool clouds floated overhead, a breeze rustled through Sarah's hair and Lady was exploring, running wherever her nose indicated the most exciting smell. Sarah knew Betty was running with them, three companions in perfect harmony, no words being necessary, they all knew the unconditional love that existed between them.

It was a long time since Sarah had felt so happy. As she walked along the crest of the moors, enjoying the wild scenery that fell away either side of her, she decided that the time was right to make her suggestion to John, to ask him the question that would change their lives for ever.

John still wasn't home when Sarah and Lady returned from their walk.

"What on earth is he planning Lady?" she said.

She passed the early afternoon pottering in her garden, partly so she could keep watch for John's return. She couldn't wait to see what he had done. She had a strange feeling in her stomach, a feeling she had never experienced before, a mix of excitement and anticipation.

By 4pm there was still no sign of John. Sarah told herself not to worry, he seemed fine this morning.

"Happy birthday Sarah," Anna shouted as she walked up the lane. "Are you having a lovely day?"

"I think so," replied Sarah.

"You only think so?"

"I haven't seen John since he brought me breakfast in bed this morning."

"I'm sure he'll be fine. He'll be planning something wonderful for you."

"That's more or less what he said this morning."

"There you go then, don't worry."

Anna handed Sarah a small neatly wrapped birthday present.

"I'm sorry it's not much but the lady I work for doesn't pay me well," she said with a grin on her face.

"Cheeky," Sarah said as she carefully opened the present. As she pulled off the wrapping paper, a dog design of course, tears welled up in her eyes. "It's beautiful, how did you ...."

"John helped me. He took the photo out of your bedroom when you were out. I took it to a photography shop in Manchester and here it is. That's why I am so late coming round today, I had to go and pick it up. It wasn't ready when I got there so I had to wait.

Sarah found words hard to come by as she held the beautiful picture on canvas of Betty. Betty sat, head raised with that look that was so distinctive of her.

"Thank you Anna. You couldn't have got me a better present. It's perfect."

They both chatted away for about half an hour before Anna had to go.

"I've got an assignment to finish this weekend, it has to be handed in on Monday. Have a lovely time tonight."

Sarah wondered if Anna knew what John had planned but didn't ask.

By 5pm there was still no sign of John.

Steve and Katy called in on their way back from visiting Katy's sister in York.

"Hello birthday girl," Steve said.

"It's a long time since anyone called me a girl. Perhaps you should make an optician appointment." They all laughed.

"Happy birthday Sarah," Katy said as she gave her a kiss on the cheek. "Are you having a good day?"

"Well yes I suppose."

"That's a strange answer."

"I don't know where John is."

"Oh I'm sure he will turn up soon and whisk you off for a wonderful evening."

"Maybe you are right. I hope so."

"Don't worry. If there was anything wrong he would have let you know."

Sarah knew that wouldn't necessarily be the case.

They gave her a beautiful bouquet of flowers.

"We had no idea what to get you. I hope these are alright," Katy said.

"They are more than alright, they are gorgeous. And at least you haven't been plotting behind my back."

"What are you on about?"

She showed them the picture that Anna had given her and explained John's involvement in the subterfuge.

They would have loved to stay longer but knew they had to get home. "We'll have to go now and give Cuddles his tea, and let him out for a wee. He'll be desperate." Katy's sister was allergic to dogs therefore Cuddles had to stay at home when they visited her.

It was 6pm and still no sign of John. Sarah decided that Lady would have to miss her second walk today. It wouldn't do her any harm for once. She had the small garden to do her necessaries in. She wanted to be here when John came back. She hoped it wouldn't be long before he came striding down the lane. Although with an OCD suffered nothing could be 100% guaranteed, she knew that.

It was beginning to get a little chilly so Sarah went back into the house. She sat at the kitchen table, the nearest seat to the door John would walk through. There on the table was the morning newspaper. John loved having the newspaper delivered, a luxury that hadn't been available when he lived at his farm. He enjoyed reading it while he was having breakfast. This morning would be no different. After he had taken Sarah's breakfast up to her he would have sat having his breakfast whilst reading the news.

Sarah rarely bothered with the newspaper but decided to have a flick through it to pass the time until John returned. She hoped it would occupy her mind which had begun to imagine all sorts of things that could have happened to John. She only scanned the headlines and pictures until she saw it – on page 9. There in big bold letters was the headline that told her something was wrong.

'OCD the Most Selfish Illness.'

Then the sub heading.

'Family and Friends suffer in silence.'

"Oh my god. What has he done?"

The article went on to say, in great detail, that OCD sufferers never knew the full extent to which those close to them suffered along with them. That they were very unfair to put family and friends through such a horrendous time.

There was an element of truth in the article but it had been dramatized to a significant degree. John wouldn't understand that though. She doubted that the reporter had any direct experience of OCD. Talk about a little knowledge being dangerous, it certainly was in this case.

She had to find John quickly.

Just then her phone beeped to signal that a text had arrived. She grabbed the phone out of her bag as quickly as possible and pressed to read the text. She was horrified by what she saw.

'I can't put you through this anymore. I had no idea what I was doing to you. Forget I ever existed. Thank you for everything you have done. Please have a happy life.'

John had gone. Gone forever the text implied. She had to find him. She couldn't give up on him now. Where would he go? There was one place that was foremost in Sarah's mind. She hoped she was right.

The journey was seeming to take forever. Her tears made visibility very poor. Her turmoil of emotions made logic difficult to see. Was she on the right track? Would she end up in a ditch? The glowing eyes of animals made her slam on the brakes several times. Would she be in time? Her rescuer had to be rescued from himself. "Help me," she cried to no one.

Even though it was dark she drove up to John's farm – there was one dim light in the distance, up on the hill, behind the farm, a torchlight – she was scared but walked towards it. The more she tried to rush, the more she stumbled. Her knees and hands grazed and bloodied. How would she deal with John with blood on her hands? Was it John? She had no reason to know from this distance but her heart told her it was him.

She saw John knelt on the ground besides his parents' final resting place. Sarah had guessed right. He must be aware of her approach by now but he didn't move.

Then she saw the knife held in his outstretched hand. Just like in the shepherd's hut. Her torch glistened on the blade.

"No John" she screamed as she ran towards him over the rough ground.

As she got closer she heard him say, "Mum, Dad I'm coming. Tell Christine that I will be with you all again very soon."

He lifted the knife.

"No! Please don't John. You can't give up now. We can't give up now."

He turned to look at her and softly said, "It's better for everyone."

"We can't quit now. Please put the knife down. I refuse to fail."

He turned the knife towards himself and brought it closer to his chest.

"You haven't failed Sarah, I'm the one who has failed. The OCD has had the last laugh. I wasn't strong enough to fight it."

"You were doing so well John. I'll get you more help, anything, please don't go."

"No one can help me. You tried and I failed. I really failed Sarah."

For Sarah everything went into slow motion. She watched the knife edge closer to John's chest. Millimetre by millimetre until it was touching him. She was frozen with fear.

She doubted that John would actually kill himself from her limited knowledge of OCD. But what if?

Sarah was close enough to see John begin to increase the pressure on the knife. So close yet powerless to help.

John continued to push the knife further very slowly, as if he was trying to conjure up the courage to give the final push. Suddenly the knife fell to the ground as John slumped onto his side. Sarah rushed to him, put her arms around him and held him close to her, his head resting on her breast. Like a baby snuggling up to his mother. He relaxed a little.

"I couldn't do it Sarah."

"Come home John."

"This is my home. I tried it your way and it didn't work."

"You can't give in. You were doing so well. Why let one article in a newspaper spoil everything. An article written by someone who has no idea what OCD is really like."

302

"Yes but what if he is an expert."

"He is just a local reporter. One day he is reporting on the football match and the next day he is writing about an illness that I am sure he knows nothing about. He is just filling column inches, that's all."

Suddenly she felt all John's tension return.

"Go away Sarah. Go and live your own life. The world is much better without me. I guess I always knew that."

Sarah didn't move.

John sat up and screamed, "Get out of my life."

Shocked by the tone of his voice Sarah jumped up and quickly walked a short distance away, a safe distance. Then she turned to face John.

"John please come with me. Remember how you enjoyed going for the meal with our friends."

She very slowly moved towards him as she spoke, inch by inch.

"Why did you say our friends? They are your friends."

"No John, they are just as much your friends now as they are mine. I didn't really know them either until I met you."

She saw the tortured look on his face ease ever so slightly again. Was she slowly getting through to him?

"And what about Lady? She loves you and you know you love her."

"Lady is your dog."

"She is our dog John."

"Anna thinks the world of you too. You saved her life, remember?"

"I like Anna, I like all of you." he said softly.

Sarah was now just a couple of feet away and knew she was having an effect on him. Her words were working.

"John did you not enjoy some of the time we were together, some of the things we did?"

"Of course I did. I never thought that I would ever relax and enjoy anything again. But I know now that my OCD will never release its grip on me. Up here I'm safe, no one can get to me."

Sarah held out her hand. "Come with me John.......................
please!"

"No Sarah. Go home now. I can't put you through all this pressure any longer. You will never be happy and relaxed while I am with you."

She was now inches away from him. "John I have grown to really like you. I want to spend the rest of my life with you."

"Don't be foolish. I would destroy your life too."

Sarah was shocked by the despair in his voice. John knew that his words were true. He had to protect Sarah. He had to protect her from the torment he was causing her.

He calmed slightly as he watched the tears roll down her cheeks in rivers of misery.

"Sarah," he said softly, "I know I am no longer taking away your physical freedom but I am sure as hell still taking away your mental and emotional freedom. You deserve to be free. Go back to feeling the wind in your hair as you walk the moors with Lady. Go back to days of happiness and freedom."

They stood looking at each other for some time. Statues frozen in time. John knew he couldn't live without Sarah but he also couldn't live with her. She was the first person since he was a child that had shown him true kindness but she needed to be free. He had to put Sarah first, even if he had to be cruel to achieve that.

"Sarah just go." He snapped. "It was good for a while but I am fed up with being your puppet. I am fed up with just being the trophy you show off to your friends. I don't want to be part of your life any longer."

He was amazed that he was managing to control the kaleidoscope of emotions storming through his mind and body.

What John had said was like a knife piercing her heart. He let go of her hand and turned his head away. His mind and his heart were in turmoil. He was saying and doing things he didn't want to say and do but his mind told him that he had to. "My bloody OCD has won again," he whispered quietly.

He raised his voice and shouted, "Go away Sarah. I never want to see you again."

She ran down the hill, stumbling several times. John didn't come to help her. Back in her car she held her head in her hands and sobbed. She sobbed for the man she loved. She sobbed for the man who had stolen her heart and had now broken it. She rocked in her despair hitting her head on the steering wheel, relishing the pain as she vented her frustration. After a while she calmed and scrubbed her wet and raw eyes on her grazed knuckles. 'Not surprising he doesn't want me' she thought ruefully as she caught sight of her blood smeared face in the mirror.

Still her spirits lifted slightly at the thought and she knew she would be back, maybe not tomorrow but one day she would break through to him again. Or die trying.

Author's Note

My wife and I are the parents of a multi aspect OCD sufferer and my first novel, *'But What If?'*, although fictional, is based on the horrendous problems and struggles both our son and ourselves have had to face over the last twenty years plus.

The content is based therefore on first-hand knowledge. It is written both from the heart as well as the mind. The only aspect that doesn't reflect the reality we have faced is that an OCD sufferer would never hold someone captive, as John did initially with Sarah at his farm, nor would they actually harm anyone. This aspect was included to add dramatic effect to stress the magnitude of the dilemmas sufferers face.

OCD always bullies the sufferer by telling them to complete a compulsion or something bad will happen, usually to those they care for most. It knows that they are caring people and it attacks this weak point. The OCD sufferer's main concern is to protect other people no matter what the cost to themselves.

OCD sufferers are notorious for not wanting people outside their immediate family knowing of their condition and it is largely for reasons of my son's anonymity that this book is written as a fictional work. The OCD aspects however are all extremely closely based on our experiences although some details such as times, locations and names have been changed to maintain anonymity. Never the less this is a true reflection of our very stressful journey, a journey I do not wish on anyone.

Our son, now in his thirties, is currently managing his OCD fairly well and has a successful career. However you can never relax. You are always aware that the OCD is waiting to attack. OCD is still a constant in his life, every minute of every day.

I have written this book for two reasons. First of all I am immensely aware of what my son has achieved with all the problems he has had to face. I write this book first and foremost as a tribute to him.

The general public's knowledge of OCD is, from our experience, extremely limited. They see it just as washing your hands a lot or placing things in neat rows, if only that was all there was to it. I get angry when I hear jokes about OCD. Whilst I know those telling the jokes do so in ignorance and mean no harm, OCD is certainly no joke. The second reason, therefore, for my writing this novel is the hope that it may just improve at least a few peoples' knowledge and understanding of OCD.